KILLING DYLAN

Alastair Puddick

Published by Raven Crest Books

ISBN-13: 978-0-9934439-6-1
ISBN-10: 0-9934439-6-6

DEDICATION

For Mum and Dad

PROLOGUE

THE EXPLOSION HAPPENED at 10.37am. Nobody saw it coming. Least of all the postman.

It was a cold Wednesday morning. Mike Chapman kissed his sleeping wife goodbye, left his home at 5.57am, took the short walk to work, and clocked in for his shift at precisely 6.15am. After forty-five minutes of processing and sorting, he slapped his good friend Keith on the back, double-checked the arrangements for that evening's game of snooker and beers, and then headed out to make his deliveries.

It was extra chilly that morning. The pavements were twinkling with a light sheen of frost. Blades of grass pointed up in jagged white peaks. Tiny clouds poured from Mike's mouth as he breathed. His fingers tingled slightly as the cold air nipped at them. The sun was still rising, the world not quite woken, as he stepped out of the depot and climbed aboard his trusty bike.

Despite the cold, Mike was in a good mood. His wife, Justine, had been more than a little amorous the previous evening. After she'd cooked him his favourite dinner of steak and chips, they'd headed to bed early. The steak had given him a bit of extra stamina as, not only had they done it twice, he'd even managed to stay up and watch the end of the Chelsea match on Sky Sports 1. He whistled as he rode – something of a cliché, he knew, but he couldn't help being cheerful.

Mike enjoyed his job as a postman. Most people wouldn't like the early mornings, or being out in the cold, but Mike loved it. He was happy getting up before the rest of the world. He enjoyed seeing the sun rise. Revelling in that quiet stillness you only ever feel before the rest of the world comes to. The streets still empty, before they start humming with rush hour commuters trundling their way to work.

And he enjoyed his job. He liked the freedom, being out in the open air. Making his way from house to house, delivering letters and parcels. He still always smiled when he had a greetings card to deliver, imagining the grinning face of the recipient as they opened it. It wasn't much, but it always gave him a nice warm feeling, especially on the days when he wasn't so cheery.

Mike's deliveries had gone pretty well that morning. Thankfully there was nothing too heavy weighing him down, so he got round his route in good time. He'd said good morning to the people he usually spoke with. And, for once, he'd managed to avoid old Mr Kirkwell, who always stopped Mike whenever he saw him for a protracted chat about anything from politics, to the state of his garden, to the price of dog food. And Mike was far too polite not to hang around and chat. But this morning he'd raced round in near record time. He was looking forward to posting his last few letters, then getting home and maybe even recording a new song for his demo tape.

At 10.29am Mike turned the corner from Cale Street onto Jubilee Place and stopped outside the Arundel Court block of flats. He leaned his bike up against the wall, delved into his bag and pulled out a stack of letters, neatly held together with a red elastic band. He scanned through the post in his hand, quickly double-checking the addresses and flat numbers.

At the bottom of the stack was an A5-sized, brown jiffy bag for Flat 29. There was nothing particularly interesting or unusual about the package, but Mike couldn't help looking at it. He felt strangely drawn to it, suddenly very curious about what might be inside.

It wasn't as if Mike had never seen a brown jiffy bag before. He'd delivered hundreds of the things over the years and never given more than a passing thought to their contents. But for some reason he held this one in his hand, staring down at it, examining every crease and wrinkle of the shiny paper. He ran his index finger over the brown parcel tape used to secure either end. He raised it to his ear, shaking it gently, listening closely for any audible clue. He looked at the handwriting of the address, wondering whether that might give him some small hint.

He gave the package a slight squeeze, careful not to press too hard in case he damaged anything inside. The envelope gave slightly under his fingers. So Mike squeezed again, slightly harder. Then slightly harder again. And then the package exploded.

The bang was so loud that birds instantly scattered from the trees. Car alarms burst into high-pitched wailing. Distant dogs barked in houses and nearby streets. Then followed a percussion of loud, sticky squelches, as small, bloody parts of Mike Chapman rained down, splatting on the road, cars, pavements and pedestrians.

CHAPTER 1

"SO WHAT'S THIS book about, then?"

The old lady stood dripping in front of me, coils of white hair hemmed in under a soaked plastic rain hood. Small puddles were slowly forming around the edges of her patent leather shoes. Her breath smelled like eggs and butterscotch.

"It's a dark, psychological thriller, full of murder, mystery and a burned-out detective, desperate to catch a psychopath before he kills again," I said, forcing as much customer-friendly enthusiasm into my voice as I could.

"Hmmm," she said, her crinkled old face pursing into a pointed look of disgust. "All sounds a bit predictable… if you don't mind me saying."

I did bloody well mind her saying.

"Well," I said, the muscles in my face aching under the weight of my forced grin, "this one is definitely different. Lots of twists and turns. It'll definitely keep you guessing until the end."

I was standing at the back of the local Waterstones book shop, engaging in what I like to call 'Marketing Activity'. In other words, I was camped behind a small table on which I'd lovingly arranged several copies of my latest, greatest, thrilling crime novel, trying to ingratiate myself to the general public and people who, if they played their cards right, could become my newest fans. And if they played their cards wrong, might just end up with a boot up the backside.

It's not that I have a particular dislike for the patrons of the local Waterstones – certainly no more than the general disdain I reserve for all members of the human race. I just find people to be, on the whole, rather irritating. So I prefer to avoid them.

I am, however, also a realist. No matter how much we like to think otherwise, we novelists need readers. There's no point writing a book – and certainly no way to make money from one – if nobody ever reads it. And, in today's competitive world of book publishing, in order be anything of a success, a good author needs to leave the sanctuary of their writing room and engage with their readers and potential readers.

And so I found myself in Waterstones, selling my wares like a cheap market stall trader, trying not to stare at the wiry grey hairs protruding from the chin of the old battleaxe in front of me.

"Hmmmm… Frederick Winters," the old lady said, picking up one of the books and inspecting the cover. "That's you, I suppose."

"Guilty as charged." I coughed out my best fake laugh.

"Never heard of you." It was more an accusation than a statement.

"Er… well… that I can't help, I'm afraid," I said, wishing the old bat would either buy the book or piss off to the undertakers next door and book a one-way trip to the crematorium. "It's very good though, if I do say so myself. And it's my tenth book, so I should know what I'm doing by now."

"Hmmm." Her eyes returned to scrutinizing the cover, as if she were looking for some mark of quality.

"Don't just take my word for it," I interjected, trying to close the sale. "This book has twenty-seven five-star reviews on Goodreads.com. So, you know…"

Her eyebrows rose. She did know.

What she didn't know was that I'd posted all twenty-seven of those reviews myself under a series of pseudonyms.

"I'm not sure," she continued, literally weighing the book in her hand, roughly fanning through the pages. "It sounds an awful lot like a James Patterson I read recently."

"This is nothing like a bloody James Patterson," I snapped. "This is a quality, well-researched, well-written book. Not like that factory-written drivel he turns out."

To be perfectly honest, I have nothing against James Patterson. Not really. Aside from a burning, rage-inducing jealousy at the man's success. Is it deserved success? Possibly. Would I rather it was my success? Definitely. Would I sell my own grandmother for even a tenth of his annual book sales? In a second. I'd even dig up the coffin and glue the bones back together myself.

I was probably just a little tetchy on account of knowing exactly which James Patterson book she thought mine was similar to – an observation quite a few other people had made. One of those people being James Patterson himself.

The old lady placed the book back down on the table. I could see the sale slipping away from me. I had to rescue it.

"Of course, if you like James Patterson, you'll love this."

"Really?"

"Oh yes, many of my fans have told me it's as good as, if not better than, any Patterson they've read." This, technically, was true. I do have fans. Four to be precise. The fact that I've had to take out a restraining order against one of them, and two are currently serving jail sentences for arson and murder respectively, is neither here nor there. The fourth one is worse. He works in a shoe shop and his name is Norman.

"Well, I suppose it looks like a fairly easy read," she said.

I bit my tongue, almost to the point of bleeding.

"How much?" she asked.

"Ten pounds. Or I can give you a signed copy for twelve."

"Two pounds for a signature?"

"You'll double your money if you sell it on eBay," I lied. If she actually found a buyer, she'd be lucky to only halve her investment.

"Really?" she cooed.

"Oh, definitely."

"Well, I only have ten pounds on me," she said, reaching into her bag and pulling out a ten pound note. "You couldn't sign it for free, could you?"

She attempted to bat her eyelids at me in a coquettish fashion, but the muscles in her face had stopped working and it looked more like she was having a stroke.

Maybe it was the stiflingly warm book shop air, the ache in my back, or the fact that I'd been standing there with no success for forty-five minutes, but I picked up a copy, sighed and shrugged, and flashed her a warm smile.

"No," I said, plucking the tenner out of her hand and replacing it with the unsigned book.

"Oh," she said, watching as I deftly thrust the note deep into my pocket. "Well... but, shouldn't I go and pay at the till?"

"Oh, no need for that," I said. "I'll save you a trip and take it over in a minute."

"But what about my loyalty points?" She pulled out a small plastic card from her bag.

Oh, for God's sake.

"Fine, hand it here," I snapped, snatching the card from her hand and pulling my mobile phone from my pocket. I pressed a few random buttons, making it beep a couple of times, then pretended to scan the card with the built-in camera. "There you go, that's your points all logged."

"What was that?" she said, unimpressed.

"I just scanned your card."

"No you didn't! That wasn't a scanner. That's your mobile phone. I'm not a fucking idiot."

"Fine," I huffed, "wait there." I stomped off in the direction of the till, then dove behind the *Mind, Body & Spirit* display. I waited a few seconds then slowly walked back and handed her the card. "There you go. All done."

"That's better," she snapped. "You know, you could really do with working on your customer service skills, if you want people to buy your books."

"Apologies," I said fixing the smile back onto my face. "Enjoy the book. And have a lovely day."

"That's better."

"Oh, by the way," I said, as the old bag gripped the handle of her tartan, wheeled shopping trolley and turned to leave. "The brother-in-law is the killer. All sales are final."

Her mouth opened as she prepared to protest, but I was already staring at my phone, pretending to compose a text message. I looked up to see her storming off – well, trundling slowly – in the direction of the sales desk. This wasn't going to be good.

A few moments later Todd, the assistant manager, came bounding through the shop, seething with indignation.

"Right, you!" he yelled. "You've been warned about this before. You know you can't just come in here setting up fake signings and selling your own books. It's against the law."

"Technically, it's not a fake signing," I countered. "I have signed a few of the books."

"You know what I mean. The manager said if I catch you again I'm to call the police."

"Oh, calm down Todd, there's no need for that."

Todd's eyes glanced down at the table in front of me, noting the small piles of my books.

"Where are the books that were on this table?"

"Sorry Todd, I don't know what you mean." I did know what he meant.

"The books that were here. The special promotion. Two books for £7. It took me over an hour to arrange them."

"No idea, I'm afraid Todd. This table was empty when I got here.

Maybe they all sold out."

Todd eyed me suspiciously. The table had not been empty when I'd arrived. It had, as Todd correctly stated, been covered in other writers' inferior work. And I'd needed a place to set up. So, I'd carefully removed the special offer sign, then gone about the store placing the books higgledy-piggledy on random shelves, with no regard whatsoever for genre, author or alphabetical order. But it would be several hours before Todd found that out.

"You can't keep doing this."

"And why not, exactly? You let other authors come in and do book signings?"

"Yes, ones that we invite in. Ones that people actually want to meet. Not just random nutjobs that turn up unannounced and flog their own books at the back of the shop."

Okay, so technically I wasn't supposed to be signing and selling books in Waterstones. According to the store's obnoxious, triple-chinned manager, I was barred from the branch for previous indiscretions and shouldn't have been in there at all. But it's a cutthroat world, and you have to make your own sales opportunities where you can.

Of the several thousands of books published each year, really only a handful will see a great deal of success. It's okay for your J K Rowlings, Dan Browns and James bloody Pattersons. But for the rest of us, it's hard enough earning enough money to feed ourselves, let alone deciding what colour interior we want for our new yacht.

And with my landlord, Mr Singh, sending me daily emails threatening eviction if he doesn't see some of the back rent I owe him, sneaking into Waterstones in disguise, setting up my own book signings, and keeping the cash for every copy I sell is, unfortunately, what I am reduced to. It's either that or get a real job.

Naturally, I resented the 'nutjob' accusation. But having dealt with Todd on several previous occasions, I knew he was not a man to be reasoned with. He was not blessed with more than a handful of brain cells at best, so any reasonable argument was usually lost on him. Besides, he was literally twice the size of me and had threatened physical violence several times in the past – something I'm always more than keen to avoid when possible.

I thought it prudent, therefore, to retreat before he called the authorities. So, I packed my books into my duffel bag, along with a carefully secreted copy of the new Lee Child hardback I'd picked off the shelf – I'm not above the occasional bout of shoplifting, especially when it's a book I'm secretly hoping to hate.

"You wouldn't know good literature if it rearranged your special offer books randomly around your stupid little shop, Todd," I said.

He looked at me with bemusement, my barbed comment falling on stupid ears. But the penny would drop soon enough, when he found a Jo Cox rammed in between his Trollopes.

I picked up my bag and swept past the old lady, hurrying out of the shop before anyone realised she'd just paid a tenner for a book that was supposed to retail for £6.99.

******

A few hours later I was sitting in the local Starbucks, staring at the ominously white screen of my laptop. At the top of a fresh, crisp Word document I had typed the word *Ideas*. I had centred it, set it in Times New Roman, changed the font size to 12pt, set it as bold, decided I didn't like the pomposity of the bold letters staring at me so changed it back, and then underlined it. I had yet to write down any actual ideas.

I took a sip of the latte I'd been nursing for forty-five minutes. It was stone cold and milky, and tasted slightly of cigarette ash. But it was wet and mildly refreshing. And whilst I still had at least a small amount of liquid in my cup, the staff were technically forbidden from either ushering me out the door, or asking me to hurry up and free the table for other patrons – although that doesn't stop them staring daggers at me, rolling their eyes whenever they clear nearby tables or, in the case of Magda, the grumpy Polish barista, muttering strange foreign words under her breath. I can't understand them, of course, but I'm fairly certain they're less than complimentary and aimed directly at me.

I like Starbucks. I know I shouldn't, what with the whole tax-dodging, corporate globalisation thing. But they do nice coffee. And nice cakes. And it's warm. And they have free Wi-Fi.

I like Costa Coffee too, and Café Nero. In fact, I like most of the chain coffee shops. I like getting out amongst people – whilst still carefully avoiding any real interaction, of course – and taking a snapshot of the world. I like immersing myself in society, peeling back the mask and exposing the murky underbelly of human existence. I find it helps me construct an authentic, believable world.

But mostly I like the free Wi-Fi.

Much of my writing is done in coffee shops. It's a cliché, I know. And just about every coffee shop you go into nowadays seems to have at least one dickhead sitting in the corner, their laptop plugged into the shop's power socket, as they work on their novel, or screenplay, or sitcom. And there's a very good reason for that. It's fucking boring at home.

I live in a perfectly reasonable two-bed flat. Okay, it's absolutely tiny, and not so much a two-bedroomed flat as a one-bed with a generous sized cupboard. But I have all the modern conveniences and hot beverage-making facilities a man could possibly want. I've turned the cupboard-bedroom into a serviceable office/writing room, and I am more than happy to tinker away at the laptop at home. But even I can only endure my own company for so long.

So, I head out and spend as long as I can nursing a small latte and struggling to come up with ideas for my next big bestseller – well, mediocre seller. All right, crappy seller.

It's important to state, at this point, that I am a properly published novelist, not just a go-it-alone, vanity self-publisher. I have a real agent, who gives me about two per cent of his attention each year. And I am published by a real, proper publisher. They're a fairly small business, which operates from a tiny unit in a local industrial estate – more Harpo Marx than Harper Collins. But they are, technically, and to all intents and purposes, a real book publisher.

Amongst their authors they are lucky to count: myself; noted historian Max Billingham; disgraced politician the (no longer) right honourable Jeffrey Hinchcliffe; romance novelist Dame Phyllis Babstock; Buster the Juggling Dog (although I'm not convinced he actually writes his own stuff); and a handful of small-time science fiction writers.

My book sales have never been exactly astronomical, but I just about manage to scrape a living from writing – well, an existence anyway. Of course, I'd like to find myself sitting on top of a bestseller list at some point. But for the time being, when books are being sold for 10p online, and the only way to guarantee a sure-fire hit is to either offend the religious nuts or include enough hardcore porn to get the housewives dripping, I'm happy enough just getting by. Well, not happy, but you know.

And so my life is writing, and my workplace is coffee shops. My record to date for drinking just one small coffee is two hours and forty-one minutes. And I could have lasted longer, were it not for the severe pain in my left buttock, caused by the hard wooden surface of the cheap Starbucks chair.

"Ahem," said a timid voice at my side.

I looked up from my laptop, with the hardened, 'what-do-you-want?' glare I save for high-street market researchers, children, overly-helpful shop assistants, the elderly, telephone cold-callers (they can't see it, obviously, as they're on the other end of a phone, but I like to think at least part of it carries over in my tone of voice), grumpy Polish baristas, and anyone who bothers me while I'm working – or at least trying to work.

"Oh, sorry to bother you," said a small, dowdy woman with mousy brown hair and too little make-up for her plain face. "Is anyone sitting here?"

She pointed at the empty chair across the table from me. I remained silent and increased the intensity of my stare, but she didn't move. She just stood there looking hopeful.

"Would you mind if I joined you?" she said finally. "It's very busy and there aren't any seats left."

I looked around the room, double-checking what she'd said. There were no empty tables.

"Fine," I huffed. "You can have the chair."

"Oh thank you," she said, placing a large cappuccino down on the table.

"But not the table," I quickly spat out. "You can have the chair, but you're not sharing my table."

"Sorry... I... what?" she said, surprised.

"You can have the chair. The chair is yours. Take the chair, go somewhere else and enjoy the rest of your life. But you're not joining me."

"Sorry?"

"So you should be, I'm trying to work and you're interrupting me."

"No, not sorry," she said. "I'm not sorry, I just meant... sorry? Pardon? What do you mean I can have the chair but not the table?"

"Exactly what I said. Which part are you having trouble with?"

"It's not *your* table, you know. You don't own it."

"No, but I'm sitting here, and I don't want company."

"I wasn't actually asking permission. You don't have the right to stop me sitting here."

"Yes, I do."

"No you don't."

"Then why did you ask?"

"I was just being polite."

"Fine. Well, the answer's still no. So would you please politely bugger off?"

She stared at me open-mouthed, as if she couldn't actually believe what I was saying. I looked back to my empty Word document, raised my hands and flapped my fingers in a dismissive gesture.

"I... I... you really are the rudest man," she said, picking up her coffee and shuffling in the direction of some other poor sap whose table she intended to invade.

"Not quite," I called after her. "I'm still practising."

I stared again at the screen and my complete lack of ideas. I'd been trying to think of a good plot for my new book – the next exciting mystery to perplex my hard-drinking, chain-smoking private detective, Dick Stone. So far, in my previous novels, Dick had gone up against people traffickers, drug cartels, serial killers, bent coppers, femmes fatales, corrupt politicians, hired assassins and one particularly vicious lollipop lady who turned out to be a drug baron using the children on her crossing route to deliver the drugs.

Recent books hadn't been selling so well, and I'd heard rumours my publisher was thinking of dropping me. I was also currently making barely enough money to sustain a goldfish, let alone a coffee-guzzling author, so I was in desperate need of a cash injection. I needed an amazing story and all I had so far was the word 'Ideas'.

I heard the shuffling of shoes next to me again. I looked up expecting to see that dithering woman coming back to complain about my rudeness. But it wasn't her. It wasn't even Magda, swooping by the table to check the level of my coffee cup, or to relay the details of another customer complaint against me.

It was a face I hadn't seen for some years. A face I wasn't sure I'd ever see again.

"Hello Freddie," he said, in a deep, sombre voice. "I need your help. I think someone's trying to kill me."

CHAPTER 2

"WHAT THE HELL do you mean, someone's trying to kill you?"

I looked up at the pale face before me, the eyes filled with worry. Dylan St James used to be a friend, back when I was younger and more open to the notion of socialising. It was at least six or seven years since I last saw him. Of all the people I'd expected to encounter, he was right down at the bottom of the list.

"Please Freddie, I'm desperate. I need your help." He sounded genuinely worried.

"Well, you'd better sit down," I said. "I'd offer you a chair, but some old hag came and pinched it." I said it loud enough that the dowdy woman could hear me from across the room. She coughed in disbelief, peppering her blouse with droplets of spat-out coffee.

"No problem," said Dylan, grabbing a chair from another table and pulling it over. He sat down across from me, his hangdog jowls drooping like he'd won the lottery but forgotten where he'd put the ticket. I suppose someone living in fear of their life probably would be a bit glum, but this was nothing new for Dylan.

"So, what's all this nonsense about someone trying to kill you?"

"It's not nonsense. I'm serious."

"Come off it. What makes you think that?"

"It's a feeling I have."

"A feeling? Oh, well, why didn't you say so? We'd best get Scotland Yard on the case. I hear they have some great people working on 'murderous feelings' nowadays."

"Not just a feeling, you smug git. There have been incidents."

"Incidents? Blimey. What sort of incidents?"

"There was the fire at my house. The whole thing burned to the ground. I only just made it out alive. The police haven't ruled out foul play."

"Accidents happen, Dylan. Houses burn down. It doesn't mean someone's out to get you. Probably just dodgy wiring or something."

"There are other things. The other day I was getting the tube at Warren Street. It was pretty crowded down there, and just as the train came into the station I felt a shove in my back. I nearly went on the tracks. The only thing that saved me was this tall goth kid who grabbed my jacket and pulled me back."

"That doesn't prove anything," I chuckled. "I'm sure it was just an accident. You know what the Tube's like – half-brained morons shuffling and banging into each other on crowded platforms. It's a wonder more people don't get accidentally bumped to their deaths."

"The other week I was nearly run over," said Dylan, getting more agitated. "I was just walking along, minding my own business. I crossed the road – and, before you ask, yes I did look both ways. Out of nowhere this white van comes belting round the corner and nearly flattens me. I only just about managed to jump out of the way. And I gave myself a really badly grazed knee."

"Oh diddums!" I said. "Come on Dylan, you're pulling my leg now. I was nearly flattened by at least three white van men last week alone. It's the price of living in a world where they allow half-brained, inbred, knuckle-dragging oafs to drive service vehicles."

"I see you haven't lost your good nature," he chided.

"Never had much to start with," I smiled.

"There's this strange car, as well. I see it everywhere I go."

"A car? Really? In London? It's not a big black thing is it? Orange light on the top that says Taxi?"

"There's no need to take the piss, Freddie," he said.

"Okay, what car?"

"It's this big car... saloon... dark blue... Ford, I think. I see it all over the place. It's been parked outside my house. I've seen it outside my agent's office. It's driven past me in the street several times."

"Well, I'm not being funny Dylan, but dark blue Fords are not exactly uncommon."

"I'm telling you this is the same car each time. It has this weird lettering on the licence plate, and one of those old Garfield things on suckers in the back passenger window. I'd know it anywhere."

"Garfield," I chuckled, "I haven't seen one of those in years. Seems like every dickhead had one of those in their car at one point. Do you remember?"

"Yes," said Dylan, grimly. "I had one. You know I did."

"Oh yes. Point proven," I laughed. "But come on, just because you've seen a car about a few times, I still think you're jumping to conclusions."

"I'm telling you Freddie, there's something not right about this car. I can feel it."

I frowned and rubbed my eyes. Dylan was not usually one for flights of fancy, but I did wonder whether his creative mind was playing tricks on him.

"You're probably just imagining it. I dare say you've been under a lot of pressure recently, figuring out how to spend all your millions of pounds. It must really take it out of you. What shall I buy today, the sports car or the private island? Personally, I don't know how you cope..."

"I'm serious, Freddie. I really think someone's trying to kill me. I'm bloody terrified. I haven't slept in days."

He hung his head even further. The tiniest of tears glinted in the corner of his eye. He looked genuinely terrified.

"You vont caffay?" Marta, the disgruntled Starbucks barista, had sneaked up behind me and was eagerly eyeing the half mouthful of cold dregs lingering at the bottom of my cup. Normally, I would have held my ground, but she looked particularly grumpy today. And her snarling lip made her look like she might actually start breathing fire if I didn't order another drink.

"Fine," I said, "I'll have another latté, please Marta. My friend is paying."

I smiled at Dylan, who sighed and shook his head.

"Vot size you vont?" she barked.

"Large, please?" I said.

"Large? Vot 'large'? You mean 'Tall', 'Grande' or 'Venti'?"

"No, I mean none of those." I smiled sycophantically. "None of those are actually sizes of beverage are they, Marta?"

"Yes sizes. Look at board. Tall, Grande, Venti. Vot size you vont?"

"I'll have a large, please, Marta."

"Large not on board."

I sighed, pinching my nose between thumb and forefinger. "Very well, if we must go through this again... I'll have the largest size you offer. Thank you."

She sneered down at me, and through gritted teeth growled, "Ve-e-e-enti."

"Whatever you wish to call it is fine by me, so long as it comes in a *large* cup," I smiled.

"Vot you vont?" she snapped at Dylan.

"Oh... er... I'll have the same, please," he returned, quivering slightly.

Marta sneered, snatched up my cup and stomped off back toward the counter.

"Do they usually do table service in here?" asked Dylan.

"Generally no," I smiled. "We have something of an... arrangement. They don't like me tying up the tables, sitting here nursing a coffee for hours at a time. So they come and harass me, insisting I need to buy something if I want to stay here. Before they know it, they're taking my order and bringing me coffee. Quite funny really. I don't think they even know they're doing it."

"You always were a sneaky fucker," said Dylan, a smile creeping across his face to replace the worried look.

"Okay," I said, returning to Dylan, "say I believe you, and somebody wants you dead. Who is it? Who wants you dead? And why?"

"Well, I don't know that, obviously. If I did, I wouldn't need help."

"But you're convinced someone's out to get you. So who? Do you have any enemies? Psycho stalkers? Disgruntled ex-wives, perhaps? Have you upset the man that delivers your Tesco shopping? There must be something."

"No, nothing. No enemies. No stalkers – well, one, but she doesn't seem like a psycho. She's actually very nice. She knits me jumpers.

"The ex-wives and I all parted pretty amicably, and we're all still on speaking terms. Apart from Corinne, but that's... well... a bit tricky. And they were all well taken care of in the divorce settlements, so they've got no reason to be disgruntled.

"And I don't get shopping delivered from Tesco. It comes from Waitrose. I am rich, you know." He smiled a slight, roguish grin. It was good to see him smile. It reminded me briefly of old times and the fun we had teasing each other.

"What about blackmail? As you say, you're a rich man. Maybe they're not murder attempts. Perhaps they're just trying to scare you. Have you had any demands for money, recently?"

"No, nothing like that."

"But you're convinced someone wants you dead?"

"I know it sounds a bit crazy," he sighed, "but I'm serious. I'm really worried."

Dylan looked around suspiciously, scanning the faces of the other people in the coffee shop, looking at the street outside.

"So, why are you telling me all this? What do you want me to do about it?"

"I thought you might be able to help somehow. Investigate or something?"

"Why me? Why not the police?"

"This is what you do, Freddie. It's what you're good at. You've always been good at it. Puzzles, conspiracies, murder plots. Your books are always great – well-plotted, intricate and detailed. They keep you guessing about who did it, right to the very end. They're very clever."

"Really?" I said, slightly taken aback. "You've read my books?"

"Of course I have. I've read all your books. I love them. Well, apart from that last one. Read a bit like a James Patterson, I thought."

"Piss off," I said.

Marta appeared at my side, banging the two coffees down onto the table with a loud thud. Dylan handed her a ten-pound note and told her to keep the change. She smiled at him, suddenly re-evaluating the disdain she felt towards anyone who would willingly sit chatting with me. She turned round, grimaced at me, and trod on my foot as she waddled off back towards the till.

"You deal with murderers in your books every day," said Dylan, as I rubbed my injured toe. "You have a knack for investigating and finding out who's done it."

"Yes, but I make it up," I said. "I decide who's going to get killed, and who's going to do the killing. I already know who the killer is."

"Yes, but your detective, Dick Stone, doesn't. He figures it all out."

"You do understand how writing works, don't you?" I laughed. "You do know Dick isn't real? He's made up. The reason he knows how to find the killer is because I tell him who it is."

"Yes, but you still write the investigation. You plot it out, set up the red herrings, put the motives and alibis in place. You could do the same here – just, sort of in reverse."

"And how would that work?"

"You don't know who's trying to kill me, but you could investigate as if it was one of your books. Just do things how Dick Stone would do them – look at the evidence, and find the killer."

"Would-be killer," I corrected. "You're not dead yet, and we still don't know for sure that someone is trying to kill you."

"No, but you could investigate and figure out what's going on."

I must admit the idea did seem quite intriguing. It might be a bit of

ALASTAIR PUDDICK

fun playing detective for a few days. And if it did turn out that someone was trying to kill Dylan, not only could I save a friend's life, it might also serve as a useful distraction from trying to think of ideas for the book I was supposed to be writing.

"How much does it pay?" I said.

"What?"

"Surely you don't expect me to do this all for free, do you? We're talking several days here, at least."

Dylan shook his head with disappointment. "Same old Freddie, I see."

"Hey, I'm a busy man," I said, pointing at the laptop in front of me. "I have books to write, marketing to do, readers to engage with. I can't just take time off because you're worried. The world keeps on spinning, even though the great Dylan St. James has a case of the willies."

"Fine, how much do you want?" he said.

"Oh, I don't know. I'm not an unreasonable man. Call it... £500 a day?"

"Five hundred quid?"

"Plus expenses," I added.

"God, you really know how to help out a friend in need, don't you, Freddie?"

"Hey, we all have bills to pay. And you do keep reminding me how rich you are. Of course, if you don't want my help, you could always go to the police."

"I can't go to the police."

"Why not?"

A look of frustration flashed across his face. "Because I've already been to them, all right? They told me I was probably just imagining things, and they couldn't investigate unless I had actual proof someone was trying to kill me."

"And so we come to the real reason you've come to see me," I said with mock outrage. "Well, then, I guess you've got no choice, have you? Five hundred pounds a day, plus expenses."

"Fine," said Dylan, grimacing slightly.

"Anyway, how did you know I'd be here?"

"It's 3.27pm on a Thursday afternoon," he said. "And you weren't in Costa... so, where else were you going to be?"

"I might have been at a book signing," I said, slightly peeved at my apparent predictability. And even more annoyed that I didn't actually have anywhere better to be.

"You still pulling that old fake signing trick, Freddie?" he laughed.

"If you sign some of the books, it's not technically a *fake* signing. Besides, some of us have to work for a living. We don't all have the world handed to us, Dylan."

"We both write books, Freddie," he snapped, sounding genuinely wounded. "It's not my fault that mine are a bit more popular than yours."

"Yeah, well…" I huffed. I didn't know how to finish the sentence so instead I screwed up my nose and pressed my tongue hard into my bottom lip. I looked like a tit, but he got the message.

******

I first met Dylan at University. We were studying for the same English degree and, as we had many of the same classes, we found ourselves constantly bumping into each other. We quickly became friends and ended up sitting together in class, studying together in our spare time, and we even set up our own little creative writing social group. We didn't have very many takers.

Back then he was just plain old Dylan James. That was before some moron at his publishing company decided he'd sound more literary – and shift a few more units – if he added the 'St' in the middle. And so, much like crime novelist Bateman dropping the 'Colin' his mother gave him, Dylan inserted an erroneous St into his name.

I remember us laughing at the idea, and him saying how daft it all was. But thirteen years, and millions of worldwide book sales later, I guess the moron wasn't quite such a moron after all.

Dylan was a fairly shy boy when we first met. Quite introverted with long floppy hair and a constant look of despondency. And didn't the girls just love that whole tortured soul act.

I was a bit of a cocky prick, with hair that never did what it was told, and I looked more clown than cool. I could never afford the clothes that made you look the right kind of scruffy. Instead, I just looked dishevelled and poverty-stricken. Needless to say, the girls didn't love me as much.

Dylan and I were kindred spirits. We'd study together, drink a lot, read each other's work, offer notes and hints, and help each other to become better writers. We stayed friends long after university, sharing a tiny, cramped flat in the very bum hole of London. We took terrible, underpaid jobs while we tried to make something of ourselves.

The dream was always to become published, of course, and neither of us doubted we were going to be the next big bestselling author. My own self-belief has waned somewhat over the last seventeen years, since it still hasn't happened.

We continued to write, always taking an interest in each other's work – his slightly better than mine. We both got agents around the same time – his a lot more enthusiastic than mine. And then we got publishing deals around the same time, too – his a bloody, great deal better than mine.

And it's fair to say that Dylan's career has been vastly more successful than mine. He turns out that God-awful, romantic, heart-breaking 'literary' fiction. The sort of thing that always seems to feature a secret abortion in 1940s London. Or a dying grandmother desperate to track down the secret daughter she abandoned. Or some miserable wanker droning on for 340 pages about the fact that his father never really loved him, and he feels incapable of loving anyone else as a result – and then he rescues a baby from a burning building, and he can start to rebuild his life. That sort of old toss.

It's the kind of stuff that has me choking on my own bile. Fortunately for Dylan, however, it's the same type of stuff that has middle-aged, middle-class women recommending it to their book clubs; awards judges throwing gongs at him; and critics praising the 'visual undertones' of his writing. Bollocks, if you ask me.

But people certainly seem to lap his books up, and his success as an author has been nothing short of phenomenal. He's won countless awards. All five of his books have spent several weeks at the top of the bestsellers lists. He's been in the Richard and bloody Judy Book Club twice. And he's appeared on TV more times than I've paid my TV licence.

One of his books was even turned into a big-budget Hollywood movie, starring Keira Knightley. *Keira Knightley*, for fuck's sake!

Dylan moved out of the flat when his first book really took off. He bought himself a big, trendy house in the city. I still live in the tiny, cramped flat.

We never officially stopped being friends. I suppose we just started drifting apart. He was always away at big book signings, literary festivals and swanky parties with his new celebrity friends. I was at home writing and trying to come up with a book that would sell more than a couple of hundred copies.

And it gets hard to remain friends with someone when you spend all your time resenting their success and wishing you could be happier for them. So we stopped hanging out, stopped emailing and eventually just stopped.

I missed his friendship, more than I'd like to admit. But of course I couldn't let *him* know that.

Despite being one of the most successful novelists of the past 10 years, with all his millions of pounds, beautiful wives, big house and fancy expensive clothes, Dylan has always been one of the most glum, depressed, unhappy people I've ever known. It's no wonder, really. Aside from finding huge success with his writing, his life has been a lot less blessed.

Some people have bad luck, but Dylan is in a whole league of his own. You could fill a book with all the upsets, problems, ill-health, accidents and general misery the man has encountered in his life. It's a wonder the poor guy never topped himself. And no wonder his books are so bloody dreary.

"Anyway, enough about me," said Dylan, taking a sip from his overly-large coffee, "how have you been Freddie?"

"Oh, just peachy. My publisher's thinking of dropping me. I can't sell a book for love nor money. And I can't afford to pay my rent. So I'll probably be homeless soon as well. All I need now is to find a lump on my balls and I'll have the full set."

"God, that's rough," he said, sounding genuinely sorry for me. "Sounds like we've both been through the wringer a bit recently."

"Yes," I replied, suddenly feeling a little ashamed and self-absorbed. "I heard about the cancer. Sorry to hear that. You're feeling better now, though?"

"Yeah, in full remission, thankfully. Second time I've beaten it now. And no more chemo, thank God. You know, I sometimes wonder what's worse, the disease or the cure. It makes you feel so sick and tired. And constantly dizzy. It's so bloody draining."

"Yes, of course... Well, at least you're on the mend."

"Yeah," he sighed, "I suppose."

"And you've got that pretty young wife to take care of you."

"Well, no... we've been divorced for about a year now." His pallid face dropped even further.

See what I mean? You couldn't make up that level of bad luck.

"Another one?" I half choked. "That's got to be the third…"

"Fourth," he cut in.

"Fourth wife? Christ. Sorry to hear it. That is rough."

"Yeah," he sighed. His shoulders sagged, his head bent down. I thought he might just break down in front of me. "Fourth wife, third divorce."

"Yes, of course. Sonia," I said, looking down at my hands.

Sonia was Dylan's first wife, and definitely the love of his life. She used to hang around with us at Uni, and went through all the bad times with us. They really were made for each other, and I missed her as much as I missed Dylan. They were only married for a year before she died. She caught a cold, somehow developed pneumonia and was dead within just a week. Poor Dylan went into a very deep depression, and never really seemed to recover.

Bizarrely, it was shortly after Sonia's death that Dylan wrote his best book, and by far his biggest seller. He won the Booker Prize for it, and was literally catapulted into fame and fortune, going from bestselling author to worldwide literary star overnight. But I don't think he ever managed to really appreciate the success, because he didn't have Sonia to share it with.

"Man, your fortune must have taken a pretty big hit after three divorces," I laughed, trying to rescue the mood.

"No, not really. Something my agent, Mortimer, took care of. He always insisted I got the girls to sign pre-nuptial agreements before getting married. Pretty clever, really. Probably saved me a fortune over the years. But it's not about the money, is it?"

"No, I suppose not," I said, thinking completely the opposite. Isn't everything about money?

I wished I'd had the common sense to get my errant wife to sign a pre-nup. The last time I saw her, she was throwing a lava lamp at me and calling me a shrivelled up ball-bag. In fairness, the marriage had been dead long before that, but the experience of washing glass and lava lamp wax out of a six inch cut on my forehead really nailed the coffin lid shut.

I don't suppose we were ever that well suited to one another. The only thing we ever really had in common was that she wanted to marry a rich, successful man. And I wanted to be one.

She got fed up waiting for my bestseller to arrive, and the fortune I'd assured her would come with it. She very quickly tired of living in a rented flat and scraping by on the meagre earnings of an unsuccessful crime novelist. And I can't really blame her. I'm pretty fucking tired of it myself.

I knew she was more interested in my potential earnings than my warm heart and tender personality when I met her. And I promised her things I couldn't deliver.

The last I heard she was living in Rotherham with a used car dealer called Pete. She's never asked me for money – primarily because she knows there's no chance of getting any. But I can't shake the feeling that, should I ever have more than a tenner in my current account, her booze-addled bones will come rattling back in my direction, demanding her fifty per cent.

"Hang on," I said. "Mortimer? Mortimer Bunkle?"

"Yes," said Dylan. "Why?"

"God, you're not still letting that old has-been represent you, are you Dylan?"

"Hey, he's always done all right by me, Freddie. He discovered me. And he always gets me a good deal."

"Well, of course he does. You're one of the country's top authors. Any agent could get you a good deal. Even my excuse for an agent could get you a good deal – a damn sight better than mine, anyway. You must be Bunkle's only remaining client. The only one that makes him any money, for sure. Everyone else decent jumped ship years ago, after… well, you know."

"Mortimer explained all that. It was just an oversight on the part of his accountant."

"Believe what you like, the man's crooked and you're his only revenue stream."

"Yeah, I know. That's why it makes it harder to let him go. I think he'd be a bit screwed without me as a client. And he's always been good to me. He's helped me out a lot. He introduced me to the third and fourth wives… although, in retrospect, maybe that wasn't such a great kindness."

"Well, if I were you I'd have given him the bullet years ago," I said, secretly wishing I had the literary pull to give my agent the shove, rather than cling on like a toddler wrapped around their mother's leg.

Dylan sighed and smiled wearily. In the corner of the coffee shop, a clumsy teenager spilled a bright red, fruity drink onto his table – his three friends scattering in all directions to escape the rapidly advancing crimson puddle. An old lady repeatedly rattled the door handle of the one and only toilet. At the counter, an apparently aggrieved businessman was giving poor Marta merry hell over the inadequate internal temperature of his brie and bacon panini. I couldn't help but smile.

"Look, I've been thinking," I said. "Where are you staying now, since your house burned down?"

"I'm in a three-bed apartment in Chelsea that Mortimer found me till the house gets rebuilt. Why?"

"I'm just thinking about this car you've seen hanging about."

"Oh, you believe me about that now, do you?"

"Hey, I have to consider every possible lead, Dylan. And I'm not sure it's safe for you to be on your own at a time like this. What with dangerous killers lurking in dark blue Fords."

"Right..." he said, not quite following.

"So, I think it's safer all around if I move in with you – just for the length of the investigation, of course."

"Of course," he sighed. "And how long do you expect the investigation to last, exactly?"

"Oh... five or six days," I said. "Maybe a few weeks. Month at the absolute most."

"At five hundred pounds a day?" he coughed.

"Well, you don't want to rush these things, do you?"

I figured I could do with a bit of fancy living for a few days, swanning about in a luxury flat and eating all of Dylan's Waitrose grub. Plus the credit on my electricity meter was getting dangerously low. And being away from my flat meant there was less chance of bumping into Mr Singh and his infuriating demands for rent.

"Fine," said Dylan. "You can come and stay for a few days."

"Excellent," I said. "Perhaps we should retire to your place now, to go over the details and form a plan. I'm a bit hungry actually. We could get a pizza delivered – on expenses, of course. And we can stop at a cash machine, so you can get me my first day's pay."

CHAPTER 3

TWO PIZZAS AND a fair few glasses of wine later, Dylan and I were sitting in the living room of his luxury pad, a little worse for wear.

"So, this hitman who's hunting you down," I said, "have you seen any credible suspects? Giant brutes following you round the supermarket? Suspicious-looking passers-by pressing fingers to their ears and talking into their sleeves?"

"I never said it was MI5, or anything. I'm not completely tonto. It's just the feeling, and all the recent things that have happened. And that car."

"Oh yes, the car. But you've not seen any odd looking people hanging around?"

"Well, I don't tend to leave the flat very often. I don't get out much at all, to be honest. My therapist says I should limit my interactions until I'm feeling a bit less... well, you know... depressed. He says I need to close myself off, get in touch with the inner me. Ask myself why I'm not happy."

"Sounds like pretty crap advice, if you ask me. I'm not one for socialising, as you know..."

"Really, Freddie?" he cut in, laughing. "You surprise me."

"But, surely, sitting in on your own all the time isn't going to help. You need to get out and meet people. Have a laugh. Get pissed. Get your end away. Do something to cheer yourself up."

"Well, that's what you'd think, but Dr Jeffries is quite against that. He says I need to fix myself before I can function happily in society. He has me on a strict plan to healthiness. I meditate and get regular exercise. I eat a healthy diet. I certainly shouldn't be eating this," he said, picking up a slice of meat feast pizza and taking a bite.

"What the hell's wrong with pizza?" I said, actually slightly offended.

"The cheese... God knows what additives are in the sauce... And you really shouldn't eat red meat."

"It's not red meat you wanna worry about mate," I scoffed. "It's the fuzzy green meat that'll kill you."

Dylan just screwed his face up and took another bite.

"But seriously, though. A trained therapist told you the best way to deal with your depression is to lock yourself away and avoid people?"

"I don't completely avoid people. I've got a book signing tomorrow. And I do work things. He just says I should cut my social life right back until I'm feeling better."

"Sounds like a fucking quack to me, Dylan. Follow that advice and you'll end up even more miserable than I am," I laughed.

Dylan chuckled and raised an eyebrow. Again, a slight flicker of the old him seemed to glint in his eyes.

"So what do you do with your time?" I said. "Sit at home writing those depressing books of yours? Can't see how that's gonna cheer you up."

"Not everyone finds my books depressing, you know. Some people find them very uplifting. I've had plenty of fan mail from people telling me how much they've changed their lives."

"Really? They never changed *my* life – well, apart from losing me a flatmate."

"Oh, so you've read my books as well, then?" he smiled.

"Yeah, I've scanned through them," I said. "I like to use them as a 'how *not* to' guide, when I'm working on my own stuff." I was lying, of course – Dylan is an incredibly good writer. Not my cup of tea in terms of genre, but he is very gifted and has a really beautiful way with words. "And they're a pretty good cure for insomnia."

"Well, I'm glad you've found them useful," he smirked, not quite believing me.

"But seriously mate," I said, "are you sure about this therapist of yours? I'm no expert, but it doesn't sound like his advice is all that great."

"He comes very highly recommended."

"By who?"

"Er... well," he stumbled slightly, looking a little embarrassed. "By Mortimer, actually."

"I might have known."

"Dr Jeffries is a great therapist," said Dylan, indignation ringing in his throat. "He's really helping me. I think..."

"Really?"

"Yes."

"Are you still depressed?"

"Well... yeah... a bit, I suppose."

"He can't be that fucking good then, can he? Why do you stick with him? His therapy's clearly not working, despite what you want to tell yourself."

"I don't know, Freddie. Life just feels so hard sometimes. Ever since Sonia, nothing ever seems to go right. Every time I get anywhere near to happiness, it just gets snatched away again. I meet a woman, I fall in love, and then she leaves me. I spend a year building a perfect house and five weeks later the bloody thing burns down. I've had cars stolen. I've been burgled three times. That jealous knob Carlisle Philpott is always having a pop at me in the press... I've had good friends walk out on me..."

He gave me a look as if to say, *Yes, I'm talking about you!* I looked at my feet, feeing slightly ashamed.

"I've had cancer twice, for God's sake," he continued. "I even bought a puppy to cheer myself up and some fucker poisoned it. Fed it slug pellets. Poor little thing.

"I'm telling you, nothing ever goes right. I'm destined to be miserable. But at least for one hour a week, Dr Jeffries listens to me. He gives me hope. And it makes me feel a bit better."

"Hey, at least you've got plenty of source material for those dreary books," I laughed, trying to find something consoling to say. "And it certainly hasn't hurt your sales."

He laughed, small tears glinting in his eyes.

"Yes, of course," he said. "My books. At least my writing hasn't suffered."

A long silence hung in the air between us.

"She'd be really pissed off with us, you know," said Dylan.

"Who would?" I asked.

"Sonia, of course," he snapped, annoyed that I hadn't instantly realised whom he was talking about.

"Pissed off? Why?"

"Because we stopped talking. Because we stopped... being friends." The last word caught in his throat. "You, she'd expect it from. You always were an antisocial prick. But she'd be annoyed with me for letting you ignore me. If she were still here, she'd have made me call you, or text you, or pop round with a bottle of wine and a pizza," he said, throwing a crust into the empty box on the floor.

"I did call, you know," he said, his words slurring. "Several times. And text. And I sent you Christmas cards. But you never picked up or replied, so I figured... well, I don't know what I figured..."

27

I looked at my feet, suddenly feeling very guilty. It was me who'd broken off the friendship. Me who'd ignored his calls and messages. And he was right; Sonia would have been annoyed with us. We'd been such good friends. Been through so much together. And it had all gone because I'd been too petty and jealous to deal with my best friend's success.

"Sorry," I said. "Really. I am sorry. I was just really busy. And you were... you were..."

"I was what?" he said.

"Well, you were always off at big fancy parties, or winning awards, or signing million pound book contracts."

"So you stopped calling me because I was successful?"

"Well... yeah, I suppose."

"Really?" he said, incredulity singing in his voice. "Seriously? You stopped being my friend because I was successful? You prick!"

"Sorry," I said. "I'm not exactly proud of it..."

"You prick. You jealous prick."

"Yeah. Sorry."

"No, seriously, you fucking prick!" He flopped back onto the sofa and drained the last mouthful of wine from his glass. "Well, I suppose it doesn't really matter now."

"No, I suppose not," I said.

"She really was a great girl, though. My Sonia."

"She was," I agreed. "One of the best."

"Things have never been the same since she... you know..."

"No," I said.

"I mean, I've been married again... too many times for my own good," he chuckled. "But it wasn't the same. I mean I loved them... But it was never the same, you know?"

"Of course," I said. "Sonia was one in a million. And you too were... well, you were right for each other. Perfect. I miss her too."

"She was one of the only people who believed in me," he said. "And we didn't have much back then."

"Don't remind me," I agreed. "I remember, I was there. And some of us still don't."

"But we had each other, and that was fine. She had her teaching job, and I wrote my books, and we managed. But she believed in me, probably more than I did myself. Then the first book sold and people liked it. Finally we had a bit of money. We were getting somewhere. We were planning a family. The future really started to look good. And then she went and died."

He looked down at the ground and sighed heavily.

"I know mate, it's not fair. It's really not."

"It's a fucking joke, is what it is," he said. "You work hard; you try and make something of yourself and what? It all gets taken away. And the fucking irony is I did make it, didn't I? I did get the success – she was right to believe in me. But it was all too late. Because she wasn't here to see it.

"I thought things were changing when I met Corinne. She was different. I really loved her and she loved me. At least I thought so. I don't even know what went wrong. I don't know why she left. I just came home from a work trip and she was gone."

"I know mate. Life is shit, and we're the poor saps wading our way through it," I said, not quite sure how you're supposed to raise someone's spirits. "Hey, it could be worse, though – someone could be trying to kill you."

"Ha! Good old Freddie. Always one to make a joke in the face of real feelings," he said, smiling.

"I'm not good for much else."

Dylan stood up, his knees wobbling slightly with the booze, and he nearly went tumbling back down onto the sofa.

"Well, I think I've had quite enough to drink tonight," he said. "And I've done far too much whinging. So, I think I'd better quit whilst I'm ahead and go to bed. Yours is the room at the end of the hall."

"Thanks Dylan," I said. "And don't worry, things will get better, I promise. We'll figure out this whole assassin business in the morning." I gave him a reassuring wink.

He flashed me a melancholic smile, one eye half-closed with drunkenness, and then burped loudly. "It's good to see you again, Freddie," he said. "Really good to see you."

Then he turned and staggered off down the hall, knocking a pot plant onto the floor as he went.

I poured myself another glass of wine and set about trying to think of all the reasons someone might want Dylan dead.

******

I woke up on the living room floor in just my underpants. I had a thudding headache and a taste like something had died in my mouth. It couldn't have been my sense of shame – that had passed away several years earlier.

With one hand I held my head, trying to stop the world from spinning round it, and with the other I rubbed at my aching back. I couldn't remember falling asleep, let alone the decision to sleep face-down on the floor rather than the more-than-adequate Queen-sized bed. And I certainly didn't remember shedding my clothes – or, indeed, the thinking behind using them to dress the Yucca plant, which I had apparently left outside Dylan's bedroom door, with a scary face and a kitchen knife sellotaped to the long green leaves, and a note saying: 'I'm going to kill you'.

I can only assume that, in my drunken state, it had seemed like a particularly good idea. I often get particularly good ideas whilst drunk. And they invariably turn out not to have been such inspired choices when the cold light of soberness flicks on the headache switch and the horror of what I've done comes flashing back.

It's the same drunken thinking that, in the past, has seen me purchase every copy of one of my books from a bargain bin at *The Works*, sign them all, and then walk around Soho handing them out to Japanese tourists. The same drunken mentality that saw me sneak into Christopher Brookmyre's hotel room after a crime writing festival in Bristol and empty a whole pack of chocolate mousse all over his crisp white sheets. Apparently, he still gets funny looks from the cleaning staff.

I once even head-butted a living statue in Covent Garden to prove to the gathered crowd that he was actually a real, moving person. I then snatched a great handful of helium balloons from a nearby balloon-seller and tried to make my escape by flying off into the air. Needless to say, it didn't work. And I was rewarded with a night in the cells for my efforts – the charges being assault, theft, drunk and disorderly behaviour and, just for fun, the arresting office scribbled down 'attempting to fly whilst under the influence'.

I picked myself up off the living room floor and stumbled into the kitchen. I found paracetamol in a drawer and washed down three pills (the two the packet recommended and one for luck) with a whole carton of orange juice.

Dylan had left a note stuck to the fridge with a magnet. It said:
Thanks for leaving that fucking thing outside my bedroom door. It scared the life

out of me, you dick! You're not as funny as you think you are!

I'll be out most of the day. I have a meeting with Mortimer in town, then I have a reading to do at a Waterstones in Oxford this arvo. Probably be back quite late. Make yourself at home and help yourself to whatever you find in the kitchen – if you haven't already!

Dylan

I searched the kitchen cupboards and found nothing but health food and disgusting looking things like muesli, brown bread and herbal tea. Certainly not the sort of food required by a man in my delicate condition. Even if it was free.

It was already 10.25 and my stomach was rumbling with a deep, nauseated growl. I needed something to fix me, so I pulled my clothes off the yucca and headed to the café at the end of the road.

A full English breakfast and three mugs of sugary tea later, I was feeling much restored. So, I pulled my trusty notepad and pen from my jacket pocket and started to think about who might possibly want Dylan dead.

I had a certain amount of experience in criminal investigations, having shadowed a young detective constable earlier in my writing career, to learn more about police procedure and to help get my facts straight. And Dylan was right: I'd written enough crime thrillers in my time that I should know roughly what I was doing.

But I needed to think like a real detective. So, I took Dylan's advice and tried putting myself in the shoes of my fictional detective Dick Stone, so I could look at the case with fresh eyes.

One thing I knew from writing my books is that you first have to list out all the potential suspects, no matter how unlikely. You need to figure out all the possible motives for wanting him dead. And establish all the red herrings – the characters you think might have done it, but turn out to have sound alibis or reasons to want him still alive.

I started sketching out a list of names. I tried to think of anyone who might have felt like they'd been wronged by Dylan, or anyone who was spiteful enough to want to see him harmed because of his success. I considered all the people I knew, all the people I knew that Dylan knew, and anyone else I could think of. Rather annoyingly, the first, most likely, candidate that seemed to fit the bill was me. But as I knew I wasn't trying to kill him, or following him around in a mysterious blue Ford, I immediately scored a line through my name.

So, who could want Dylan dead? The next most obvious candidate –

or trio of candidates – were Dylan's three ex-wives. He'd said they had all parted amicably, and had been taken care of in the divorces, but in my experience things are never quite that simple. Maybe the splits weren't as amicable as Dylan thought. Or maybe they weren't quite as happy with the terms of their pre-nuptial agreements as he assumed. As a first step, I decided to make visits to all three and find out more about them.

When it comes to murder, they say you should always look at family members first. But Dylan didn't have any. His parents died when he was young. He had no brothers or sisters. And he'd certainly never mentioned any aunts, uncles, cousins or murderous distant relations. I wrote down *No family* in my pad.

I definitely wanted to talk to Dylan's agent, Mortimer Bunkle. He wasn't a suspect, but he'd represented Dylan throughout his whole career. He knows Dylan better than anyone, and if something untoward was going on he might be able to shed some light on it. And if Dylan was just being paranoid, talking to Mortimer might help me to prove it.

I'd also have to look into the mysterious blue car. I wasn't quite sure how you went about tracking down mysterious cars – or exactly what I was going to do if I did manage to find it – but I wrote it down on the list anyway.

CHAPTER 4

I HEADED BACK to Dylan's flat and logged on to his computer. It took all of five seconds to break his highly unsophisticated password – KATMANDU. It was the name he gave to the ginger moggy that used to wander into our flat in London, sleep on our sofa, beg us for food and then disappear to wherever it actually lived.

Dylan, being Dylan, instantly fell in love with the flea-ridden bag of fur – me far less so – and he took to leaving out little plates of food for it, christening it with a comedy moniker and even spending twenty quid on a sodding cat bed for the thing when it deigned to visit. We never did find out who its real owners were, but it came to see us four or five times a week – no doubt doing the rounds of the neighbourhood and picking up free meals from all the suckers who let it in.

Dylan had thought his comedy cat name so hilarious that he'd taken to using it for all his online and computer passwords. He thought I didn't know, but it was too obvious. Apparently, about ninety per cent of idiots around the world use a beloved pet's name for their computer password. Dylan was one of those idiots.

I had to laugh at his predictability. And I now had instant access to his laptop and probably his bank accounts, Facebook, Twitter and mobile phone.

I had a quick check through his emails. Nothing particularly salacious or suspicious jumped out at me, so I scanned through a folder on the desktop named pictures. Inside were folders marked: *Christmas, Holidays, Sonia, Katmandu, Funny Pics, Me & Freddie, Book Covers* and *Wedding Pics*. I clicked on the wedding pics folder and inside found four more sub folders named: *Sonia, Georgina, Corinne* and *Chantelle*. He really was making this too easy for me.

I scanned through the pictures inside the folders, all of which featured snaps of Dylan and his various brides. I sighed as I looked through the folder named *Sonia*. It brought back memories.

I had, of course, been Dylan's best man and there were lots of pictures of me and him smiling and joking, wearing our silly looking, ill-fitting suits. There were snaps of me and Sonia hugging; pictures of us all at the top table; shots of people falling about laughing as I delivered my hilarious best man's speech – one picture featured Sonia's mother literally shooting wine out of her nose as I revealed the details of one of Dylan's late-night, naked, drunken parades through the halls of residence.

I clicked through the pictures of Dylan's other weddings, feeling more than a little shamefaced at having not attended any of them. I had, of course, received invitations to all of them. But, by that point, my jealousy and arrogance had reached its peak and I'd thrown them all straight in the bin.

I checked the dates on all the pictures, quickly surmising that Georgina had been Dylan's second wife after Sonia. Corinne had been his third wife. And, finally, Chantelle had been the fourth. All three women were very beautiful. Georgina had dark bobbed hair, a pretty face, a very toned physique and a demure look. Corinne looked similarly classy with flowing, brunette hair, a beaming smile and also a slim figure. I could certainly see what Dylan saw in them.

Chantelle, however, didn't look exactly Dylan's type. She was a good seven or eight years younger than the other women – I'd have guessed her age at maybe twenty or twenty-one. She had long, blonde hair, big boobs, a tiny waist and a serious pout on her face – every bit the playboy bunny type. In every single picture she looked far more interested in the camera than in her new husband. And Dylan, I'm sad to say, looked more embarrassing old sugar daddy than blushing, happy groom.

I opened up the contacts book on the laptop, cross-referenced the three wives against the names found there, and soon I had phone numbers and addresses for all three. I smiled smugly, impressed at my own research skills. The investigation was fully under way and I started to psych myself up into full-on interrogation mode.

Just as I was about to shut down the laptop, another folder on the desktop caught my eye. It was simply titled *Books*. I clicked it open. Inside were individual folders for all of Dylan's novels – *The Merchant of Sorrow*, *A Chance for Happiness*, *Once Upon a Never*, *The Christening of No One's Child* and *Let It Be Me*. A bloody depressing looking reading list if ever I'd seen one.

But there were two other folders inside – one entitled *New Book: Final Draft* and another called *Rejected Books*. Naturally, I assumed the first folder would contain a manuscript for Dylan's newest project. There had been press speculation that he was due to deliver his long-awaited new book to his publisher soon. Anyone who'd seen even a paragraph of a preview copy was claiming it to be his best yet, and sure to win all this year's prizes. I figured I might pinch a copy and have a look over it when I had time. But I was far more intrigued by the second mystery folder.

I clicked it open and found four full manuscripts for novels I had no idea Dylan had written. The folders were called: *The Redemption of Alicia Sweet*, *Falling for You*, *Happiness at Last* and *Love in Calmer Waters*.

Had Dylan really written so many books that had never been published? Possibly even rejected? I'm ashamed to admit I was a little bit pleased. Perhaps he wasn't as infallible as everyone thought. This would certainly warrant a little further investigation. But, for the time being, I was keen to crack on and track down Dylan's ex-wives.

So, I copied the whole *Books* folder onto a memory stick, powered down the laptop and phoned for a taxi to take me to Victoria train station.

******

I strolled up the pathway of the semi-detached house in the small Sussex town of Haywards Heath. It was a fairly modest property – modern and well-maintained, though a little small and somewhat ordinary looking.

Dylan married Georgina about three years after Sonia died, and after his second novel, and first big success, was published. But they separated before he achieved the astronomical success he now has. She had clearly cashed her chips before the big windfall came, and her divorce settlement would presumably have been smaller than wives three and four. Hence the modest-sized house and not the million pound apartment wife number three apparently resided in.

Maybe I'd found my motive already – spurned former wife, jealous at having less money than she felt entitled to, striking a blow for revenge? Stranger things have happened.

The door was answered by a petite, attractive woman with dark hair and a warm smile. She looked a little older than the pictures I'd seen of her, and her hair was double the length, but she was still very pretty.

"Hello?" she said, with the sort of dismissive politeness people generally reserve for vacuum cleaner salesmen.

"Hello," I said. "Mrs St James?"

"That's right. What can I do for you?"

"My name is Freddie Winters. I was hoping I could talk to you about your ex-husband."

"Dylan?" she said with genuine concern. "Is everything all right? Has something happened to him?"

"Oh no, nothing like that," I said, with a reassuring smile. "Well, not yet, anyway."

"Not yet?"

"Dylan thinks someone might be trying to... well... kill him," I chuckled dismissively. "And he's asked me to... look into it. Perhaps I could come inside?"

She welcomed me through to the living room and came back a few minutes later with a pot of tea. She poured us both a cup and sat on the sofa across from me.

"So, who are you?" she asked, almost accusingly.

"My name's Freddie. I'm an old friend of Dylan's."

"Freddie..." she said, thinking. "Hang on... Freddie? You're not *that* Freddie, are you?"

"Erm... possibly..." I said.

"Hmmm... Freddie Winters," she said with disapproval. "I thought I recognised the name. Dylan's old university friend?"

"Yes, has he mentioned me?"

"You could say that."

"None too favourably, I presume?"

"On the contrary,' she said, sneering slightly. "Dylan never had a bad word to say about you. Always talking about his great friend, Freddie. It's me that doesn't much care for you."

"Ah," I said. "Nothing like first impressions, eh?"

"He was really hurt when you stopped answering his phone calls, you know," said Georgina. "Kept saying he didn't know what he'd done to upset you. I told him not to worry about it – some people are just uncaring twats." She said the last word with real venom.

"Well, I can't argue with that," I said. "But we've had something of a... reconciliation just lately."

"You mean you've stopped being a dick?"

"Not entirely," I laughed, "but I'm working on it."

This raised the slightest hint of a smile from her, and she let her guard down just a little.

"So what's all this about Dylan, then? Someone's trying to kill him?"

"That's certainly what he seems to think."

"I take it the threat can't be that serious. Or there'd be a policeman at my door, not a failed novelist." Again the last words were delivered with more than a hint of menace.

"Quite," I said. "But Dylan's concerned, so he asked me to look into it and see if there was any credible threat."

"And what exactly qualifies you for this dubious honour?" she said.

"Well, nothing really. Dylan seemed to think that because I write crime novels, I might have some useful insights."

"And as you're here questioning me, should I assume that I'm some kind of a suspect in all this?"

"Of course not," I lied. "I'm just doing the rounds, talking to people, trying to figure out what's going on and ease the poor guy's mind."

"Well, it shouldn't need saying, but just for the record, I'd never do anything to harm Dylan. I still care for him, very deeply."

"Of course," I said, pulling my notepad and pen from my pocket. "So, how exactly did you and Dylan first meet?"

"Well..." she said, with a melancholy sigh, "it was about eight years ago now. I was working as an assistant to Dylan's agent."

"Mortimer Bunkle?"

"That's right, do you know him?"

"Sort of. I mean, I used to," I said.

"Well, anyway, I was working for Mortimer, and Dylan used to come in to the office quite often. He looked so sad in those days, like a little lost puppy. I felt quite sorry for him."

"And you hit it off straight away?" I said.

"Not exactly. He was a bit shy, but we always chatted when he came in. I thought he was cute and really charming. Then one day he surprised me by asking me out. We dated for a bit and we fell in love."

"Hmmm..." I said, closing my eyes into thin slits. "And how long were you together?"

"We dated for six months, and were married for just under two years. Such a shame it ended, but you know..."

"Not really. Tell me about it."

"Well, you know Dylan. He's the loveliest, kindest, sweetest man in the world, and when we first met I knew he had problems with his depression. His first wife, Sonia, had died a few years before, and he was still grieving. But I genuinely thought I made things better for him. For the first year we were really happy."

"And then?"

"He was working on a new book. We went out lots and had fun. He really seemed like a new man. And then it all started to go wrong."

"Wrong? How exactly?"

"It started when he got bad feedback from his publisher about his new book."

"Really? What did they say?"

"No idea. He wouldn't tell me. But I assumed they didn't like it."

"So what happened?"

"It's hard to explain. He just sort of drifted away from me. It happened slowly at first. He locked himself away in his office for days at a time. He barely talked to me."

She seemed genuinely saddened as she spoke.

"That must have been pretty hard," I said.

"It was devastating," she said. "I could see him sinking back into himself, and there was nothing I could do. I tried to be there for him… give him support and be his wife. But the more I tried, the more he pushed me away. I think that was the worst of it. He wouldn't tell me what was wrong, and he wouldn't let me help him."

"He always was a sensitive soul," I said. "Never did like criticism – though, I suppose, who does?"

"There was only so much of it I could take," she said. "He'd spend days away from the house. Then the days became weeks. I barely saw him; we never talked. All he ever did was work. And the rare times I did see him, he was always so down and depressed. In the end, I had to leave. It was no kind of life, and I was worried that if I stayed any longer I'd end up as unhappy as he was."

She wiped a tear from the corner of her eye and forced a smile.

"Of course, as it turns out," she said, "I suppose he made the right decision. That book was even more successful than his previous bestseller and won him his first big award. I'm sure the publishers were over the moon about that – even if it did cost me my marriage. And you know, I don't think I've ever seen him genuinely happy since."

"You still see him?" I asked.

"Not so much, really," she said. "We keep in touch a bit. And I see him on the telly every now and then. He always has such sad eyes, like they were when I first met him."

"Yes, he is a bit of a sourpuss, isn't he? So, can you think of anyone that might want to hurt Dylan?"

"No," she said, shaking her head. "No one. Dylan really is the sweetest, nicest man. I can't imagine anyone wanting to hurt him. Certainly not kill him. When he's not in one of his dark moods he really is so nice – he'd do anything to help anyone. He always has time for his fans. He once even paid a £200 taxi fare for a woman who queued up so long to get her book signed that she missed her train home."

"Yes, he is quite annoying, isn't he?" I said.

Her look told me that she didn't agree.

"And how are things with you?" I said, sitting back in my chair and raising an eyebrow.

"How are things with me?" she asked. "I assume this is the point at which you try and create some kind of motive for me wanting to hurt Dylan, is it?"

"Motive? What motive?" I said, trying out something I'd seen police detectives use in the past to trick suspects into revealing more than they meant to. "I never said anything about a motive." It didn't quite work, but she got the point.

"Oh stop pissing about, Mr Winters," she said. "What madcap theory have you got floating about in your tiny little brain?"

"Okay," I said. "Money. You divorced Dylan before he became vastly rich. If you'd hung around long enough, you might have got more out of him. You might be living in a million pound mansion, not a two-bed semi. Maybe you're unhappy about that?"

She laughed at my theory, shaking her head. "Very good," she said. "Except you're completely wrong."

"Really?"

"Yes. Firstly, it's a three-bed, not two. Secondly, I bought my own house and I am more than pleased with it. Thirdly, Dylan and I signed a pre-nuptial agreement, so I wouldn't have got any more than was originally agreed."

"Really? You weren't upset that Dylan asked for a pre-nup?"

"Not really. I knew what I was getting into when I married Dylan. He was already quite established. And, to be honest, it seemed quite sensible. It was Dylan who was embarrassed when he asked me to sign it."

"How did he bring it up?"

"I don't remember, it was years ago. I think he just told me he'd been given some legal advice, and said it was best to get everything down in a contract before we got married."

"Legal advice? From who?"

"I don't know. I didn't ask. A lawyer, I suppose."

"And you really didn't care?"

"No, I didn't care. I loved Dylan and I wanted to marry him – not his money!"

"Still, without that bit of paper, you'd have got a bigger settlement,"

I said.

"Believe it or not, I actually have a very good job as a literary agent, which I got when I quit Mortimer. So I have as much money as I need. I choose to live here because I like it. It's outside London and I get to work from home. And lastly, as far as I know, I'm not in Dylan's will. And I'm not named on any insurance policy. So if Dylan dies, how exactly am I supposed to profit from it?"

"Maybe it's not about money. Maybe it's about revenge."

"But I have no reason to want revenge. I was sad that the marriage ended, but it was my decision to leave. And you know what Dylan's like; if I really wanted money all I'd have to do is ask and he'd just give it to me."

"That is true," I said, feeling the bulge of notes in my pocket, "he is a bit of a sucker for that sort of thing."

"If you're really looking for someone with a motive to hurt Dylan, maybe you should go and speak with his third wife," said Georgina.

"Corinne? Why do you say that?"

She turned away, hesitating to speak. "Oh, I've said too much already."

"No, come on," I insisted, "you can't say something like that and then not follow it up."

"Look, it's nothing, really," she said, "probably just me being bitchy. But I just never really bought it when they got married. I didn't believe she really loved him. And she was quick to divorce him, too. If anyone married Dylan for his money or his status, it was her."

"Really?" I said. "Did you know her?"

"Not very well. She was another client of Mortimer's. She wrote one of those tacky kiss-and-tell books. Desperate to become famous at any cost. I never could tell what Dylan saw in her. Well, aside from the obvious…"

"Yes, she is a bit of a stunner," I said.

Georgina raised an eyebrow. "Yes, I suppose she is."

"And what do you know of Dylan's fourth wife?"

"Nothing," she said, dismissively. "Never met her. I saw the pictures on the internet, of course. Another weird choice, if you ask me. And I don't think anyone was surprised that marriage ended. How long was it? Six months?"

I drained my cup, looking hopefully at her for a refill. She responded by lifting the pot from the table and walking it out into the kitchen.

"If those are all your questions," she said, coming back into the room, "I have lots of work to do, and I think I've been accused of quite enough for one day."

"I do have one final question," I said, peeling the scowl from my face and replacing it with my best smile. "You say you're a literary agent now. I don't suppose you're taking on new clients?"

"Only good ones," she said, smiling sycophantically and gesturing me towards the door.

I scowled again, standing up and walking out of the room. "Thank you for your time."

"Wait," she said, suddenly.

I stopped on the other side of the door, turning back towards her.

"If you see Dylan, tell him to give me a ring."

"I will do," I said.

"And make sure you look after him. Make sure he's all right."

And then she called me a wanker and slammed the door in my face.

CHAPTER 5

AFTER A MISERABLE half hour waiting at Haywards Heath train station, a forty-five minute journey in a piss-smelling train carriage, and a ten-minute delay on the Tube, I was thankfully back in London, and back in the luxury of Dylan's flat. He'd sent me a text message to let me know his reading had overrun. Rather than getting a late train back, he'd decided to check into a hotel in Oxford and travel back in the morning.

No doubt it was Dylan's fault the reading had overrun. He'd probably spent hours playing the saint, signing more books than he was contractually obliged to and talking at length with his adoring fans. Some people really are too nice. But, no matter. It meant I had the place to myself for the evening, and more time to think about the case at hand. And if I got really bored, I could even do some actual work as well.

The train back from Haywards Heath had taken me directly past Gatwick Airport. I'd gazed out at the twinkling lights of the runway as we passed, watching as a plane came down over the top of the carriage and landed just yards away. I'd wondered where the plane had come in from. It was an EasyJet, so more likely a returning booze-up from Magaluf than a stunning Caribbean destination, but no doubt more exciting than boring old England.

I'd thought about all the passengers crammed in at the airport, awaiting their flights to a multitude of destinations. Sandy beaches, snow-capped mountains, historical cities… the options were limitless. I imagined how excited they all were – the lucky bastards.

And then I felt the wad of notes Dylan had given me last night, stuffed into my trouser pocket. I had a sudden urge to head to the airport, buy the first ticket to anywhere and just get the hell away. I had about £460 left, so it wouldn't get me far, but it would get me somewhere more exotic than London. How nice it must be, I thought, to be able to just get away. To escape. To go where your heart desires and just do what you want.

How nice it must be to have Dylan's kind of money – serious wealth, where you can do whatever you want, go wherever you want to at the drop of a hat. Have as much fun as your money could buy. And yet the miserable bastard spent all his time sitting at home, moping about, barely spending a penny and not having any fun at all.

Surely the best thing for a man in his position would be a decent bloody holiday. Forget about his problems and sit on a tropical beach, drinking cocktails out of a coconut and cavorting with bikini-clad girls in the sea. I couldn't believe his so-called expert therapist had advised against any of that, and instead told him to lock himself away. How was that supposed to help? I made a mental note that I'd have to go and question Dylan's shrink, as part of my investigation. And give him a bloody big piece of my mind when I was there.

Thankfully, Dylan had also sent me the code for the little security box on the wall that held the spare keys. So I let myself into the flat, checked that nobody was home and gave myself a quick tour of the place. I'd been too involved in reminiscing with Dylan the previous night. And I was so hungover and keen to get out investigating that morning that I'd neglected to familiarise myself with my new temporary home.

The flat was enormous. There were three bedrooms – one giant master bedroom and another two decent-sized doubles, all three with en suite. The living room was also huge, at least the size of my entire flat, leading out into a long hallway that branched off into a large kitchen with flashy, expensive appliances and one of those poncy central worktop islands. There was a spacious dining room with a long mahogany table that looked as though it had never been used. And a great big bathroom with a giant whirlpool bath.

My own bathroom at home is a good sixteenth the size, with a bath so small no reasonable-sized human could possibly fit into it comfortably. There's so little floor space that you literally have to squeeze your legs into the gap between the loo and the edge of the bath when you sit down – and you daren't take longer than a five-minute poo or the circulation in your legs cuts off and you're risking near-fatal levels of deep vein thrombosis.

The décor throughout Dylan's place was modern and somewhat lacking in personality – the standard plain walls, inoffensive furniture and nondescript trinkets you'd expect to find in any short-stay rental apartment. There was nothing of Dylan's on display. But then, he was only staying there short-term. And I guessed most of his stuff had probably gone up in flames in the fire at his house.

Though lacking in charm, the place was definitely very plush. I dreaded to think how much rent Dylan must have been paying. And I was already starting to feel quite at home – as if I'd finally made it to the kind of living I should have been enjoying all these years. I'd certainly have to see if I could drag the case out for a few weeks longer, and enjoy this new life of luxury, before returning to my own disappointing home.

At the end of the hall was Dylan's office. I'd been in there that morning, to crack into Dylan's laptop. But I'd been so keen to get the investigation under way that I'd barely looked around. It was only now that I stopped to take it all in.

It was an average-sized room, with a long desk and an expensive-looking leather office chair. One of those dreadful inspirational posters adorned the wall, with a picture of a penguin leaping from a giant block of ice. Underneath were the words: *Courage: Sometimes you just have to take that leap of faith!* It was so 'inspirational' I was almost sick in my mouth.

I noticed a shelf above the desk; two heavy, metal book-ends sitting either side of a selection of books. My books. Every single one of them.

I looked closely at the paperbacks. Each one had a cracked, battered spine – visible proof that they'd all been read, probably more than once. I felt embarrassed. Dylan's dedication to our friendship once again put me very much to shame.

There was a small two-seater leather sofa in the corner of the room. A thick, woollen cardigan lay draped over one arm, and several dirty mugs sat on a small coffee table by its side. I guessed this was the room Dylan spent most of his time in. No wonder he was so bloody depressed.

Dylan's laptop sat in the middle of the desk, surrounded by piles of books and uncorrected manuscripts. I guessed they were samples sent to Dylan in the hope he might read them and endow them with a glittering endorsement for the final printed cover. There's nothing like a recommendation from another big-named author to help you shift units – I should know, I've been legally obliged to remove several from my website over the years, due to the minor technicality of the authors I'd quoted claiming to have never actually endorsed me, or even read any of my books. Bloody Ian bloody Rankin and his bloody lawyers.

Most of the books looked as though Dylan had at least skimmed through them. On top of one of the piles was a manuscript entitled *The Art of Love in the Time of War and Death* by Carlisle Philpott. Stuck to the front cover was a yellow Post-it note with the words 'Fat chance, dickhead!' scribbled on it.

Carlisle Philpott was Dylan's nemesis, or as close to one as someone like Dylan could have. He, too, was a reasonably successful writer – on the scale of things much better off than me, but still far short of Dylan. He wrote the same kind of morbid, dreary 'literary' fiction as Dylan, hence the coma-inducing title of what I assumed was his latest masterpiece.

Carlisle was pretty well respected. He was considered to be a decent writer, and certainly had the sales to back it up. The only problem he had was Dylan. It seemed as though every time Carlisle released a new book, Dylan's latest came out the very same week, soaking up the majority of sales from that market and leaving Carlisle's offering very much in second place.

They always seemed to be short-listed for the same awards. And on the rare occasion that Dylan didn't take first place, he still finished higher up the list and took all the press attention that Carlisle craved. Dylan was invited to appear on the Late Review show, whilst Carlisle had to watch it from home. Dylan always had the longest line of autograph hunters at the book festivals, and the prettiest fans. And whenever Carlisle was interviewed in the paper, or on TV, the one question he was asked more than any other was what he thought of Dylan's work.

It was all far too coincidental for my liking. No doubt the work of the same marketing geniuses that convinced Dylan to change his name and helped him to build his 'brand'.

At first Carlisle seemed to take it all in his stride, fixing his best fake smile and pretending it didn't bother him. But I guess there's only so much you can take when you see someone else getting the fame and success that could – or should – be coming your way. Because without Dylan, Carlisle would be cleaning up on sales, appearing on late-night BBC2 and fending off pretty book groupies.

So it wasn't long before jealousy reared its ugly head and, clearly having had enough of standing in Dylan's shadow, Carlisle started to fight back. He'd rubbish Dylan in the press at every opportunity. He wrote mean-spirited, derogatory reviews of his books. He had a pop at him on Facebook and Twitter on a near daily basis.

Dylan didn't take too kindly to any of it – after all, he was only writing books, not purposefully going out of his way to sabotage the man. After several attempts to make the peace, he had to accept that the two were pretty much enemies.

And when the marketing boys got hold of the dispute between them, they spun it out of all control. Soon the press were talking about the bitterest literary feud of all time, and things just got worse.

Naturally, Dylan came off as the injured party, which only saw his book sales increase, his TV appearances become more frequent and his autograph hunters double in number. Which must have really, really annoyed Carlisle.

I smiled at the thought of Dylan being asked to endorse his book. And then I laughed as I imagined the stream of verbal abuse the poor publicity sap at Carlisle's publishers would receive if he ever found out that they'd sent a copy to Dylan.

I pulled out my notepad and wrote *Carlisle Philpott* at the top of one of the pages, then underlined it three times. He would definitely need some further investigation. After all, who was likely to benefit the most if Dylan was suddenly out of the way, if not the writer who felt he'd been holding him back for his whole career? If this threat against Dylan was real, the list of suspects was growing bigger all the time.

I powered up Dylan's laptop, hacked into his Facebook account using his one and only password, and scanned through his most recent interactions. He wasn't the most active social media user. His page was filled with unanswered friend requests from fans, hundreds of birthday greetings on his wall and numerous unread messages. There were over 100 messages – more than three per day – from one of Dylan's 'friends', who went by the name of DylansBiggestFan. I wondered if she might have been the jumper-knitting stalker Dylan had mentioned.

There were no status updates from Dylan, no posts of any kind and no indication he'd even logged in over the last six months. Unlike myself, who dedicates a good hour each day to spamming anyone and everyone with friend requests, links to where people can buy my books online, or details of where they can come and see me at one of my impromptu readings or signings. I guessed Dylan didn't need to bother with his own marketing activities. His 'people' probably did that all for him. In a far more professional manner.

Dylan's Twitter account was equally sparse, offering no tangible leads whatsoever. So I clicked on his email account and started reading through messages.

Again, there were hundreds of emails from DylansBiggestFan on various subjects ranging from how much she loved his latest books to the theme she was thinking of for his next jumper, questions about his childhood, how he thought up the plots of his books, and lots of questions about different aspects of his characters. And there were lots of pictures of cats wearing various articles of clothing, which she'd emailed to Dylan because she thought they were 'cute'. I couldn't tell if she was quirky or deranged, but she didn't seem particularly dangerous.

I wondered how she'd managed to get hold of Dylan's email address. Had she hacked into his online accounts to extract the information? Had she phoned him under elaborate false pretences and tricked him into telling her? Knowing Dylan, he'd probably just given it to her.

I scanned through the rest of the Inbox. There were a handful of emails from his second wife, Georgina. It was all standard keeping in touch stuff – asking how he was, commiserating about the house fire, expressing her hopes that he was okay. I continued down the list, scouring through all the usual junk mail offering PPI reclaims, cheap deals on electronics goods and 'highly effective' penis-growing medicines. And there were about a thousand unopened emails from Amazon, flogging all manner of crap.

I found several emails from Dylan's agent, Mortimer. They talked about Dylan's newest book and how excited the publisher was to read it. In another email, Mortimer talked about trying to get Dylan a better deal. Another asked how Dylan felt about putting the book out for auction. Dylan had replied to say that, even though he was out of contract with them, he would prefer to stay with his current publisher.

Naturally, Mortimer had come back to say that he thought Dylan could get much more money if he went elsewhere. He urged him to reconsider sending it out to other players in the field. There didn't seem to be a reply to that one.

I clicked on an email from Dylan's most recent wife, the young Barbie-doll lookalike, Chantelle. There was very little warmth to what she wrote and barely a word spelled correctly. Either the woman was on a self-imposed punctuation ban, or she was experimenting with streams of consciousness. Or she was just an illiterate idiot. I guessed probably the latter.

She started off talking about how "guttid I woz the house burnd down" and "I sore you on the telley last week". The rest of the email was nothing more than a blatant request for money. She explained how she'd been struggling to get much work recently and, having spent a fortune setting herself up in LA with a view to picking up acting work, she'd yet to be given a part. She'd run out of cash and had to return to the UK.

She went on to say that she'd spent all of the money she got from the divorce, and asked if he would reconsider the terms of their pre-nup and give her some more.

I stretched and yawned and rubbed my tired eyes. It was getting late and, having extracted everything I reasonably could from Dylan's emails, I decided to call it a night. I clicked on the website for the local Chinese takeaway and ordered a delivery big enough for three people. While I waited, I thought I might as well try out Dylan's giant bath and all the fancy soaps and potions in the bathroom cabinet.

I closed the lid of the laptop and made my way towards the hall. As I passed the window, something caught my eye on the street below. It was the merest flicker of light – a tiny amber spark as someone lit a cigarette in the driver's seat of a car. But it was enough to make me stop.

I looked closer. It was dark outside and it was hard to see, but the car was clearly a Ford Mondeo – one of the older, rounder models. I couldn't tell exactly what colour it was, but it was either black or dark blue. A cold shiver ran the length of my spine.

I couldn't clearly see the licence plate, but there was something stuck to the inside of the rear passenger window. I squinted my eyes, straining to see and… yes… it was… a cuddly fucking Garfield. Dylan had been right about the car after all.

I dashed out of the room, down the hallway and out the front door. I sprinted down four flights of stairs to the ground floor, burst out of the main building and out onto the street.

I saw the car on the other side of the road and strolled purposefully over. But the driver must have seen me, as the engine suddenly roared into life. The lights flicked on full beam, half blinding me. I raised a hand to shield my eyes, squinting hard as I stepped out into the road.

The car's tyres squealed as they spun on the cold tarmac. I stopped dead, watching as the car lurched into life, peeling out of the space and hurtling towards me at speed. My legs took over and I jolted to my side, throwing myself over the bonnet of another parked car. I landed face down on the windscreen with all the grace and poise of a sumo wrestler.

The speeding car missed me by just a few inches. It narrowly avoided the car I was spread-eagled across. It clipped the wing mirror of the next car in the row. And then it hurtled off down the street and disappeared into the darkness.

CHAPTER 6

MARTA, THE GRUMPY Polish barista, was glaring at me from behind the counter. I'd been ensconced at a table in the corner of Starbucks for one hour and forty-three minutes, and I still had a full two thirds of a cold, small cappuccino idling in my cup. I was finding Dylan's flat a little too luxurious, and his big screen TV too distracting. I'd needed to get out and find somewhere that I could think more clearly, so I relocated to my favourite coffee shop.

I'd also wanted to get out before Dylan got back, so that I could take his laptop rather than my own. There were still a few things I wanted to follow up, and I hadn't quite finished snooping through it. My own laptop, with its incomplete page of 'ideas', was also little more than a constant reminder of how far behind I was with my own work. At least I was getting paid to look into Dylan's mystery.

After the previous night's encounter with the kamikaze Mondeo driver, I was taking things a lot more seriously. Either they were auditioning for a part in the Wacky Races, or they had been deliberately trying to either kill or seriously injure me.

Dylan had been right about the car. I had no idea how long it had been parked outside the flat, but as soon I came out the driver had fled.

Was it a hitman, lying in wait for his prey? I couldn't tell. There was still nothing to suggest more than a little light stalking. But it was certainly suspicious. And the fact that they'd panicked and tried to squash me under their wheels suggested something strange was definitely going on.

I pulled out my notepad and reviewed my list of suspects. I made a note next to Georgina's name, ruling her out of the investigation. She'd seemed genuine in her affection for Dylan, and I really couldn't see her wanting to hurt him. There was no tangible motive, either. I'd spent twenty minutes Googling her, and she did indeed work as a literary agent for a reasonable-sized firm. She had a couple of decent clients, so she wasn't exactly poor. I had no idea how much she'd received in the divorce settlement, but even though it was likely to be less than wives three and four, she hadn't seemed aggrieved about it.

The next name on my list was Corinne Handley, Dylan's third wife.

I typed her name into Google and it came back with thousands of results. The first was a link to her website. The second went to a Wikipedia page about her. The third linked to a selection of her books on Amazon. There were also several links to interviews with her, articles about her, reviews of her books (both positive and derogatory, depending on which site they were on) and plenty of other pages dedicated to her.

As Georgina had mentioned, Corinne was a fellow writer. According to Wikipedia, she had come to fame at the tender age of twenty-three, after writing a kiss-and-tell book about an affair she'd had with the then England football captain. The affair had apparently caused major upset and scandal, partly due to the sordid nature of their sexual interactions – which included drug taking and light bondage – and partly due to the footballer's wife being pregnant at the time.

The affair had seen the football star kicked out of the national squad, quickly divorced, and then sold by his premiership team to a dwindling side in the lower leagues. Corinne, however, made over three million pounds from her book. It was also serialised in the Daily Mail (no surprise!), and she went on to establish a successful career as a writer.

Her disreputable canon of work included her first kiss-and-tell book; a second kiss-and-tell, in which she spilled the beans on a prominent cabinet minister (really, he should have seen it coming); two erotic novels; and a third kiss-and-tell with a gormless, married TV quiz show host (seriously, he only has himself to blame). She'd also apparently tried her hand at writing a serious fiction book, which was heavily panned by the critics and sold next to no copies.

There appeared to be several hundred pictures of Corinne plastered all over the internet. She was thirty-two years old, but still looked several years younger. She had long brunette hair, sparkling brown eyes and full, red lips. Some of the pictures showed her at book signings, some were 'serious literary shots' for the weekend papers, and there were countless lads mag spreads in which she appeared in just her underwear and a smile.

The Daily Mail website also had several hundred paparazzi pictures of her doing such exciting things as shopping, filling her car with petrol, walking her dog or just breathing.

She was very beautiful, and I could certainly see why so many men had fallen for her charms – and why they'd lied to themselves that they weren't in line for the same treatment as the kiss-and-tell victims before them. I could also see how Dylan might have been drawn to her. He would have been the easiest mark – rich, successful, very much in the public eye and also very depressed and lonely. She'd barely have had to flash a smile in his direction, and she'd have him hook, line and sort code.

Despite that, there was no evidence that Dylan had been a mark to her at all. She'd certainly never written a book about their time together, and appeared to have no plans to. I found several interviews with her, asking about her relationship with Dylan, and it actually seemed quite genuine. When they first married, she told an interviewer from the Sun that 'this marriage is for real' and it was 'the happiest I've ever been'. Since their split, she had apparently refused to ever discuss Dylan at all.

In fact, several of the interviews I found with her displayed the same surprise as I had that she was unwilling to reveal the more intimate nature of their marriage.

So, had the marriage been for real? Or had she found herself outwitted by Mortimer Bunkle and his mysterious pre-nuptial agreement? If so, why had she gone through with the marriage, instead of just shagging the poor guy for a few months then selling the story? The tabloids would have been salivating over the chance to expose the country's top literary talent in a shameful sex scandal.

The front page of her website held a large advert for her forthcoming book – *Cash and Tell: How to make money from cheating men*. It would appear that she had gone back to her roots and, rather than actually kissing and telling herself, she'd written some kind of instruction manual for other would-be gold-diggers. According to the blurb, the book outlines the best ways to attract rich men, what to do to them, and then finally how to either blackmail them or sell the story to the highest bidder. It was an absolutely loathsome idea, which was bound to sell in the millions. I cursed myself for not coming up with it.

So, Dylan's third wife had a history of screwing men for money. Would she also be open to the idea of killing them for it? I scribbled a big question mark next to her name. She would definitely have to be next on my list to interview.

I opened up Dylan's emails again. There were sixteen new messages. One was from Mortimer Bunkle, asking how Dylan's reading had gone yesterday and again enquiring about the possibility of taking his new book to other publishers. There was an email from Georgina, asking how Dylan was doing and letting him know I'd been to see her. She went on to outline her less than charitable opinion of me in a long sequence of expletives.

There were two new innocuous emails from DylansBiggestFan; one offer of a new credit card; two PPI emails; and another offering a revolutionary penis enlargement procedure. Just for fun and badness, I clicked on the link to request further information. I typed in Dylan's phone number, so a representative could 'call to discuss your penis enlargement needs'.

One email really stood out to me. It was another from Chantelle, Dylan's fourth wife, with the subject line: *I only want wots fare*. I assumed she meant 'what's' and 'fair'.

I opened the email to find yet another poorly-written, dreadfully-spelled request for money, in which she urged Dylan to 'look in you're hart' and 'giv me wot Im entiterled too'. Honestly, the standard of education in this country today. Personally, I blame Heat magazine. And James Patterson – but then, I tend to blame him for most things. I'd blame God, too, if he existed.

Again, I was intrigued by the notion of what she felt she was 'entitled' to. I'd never met the girl, but from her standard of written English, I'd be surprised if she'd ever heard the word, let alone knew what it meant.

I thought back to what Dylan had said. They'd been divorced for about a year, and I assumed she'd have received everything she was entitled to after the divorce. But she was clearly quite desperate for money. And maybe she'd be in line for a big inheritance if Dylan were suddenly no longer around? As his most recent wife, she could potentially stand to control his whole estate. That would certainly be a clear motive for wanting him dead. I made a note in my pad that I'd have to ask Dylan about the contents of his pre-nuptial agreements, and who stood to inherit his money if he died.

Marta swooped past my table in one of her coffee-level-inspecting fly-bys. She bumped my table as she went, grumbling something in Polish and tutting loudly as she saw how half-full my cup still was. I made another note in my pad that I'd have to learn Polish at some point, just so I could find out how insulting she was being towards me. And then report her to Starbucks High Command, and hopefully get her sacked, or deported. Or at least get a couple of free muffins as compensation.

I'd usually have entered into a heated dispute with her about the rights of the customer to consume their beverage as quickly or slowly as they deemed fit, but I suddenly caught sight of the clock in the corner of Dylan's laptop screen. It was 11.45am and I had somewhere to be. So, instead, I quickly packed up my bag, deliberately spilled the remaining contents of my cup onto the table, and dashed out of the shop.

******

"Okay everyone, gather around," I said in a loud whisper, keen to be heard but still wanting to remain relatively inconspicuous. "Let's be having you. We haven't got all day." I waved my arms wildly, trying to attract attention.

A selection of slightly bemused pensioners glanced over in my direction.

"Come on, don't be shy. Come in as close as you can. There's plenty of seats here at the front. And make sure to turn your hearing aids up, if you have them. The reading will be starting in just a few minutes." I pointed to a handwritten sign I'd sellotaped to the edge of a bookshelf that read:

READING TODAY
World famous author Frederick Winters
reads from his latest crime thriller
DEATH OF A RUSSIAN BILLIONAIRE

Gradually, a cluster of white-haired old men and women trundled their way over and sat down in the seats I'd hastily assembled in a semi-circle around me. They'd just finished their *Silver Surfers: Internet for the Elderly* class, so I had a captive audience.

I'd waited just long enough for the class instructor to disappear, and made sure none of the busybody librarians were hanging around, before I'd thrown up my sign, rearranged the seats in the computer room, then corralled the old duffers back in and shut the door. I perched on the desk at the front, on which I'd arranged a selection of my own books, and another sign on which I'd written 'Books: £10, Signed copies: £12' in extra-large writing so the old bats could read it.

Pensioners are a good market for me. They tend to be big consumers of crime and mystery books, they always have cash on them (tending not to trust banks, debit cards or anything too shiny and new), and they're usually quite forgetful – which means you can trick them into buying books they've already read, and they rarely remember your face when they come back for a refund.

Also, they often have very little to do. So, if you happen to know when and where they'll be gathered in large enough groups – like the Silver Surfers class, Wednesdays 11am-12pm in the local library, for example – and if you're quick on your toes (at least quicker than a pensioner on a Zimmer frame), you can gather up a group of potential customers with little effort.

I was pleased to see that a few other, slightly less decrepit, customers had also wandered in, no doubt curious what all the fuss was about. An eager-looking middle-aged woman in expensive clothes perched at the end of one of the rows, possibly assuming I was more "world famous" than I really am. A hoodie-clad youth plopped himself down on a seat at the back, then promptly fell asleep. A busy looking man in a suit strolled into the room, read my sign, and then walked straight back out again. And then a rather attractive woman walked in.

She was mid- to late-thirties, with mousy brown hair and an average figure – just a little too podgy to be called slim, but by no means a fatty. She was wearing bright red jeans and a rather unique, overly colourful jumper with a picture of a cat on it. Her questionable fashion-sense aside, she was very pretty and had a nice smile. If she didn't leave during the reading, I'd be sure to give her a private audience. I might even let her off the two quid for a signature.

"So who are you, then?" asked one of the old biddies in the front row.

"Please keep all questions until the end," I said, picking up a book and opening it.

"Is this the computer class?" called out an elderly man in glasses and a brown cardigan, in the middle of the group.

"No, you old fool, we've just had that," shouted the old lady next to him. "This man's from the council. He's doing a reading."

"Well, I'm not from the council," I corrected her, "but yes, I am going to do a reading for you."

"Death of a Russian Billionaire?" said another old woman, reading my sign. "Sounds like a James Patterson I've read..."

"It's nothing like a bloody James Patterson," I snapped, starting to get annoyed.

Another old bag looked ready to join in the conversation, but I managed to cut her off before she could open her mouth. "Okay then. Let's begin."

I flicked through the book to one of the more exciting chapters and began. I managed to get a full six minutes into the reading before the door to the computer room swung open and in walked a dowdy woman with a laminated badge swinging on a lanyard around her neck. She shook her head, looking at me with a mixture of anger and pity.

"Sandra," she shouted, poking her head back out the door. "Sandra, he's doing it again. That nutcase has kidnapped the Silver Surfers and he's reading to them."

******

I retired to the safety of a nearby Café Nero, and sat up by the window with a small mocha latte. I'd only just managed to pack up my bag and scarper before Bruce, the heavy-handed library security guard, came bundling into the room and chased me down the stairs and out onto the street. My aged audience mistook the calamity for an impromptu dramatic performance of my book, and sat oohing and aahing as the big oaf stomped about trying to grab hold of me. They were probably still sitting there, waiting for Act Two to commence.

Sadly, I hadn't managed to make any sales to the Silver Surfers, and still had a bag full of slightly battered paperbacks. But I consoled myself that with Dylan's investigation money I'd at least be up another £500 by the end of the day. And just in case I didn't catch up with him, I thought it only sensible to break into his online bank account and transfer the money across to myself. Unfortunately, the website required the 16-digit number from his debit card, which I didn't have. So, I made a note in my pad to write the number down next time I was in the vicinity of his wallet.

I once again opened Dylan's email account, but there were no new messages. I had another scan through the various other files on the machine, but found nothing of interest.

I clicked back onto Corinne Handley's website. The news section listed details of forthcoming signings at a selection of bookshops – one of which just so happened to be the next day at Foyles on Charring Cross road. It was easy to get to and would save me a lot of work in tracking her down. I could simply show up at the shop, confront her and question her about her marriage to Dylan. I made a note of the date and time in my notebook, and planned to pop along the next afternoon.

Next, I clicked onto the website for Carlisle Philpott. Unfortunately, his news section had not been updated in over six months, and there were no listings for any similar events. I'd heard that Carlisle had become so paranoid of Dylan stealing his thunder that he had taken to never advertising his public appearances, just in case Dylan's marketing men somehow scuppered the event. It appeared the rumour was true, so if I was going to use the same kind of ambush tactics, I'd have to be a bit sneakier about finding out where he would be.

I felt a presence next to my table. I was all set to repel any over-eager Café Nero employee with a well-versed justification for my slow drinking speed, when I looked up to see the woman in the cat jumper from my hastily abandoned reading at the library.

"Hello. It's Mr Winters, isn't it? Frederick Winters?" she said.

She was even prettier up close, and slightly less podgy than I'd originally thought. She was grinning down at me with a nervous, excited glint in her eye.

"Yes, that's right," I said, smiling. "But please, call me Freddie."

"I was at your reading just now. I was really enjoying it. Such a shame it ended so quickly. Was there some kind of mix up with the room booking, or something?"

"Eh? Oh yes," I said. "Mix up. That was it. They forgot I'd booked it... all got sorted out in the end."

"That security guard certainly looked a bit miffed. What was that he was saying about calling the police if he found you abducting library-goers again?"

"Oh, him? Well, he's not quite right in the head... I believe the library took him on as a favour to his mum after he was injured in Afghanistan," I lied. "Took a hand grenade to the head. Blew literally half his brain out. That's why he gets a bit confused. And why he's so bloody ugly."

I laughed out loud. She didn't join in. Instead, she just gave me a confused look, not sure whether to be amused or outraged.

"Would you like to join me for a coffee?" I said, trying to rescue the situation.

"Oh, that would be lovely, thank you."

She sat down, I ordered her a drink and we chatted for over an hour. She told me all about herself, and how she loved to read. Her name was Caroline, she lived in Hackney and she worked as a communications manager for a law firm just down the road from the library. She'd popped in during her lunch break to find something to read and happened upon my impromptu gathering. And aside from the quirky cat jumper, she seemed relatively normal.

"Do communications managers for law firms usually wear cat

jumpers to work?" I asked.

She looked down at herself, suddenly blushing red, as if she'd forgotten what she was wearing. "Oh, God, you must think I'm quite strange," she said. "No, this isn't what I'd usually wear to work. It's a charity thing. Tacky Jumper Tuesday. Everyone pays two pounds for the privilege of looking like an idiot for the day – not to mention the tenner I had to spend on the jumper in the first place. But you know what offices are like – you end up looking even dafter if you don't get involved. At least it's for a good cause."

"Well, that's a relief," I smiled. She was growing more attractive by the second.

"So, do you know many other writers?" she asked me.

"Yeah, sure, I know a few. You meet them at book festivals, readings, author events, you know…" I said, trying to make myself sound more impressive than I really am.

"Wow, that's amazing," she said, looking more excited than she really should have been. "Do you know any famous writers? Any big names?"

"Oh, a few…"

"Do you know J K Rowling?"

"No, I haven't had the honour. But her editor did once turn down one of my books."

"Wow," she said, "that's brilliant. Do you know Dan Brown?"

"Not personally, but we used to share an agent," I lied, getting carried away.

"What about James Patterson? Do you know him?"

"Don't talk to me about James fucking Patterson," I sneered. "The man's an arse. I taught him everything he knows. And he's stolen half my ideas. Alex Cross? I came up with that character over a game of cards," I lied. "And the sod bloody wrote it up before I had the chance."

I've never played cards with James Patterson. And I can't truthfully claim to have invented any of his characters. But I was really getting into the deception now, and my lies, it seems, knew no bounds.

"Wow, I never knew the world of writers was so exciting," she said, practically frothing at the mouth with enthusiasm. "Do you know anyone else famous? Do you know…" she thought for a moment, "ooh, do you know Dylan St James?"

"Know him? He's one of my dearest friends. I'm actually staying at his place at the moment."

I instantly regretted letting that piece of information slip out – partly because I didn't want her asking questions about why I was staying there, and partly because it suddenly occurred to me that I could have invited her back to the fancy flat and passed it off as my own.

"Oh my God," she shrieked. "Dylan St James? Really? Oh, I love him."

"Yeah, he's all right, I suppose."

"No, seriously, his books are like… well, they just… they speak to me."

"Really? You like all that dreary stuff," I said, a little annoyed at Dylan upstaging me without even being in the room. I suddenly had a lot of sympathy for Carlisle Philpott.

"Oh, I mean, I read all kinds of things," she said, pandering to my obviously pouting face. "Literary fiction, chick-lit, a good crime novel… I love all books, really."

"And have you ever read any of mine?" I asked.

A long pause.

"No… sorry," she said. I must have looked even more wounded, because she followed up immediately with, "but I was really enjoying your reading earlier. Really good characters and the plot seemed very exciting. I'm sure I'd love your books."

Well, of course she would. I mean, who wouldn't?

"Well, that could certainly be arranged," I said, digging out my very best flirting smile and slapping it across my face.

CHAPTER 7

MY HEAD WAS pounding again. Thin beams of light slashed through gaps in the curtains. They pierced the room, stinging my eyes and making my head throb even more. It took a few seconds for my gaze to come into focus.

I scanned the room, not quite sure where I was. It certainly wasn't my own bed – far too big and comfortable. The room was littered was soulless, anodyne IKEA furniture and pointless, inoffensive trinkets, vases and coloured candles. For a brief moment, I thought I'd woken up in a furniture store display bedroom. And not for the first time.

And then I remembered. Dylan's fancy rental apartment. I scratched my fingers through my dense messy hair, gagging on the dry alcohol stench in my mouth.

On the pillow next to me was a hand-written note. It came flooding back. Caroline, the cat jumper lady.

The note read:

Sorry I had to dash off, but I've got an early meeting.
Last night was amazing, I had such a fantastic time.
I hope we can do it again soon.
Call me, Caroline.

Every lower case 'i' was dotted with a tiny heart. I couldn't decide whether it was charmingly cute or the sign of a seriously deranged mind. I decided I should probably withhold judgement until I'd had the chance to sleep with her at least once more.

But how was I supposed to call her? She hadn't written her number on the note. I clawed at the bedside table, grabbing for my mobile. I squinted at the glowing screen. There were no missed calls or text messages. And then I noticed that Caroline had taken the liberty of adding her phone number to my directory, along with a very smiley picture that she'd taken of herself. Pretty bloody keen, I thought. Almost quite creepy.

I carefully sat up in bed, holding my delicate head in my hands, groaning and sighing, and breathing heavily. I managed to open my eyes fully without my brain exploding, and tried to piece together the previous night's events.

Caroline and I had shared another coffee and, to my delight and – I'm not ashamed to admit it – complete surprise, she had suggested moving on to a bar down the road for something a bit stronger. We shared a few glasses of wine. We laughed and chatted and really hit it off. And I was just working my way towards asking for her phone number, when she beat me to the punch and suggested coming back to my place.

Now, I'm no expert in the arts of attracting female attention. In fact, it's fair to say that my limited sexual success with women over the years has all been pretty hard won. Unlike Dylan, who barely had to smile at a girl to have her dropping her knickers, any sexual congress I had my sights set on generally took a good few weeks – or sometimes months – of strategising, scheming and planning to pull off. It would often involve ingratiating myself with a key close friend, hanging around for hours on end to repeatedly 'bump into the target by accident', or sending numerous texts and emails until they felt so sorry for me that they'd just give in.

So, to have a woman ask to come back to my place after just a few drinks was not only a huge compliment, it was an enormous surprise. I practically fell over my own feet as I ran into the street to hail a taxi.

I certainly had no intention of taking her back to my tiny dwelling, so it had to be Dylan's flat. I knew it was going to be empty, as Dylan had already sent me a text message to say that his agent, Mortimer, had surprised him with another last minute book signing in Reading. So, he wasn't going to be back now until the following day. I was still kicking myself at missing the opportunity to pass his place off as my own. But I figured if she asked, I could always tell her I was staying there because my million pound mansion was being refurbished. I'd already started our relationship on a succession of lies, so it seemed quite reasonable to keep on going.

I remembered getting back to the flat and her being highly impressed with the place. A little too impressed, in fact. I had vague memories of her demanding a full tour, wanting to see each room, every nook and cranny. Even down to the type of washing machine Dylan had, and where his sofas were from.

Of course I had no idea, so I remember pilfering a bottle of wine from the rack in the kitchen, then set about distracting her by getting her – and myself – even more drunk. After that it was a complete blank.

I crawled out of bed, lamenting the fact that I couldn't actually remember any of the previous evening's sex, and stumbled down the hall to the living room. On the small coffee table sat three empty bottles of Dylan's expensive wine – I really was turning out to be the most ungracious, rude, expensive houseguest. How much of the wine had I drunk? And how much had she had? From the throbbing in my head, I guessed I'd probably had the lion's share.

Had the sex been any good at all? I'd hate to have given a poor performance on account of too much booze. But then her note had practically sung with satisfaction, so maybe I'd given my usual sterling effort after all.

Large grey clouds hung ominously outside the living room window. The world outside looked cold and miserable, like the inside of my head. I stumbled my way into the kitchen, found another handful of paracetamol and pulled an empty orange juice carton from the fridge. I loudly cursed the miserable sod who'd finished the last drop, then remembered it had been me the previous day. I then cursed Dylan's lack of forethought in having not foreseen my selfish behaviour and bought in a spare carton. I put the empty box back in the fridge and gulped water straight from the tap to wash down the pills.

I flung open cupboards and drawers, swearing and scowling as I failed to find anything that looked any more appetising than the previous day's trawl of health foods. Dylan's apparent dislike of any foodstuffs that contained a decent amount of sugar, fat or preservatives was quickly threatening to turn me against him. There was no bacon, no eggs, no fizzy drinks, chocolate, cakes, tins of beans, white bread, pies, pizzas or anything with any flavour whatsoever. I mean, what the hell did the man live on? There wasn't even a random Pot Noodle hidden at the back of one of the cupboards. Who doesn't have at least one random Pot Noodle hidden in the back of a cupboard?

I know Dylan had said he'd embraced healthy eating in a bid to get better, but seriously. Given the choice between living another ten years chowing down on Ryvitas, fruit and wholemeal bread, or living your last two months in a blaze of Wotsits, hot dogs and chicken wings, I know what I'd choose.

Resigning myself to another shaky, hungover walk to the café down the road, I slinked off for a long rejuvenating shower. I still hadn't been back to my place to pick up a change of clothes, and my current outfit was looking and smelling a little bit funky. So, I had no choice but to raid Dylan's wardrobe. His clothes were far nicer and vastly more expensive than mine, and way more stylish than anything I was used to. I pawed my way through jeans, t-shirts, trousers, jumpers – every single item a designer label of some kind. In the end, I settled for a simple, black, single-breasted Hugo Boss suit and a pale blue Ralph Lauren shirt.

Thankfully, Dylan is roughly the same build as me – if about half a foot shorter. So, despite the trousers falling just the right side of ankle swingers, the clothes were a pretty decent fit. Unfortunately, Dylan has small feet and his expensive Italian loafers were nipping at my toes. So, I had to settle for my own, tatty grey-white converse trainers instead. They looked a bit odd with the rest of the expensive clobber, but I think I just about pulled it off. At the very worst, people would think I was eccentric.

I looked at myself in the mirror, sighing once again at the life and lifestyle that should be mine. This one outfit probably cost more than my month's rent.

The pounding in my head had all but subsided and my stomach was rumbling as I prepared to leave the flat. I checked my watch – 10.36am. I still had a few hours before I had to head over to Soho to ambush Dylan's third wife. I wrapped a thick, soft scarf around my neck and headed for the front door.

And then: bang!

The noise was so loud that at first it didn't quite register. As if I had imagined it. A small eruption of my hangover, rattling against the inside of my skull.

Less than a second later the street outside erupted with a chorus of fluttering birds, barking dogs and wailing car alarms. A woman screamed somewhere in the distance. Glass shattered and crashed to the ground, tinkling and singing as it fell. Then came a curious series of dull, wet splats.

I ran over to the living room window, staring at the scene outside. Thick white smoke billowed up into the air. Orange hazard lights blinked along the row of screaming cars. A teenage boy hunkered down behind a car across the street. He was looking this way and that, rubbing red liquid from his face. A dazed old woman gripped tight to her Zimmer frame. She tried to remain on her feet as a yappy dog barked and jumped frantically on the end of the lead in her hand.

A young mum, pushing her child in a stroller, screamed manically.

She, too, was swathed in red, clawing madly at the pushchair to check her wailing child. Across the street, people stared out of random windows. I followed their gaze to the foot of the building I was in. At the end of the short path was a huge, great splat of red, as if someone had dropped a giant water balloon full of paint from a great height.

The gooey red liquid spread outwards from a scorched black centre. It was painted up the sides of cars. Splattered up the path. Stretched out into the road and over the small patch of grass at the front of the block of flats. I could tell instantly that it was blood. There was something about the look, the colour, the consistency that told me. Also, I could see half a leg on the grass, severed at the knee and still wearing a white sock and black shoe.

******

You would think that seeing the remains of a human being literally splattered across a residential street would be enough to put me off my breakfast. But the stomach is a mysterious thing. And after two hours being trapped in the flat, and a further thirty minutes spent telling a uniformed police officer than I'd seen nothing of any note aside from a puddle of person, I was absolutely ravenous. I retired to the café at the end of the road and, as it was now gone 1pm, I ordered the mixed grill.

The police had arrived at the scene relatively quickly after the explosion and immediately cordoned off the whole area. They then went from door to door, questioning people. What with recent terrorist activities, explosions in London tend to get quicker response times than the average mugging. And the police are always extra twitchy. So, before I could get out and head off for breakfast, I found myself confined to the flat.

The 14-year-old police constable (I mean, he wasn't actually, but he really looked it) who took my lack of a statement was more than just a little wet behind the ears. Unsurprisingly, he had no clue as to what had happened outside. Or if he did, he wasn't saying. By the time I was finally allowed out of the flat, a small group of journalists had assembled, flashing their camera bulbs and jostling for position behind a police cordon. They were a lot more loose-lipped, thankfully, and revealed that apparently a postman had inexplicably exploded whilst out on his rounds. Of course, the police weren't saying anything. The journalists' running theory was that he'd fallen victim to a letter bomb intended for a target in the immediate area.

Naturally, the coincidence between Dylan suspecting someone wanted to kill him and a postman exploding in the street outside his flat didn't escape me. But it wasn't something I wanted to share with the police just yet. For one thing, I couldn't be absolutely certain that the two things were definitely related. Secondly, I wasn't the biggest fan of the local police, or they of me, due to a number of unfortunate, unresolved issues. If there really was someone out there trying to kill Dylan, I was pretty sure I could get to the bottom of things before involving them.

I washed down a mouthful of sausage with a big glug of full-fat coke (the best friend to any hangover sufferer) and pulled out my notebook. I jotted down a few lines about the morning's incident.

The latest development was something of a concern. It seemed pretty clear now that someone actually was trying to hurt Dylan. The incident on the underground, the mysterious car that had almost flattened me, and now an exploding mail carrier. It was all too much of a coincidence. Maybe the fire at Dylan's house hadn't just been an accident after all.

So, had the letter bomb been addressed to Dylan? As there had been very little left of the postman, I assumed there would also be little left of the letter. So there might be no way to tell. I figured it would be a while before the forensics teams had extracted anything useful from the crime scene. Quite how I was going to get that information, I wasn't yet sure. I still had a few police connections, but they didn't particularly like me. I'd have to cross that bridge when I came to it.

Had it even been a letter bomb at all? It was just a working theory spouted by a bunch of journalists, and they're hardly the most trustworthy sources. But it seemed the most likely explanation. After all, postmen didn't tend to just randomly explode, did they? And it seemed unlikely that he was a suicide bomber. If he was, he was possibly the least successful one ever.

The stakes had been raised and I needed to warn Dylan. I pulled out my mobile and dialled his number. Straight to answerphone. I left a short message telling him to be on his guard, without giving away too many worrying details.

So, who was behind this? The use of explosive devices in the post was a worrying escalation, and seemed unlike the sort of thing anyone on my list was capable of. An ex-wife could certainly bump you in front of a tube train, maybe even set fire to your house. But constructing a bomb and sending it through the post seemed a little too hard core. And way too technical. Maybe the killer had contracted out to hired help? But why had the bomb gone off before it had reached the target?

I finished off the last of my lunch, drained the remaining cola and checked my watch. It was 13.42 and I had just under an hour to get across London.

CHAPTER 8

A LONG LINE of slim, attractive women, with too much make-up and bright designer clothes, tottered on ridiculously high heels as they queued to get into Foyles bookshop. With their short skirts, hair extensions and fake Louis Vuitton handbags, they weren't exactly the bookstore's usual clientele. They were, however, exactly what I imagined Corinne Handley's devoted fan base to look like.

After all, her latest book advised women on the best ways to seduce and trap rich men, then manipulate them into providing a glamorous lifestyle or a big pay out. So, I wasn't surprised to find myself queuing behind an army of dolled-up wannabe WAGs, all desperate to get their signed copy of the shameful guidebook, and maybe press the scandalous author for a few extra hints and tips. A march for women's rights, it was not. They were, however, not an unpleasant sight to look at.

A mixture of blondes, brunettes and redheads, the women appeared to be aged between 19 and 25. They were slim, curvy and all fit very nicely into their tiny skirts, tight jeans and skimpy tops and jackets. I couldn't help but wonder why they felt they needed advice in attracting rich, stupid men. Just about every girl in line was stunning, and would have looked quite at home on the arm of any footballer, movie star or disgraced game show host. And if they couldn't get one of them, they could at least settle for a scumbag politician.

There were a few stragglers at the back, with far too much make-up, fingernails the size of ping-pong bats and a few too many curves squeezed into their tight dresses. I guessed they might be a little less successful. They'd probably need a full library of Corinne Handley's books to bag the premiership stars they hoped to leach off.

I queued for just over an hour, during which time three separate bimbos, having seen the expensive suit I was wearing, fluttered their eyelashes, chatted me up and asked if I was either rich or famous.

One very pretty brunette in a short skirt, knee-high boots and a top that left very little to the imagination seemed keen to get to know me better. And if I had been rich and famous, I could see myself signing over the deeds to my house just to get her into bed (such is the stupidity of man, and the reason Corinne's latest book was already shooting up the bestseller charts). I was sorely tempted to lie my teeth off and whisk her back to Dylan's pad, so I could treat her to an afternoon of disappointing sex, and an even more disappointing realisation that I was about as rich as a dry sponge cake. But I had work to do. And potentially murderous ex-wives to interrogate. So, I told her I had an afternoon of high-level stock acquisition meetings lined up. And I took her phone number for later.

Finally, I made my way to the head of the queue and found myself in front of a seated Corinne Handley. Without looking up, she reached out for a book to sign. Finding nothing there, she gazed up, confused.

"Don't you want me to sign anything?"

"Actually, yes. I was hoping you'd sign a confession," I said, pausing and tilting my head like a bad TV detective, "for the attempted murder of your ex-husband!"

I over-emphasised the last part, pausing again for dramatic effect. It was quite good, I thought, and certainly had the desired effect as the room fell instantly silent. All the women in the queue ceased their squawking and chatting, and stood open-mouthed, staring at Corinne.

Corinne stared at me. I stared back at her. She shifted in her chair. I tilted my head even further. Our eyes remained locked the whole time.

"What the fuck are you talking about?" she finally said.

It was then that I realised I didn't actually have a further sharp line to follow it up with. "I... er... I... erm... I mean..."

"Security!" she shouted. "Security, can we get rid of this nutcase, please?"

I went to speak again, but two hulking brutes appeared at either side of me, grabbed hold of my arms and dragged me backwards towards the doors. A loud cheer went up, as the wannabe WAGs whooped and hollered, clapping and shrieking as I was forcibly removed from the building. I tried to shout out, beseeching Corinne for a minute more of her time, but she already had her head down, signing another book.

The security guards dragged me past the line of women, out the main entrance and threw me down onto the pavement outside. The smaller of the two gave me a quick kick in the ribs for good measure, then told me to fuck off.

Sitting on the cold, damp paving slab, clutching at my aching sides, I wondered whether I might have gone in with slightly the wrong tactics.

******

I waited outside the shop for two and a half hours, until the queue had disappeared. I tried phoning Dylan a few more times, but still couldn't get hold of him. I was starting to get a little worried that I couldn't reach him. He'd probably just been held up at his signing, wittering on about himself and charming his female fans. But just in case, I sent him a text message asking him to call me as soon as he could.

Peering through the window of the bookshop, I could see Corinne sitting behind the desk, no further autograph hunters waiting to be seen. A busy-looking woman stood next to her, speaking into a mobile phone and gesticulating wildly. I scanned the rest of the shop. No security guards in sight. So, I stepped back through the entrance and made my way to the table.

The bookshop had returned to its usual quiet haven. The buzzing of the wannabe WAGs was replaced with hushed chatter, quiet footsteps and the occasional turning of pages. A table of three-for-two romance books was dishevelled beyond repair; the titles strewn higgledy-piggledy as they'd been lifted, looked at and thrown back down. The odour of fake tan and a multitude of strong perfumes hung in the air, and a weary looking cashier stood slumped and exhausted behind the till.

Corinne Handley caught sight of me as I approached her table. She was all set to call for security again, so I said, "Miss Handley, apologies for before. I misjudged the situation. Please can I just have a minute of your time?"

She stood up from her seat, looking all around the shop.

"Please, Miss Handley. It'll only take a few minutes. It's about Dylan."

"Dylan?" she said, turning back to me, her look changing from annoyance to sudden concern. "What's happened? Is Dylan okay?"

Just like Georgina, Corinne seemed genuinely worried about her ex-husband. Which surprised me, considering the lack of concern she'd shown for her other previous partners – with the media castigating them so vociferously, she had simply added more fuel to the fire, spilling further beans to the tabloids and profiting as she did so.

"Yes, he's perfectly fine," I said. "Well, not fine, exactly. I think someone's trying to kill him."

"Kill him? What do you mean, kill him?"

"I'm Dylan's friend, Freddie Winters. He came to me the other day, saying he thought someone was trying to kill him. Now I can't get hold of him. And a postman just exploded outside his flat."

Corinne Handley eyed me suspiciously for a few seconds. She turned to her PA, who was now off the phone and signalling that they had to leave.

"So, you're the great Freddie Winters? Dylan mentioned you. You're his friend, or at least you used to be. You write those second-rate crime novels, with that detective... what's his name... Jack...?"

"Dick Stone," I corrected her, my jaw clamped in a polite, rictus grin. She was a fine one to talk about second-rate books, considering her questionable canon of work. I would usually have let her know what I thought of her, but we'd already got off to a pretty bad start, so I thought it best to bite my tongue.

"Fine," she said, "but I'm on my way across town to do The One Show. If you want to talk, you'll have to come with us."

I followed on as the two women headed out through the back exit of the shop and into a waiting, chauffeured car. Whilst we drove, I explained all the recent goings-on and how Dylan had hired me to investigate his apparent attempted murder.

"So, you come into a shop, interrupt my book signing and accuse me of trying to kill Dylan?" she asked.

"Er... yeah, sorry about that. I just wanted to see how you'd react. You know, like in the movies, where the detective confronts the killer, they react badly and everyone knows they're guilty."

"And how did I react?"

"Pretty fairly, I'd say."

"Do you really think Dylan's life is in danger?"

"To be honest, no, I didn't. But after this morning, I think there could be some truth to it."

"And where exactly does Miss Handley fit into all this?" interrupted Corinne's PA. "You can't just go around accusing people of murder, you know." She turned to Corinne. "Would you like me to contact Martin?"

"Who's Martin?" I snapped, sneering at the annoying blonde girl.

"Martin is my solicitor," said Corinne, cutting in. "And no, that won't be necessary, thank you Sophie. Why don't you look over the interview questions for the show, whilst Mr Winters and I talk? You'll have to excuse Sophie, Mr Winters; she's very protective of me."

Sophie the PA sneered back at me, like a disgruntled child cross at being told off, and started scanning through files on an iPad.

"But she does raise a good point," continued Corinne. "What does this have to do with me? I haven't seen Dylan in about three years now. Last I heard, he'd married some bimbo actress, or something."

"Well, I'm just speaking to everyone. Trying to find out what might be going on, and see if anyone has a grudge against Dylan or any reason to harm him. Don't worry; I'll be talking to the bimbo actress as well. So, can you think of anyone that might want to kill Dylan?"

She smiled fondly. "You know Dylan," she said, "nicest guy in the world. One of the reasons I fell for him. I can't imagine anyone wanting to hurt him. The only person I've ever known to have a problem with Dylan is that guy he was always so upset about. That other writer... Carl? Carlton?"

"You mean Carlisle Philpott?"

"Philpott. Yeah, that's the guy. He was always having such a go at him in the press. Seriously jealous of his success. Dylan tried to laugh it off, but I knew it got to him. He's the only person I can think of. But he wouldn't try and kill him, would he?"

"He'd have a lot to gain, don't you think?" I said.

"Maybe. But would anyone really kill someone over book sales?"

"I can think of a few people I'd happily strangle to get a few more books sold," I laughed. Corinne did not laugh along. "But no... maybe that is a bit far-fetched."

"Well, I certainly wouldn't want to see him hurt," said Corinne, "and I don't think he ever had a problem with his wife before me. Can't speak for the most recent bimbo, of course."

"No," I said, sensing a real tension at the mention of Dylan's latest spouse. "So how did you and Dylan first... get together?"

"My former agent, Mortimer, introduced us. Dylan and I were both clients of his. He was very keen to get us together, actually. It seemed a bit odd at the time, as he'd never shown any interest in my personal life before. Then all of a sudden he's trying to set me up on dates."

"Really?"

"He made a real thing of introducing us, then suggested we should go out for dinner together. At the time, I figured he was just trying to whip up a bit of publicity – you know, get us snapped together by the paparazzi as our new books were due out."

"So, you started dating Dylan as a publicity stunt?"

"Of course not," she said, defiantly. "What do you think I am?"

"Well, no offence," I said, sheepishly, "but you have made a living out of kiss-and-tell books."

"I date who I want, when I want, and because *I* want to," she said angrily. "If the general public are interested in the men I sleep with, and want to pay to read about it, that's another matter. I dated Dylan because I liked him. I found him charming, funny, interesting and really romantic. And we worked hard to keep our relationship a secret for as long as possible, because I didn't want the press to ruin it."

"Ruin it? You mean you didn't want people to assume you were just targeting him as a subject for your next kiss-and-tell? World famous author – a lot of people would want to read about that."

"I appreciate that I have something of a reputation, Mr Winters," she said, sadly. "And in the past it has led men to be slightly wary of me. I didn't want the press to start writing stories about us and scare Dylan off."

"So, you weren't planning on writing one of your books about Dylan?"

"Have I written that book, Mr Winters? No. And I have absolutely no plans to. It was even part of our prenuptial agreement – we both agreed never to write about the intimate details of our relationship. So I couldn't write it if I wanted to."

"Really? And you signed off on that?"

"Gladly. Think what you will of me, but I married Dylan because I loved him. I was a big fan of his. I'd read all of his books, and I was so thrilled to be with him. I was heartbroken when the marriage failed."

"So, what happened exactly?"

"You tell me. We were happy for a long time. We were really in love; at least I thought we were. We'd even started talking about having kids..."

"And then?"

"I really don't know. It's not as if we even started drifting apart. Dylan was working hard on a book, and he was away a lot promoting. It seemed like every week Mortimer had him jetting of somewhere for an interview or a promotional tour. I was busy here with my books, so I didn't see much of him."

"And it was too hard being apart?"

"Of course, but I understood it and supported him. Then one day, whilst Dylan was on a long trip touring round the States, I get a phone call from a lawyer. He tells me that divorce papers have been filed, and he's been instructed to offer me a million pounds to sign them, move out of the house and end the marriage quickly."

"A million quid? Who was the money from?"

"I assumed it was from Dylan, of course. Too spineless to tell me that he wanted out of the marriage, so he goes away on a trip and instructs a lawyer to pay me off. I was crushed."

"Did you try and talk to Dylan?"

"Of course I did. I tried calling, texting, emailing, but he didn't pick up and he didn't reply. I spent weeks trying but he never returned my calls. I tried to find out where he was, so I could fly out and speak to him, but Mortimer wouldn't tell me. He said Dylan didn't want to see me, and it was best if I just took the money and left."

"So?"

"So I did. What else was I going to do? If someone wants rid of you that much, what's the point in sticking around? I've been hurt before, Mr Winters, and let me tell you, the money always helps to heal the wounds." She sounded distant then, as if she were trying to convince herself rather than me.

"And who was this lawyer?" I said. "The man who contacted you."

"No idea. Do we have a name for him, Sophie?"

The young girl glared at me, tapped away at her iPad for a few seconds, then said, "Charles Walker of... Walker, Hawkes and Byrne Solicitors."

I pulled my notepad from my pocket and jotted down the name. "And you'd never met him before?"

"Never," said Corinne. "And I haven't heard from him since. After two weeks of Dylan ignoring me, I signed the papers, sent them back and the money was in my account the next day. And that's the last I heard of it until the decree absolute came in the post."

"So, how do you know the money came from Dylan?"

"Well, who else would it have been from? Why would anyone else pay me a million pounds to divorce my husband?"

Her story didn't add up. Dylan told me it was she who had ended the relationship. He'd come home from a press trip to find all her things gone from the house and signed divorce papers waiting for him on the kitchen counter. No note, no explanation. And when he'd tried to contact her, a busybody PA had thwarted all his attempts. It didn't make sense. One of them had to be lying.

Corinne looked away from me, gazing out of the car's window, trying to hide the tears forming in the corners of her eyes. She seemed genuinely saddened about the breakdown of the relationship. Not at all like a woman who had coldly walked out on a man and left divorce papers for him to come home to.

"Former agent?" I said, picking up on what Corinne had said before.

"I take it you're not with Mortimer any longer?"

"God, no!"

"Is that because of Dylan?"

Corinne laughed, snorting through her nose. "I suppose it would have been hard bumping into him at the office… But no, I left Morty when everyone else did. You know, after all that business with the taxes. Mortimer signed me when I couldn't get any other agent, but I was in no hurry to stay with him when I didn't have to. I never trusted the old sod."

"Really? Why?"

"There's just something about him. I wouldn't trust that man with a charity tin. I was always telling Dylan he should leave too. It's quite ridiculous, one of the world's biggest authors represented by such a dodgy old dinosaur."

The car pulled up at the BBC's New Broadcasting House in Central London. The driver climbed out, walked round to the side of the car and opened the door, so we could all exit. He smiled sweetly at both Corinne and her PA, and gave me a slight, almost imperceptible sneer as I thanked him.

"And this is where we leave you, Mr Winters," said Corinne.

"Invited guests only," cut in Sophie, sharply.

"Thanks for your time," I said. "And for what it's worth, I'm sorry things didn't work out between you and Dylan. I'm sure you would have made him very happy."

"Piss off, Mr Winters," said Corinne.

"If I see you again, I'm calling the police," said Sophie the PA. Then she and Corinne turned and walked away, the sound of their heels click-clacking on the pavement as they headed towards the reception area.

******

Our little car ride to the BBC had left me not too far from Dylan's place. So, I checked my watch and headed off in the direction of Oxford Circus tube station. As I walked, I felt my phone vibrate in my pocket. The screen displayed a number I didn't recognise, so naturally I let it go to voicemail. I make it a rule never to answer the phone to unknown numbers, just in case it's someone looking for money, or my landlord looking for his rent. Or a long forgotten dalliance of the past calling to inform me of an unknown, errant offspring. Who probably

wants money.

Corinne had seemed genuinely upset about the split with Dylan. And more saddened than I'd expected, considering her shameless reputation and apparent ease of disposing with former lovers. But her story still didn't quite add up.

When I'd spoken with Dylan a few nights previously, he'd definitely told me that it had been her decision to leave. He'd been so cut up that she'd just walked out without any word of an explanation. He certainly hadn't mentioned any payment of a million pounds to get rid of her. But why would he lie about that?

If Corinne was telling the truth, where had the money come from? And why had Mortimer prevented her from getting hold of Dylan?

I took out my notepad and added the name Charles Walker to my list of people to speak to. I also put a large question mark next to Mortimer Bunkle. What was his part in this mysterious break up?

Was he disgruntled at losing Corinne as a client – one that he'd apparently discovered – and was acting out some kind of grudge against her? Or maybe he'd found out about her attempts to persuade Dylan to find a new agent, and seen the chance to split the pair before his biggest earner jumped ship. It all seemed a bit unlikely. The man was about as crooked as a witch's nose, but he was old and doddery and I couldn't see him masterminding the theft of a biscuit, let alone something like this.

So, perhaps I'd ruled out another suspect in Corinne. But the case had become even more complex and confusing.

As I neared the Tube station, I checked my new voicemail. I was hoping it might have been Dylan, calling from some payphone or other mysterious number.

"Hello Mr Winters," said a distant, tinny sounding voice when the message connected. "My name is Nurse Janet Wallace. I'm calling from the Accident and Emergency department at St. Mary's hospital. It's regarding your friend, Dylan St James."

A chill ran the length of my spine.

"Mr St James was brought in to the hospital earlier. I'm afraid he's in quite a bad way."

CHAPTER 9

I RUSHED INTO the hospital, making my way past a huddle of sick smokers in dressing gowns, puffing and coughing outside the main entrance. I glared up at the confusion of signs on the wall. There were arrows sending me this way and that for Phlebotomy, Cardiology, Gastroenterology and all manner of other confusing destinations. The red and blue signs hanging from the ceiling offered even more options. I found myself spinning like a dog chasing its tail, trying to find the right department.

After a befuddling exchange with a confused, senile old bat on reception, I finally found my way to Dylan's ward and located the nurse who had phoned me.

"Thank you for coming, Mr Winters," she said. "I'm afraid your friend is in a bit of a bad way."

"What happened? What's wrong with him?"

"I understand he was attacked earlier today. Outside Paddington station. He came in by ambulance about six hours ago."

"Attacked," I said, fearing the worst after that morning's exploding postman incident. "Attacked how, exactly?"

"Mr St James has been shot."

"Shot?"

"Yes, shot." She looked around, took a deep breath, as if gearing herself up for the next part of the sentence. "With a harpoon."

"I'm sorry, what did you say?"

"A harpoon."

"A harpoon?" I said.

"Yes," she said, "a harpoon."

I looked around too, double-checking my surroundings, eyeing dog-eared pamphlets pinned to the wall, offering advice on various ailments, and a poster of a smiling doctor asking me to let him know if I find blood in my urine. I looked back at the nurse, my forehead crinkled with stupefaction.

"I'm sorry, for a second there I could have sworn it sounded like you said Dylan was shot with a harpoon…"

"Yes, a harpoon," she said, starting to get annoyed. "One of those spear things they shoot fish with under water."

"A harpoon," I repeated again. "Did he swim into Paddington Station? Who the hell gets shot with a harpoon in central London? Did anyone see what happened?"

"I don't know too much about that, I'm afraid. The police are in with him now. They might know more than I do."

"And how is he?" I blurted. "Is he going to be all right?"

"Mr St James has been quite seriously hurt. I don't know the full extent, but I can ask one of the doctors to come and speak with you. I do know that he came out of theatre about twenty minutes ago, and the surgeons managed to remove the spear successfully. Your friend was very lucky. The spear missed his heart by just an inch. But he did suffer a punctured lung and two broken ribs. He also lost a lot of blood, and he's still unconscious."

"He's not going to... die, is he?" I asked.

"It's early days, and Mr St James is still in a critical condition. But the doctors are doing everything they can."

"Can I see him?" I asked.

"We're still waiting for him to wake up, and there's a policeman in with him now. But you can pop in and see him quickly. He's in the third room on the right."

"Incidentally," I said, "how did you know to contact me? I can't be listed as next of kin."

"When Mr St James was admitted to Accident & Emergency he was still conscious and very distressed. He kept repeating the same sentence over and over until he passed out: 'Get Freddie. Tell him Garfield.' Didn't make much sense to us, but I looked through his mobile and found your number. I assumed you were the Freddie he was after."

Garfield, I thought. It must have been Dylan's attempt to pass on a clue. Had he seen the person that shot him? Was it the guy in the blue car with the Garfield toy? And why the fuck did he shoot him with a harpoon, of all things?

I thanked the nurse and made my way down the hall to Dylan's room. I walked in to find him comatose on the bed. There was a big plastic tube taped into his mouth; another poking out the side of his chest. All manner of fancy, futuristic-looking machines stood to the side of him, blinking and beeping in a sterile, melancholy symphony.

Next to the bed, hunched over and looking down at Dylan, stood Detective Dick Stone. The real one.

******

I first met Detective Inspector Richard Stone eight years ago, back when he was still a detective constable working for the Metropolitan

Police. I was doing research for a book and he graciously allowed me to interview him several times, and follow him around whilst he investigated a number of murder cases. He answered all manner of what I'm sure must have been very tedious, mundane questions about police procedure and the criminal justice system.

We became quite good friends, spending countless hours together at crime scenes, coroner's offices, the police station and, of course, the local pub. He was a great source of inspiration. He had lots of useful knowledge and fascinating 'on-the-job' stories, and he helped me greatly in shaping the book and getting all the facts right.

In fact, he was such a source of inspiration, that he in part inspired the creation of my most famous, long-running character, Dick Stone. I thought it would be a great testament to our friendship if I named the character after him. I had assumed that Richard would see the compliment in it. But I was wrong.

When the first Dick Stone novel came out, Richard was actually very pleased. He loved the idea that he had inspired a character. And he was thrilled to have his name immortalized in print. But then he read it.

In the best traditions of detective novels, the fictional Dick Stone is a hard-drinking, womanising, arrogant, flawed genius, who has little time for authority, thinks little of his colleagues, plays by his own rules and generally acts like a bit of a wanker. But it's okay, because he always solves the case and puts the bad guys away. It's a bit of a cliché, and it's certainly been done before, but it works well for the genre and people expect these kinds of characters.

The real Richard, of course, is not that much like Dick Stone. He does enjoy a drink (but he's not an alcoholic). He's dedicated to his work. And he's not always that keen on some of his superior officers (though he'd never flagrantly oppose them). And I'm sure he has his own problems and personal demons – as does anyone. That's where the similarities end.

The fictional version was only inspired by parts of the real man. It was a heavily exaggerated version of him. A caricature. But I may have made them just a tad too similar. And using the man's actual name – or at least a version of it – was probably not wise. But it was a really great character name, and I couldn't help myself.

When Richard read the book he was horrified. He didn't like the idea that this character had been inspired by him. He thought I'd gone out on some deranged character assassination, pulling out all the worst parts of his personality and magnifying them. I tried to reassure him that it was only artistic licence, and all done for the good of the book, but he never quite believed it.

Worse than that, his fears that people might come to believe the character was a realistic representation of him also proved to be valid. When Richard's wife read the book – especially the parts where he seduced female witnesses, partook of the services of the prostitutes he was interrogating, and constantly bemoaned his evil ex-wife who'd taken his children from him – she started seeing her husband in a different light. She, too, couldn't believe that it had all come from my imagination.

Though both Richard and I assured her that he had never done anything like that, she started to distrust him. She constantly questioned what he got up to at work, and whom he was seeing. Sadly, the marriage quickly fell apart. And like the fictional version of the man, Richard also saw his wife divorce him and move his son to another town.

His colleagues at work were naturally keen to read the book based on their friend and co-worker. But when they saw how the fictional Detective Stone disliked his fellow officers and regularly mocked their ineptitude, they also took against him. I'd apparently painted the character as the only man capable of solving a crime in the whole of the Met, and all of his colleagues as blithering idiots who needed his help to solve a simple missing cat case. Again, they assumed that much of the character had come from the real man. His friends soon shunned him and nobody wanted to work with him.

Finally, when a copy of the book found its way onto the Deputy Commissioner's desk, Richard suddenly found himself hauled in front of a professional standards committee, keen to investigate his supposed hard-drinking, flouting of police procedures and highly unprofessional behaviour. Of course, they found nothing untoward about his approach to the job and there were never any charges filed or complaints upheld.

But with enough people talking, and too many of them believing the fiction of my book to be true, it wasn't long before Richard's career started to suffer. Before the book came out, Richard had been hotly tipped for promotion and quick progression through the ranks. After publication, with half the police force either hating or distrusting him, it took Richard a further five years just to make it up to Detective Sergeant.

The effect of the book spread quickly. And though it was great for me to be selling copies, it seemed the more people that read it, the more problems Richard encountered. Informants stopped talking to him. His bosses dropped every rank, petty, unsolvable case on his desk. His reputation was literally in tatters.

And, of course, the dedication – *To Richard: the real Dick Stone* – probably didn't do much to dispel the myth either.

In short, Richard hates me. More than anyone else has ever hated me. Possibly even more than I hate James fucking Patterson.

And it's for quite good reason. Understandably, he was pretty affronted by the first Dick Stone novel. The fact that I then went on to write a whole series of books featuring the hard-drinking, lecherous, rule-breaking character only increased his dislike of me. So, I've never been able to get as much as an interview with another police officer for book research since.

"Oh, for fuck's sake," said Richard, as he turned to see me standing in the doorway. "What the fuck are you doing here, Freddie?"

"Good to see you, Richard," I said.

"No, seriously, what the fuck are you doing here?"

"I'm here to see my friend, Dylan. The guy in the bed. How is he?"

"Do I look like a fucking doctor?" he snapped. "He's been shot. With a harpoon. How the fuck do you think he's doing?"

"Right," I said.

"I mean, who shoots someone with a harpoon? In central London?" said Richard, shaking his head.

"That's what I said," smiling, suddenly reminded of the fun we used to have together, drinking and waxing lyrical about the cases Richard investigated.

Richard just grimaced at me. A long silence hung between us. "I still fucking hate you," he said, finally breaking the tension. "You prick."

"Yes, I gathered," I said. "Sorry… again. How's little Danny?"

Richard didn't answer, he just stared back, his dark eyes burning into me.

"So, where are you on the case?" I said. "I take it you're investigating. Does anyone know what happened?"

"I told you, he was shot with a harpoon. I haven't gone over the witness statements yet, but I don't expect to find much. Crowded street; people doing their best to ignore each other; nobody ever really sees anything. I'm waiting to get what's left of the… murder weapon, if you want to call it that. See if forensics can find anything. Apparently, the victim kept repeating something about Garfield when he came in. Fuck knows what that's all about."

I nodded, enjoying the feeling of contributing to an investigation again.

"Anyway, why the fuck am I telling you all this?" he snapped.

"I might be able to help, you know," I said. "Dylan recently hired me to investigate a threat against him. He thought someone was trying to kill him."

"Hired you?" laughed Richard. "To investigate? That's a laugh."

"He did go to the police, you know. Told you lot about it. Of course, you weren't interested. And now look what's happened."

"Well, I don't know anything about that. I'm just dealing with what's happened today. And I certainly don't need the help of some wannabe Agatha bloody Christie. So piss off."

"Did you know about the house fire? Or that someone tried to push him in front of a Tube train? Or run him down with a van?"

"Purely circumstantial at this stage," grimaced Richard. "But of course we'll be looking into any relevant leads."

"And what about the bomb? Somebody tried to blow him up this morning. Got the poor bloody postman instead. Could have been me if the parcel had made its way up to the flat."

"You?" he said.

"Yes, I'm staying at Dylan's place at the moment."

"Typical Freddie," grimaced Richard, shaking his head, "always leaching off people."

"It's just during the course of the investigation... at Dylan's request, actually," I lied. "Just until we figure out what's going on."

"Shame the postman got it... and not somebody else," said Richard, sneering. "Anyway, we can't be certain yet that the package was intended for Mr St James. But we'll be following up that lead as well."

"Good, because I've done some digging, spoken to a few people and narrowed down a list of suspects," I said. "I've uncovered something a bit unusual..."

"This isn't like old times, Fred," said Richard, cutting me off. "You don't get to come in on this. You're not wanted."

"But I could be a big help," I insisted.

"Really? Well, next time I need to consult with a second rate hack I'll give you a call. Until then, rest assured Mr St James' assault will be dealt with by real detectives."

"Please," I urged him.

"Not wanted. Not needed," he said, coldly. He looked me up and down, shaking his head disapprovingly, then walked towards the door.

"Please," I said. "He's my friend. I'm worried about him. What if they come back? Please let me help with this."

Richard didn't turn around. He just walked out of the room and disappeared off down the hall.

CHAPTER 10

LOOKING DOWN AT Dylan, I felt ashamed that I hadn't taken his fears more seriously. Instead of being a friend when he needed one, I'd laughed off the threat as simple paranoia, instantly working out the quickest way to profit from the situation. Perhaps Richard Stone was right. What kind of a friend was I, leaching off people and manipulating them for my own means?

If I'd taken Dylan's fears more seriously, I might have got to the bottom of things sooner. Or at least made him take more precautions. Then he might not have been lying there with a harpoon hole in his chest.

Seriously, though, who the hell shoots someone with a harpoon in central London?

A horrible hospital smell invaded my nostrils, all bleach and antiseptic. The one that always makes you think of death and disease, and bedpans... rather than positive things like doctors and nurses fighting to keep people alive. I coughed slightly, gagging on the cleanliness.

A machine to the side of me wheezed and hissed. Another one blinked and beeped, as it powered away to keep my friend alive. At least, I assumed that's what they were doing. For all I knew, they could have been part of some experimental, new-wave prog rock orchestra setup. But probably not.

Dylan looked pale. If it wasn't for the gentle rise and fall of his chest, anyone would have thought he was quite dead. He looked so weak. So frail. And I really couldn't imagine why anyone would want to hurt, or kill, such a nice bloke.

He'd never given up on me. Despite the horrible thoughts I'd had about him and the cruel things I'd said. Despite all my petty jealousy. My hatred of his success. He'd never given up on me, and always held the door open for reconciliation after I'd deserted him. Despite everything, he still wanted to be my friend.

And when he really needed someone – when he was literally afraid for his life – it was me that he turned to. Me that he took in and gave a home to. Me that he was paying a ridiculous fee for helping him, when

I should be helping him for free. I felt the wad of notes sitting heavy in my trouser pocket. Again I felt a sting of shame.

I should give Dylan's money back. I should be the friend he deserved. I should help him out of love and comradeship – and because it was the right thing to do. Not fleece him for a few easy quid here and there. But then, a man has to eat. And the guy's a multi-millionaire. So he was hardly going to miss it.

My mind returned to the case and how utterly behind I was. I still had no real leads or definitive suspects. Dylan's attack had at least moved the case forward. The threat was obviously real now. The hole in Dylan's chest was undeniable proof – someone was definitely trying to kill him. And they were clearly not very good at it. But they were determined. If Dylan survived this latest attack, it was only sensible to assume that someone would be back to try again.

Their methods of assassination had, so far, been pretty random. If the same person – or people – had been behind them all, they had quickly escalated to more extreme, brutal methods. The fire and the Tube train were relatively inconspicuous – as if intended to make Dylan's death look accidental. But the bomb attack and the harpoon shooting were a lot more risky and determined. And clearly more deliberate.

There was also a certain desperation to them – especially with the last two attacks coming in the same day. As if there was a clock ticking, or deadline looming. Was there a rush to finish the job? And, if so, how long would it be before the next attack?

And what was with that harpoon? If you're going to attack someone in broad daylight, at a busy London train station, surely a gun or knife would be the weapon of choice. Something you can easily conceal and pull out at the last minute. Something that doesn't instantly scream: 'Hey look, there's a murderer coming!'

There is literally nothing inconspicuous about a man walking down the street with a harpoon spear fishing gun in his hand.

So, time was against me. Another attack on Dylan was imminent. If I had any chance of stopping it, I had to figure out who was trying to kill him – and why – before they could finish the job.

It would have been a big help if I could have consulted with the police. We could have shared leads, run down suspects together, and I could have piggybacked on their investigations. With a gifted detective like Richard Stone on the case, I would have had the help of one of the best minds I've ever known. And, of course, the wide-ranging resources of the Metropolitan Police.

But Richard's refusal to entertain any help from me whatsoever had made it very clear that I could not rely on the police. I'd have to do this on my own.

"Hello," said a voice behind me.

I looked round to see a tired man with a two-day beard, bloodshot eyes, a creased shirt and poorly knotted tie standing in the doorway. From the stethoscope hung around his neck, I deduced that he was a doctor – I'm quick like that.

"I'm Dr Haynes," he said.

See, I told you.

"Hello doctor," I said, "I'm Dylan's friend, Freddie. Is he going to be okay?"

"Your friend has been very lucky," he told me. "The spear missed his heart and we were able to remove it cleanly. The injuries he sustained are very serious, but he's in a stable condition. The next twenty-four hours will be critical. But if he gets through that, I don't see any reason he can't make a full recovery in time."

"And what about the cancer?" I said. "Will that affect his chances?"

"The cancer?" asked the doctor, yawning wide and trying to rub the tiredness out of his eyes with a thumb and forefinger.

"Yes, the cancer. Will it… you know… stop him from recovering properly?"

"I'm sorry, I don't follow."

"You know… will it, like, affect him? His immune system. Won't it be… like… degraded or something, after the chemo?"

He just stared at me blankly.

"I mean, I'm not a doctor, but doesn't it do something to your… blood cells, or something?"

"I'm sorry, I don't understand, you're saying Mr St James has recently undergone treatment for cancer?"

"Yes, he's had it twice. And recovered twice. I don't know when the last lot was, but it was fairly recent, I think."

"This Mr St James?" he said, pointing at Dylan. "He had cancer?"

"Yes, of course. That's what I've been saying."

"I don't think so," he said.

"You don't think it will affect his chances?"

"No, I don't think he's ever had cancer."

"He's never had cancer?" I said.

"He's never had cancer," he said.

"He's never had cancer?"

"He's never had cancer."

"He's never had…?"

This could have gone on for a while, so I was glad when the doctor raised his hand to stop me, sighed heavily and said, "Look, there's no mention of it in his medical records. You're saying he's been treated for cancer twice? Well, not according to his records. I checked them myself when he was admitted, and there was definitely no cancer."

"I don't understand…" I said. "Dylan told me. He was treated by one of those expensive, rich people's doctors on Harley Street."

Dr Haynes shrugged. "Well, I don't know about that. But if Mr St James had ever been diagnosed with, or treated for cancer at this hospital, the records would show it. And if he was treated for it somewhere else, Harley Street or any other surgery, there would definitely be a mention of it in his file with his GP. Which there isn't."

"So, what are you saying?"

Another long, tired sigh. "I'm saying your friend has never had cancer. Unless he self-diagnosed, treated it himself, then purposefully kept it out of his medical records. Which seems pretty unlikely."

I stood there dumbfounded, unable to speak.

"I have to go now," said the doctor, yawning again. "I'm sure your friend will be fine. He's on a lot of medication at the moment, but he should regain consciousness tomorrow. I'd go home and get some rest if I were you. I wish *I* could…"

He walked out of the room, leaving me standing alone.

******

I walked slowly down the hospital corridor, lost in thought. What the hell was going on? Why would Dylan lie about having cancer? How could he possibly benefit from it?

I'd heard cases of people faking cancer before, but there was always some desperate, devious reason for it. People pretended to be sick to stop wives or husbands leaving them. They did it to manipulate people, seek attention or have others feel sorry for them.

I remembered a story in the papers a few years back about a man called Blake Westcott – the guy who'd miraculously overcome cancer after being given just a few days to live. Doctors were flabbergasted by his recovery. No one could explain just how he'd managed it. He, of course, accredited his 'miracle' to positive thinking, determination, and just a little bit of help from Jesus.

Of course, the tabloids and daytime TV shows lapped up his story, fawning all over him. Months later he was a huge celebrity, setting up his own charity and organising multiple fund-raising events. He trekked the whole coastline of Britain to raise money, gaining plenty of TV coverage. He even had an inspirational book published, describing his desperate struggle and showing how others could overcome cancer, just as he had – all profits naturally going to his own charity. I remember seeing a copy of it on a shelf in Dylan's flat.

As always happens with these things, however, one of the tabloids that initially loved him soon started to smell a rat. After one of their famous undercover stings, Blake Westcott was exposed as a fraud. He'd never actually had cancer – he simply shaved his head, faked his medical records and went on a crash diet to make himself look deathly pale and gaunt. From there, his recovery was relatively simple – he just let his hair grow back and started eating again.

None of the money he raised through his charity ever went to any charitable causes. He siphoned off millions to a number of untouchable offshore bank accounts. By the time the police turned up at his offices to arrest him, he'd already skipped the country to a sunny, tropical, non-extradition island.

He did get his comeuppance a few years later, however. He really was diagnosed with a highly aggressive form of bowel cancer that even his millions couldn't cure. A fine example of irony and karma at work, if ever there was one. And so this time, when he was given just a few weeks to live, it turned out to be true.

So, Blake Westcott had clearly had a detestable, loathsome and highly profitable motive for faking his cancer. But what could Dylan possibly hope to achieve from it?

There was certainly no financial motive; the man was already rich by the time he was first diagnosed. And it was not for attention or fame – he had plenty of that too. And both he and his agent had worked hard to keep the story out of the papers, so that Dylan could keep it as private as possible. That's why he'd been secretly treated on Harley Street.

But that didn't explain the medical records. They're highly

confidential, so there would be no need to falsify them. The only reason there would be no mention of cancer in Dylan's file was if he'd never had it. Of course, the doctor could have been mistaken – he looked like he hadn't slept in days. But I didn't think so. He'd been compos mentis enough to operate on Dylan. And at least someone would have spotted a thing as big as cancer on the records.

So what the hell was going on? I couldn't think of a single reason why Dylan would have wanted to fake having cancer once, let alone twice. And he'd spoken so passionately about his hatred of the chemotherapy – how sick, tired and dizzy it had made him.

Could someone have tricked Dylan into thinking he was ill? And if so, had they then also tricked him into undergoing a hellish treatment regime, making him sick in the process and potentially risking his life?

My head spun just contemplating it. Surely it couldn't be possible. Who would do such a thing? And why? It was ridiculous. It was like an idiotic plot you'd expect to find in a James fucking Patterson novel.

Clearly my investigation had taken one hell of a turn. I took out my notepad, turned to a new page and scribbled down:

Doctor. Harley Street. Cancer. What the FUCK???

I would need to track down Dylan's doctor and try to figure out what this whole cancer business was about.

I came to the end of the corridor, twisting and turning as I tried to make sense of the signs pinned to the walls and hanging from the ceiling. After much confused looking, spinning, and walking this way and that, I finally made my way to the front door of the hospital. I stepped through the large, automatic glass doors. It was dark outside, a cool breeze whispering across the busy car park. I checked my watch: 21.30. My stomach growled and I felt a deep, hollow pang of hunger.

It was hours since I'd eaten, and I had a lot of thinking to do. And since my deductive powers are severely diminished when I'm hungry, I decided to return to Dylan's flat and deal with that issue as quickly as possible.

I took my phone from my pocket and pressed the little power button, feeling it vibrate in my hand as it jolted back to life. I'd switched it off in the hospital, fearful that the magnetic waves – or whatever the hell it is that mobile phones emit – might interfere with all the blinking, bleeping machines in Dylan's room. I suspect this is another fiction perpetrated by hospitals simply to prevent loud, squawking idiots shouting into their mobiles on quiet hospital wards.

But there's no sense in taking chances.

There were three text messages: one from Caroline, asking if I was free to see her tonight; one from Domino's Pizza, offering me the chance to buy two pizzas for the price of one; and the third was from a very helpful company advising me that I was owed £3,487 for the accident I had last year. I hadn't actually had an accident last year, but that didn't mean to say I was above pretending I'd had one – especially if they wanted to give me three and half grand to make up for it. I made a mental note to look into it later and checked my voicemails.

There was a message from Mr Singh, my long-suffering and grossly underpaid landlord, enquiring rather aggressively in his thick accent: "When the bloody hell are you going to pay me my bloody rent? Fucking useless bastard scum." I decided to deal with that particular thorny issue another day and pressed delete.

The second message was from my publisher, asking in a slightly less aggressive tone – though still verging on snarky – when I was intending on delivering the first draft of my new book. This was, of course, the new book that was supposed to have been delivered a week previously. And I had yet to write the first word.

The third message was from Caroline, asking if I'd seen her text, and whether I wanted to see her tonight. I decided that I did want to see her, so I typed out a quick text message telling her that I was on my way back to Dylan's and she should meet me there. I then tapped out a second message asking her to pick up a curry on the way over – I'm all for women's lib and allowing them to feel empowered by paying their own fair share. It's just the kind of guy I am.

My stomach rumbled again. I smiled at the thought of a free meal and, if I played my cards right, another night of sex. Then I hailed a taxi and headed back to the flat.

******

Caroline was absolutely devastated when I told her about Dylan. She instantly burst into uncontrollable sobs as I explained that he'd undergone surgery, and was still in bad shape, but the doctors expected him to make a full recovery. It took me a good half an hour to finally get her to stop crying – all of which time my curry was getting colder and colder in the small tin-foil trays.

It did seem a bit of an overreaction, Caroline getting so upset over a man she'd never actually met. But book fans can be a strange lot. They get so carried away with their appreciation for their favourite author that they can sometimes build up a weird emotional connection with them. They get so involved with the characters the writer creates, and the emotions they put down on the page, and it's as if the book was written especially for them.

They read interviews with the author in the press, or they see them on TV, and they build up a weird fantasy in their heads. It can feel like the author is really their friend – like they really care about each other – even though the object of their affection wouldn't know them if they ran into them naked at a swingers' club.

So, I guessed it was natural that Caroline might have felt emotional about what had happened to Dylan – in a way, it was her friend who was laid up in hospital. If anything, I was probably just a little jealous. I wished my fans were all as attractive as Caroline – rather than sweaty, overweight shoe salesmen called Norman.

By the time I'd finally calmed her down, she was quite emotionally drained. It was obvious any ideas I had about a repeat performance of the previous night's sexual marathon were destined to be dashed. And I had no desire to spend the night stroking her hair and saying: "There, there..." So, I called a taxi and sent her home.

When I finally got the curry plated up, I found that I had no idea how to operate Dylan's space-aged microwave. So, I had to sate my aching hunger with a plate of soggy bhajis, cold korma and a tepid lamb bhuna.

CHAPTER 11

I HADN'T MADE it anywhere near a shop, so Dylan's kitchen cupboards were still completely bereft of anything even nearly worth eating for breakfast. Luckily, the curry Caroline brought round the previous evening had been enough for at least four or five people. And I'd only eaten enough to feed about three. So there was plenty left.

After a frustrating five minutes of slapping, punching and swearing at Dylan's uncooperative microwave, I tipped all the remains into the one big saucepan I could find and heated it up on the hob. Several minutes later I sat down on Dylan's sofa and breakfasted on a steaming hot curry concoction, possibly never before consumed by a human.

It was a fairly unconventional breakfast, and not the sort of thing I'd usually consume before at least midday. Its constituent parts were chicken korma, lamb bhuna, saag aloo, mushroom bhaji, lamb rogan josh, onion bhaji, the curried cauliflower thing (I can never remember what it's called), pilau rice and four poppadums crumbled in for texture. So, it was a fairly dark, angry looking thing. But at least it was edible and packed full of flavour (a little too much, perhaps).

As a writer of fairly modest means, my kitchen cupboards are generally as sparse as a beggar's pocket. And I prefer to avoid mingling with the mouth-breathing plodders that block the aisles of the local supermarket. So, I'm quite familiar with 'making do' when it comes to food. It's helped me to develop a fairly hardy digestive constitution over the years, and I'm certainly no stranger to unusual meal times.

It's true that necessity is the mother of invention – no more so than when it comes to finding adequate grub to keep you going. During these times of necessity, I've often found myself rooting around in the back of kitchen cupboards, pulling out all sorts of random, unexpected ingredients, and creating some rather splendid gastronomic creations of my own: pasta with sardines and cheese spread, with a crumbled Frazzles topping; peanut butter garlic bread; beans on cornflakes (hot or cold); Marmite with cheese dipping sticks (mouldy bits cut off); rice pudding with mushrooms and chicken gravy; Digestive biscuits with tomato ketchup and sliced gherkins; evaporated milk with Ryvita soldiers; butter bean and pickled onion stew; mulligatawny soup with

Jaffa Cakes (in retrospect, I could have had these as separate courses – but when you're in a creative mood...).

The list of possibilities is literally endless – so long as you have a cupboard full of random ingredients, an adventurous nature and the desperation of a struggling artiste. Or, indeed, the food cravings of a pregnant woman. In fact, I've often thought of listing my creations in my own cookery book – *Frederick Winters' Meals for Pregnant Women and Starving Authors*.

I washed my curry breakfast down with three cups of coffee from the fancy coffee machine and made my way through to Dylan's office to continue my research. I flipped through my notebook, poring over the list of potential suspects and reeling slightly at the size of it. It seemed that every time I crossed a suspect off (or at least, thought I had), another name cropped up to take its place. The case was growing ever more complex by the hour.

The previous evening's revelation about Dylan's cancer – or apparent lack of it – was troubling me the most. I walked through to the bathroom and opened up the medicine cabinet. I pulled out bottles, jars and tubes of all different kinds and lined them up on the edge of the bath. There was a large selection of painkillers, cough medicines, cold and flu powders, herbal remedies to aid sleep and various tubes of different creams. There was also a packet of Sertraline, which I already knew to be a type of anti-depressant, and a bottle of Valium.

One small, brown pill bottle stood out amongst the rest, so I picked it up. The label on the side said Thioguanine 40mg tablets. The label showed it had been prescribed to Dylan the previous year. There were just a few pills left rattling around at the bottom.

I carried the bottle back through to the office, opened up a search engine on the laptop and typed in Thioguanine. I scanned the list of search results, the words 'drug', 'cancer' and 'chemotherapy' littered about on the screen. I clicked through to the first link, which told me:

Thioguanine is an anti-cancer medication, most commonly used to treat the symptoms of acute myelogenous leukaemia. Thioguanine is an antimetabolite class of drug and works by slowing or stopping the growth of cancer cells in the body.

So these *were* chemotherapy drugs, used to treat cancer. They had been prescribed to Dylan. And considering the bottle was nearly empty, it was reasonable to assume that he must have been taking them.

So what the hell was going on? Had Dylan had cancer or not? The doctor the previous evening had been adamant that he hadn't. So then why had he been taking cancer treatment drugs?

Naturally, I'd ask Dylan about it when he regained consciousness, but I'd heard nothing from the hospital and didn't know when that might be.

I picked up a pen and circled the word 'doctor' in my pad. Who was this mysterious Harley Street doctor? And why was he going around handing out false diagnoses and treatments for cancer? If they were actually false, of course.

I opened up Dylan's emails and started to scan the list for clues to the doctor's identity. Just then I heard a strange buzzing sound, like a mechanical mosquito, coming from down the hall. Everything went quiet, then a few seconds later the low-pitched buzz sounded again. Another thirty seconds of silence, then it sounded again.

I stepped out of the office, following the noise to its source and saw a tiny TV screen illuminated in the corner of the phone on the wall. It showed a grainy, black and white picture of a man at the entrance to the block of flats. He had dark hair and glasses and wore a thick, dark, roll-neck jumper. He was staring up into the camera, looking slightly impatient. I saw him reach forward and press something, then the buzz sounded again.

My astute detective skills instantly told me that the phone must have doubled as a security entrance monitor.

The man didn't look particularly threatening. In that ridiculous sweater, and with a limp goatee beard that barely covered his chin, he looked like he could barely snap a stick of celery. I assumed he wasn't here to kill anyone (he probably wouldn't have rung the doorbell if he was), so I pressed the button to buzz him in. He walked into the building and the screen went blank.

I waited a few minutes, allowing him to make his way up the stairs, then opened the front door of the flat to find him with a confused look on his face.

"Oh," he said, "I was looking for Dylan."

"Sorry," I replied, "he's not here."

"Well, do you know when he'll be back? We're supposed to have an appointment."

"An appointment?" I said. "For what?"

"I don't think I really want to tell…" he said, trailing off as an even more suspicious look came over him. "I'm sorry, who are you?"

"I'm Dylan's friend," I said. "I'm staying with him for a while."

"That's funny; Dylan didn't mention that anyone was staying with him."

"Are you calling me a liar?"

"No, no... of course not," he said, his face turning red as he got visibly more flustered.

"Good. Now we've established who I am, who are you? And what's this appointment? What are you? Rent boy? Vacuum cleaner salesman? Jehovah's witness?"

"If you must know," he said sharply, "I'm Dylan's therapist. We have a session booked for today."

"Oh, so you're the quack filling his head with nonsense, eh?" I sneered. "Telling him to lock himself away and avoid people."

"What I discuss with my patients is completely confidential and I will not tell..."

"Well, you'd better come in then," I said, cutting him off. I waved a hand in the direction of the hall. "Dr...?" I paused, waiting for him to fill in the gap.

"Jeffries," he snapped. "Dr Michael Jeffries." He walked past me and I followed him through to the living room. He sat down on one of the sofas, and I sat on the other one opposite him. He looked increasingly nervous and did what he could to avoid making eye contact with me as I glared at him with my best menacing stare.

After a few minutes, he looked at his watch and said, "So, will Dylan be back soon?"

"I wouldn't have thought so," I replied, "he's lying in a hospital bed with a bloody great hole in his chest."

"What? He... what?"

"Yeah, hospital. Someone shot him. With a harpoon gun, if you can believe that?"

"Shot?" He stumbled, dumbfounded. "A... harpoon?"

"I know! Who the hell shoots someone with a harpoon? In central London?"

"Jesus," he blurted. "And you didn't think to mention this when I arrived?"

"No, well I wanted to talk to you, didn't I?"

"Talk to me? About what?"

"Dylan thinks someone's trying to kill him," I said. "He actually hired me to investigate. I'd say the fact that he's in hospital after being shot indicates that he could well be right."

"Oh my God," he said, "really?"

"Yeah, someone tried to blow him up as well. Letter bomb. Poor postman copped it instead. You probably saw the police tape."

"Yes," said the man with the roll-neck sweater and stupid beard, "I was going to ask about the tape. Goodness, that's awful." He stopped for a second, looking thoughtful. "But what does that have to do with me?"

"I was just wondering whether Dylan ever mentioned any of this to you."

"I've already told you, I'm not discussing my patients," he said.

"Yeah, whatever. I was just wondering whether Dylan ever talked about it. I mean, if he thought someone was trying to harm him, don't you have a responsibility to notify the authorities, or something?"

"If every psychiatrist called the police every time a patient displayed paranoid symptoms, the lines would be inundated," he laughed, smugly.

"So, Dylan was displaying paranoid tendencies? He *did* tell you he was in fear of his life?"

"I never said that," replied the doctor, looking increasingly uncomfortable. "You're putting words in my mouth. And I've told you, I'm not going to discuss my patient."

"You call in on Dylan as a courtesy?" I said, changing tack. "That seems a bit strange."

"Er… well, no… not really…" he stumbled.

"Surely, you must have an office where people come to see you," I pressed him. "That's how things are usually done, isn't it?"

"Well, yes, generally, I suppose, but I make a special exception…"

"Really?" I said, cutting him off. "And how many of your other patients do you make special exceptions for?"

"Not many…" His composure was starting to slip. He looked all around the flat as he searched for words, desperate to avoid eye contact. Small beads of sweat formed on his brow, twinkling silver in the glow of the overhead lights. "I make an exception for Dylan because he has trouble leaving the flat…"

"Trouble leaving the flat?" I laughed. "You're the one who told him not to leave it."

"Yes… er… well, I…"

"And about that, what the hell kind of advice is that to give someone suffering from depression? Lock yourself away and ignore the world? What medieval quackery is that exactly?"

"I don't have to sit here and explain myself to you," he said, panic tingeing his voice as he stood and started towards the door. "There is such a thing as patient confidentiality you know."

"I'm just trying to help my friend," I said. "I thought you'd want to do the same."

"I'm not answering any more of your questions," he shouted, yanking open the door and stepping through it. He tried to slam it behind him but I raced forward and caught it, following him out into the hallway.

"Why won't you talk to me?" I called after him. He didn't respond. He just marched off along the hall, thudding down the stairs until he was out of sight.

"Don't you even want to know what hospital your favourite patient's in?" I called after him. But he was gone.

I walked back into the flat and poured another cup of coffee. That was certainly strange, I thought. I'd poked him with a few questions just to see what kind of a reaction I'd get. And I'd expected the whole 'patient confidentiality' thing. But he'd actually seemed a little rattled.

I powered up Dylan's laptop, opened his emails and searched for any correspondence with Dr Jeffries. I checked the list, looking for the right email address, but there was nothing from a Dr Jeffries at all.

I scanned through all the recent mails, looking for anything that could have come from him. Finally, I happened upon a curious looking address: Therapist4You@gmail.com. It looked more like some spam mail – like a PPI scam, or payday loans company. Instantly, my crime writer's sense of suspicion kicked in.

I clicked open the email and, sure enough, it was from Jeffries. I filtered Dylan's inbox to show only messages from this address. There were a handful of mails, dating back over a couple of years, containing little more than pleasantries and arrangements for convenient times that the doctor could call round for his next appointment.

This was another thing that struck me as strange. What psychiatrist arranges his own appointments? Surely even a crummy one would have a receptionist or secretary to keep his schedule up to date.

I scrolled down to the bottom of the list, finding the earliest email Dylan had received from him. It was titled: *I'm here to help*. The message read:

Dear Dylan,

I have been provided your details by your agent, Mr Mortimer Bunkle, who feels I may be of some assistance to you. Mortimer tells me you've been feeling a bit down recently, and asked if I would consult with you. I am a psychiatrist and, having heard about you, I do believe that you could benefit from some consultations with me. And I'm sure we can have you feeling much better very soon.

Please call me on the number listed below, and we can schedule an appointment so I can come and meet you and find out more about what problems your dealing with.

Sincerely
Dr Martin Jeffries

Something was definitely not right. What kind of psychiatrist randomly emails patients out of the blue? What was he, some kind of ambulance-chasing, opportunist shrink?

There was also something odd about the language he used. It was not exactly scholarly, or even terribly professional. And definitely not the sort of thing I'd expect to come from a professional psychiatrist. Especially with the obvious grammatical error on 'problems *your* dealing with'.

The email address was equally suspicious. No practice name, no official title in the email, and all through just a bog-standard Gmail account. It hardly screamed out professional psychiatrist. With a name like Therapist4You, I figured Jeffries was definitely at the lower end of the professional scale.

There were no qualifications listed, either. If there's one thing I know about doctors of any kind, it's that they're a fairly vainglorious bunch. Any chance to quote certificates, qualifications or which university they attended and they'll take it. But Jeffries didn't have so much as a PHD, DPM, or MClinPsychol after his name. Not even a LOL or PMSL.

I opened up another search window and typed in the doctor's name. Among the results for 'Dr Martin Jeffries' were: a veterinarian in Kansas; a gastroenterologist in Norfolk; a gynaecologist in Exeter; and a supposed spiritual healer in Croydon (whom I suspected had probably bought his doctorate on the internet). There were a handful of other random medical practitioners listed before Google autocorrected me and turned up results for Dr Marten's shoes and Doc Martin – a twee-looking comedy drama show starring Martin Clunes.

I messed around with the search terms, keying in a number of variations, including: Dr Jeffries, Dr Jeffries London, Dr Jeffries Psychiatrist, Martin Jeffries Psychiatrist, Therapist4You and host of others. None of them turned up anything linked to the man I'd just spoken with. I understood he might not have his own website, of course, but surely there would have been at least a mention of him somewhere.

With all the money in his bank, why wasn't Dylan seeing one of the country's leading shrinks? Why was he taking advice from this clown?

I took out my notepad and scribbled down: *Doctors – what the bloody hell is going on?*

CHAPTER 12

A LAYER OF thin blue and white police tape flapped softly in the breeze as I left Dylan's flat and walked down the path to the street. A low hum sang in the air as cars passed at the end of the road. Across the street, a teenager whizzed by on a skateboard, the gravel-grate sound echoing off the walls of the high buildings. A woman walked her dog, chatting loudly on a mobile phone – something about the price of jeans in Marks & Spencer.

The only reminder that a man had lost his life there, just a day before, was the police tape and the cordoned-off area at the end of the path. There were no police officers there any longer. They'd packed up the previous night and gone. I wasn't sure if, or when, they'd be back to carry on with the investigation.

I walked past the macabre reminder, turned right and headed towards the main road. Then I hailed a cab and asked the driver to take me to Soho.

I had so many questions about Dylan. The more I thought about things the more I realised they just didn't add up. So many of the things he'd told me had turned out to be untrue. Or, at least, the story wasn't exactly as Dylan had explained it to me. I needed answers, and if there was one man who should be able to help it was Dylan's agent, Mortimer Bunkle.

The cab dropped me outside a building on Wardour Street. On the wall next to the door was an ancient-looking entry system, with five different buzzers. A collection of signs marked out all the different businesses operating in the building, with Red Monkey Marketing on the first and second floor; Dynamic Recruitment Solutions on the third floor; and something called Blue Dynamite Media on the fourth. It sounded equally as though it could have been a documentary film-maker or a porn producer. Considering it was in the heart of Soho, I figured it was more likely to be the latter.

Right at the top was an aged silver plaque that read: *Mortimer Bunkle Literary and Talent Agency*. It had worn over time with dirt and age, and looked positively ancient compared to the flashy logos and modern typefaces of the signs below.

I pressed the buzzer next to Mortimer's sign. No sound. I tried the door and it opened instantly. I entered and walked up the five flights of stairs. At the top was another door with an identical plaque to the one below. It was slightly ajar, so I pushed my way inside.

Walking into Mortimer Bunkle's office was like stepping through a wormhole into 1976. Gaudy orange and brown carpet littered the floor, swirling off in all directions in a series of random, jagged patterns. It was like a Rorschach test in interior design – the more I looked at it, the more disturbing images I saw. It was threadbare to say the least, the once presumably bouncy, deep shag having been trampled down to a thin, hard surface. It looked as though 1976 was also the last time it had seen a carpet cleaner.

Blue-and-pink-striped wallpaper hung limply on the walls. It was faded by the sun and peeling away at the corners and the edges. It clashed violently with the colours on the floor, and it actually made me feel slightly nauseated.

In the corner of the room was a small, semi-circular bar – the type of thing it was no doubt trendy to install in offices back in the 70s. It was clad in bright gold padding, with a criss-crossed pattern. The main desktop surface had presumably once been white, but was now a faded, mucky beige colour.

An assortment of glasses hung from a wooden shelf above the bar and the far wall held a line of bottles cradled into optics. I didn't recognise any of the brands. There were things like Captain Columbo's Rum, Indian River Gin, Loch Nevis Whisky and Prussian Red Wodka. Considering Prussia had been dissolved before World War II, I dreaded to think how long those bottles had been sitting up there gathering dust.

On the other side of the room, next to a large brown door that led through to the inner office, was a small wooden desk. A computer sat on top, which looked like a relic from the early 90s, along with a large phone with around ten or fifteen different buttons and lights. I imagined back in the day, at the height of Mortimer's success, all of those lights would have been flashing, each one indicating highly important calls from authors, editors, publishers, actors or TV and film producers. Now, not even a single one was blinking. And I guessed they hadn't done so for quite some time.

Behind the desk sat a little old lady with bright white hair tied into a tight bun on top of her head. She wore tiny round glasses, perched on the very tip of her nose, with a silver chain drooping down from either side and disappearing around the back of her neck. She must have been at least ninety years old. With her head slumped forwards she looked like she was asleep. Or maybe dead.

As I walked closer, however, I could hear a strange, incessant click-clacking sound. I peered over the top of the computer and saw that she was actually intently focused on the knitting in her lap. And where the rest of her looked like it might not have moved since the dreadful carpet was installed, her fingers were working away in a blur, rattling along at an astonishing pace.

Now, I know nothing about knitting, but at that rate she looked like she could turn out a pretty decent scarf in under an hour. She could probably stock out an entire branch of The Edinburgh Woollen Mill in little over a month.

"Hello," I said.

No reply.

"Hello," I said again, a little louder this time.

Click-clack. Click-clack. No reply.

"Hello," I said, louder still, waving my hands in the air to get her attention.

Click-clack. Click-clack. Click-clack. Still nothing.

I opened my mouth, ready to shout, when the door to the side of me opened and two men came walking out briskly.

One of them I recognised as Mortimer Bunkle. The other man I had never met. He was tall and wiry, with black hair slicked back over his head and a thick layer of black stubble painted across his chin and cheeks. He was dressed in black combat trousers, a black t-shirt, black bomber jacket and heavy black boots. He looked like an army surplus store had thrown up all over him.

He seemed vaguely familiar, although I couldn't put my finger on why, or where I might have seen him before.

"We need this sorted now," said Mortimer to the other man, as they entered the outer room. "Time is…"

The sentence trailed off as they saw me. They stopped immediately where they were, both looking startled and cautiously eyeing me up and down.

Mortimer quickly forced the surprise from his face. The other man caught my eye, then instantly looked down at the ground. He marched forwards, pushing past me, bumping my shoulder as he walked towards the main door. He shoved it hard, walked through and disappeared out of sight.

"You must excuse him," said Mortimer, with an ingratiating smile. "Not really what you'd call a people person."

"No," I said, watching the door slam shut behind him. "Has something upset him?"

"Oh, hard to tell. He's just like that. Always in a foul mood since he had his little... well, you know." He said the last words in a conspiratorial hushed whisper, leaning in and winking at me.

"Sorry, no, I'm not sure I do," I said, shrugging.

"Oh, well, I guess his face has been out of the papers for a while, so no wonder you wouldn't recognise him. That's Henry Sanders."

I shrugged again, shaking my head.

"Captain Henry Sanders. The Conman Captain. The SAS Scoundrel – although don't let him catch you calling him that. Don't you read the papers?"

And then suddenly I did recognise him. Henry Sanders, A.K.A the Conman Captain, A.K.A the SAS Scoundrel, as the papers had so imaginatively titled him. He was the fake SAS captain, who had been at the centre of a huge scandal about five or six years previously.

"Yes, of course," I said, smirking. No wonder he'd rushed out of there in a mood.

Captain Henry Sanders was a famous war veteran, who had served with a special SAS unit in the Gulf War. He'd survived a particularly perilous mission, in which his whole unit had been killed and only he had survived. He evaded capture in enemy territory for two whole weeks, and then, against the odds, he managed to smuggle himself out of the country and back home to safety. Although these things are supposed to be top secret, much like Andy McNab and Chris Ryan before him, he wrote a bestselling memoir telling all the gritty details.

This was followed by a second auto-biography and a series of novels – all loosely based on his time in the service, and the missions he'd taken part in. He even got a plum job as an advisor on one of the broadsheet newspapers, writing a weekly security column and commenting on any defence stories that cropped up in the news.

He had a highly successful career. His book sales were more than I could ever dream of, and he had a huge following. For a while he seemed to be all over the TV as well. He was always commenting about foreign affairs on the news. He trained a group of middle-aged housewives how to survive off the land and evade enemy capture, in a poorly thought out Channel 4 show called *Mum's Army*. And he became the general go-to expert for any military issues. There was even a rumour that he'd turned down a hundred grand to appear on Celebrity Big Brother.

He was incredibly popular, well-respected and people really loved his whole legend. So, of course, it wasn't long before the press got tired of talking about what a great guy he was, and instead decided to dig up whatever dirt they could find. And they found plenty.

When they looked into Sanders' supposed miraculous survival story, they found more than a few inconsistencies. The dates didn't quite add up. His recollections of the terrain and surrounding countryside didn't really fit. He couldn't quite remember the exact route he took out of the country, and struggled to point it out on a map. He blamed it all on fatigue, malnourishment and the debilitating effects all the stress and fear had on his brain.

When the papers dug a little deeper, they struggled to find anyone who recalled serving with him in the SAS. And there was apparently no record of his service at all. He claimed this was due to the highly covert nature of his missions, and the fact that all his records had been sealed as a matter of national security. But even his staunchest supporters started to smell a rat.

It took a TV interview with Jeremy Paxman, in which the bulldog interviewer asked him outright thirteen times in a row whether he'd ever actually served in the SAS, before he finally broke down and admitted it was all a con. He had genuinely been in the army, serving as a Lance Corporal, but had never seen any real action. He had tried out for the SAS, but had been sent home during the very first phase of the selection process. His survival story and subsequent memoirs had all been a complete lie.

The day after the interview, he was very publicly dropped by his publisher and all of his books were withdrawn from sale. He quickly lost his TV work, and the planned big-budget ITV drama based on his series of novels was cancelled before the first script was even written.

The press hounded him for a few weeks, before moving on to bully their next target. And ever since, he'd dropped completely off the radar.

"Used to be one of my best clients," said Mortimer, with a sad look. "Now he couldn't sell a Post-it note, let alone a book. Real shame."

"So, did you know?" I asked.

"Know what?"

"Did you know he was a fake?"

"Now, that would be telling," he said, smiling coyly. "Hang on a sec…" He squinted his eyes, looking hard at me. Then a look of realisation spread across his face and he raised his hand to point a large, fat finger at me. "Freddie Winters. I thought that was you."

"Hello Mortimer," I said.

"Freddie Winters," he said again, coming over all nostalgic. "God it must be… ten years since I last saw you. How the devil are you?"

"Can't complain," I said. "Sorry to pop in on you unannounced. I was just trying to get your assistant's attention to see if you were free, but…"

"Oh, no use trying to get anything out of her," said Mortimer, turning to wince at the old lady. "Old bat's as deaf as a post."

He waved his arms at her. No reaction. He knocked loudly on top of the computer. Nothing. He leaned over the desk and tapped her gently on the shoulder.

Her head jolted back, a look of terror on her face. The knitting shot out of her hands, arcing high up into the air and landing with a thud on the computer. Her glasses tipped forwards off her nose, catching on the chain around her neck. She looked up, startled, and for the first time I could see just how wrinkled and worn her face was.

I found myself wondering what would happen if she untied the bun in her hair. Was it there for structural support? Would all the skin tumble down into loose flaps around her head, like one of those droopy-faced dogs?

"I said you're as deaf as a post," Mortimer shouted at her.

"Eh? What?" she shouted back at him.

I'd have to remember to try and flog her a book on the way out.

"Oh, go back to your knitting," said Mortimer. "You know, I've no idea why I keep her around. She hasn't done a stitch of work in years, the old bag. I bought her this computer to help with the filing and I don't think she's ever even turned it on. She keeps the keyboard in a drawer. I should let her go, really, but I keep hoping she'll have a heart attack and save me the bother. Still, what can you do? Mothers, eh?"

I wished I had a mouthful of water, just so I could have spat it out all over the place in shock. Instead, I had to make do with looking mildly discombobulated.

"Goodness. Freddie Winters. Great to see you. Won't you come through?" He ushered me into his office and closed the door behind him.

Mortimer was a large man, with ruddy cheeks and a pockmarked nose, reddened through years of too much booze. A bright white shock of hair sat atop his head, coiffured into an elaborate, thick, wavy quiff. He wore an expensive-looking navy suit that clung tightly to his large girth, and a crisp white shirt with high, wide collars. Shining out brightly, cutting his multitude of chins in two, sat a garish red bow tie.

Amazingly, Mortimer didn't look much different than he had when I'd known him fifteen years previously. Maybe just a little plumper. He'd always looked antiquated – like he was lost in the wrong century. I remember joking with Dylan that he spoke like a character from a Charles Dickens novel, and that he'd probably been around when the very first book was published.

For a group of young aspiring novelists, who thought the world of ourselves, and genuinely believed we were ushering in a new age of publishing, he'd been the very embodiment of everything we thought we were opposed to. So, when Dylan signed with his agency, we thought he was crazy.

We told Dylan to hold out for better offers, and that an agent more on our wavelength would come along and snap him up. But Dylan was adamant. Mortimer had seen something in his writing that no one else had.

It was all just jealousy, of course. Mortimer was a highly successful agent back then, with a number of big name clients from the worlds of literature, music, film and TV. Any of us would have bitten his hand off for the chance to be represented by him. But because he hadn't picked us, it was easier to pretend that we'd reject him given half the chance.

Mortimer would regularly come to the pub with Dylan, then hang out with us as well. We'd accept the free drinks he bought us, then mock him behind his back. We'd say that it was people like him that were ruining the publishing world with his outdated attitudes and 'old boys' club' mentality. People like him, and short-sighted publishers, that stopped the general public from getting the chance to discover our genius. All just sour grapes, of course.

And Dylan had been right. Mortimer got his first book published with a keen young editor willing to take a risk, and the book did pretty well. Then the next book did better, and the next, until Mortimer guided Dylan to becoming one of the country's top literary talents. All while the rest of us were still sitting in the pub waiting for our big breaks to come and find us.

"So, Freddie, how have you been?" said Mortimer. "How are book sales? You write those terrific crime books, with that police chap... Rick something..."

"Dick Stone," I corrected him. "So, you like my books?"

"Oh, yes," he bellowed, enthusiastically. He paused for a beat, thinking, then said, "Haven't actually read any of them, but I've heard great things. Dylan was always raving about them."

"Oh, well at least you've heard of them. That's more than most people."

Mortimer strolled around behind his expansive mahogany desk and threw himself down into an ageing leather chair. It creaked loudly under the strain of his weight, a gust of air hissing out sharply from a crack in the upholstery. Then he reclined back, his face just about visible over his bulbous stomach. He rested his arms languidly on top of the mass, the hands not quite able to meet in the middle.

I sat down in a chair opposite his desk.

"So, what can I do for you, Freddie?" he said. "Are you looking for new representation?"

Like I say, fifteen years ago I would have jumped at the chance. But things had taken a huge slide for Mortimer. A rather high-profile tax scandal a few years previously had seen his business dwindle to near non-existence. It was nothing too suspect, apparently. He hadn't been siphoning off any of his clients' money, or investing in phoney businesses. He just hadn't 'remembered' to pay his own taxes. For more than ten years.

Of course, the rich and famous prefer not to be associated with that sort of thing, and the majority of his clients jumped ship overnight, before the press or the tax office started looking too closely at their own affairs. After Mortimer had repaid Her Majesty's Revenue Officers' over-inflated bill, he was just about broke. He lost his big house and his fancy cars. His business came close to going under, save for the generosity of Dylan. He was the only big name to stick with him. But then, Dylan always was too loyal.

It was Mortimer's reputation that took a real beating, though. Far bigger than the one his bank balance took. All the producers, publishers and directors that used to be queuing up at his door suddenly stopped answering his calls. Without any big name clients, he couldn't get a meeting with anyone. And with no meetings, he couldn't attract any new clients. Without his 15% income from Dylan, he would have been literally destitute.

"Not today," I replied. "I still have an agent. Although I'm not entirely certain what he does for his money."

"Well, if you ever feel like a change," smiled Mortimer, "you know where we are."

"The reason I'm here is because I actually wanted to talk to you about Dylan."

"Dylan?"

"Yes, I'm staying with him at the moment. He's actually hired me to do a job for him."

"A job. That sounds intriguing. What sort of a job?"

"He's hired me to find out who's trying to kill him."

Mortimer lurched forward, his arms flapping wildly, the chair creaking and farting as it snapped upwards. I braced myself as I thought the thing might propel him right across the desk at me.

"Kill him?" he snapped, quizzically.

"Yes, he came to me a few days ago, scared out of his mind. Rambling that someone was trying to kill him."

"Nonsense," he half laughed, half coughed. "Who would want to kill Dylan? It's ridiculous."

"Well, he is lying in hospital with a big hole in his chest."

"A what?"

"A big hole. You mean you haven't heard?"

"Heard what?"

"Someone shot Dylan. With a harpoon."

The man's face went pale, all the colour rushing from his bulbous, red nose. He leaned back in his chair, his mouth hanging wide open and a look of total bemusement in his eyes. "My God," he said, finally. "I had no idea. Is he all right? Will he be okay? What have the police said? I must get down there right away. I must be with him."

"I'm sorry, I thought you knew. I assumed the hospital would have called you."

He grabbed onto the edge of the desk, pulling himself up out of the chair, and waddled around the desk towards the door. I stood up and followed him out of the office.

We rushed down four flights of stairs and out onto the street outside. He moved remarkably quickly for a big man, and within just a few seconds he'd managed to hail a taxi. We hopped in and told the driver to take us to the hospital. Mortimer flopped back, taking up nearly the whole back seat and I perched opposite him on one of the fold-down chairs.

"So, you have no idea who might have it in for Dylan?" I asked Mortimer.

"No, of course not," he said. "Are the police sure the harpoon was definitely meant for Dylan? I mean, might it not just have been an accident?"

"An accident?" I laughed. "Where the shooter runs away? I don't think so. Besides, there have been other attempts."

"Other attempts?"

"A van nearly knocked him down. And there was the mysterious fire at his house."

"My God," said Mortimer. "Are you sure those were attempts? I mean, people nearly get knocked down in London all the time. And that fire was just an accident, wasn't it?"

"There's a car, as well. Blue Ford. It's been following him around."

"There are lots of blue cars in London. And plenty of them must be Fords, too."

"Okay, well, how do you explain the postman then?"

"Postman?" he said.

"Yesterday a postman blew up outside Dylan's building."

"Blew up?"

"Letter bomb, apparently. I think it was meant for Dylan, but it exploded before it could reach him."

"My goodness," said Mortimer, reaching into his pocket and pulling out a paisley handkerchief, which he used to mop his brow. Beads of sweat twinkled on his upper lip, a thin stream running down his face and disappearing down the side of his tight collar. I couldn't tell whether it was caused by the stress of the news or the exertion of trundling his bulky frame down all those stairs.

"How well do you know Dr Jeffries?" I asked.

"Jeffries?" said Mortimer, a completely blank look on his face.

"Dylan's therapist. I met him this morning. I believe you recommended him to Dylan. So, how well do you know him exactly?"

"Oh, yes... Jeffries. Of course. Therapist chap. Erm... not well, I'm afraid. Not at all, really."

"But you recommended he should contact Dylan. You told him

Dylan needed his help."

"I did? Oh... er... yes, of course. Of course, I did. I, er... well, I knew Dylan was having a few problems and what-not. What with his divorce and his illness... well, you know what Dylan's like. He seemed a bit depressed. I thought maybe having someone to talk to might help him. So, I made a recommendation that he should seek some counselling. He was a bit embarrassed and didn't want to go to his doctor or anything. So I, er... recommended Jeffries. Dylan is a client and a friend, and I was just trying to help."

"So you knew Dr Jeffries from before?"

"Not really. Someone recommended him to me and I just sort of passed it on. Sorry... what is this about? And what does it have to do with people trying to kill Dylan?"

"I don't know yet. I'm just looking into all the leads I can. I'm just trying to help as well."

"Yes, of course. Of course you are."

"Let me ask you," I said, changing subjects, "what do you know of Dylan's ex-wife?"

"Which one, old boy? Chap's had a few."

"Corinne Handley? I believe you introduced the two of them. She says you were quite keen on the two of them getting together."

"Oh, don't believe a word of what that woman says," he huffed. "She can't be trusted."

"Funny, she says the same about you."

"Yes, well, of course she would. You know her reputation, I take it?"

"I'm familiar with her... work," I said.

"Well, there you go then. She is of dubious character, and no mistake. She begged me to introduce her to Dylan, and in the end I did, just to get her off my back. Then the silly fool goes and falls in love with her. What a mistake."

"Really? I thought they were in love?"

"He might have been. But her? No, I never bought it. I was always waiting for her to turn on him and sell the story to the press. That's why I got Dylan to write it into the pre-nup, when he told me they were getting married. I wasn't having her spilling the beans to the bloody tabloids."

"Yes, she told me about that. She also said that someone paid her a million pounds to divorce Dylan. She said it was he who left her, and when she tried to call Dylan you wouldn't let her speak to him."

"Oh, she did, eh?" said Mortimer, getting visibly agitated. "Why the hell would someone pay her a million pounds to divorce Dylan? It doesn't make sense. And how exactly could I have stopped Dylan from speaking to her? No, believe me, that woman is a compulsive liar. I had to put Dylan back together when she left him. And that's what she did, you know. Just upped and left. Poor sod came home to find divorce papers in the house."

"Yes, that's what he told me. He says he tried to contact Corinne, but she refused to speak with him."

"Well, there you go then. Who are you going to believe, your friend, or a known harlot who sleeps with men and then brags about it in the papers?"

He made a good point.

"So, what do you know about Dylan's illness?" I said, keen to ask as many questions as possible before we arrived at the hospital.

"Illness?" said Mortimer, starting to look slightly uncomfortable. "What about it? He had cancer. Terrible thing."

"Yes, he told me about his cancer. He told me how sick he was, and how bad the treatment made him feel. I even found some of the medication in his bathroom."

"Mmm… it was a horrible time for him."

"And I believe he was treated by your own doctor, wasn't he?"

"Not exactly," said Mortimer, my questions clearly starting to annoy him. "Not my doctor. Just a doctor I happen to know."

"But you referred him?"

"Yes. It's not that unusual, you know," said Mortimer, forcing a chuckle. "I'm his agent, so I do everything I can to help him. That sometimes extends to recommending things. I recommend wines, and shops and restaurants too."

"But you trust this doctor?"

"Yes, of course. I wouldn't recommend him otherwise. Look, I'm sorry Freddie, but what exactly are you getting at?"

"It's just that I was talking to Dylan's doctor at the hospital last night, and he says Dylan never had cancer. No record of it, anywhere."

"What do you mean? Of course he had cancer. You said it yourself, you even saw his medication."

"I know," I said. "That's what's really confusing me. He was clearly taking the medication, and he obviously thought he had cancer. But why would the doctor say he hadn't had it? No record of it. And the doctor was adamant about that. There should have been some mention of it in his file. Clearly someone's wrong. Or worse – someone's lying."

"Well, I wouldn't know about that I'm afraid," said Mortimer turning to look out the window as the taxi slowed down. "Oh God, the bloody vultures are here already."

I looked out the window to see a group of scruffy looking men outside the main entrance to the hotel, huddled alongside the sickly smokers in their dressing gowns. Each one had a large camera with a zoom lens hanging around their necks.

"Bloody paparazzi," snarled Mortimer. "How the bloody hell did they find out about this before I did? I'm his bloody agent, for God's sake!"

The taxi pulled up outside the front of the hospital and the photographers turned in unison to see who was inside. They raised their cameras, peering through the zoom lenses, presumably to see whether any of Dylan's celebrity chums had come to pay him a visit.

About a hundred yards up the road sat two large vans with huge satellite dishes perched on the roofs. Two men with large TV cameras stood aimlessly, checking their equipment and gazing all around for the best places to set up. Men in suits and anoraks stood around talking to them, waiting for their live-to-camera reports. I thought I recognised a pretty, blonde female newsreader from the BBC in the middle of the crowd.

"Fucking vultures," hissed Mortimer, as he clambered forward in his seat and flung the taxi door open.

Clearly, Mortimer and I weren't a big enough draw for the paps. As soon as they saw we were nobody special, they lowered their cameras, turned away and went back to their previous conversations, without so much as a single flash going off.

The taxi dipped and then rose on one side as Mortimer climbed out onto the pavement. He turned back to look at me, still sitting in my seat.

"Aren't you coming?" he said.

"No," I replied. "I'll let you be alone with Dylan for a while. I have a few more leads to chase up, so I'll pop in and see him later on."

As far as I knew, Dylan still hadn't regained consciousness. And there was no point sitting around in a hospital room with Mortimer. I'd asked him all the questions I could for the time being, and I got the distinct impression he wasn't keen on answering any more.

Mortimer slammed the car door shut and thundered off towards the hospital entrance. I checked my phone for messages and asked the driver to take me back to Soho.

CHAPTER 13

"IT'S SO AWFUL," said Caroline. "I mean, I just can't believe it. Who would do such a terrible thing?"

I was sitting on Dylan's sofa, eating a Chinese takeaway that Caroline had brought round. When I'd checked my mobile in the taxi, I'd found four missed calls from her. There were three voicemails, asking if I was all right, and whether there were any updates on Dylan. There were also four text messages asking pretty much the same thing, and whether I wanted her to come round that night and cheer me up.

It was early afternoon when I left Mortimer at the hospital, and I hadn't fancied going back to Dylan's place and sitting there alone. So, I instead headed to the Crown and Two Chairmen pub on Dean Street. I thought I'd get some perspective by taking my mind off the case and doing a bit of my own writing. But I just couldn't get into it. The more I tried to think up new cases for Dick Stone (the fictional one) to investigate, the more I thought of Dylan's real-life case and how little progress I was making.

Without the police allowing me to share their insights or leads, I was feeling second rate and very alone. And I wasn't sure how to progress. I tried calling Detective Stone (the real one) but, unsurprisingly, he wasn't answering his mobile. I phoned him at the police station, but was greeted by a grumpy desk sergeant, who told me, "Detective Inspector Stone is currently busy. And he's left instructions that he doesn't want to be bothered by any amateur sleuths or wannabe Miss Marples." I sent a text message, asking whether he'd agree to meet me, but I didn't expect a reply.

Before I knew it, I'd polished off five pints, and was feeling that strange mix of lonely, depressed and horny that alcohol is so good at creating. That's when I'd called Caroline and told her I did need cheering up, and it would be lovely to see her – and could she pick up some dinner on her way round?

"I mean, it just doesn't make sense," she continued. "Dylan St James is one of our greatest writers. He's brought so much happiness to so many people. Why would anybody want to hurt him?"

Her breath quickened as tears welled in her eyes. She was taking this all much harder than I'd expected. "There, there," I said, placing a hand around her shoulder. "Don't worry. I'm gonna find out who's behind this. Nobody's gonna hurt him again. Are you eating that last spring roll?"

We were watching the evening news. The woman I thought I'd recognised at the hospital that afternoon was doing a piece to camera.

"Celebrated author Dylan St James is still recovering in hospital tonight, after suffering a vicious attack yesterday.

"Mr St James was walking along Eastbourne Terrace in central London, after exiting Paddington Rail Station, when he was hit in the chest by a spear from a spear-fishing gun. Police are looking for anybody who may have seen the attack. However, no witnesses are forthcoming at present.

"Paramedics attended the scene and brought Mr St James here to St Mary's Hospital, where the author underwent surgery to remove the projectile. He remains unconscious, but in a stable condition, and doctors expect him to make a full recovery. However, had the spear been just one inch to the right, it would have entered the victim's heart, and surgeons believe the attack would have been fatal."

"A small number of Mr St James' fans have gathered here this evening, to hold a candlelight vigil and wish the author well."

The camera then cut to a shot of the front of the hospital, where a group of people stood with bunches of flowers and large placards – much to the chagrin of the sickly smokers, who had been forced to move a further ten metres from the main entrance. One effeminate looking man held a sign saying: *Get Well Soon Dylan.* A frumpy woman in a bright anorak held a bunch of flowers and placard stating: *We love you Dylan.* And one grey-haired, old lady with glasses had gone completely over the top with a large banner proclaiming: *Dylan St James – Prince of our Hearts.*

"Currently, the police have no suspects, but are chasing up a number of possible leads."

The camera cut to footage of Detective Inspector Stone leaving the hospital earlier that day. He side-stepped the gathered journalists and cameramen, clearly trying to avoid punching them or pushing them out of the way, as he refused to answer their questions.

The camera cut back to the female journalist, who went on to give a short biography of Dylan, his books and all the awards he's won in recent years. Then she signed off and handed back to the studio.

The camera cut to the main anchor, looking solemn behind his desk. He turned to a large video screen on his right. Up popped a live image of Salman Rushdie, who they'd drafted in to give his opinion on the attacks, in light of his own past death threats.

"Salman Rushdie," I said. "They always get Salman fucking Rushdie on for these things. Honestly, you get one fatwa issued against you, and that makes you an expert on all attacks against authors? If they want real insight, they should have got me on there. I actually know Dylan. And it might even have helped with sales..."

Caroline screwed up her face, blowing air out of her nose.

"I mean... not that I would have agreed," I said, realising how wrong I'd read the room. "Far more important things to do... like find out who's behind all this."

Then I thought about how far I actually was from finding out who was behind it, and I suddenly felt very deflated again.

"You know, you look very tired," said Caroline, slipping off the sofa and kneeling before me. "Maybe if we were to do something a bit more fun, it might relax you. Then you might be able to think more clearly."

"Erm... well... I suppose anything's worth a try."

"Now," she said, slowly unfastening the zip on my trousers, "what can we do that's a bit more fun?"

******

I woke with a start. I'd been dreaming about Dylan. I was walking down the street, following after him as he marched along ahead of me. A blue car pulled out from a side-street, everything moving in slow motion. I called to Dylan to look out, but he didn't hear me. He just carried on walking.

The car continued down the road and I called out again. I tried to run, desperate to get to Dylan before the car did. But I was stuck in place. Unable to move, like my feet were glued to the pavement. All I could do was try to shout, as the car drove past me. I stared at the window, trying to make out the driver, but all I saw was the ghostly shadow of a face.

The car's window wound down. A long silver spear poked out. And then, a loud bang.

And then I woke up – panicked, sweating and breathing heavily. I gazed around the room, still trapped somewhere between sleep and awake, as I reassured myself I was safe and sound in Dylan's guest bedroom.

The clock by the bed shone out a red 4.32. I was just about to roll over and go back to sleep, when I became aware of the emptiness next to me in the bed.

"Caroline?" I said, sitting up and turning on the bedside lamp. Her skirt and bra were still lying in a heap on the floor, so I assumed she hadn't sneaked out early. "Caroline, are you okay?"

No reply. Then, as I cocked my head to one side to listen out into the darkness, I heard a strange noise coming from somewhere in the flat.

"Caroline?" Again, no reply.

I climbed out of bed, and went into the hall, scratching my head. There were no lights on anywhere in the flat. The extractor fan in the bathroom was not kicking out its usual loud, mechanical whirring. "Caroline?"

I walked down the hall, checking the kitchen and the living room, but she was nowhere to be seen. Then I heard the sound again, like a deep, wooden, scraping noise. It was unmistakably coming from inside Dylan's bedroom. I tip-toed back along the hall and very carefully, and very slowly, pushed the door open.

The room was illuminated in a silvery glow, as moonlight shone in through the open curtains. The room was a mess. The wardrobe doors hung wide open and clothes had been pulled out and strewn all over the floor. The duvet had been pulled right back and hung limply from the end of the bed. The drawers of the bedside cabinet were pulled right out.

I was just about to run to the kitchen and call the police, when I saw a figure in the corner of the room, hunched over the chest of drawers.

"Caroline?" I said, flicking the switch and lighting up the room. She just stood there, facing away from me and glaring at the wall in front of her.

I walked across to her. "Caroline?" I said, taking her shoulder and spinning her round until she faced me. No reply. She just looked through me, like I wasn't even there. "Caroline!"

I took her shoulders and shook her gently. Her eyes shifted, slowly coming into focus until she was looking me right in the eye. And then she screamed.

"Shit! Shit, Freddie..." she cried out, her legs buckling beneath her, as she fell back to sit on the edge of the bed. "What the fuck? How did I get in here?"

120

"Don't ask me, I just came in and found you like this."

"Oh, Christ, I must have been sleepwalking again. You know, you shouldn't wake people up when they're sleepwalking, it can be really dangerous."

"Sorry, I had no idea. Is this... something you often do, then?"

"No," she said, red-faced with embarrassment. "It hasn't happened in years. I thought it was all over. Oh, God..." She held her head in her hands.

"Well, it's a new one on me," I said, forcing a laugh to try and make her feel better. She smiled back at me, still embarrassed, but at least it was easing off. "So what's the deal with all the mess? Is this all part of it?"

"I've no idea," she said, looking around the room. "Was this all me?"

"I guess so."

"Oh God. I'm so sorry. I've never done this before."

I'd read about this sort of thing. People that have been found walking round 24-hour supermarkets in their pyjamas, with no idea how they got there. And then there are the lazy bloaters, who can't understand why they're getting fat, and swear they eat a healthy diet. Then they set up webcams in the house, and it turns out they're sleepwalking down to the kitchen in the middle of the night and filling themselves up with cakes and biscuits.

"One time an ex-boyfriend found me out in the garden at 3am," said Caroline, "digging up plants in my dressing gown. That's as weird as I've ever had. Funny thing was, I gave him hell the next morning for walking muddy footprints in through the kitchen. I'd never have believed him if he hadn't thought to record it all on his iPhone."

"What do you think you were doing in here? It looks like you were looking for something. Hey, are those Dylan's pants?"

She looked down at herself in shock. I'd been so surprised to see her in here, it hadn't registered what she was wearing. But all of a sudden I realised she was in one of Dylan's shirts, with the sleeves rolled up. And a pair of his boxer shorts.

"Oh my God," she said, her eyes starting to well with tears. "I had no idea. Oh, you must think I'm totally crazy."

"Don't be daft," I lied. "You just need some rest. Come on, let's get you back to bed. I'm sure Dylan won't mind lending you a pair of pants for one night."

I took her hand and led her back through to the guest bedroom.

When I awoke the next morning, Caroline was already gone. There was a note on the pillow next to me, thanking me for a lovely evening, apologising for her strange behaviour, and promising to make it up to me. The note said she'd call me later, and that she couldn't wait to see me again. It also said that I should call her if I wanted her to go with me when I went to visit Dylan. Then she signed off with the words: *What takeaway shall we have tonight?* I winced when I saw that she'd dotted the 'i' in 'tonight' with a tiny heart.

I checked Dylan's bedroom and she had already been in and tidied everything away. "Christ," I said to myself, rubbing the sleep out of my eyes, "why do I always end up with the crazy ones?"

CHAPTER 14

"WELL, YOU LOOK like shit."

Dylan's tired, pallid face looked up at me from the crisp white of the hospital pillow. His eyelids hung low and he coughed lightly as he fought to keep them open. The busybody nurse, fiddling with Dylan's IV bag on the other side of the bed, raised one eyebrow and gave me a look that could curdle milk.

"Only joking mate," I laughed, "you're the absolute picture of pasty health. But seriously, how are you feeling?"

"I feel like I've got a bloody great big hole in my chest," he muttered, wheezing slightly with the effort.

"Yeah, well... that's probably because you do."

The nurse took hold of Dylan's wrist, gazing down at the little watch attached at her waist. After a few seconds, she placed his hand gently back onto the bed, and said, "Now, don't you let your friend keep you talking for too long. You need your rest."

Dylan turned his head towards her, smiling a sickly grin.

"And you," she said, turning to me, "I've only let you in here as a favour to Dylan. He's not really up to visitors, so don't stay too long. And don't get him too excited."

"Oh right," I replied, pulling my phone from my pocket and holding it up towards my ear. "So, should I ring and cancel the stripper, then?"

She raised her eyebrow even higher, sucking in her cheeks, and blowing air out of her nose. Then she turned around and walked out of the room.

"Same old, Freddie," said Dylan, in a gravelly whisper. "Always determined to get on the wrong side of people, aren't you?"

"Well... what does she think I'm gonna do, lead a bloody marching band through the room?"

He just looked up at me, eyes half-closed, shaking his head. He looked so weak, like a baby bird with a broken wing. I'd never seen him look so frail, and I suddenly felt very worried about him. We hadn't been in contact for many years, but he was still my best friend – probably my only friend, really. And I didn't want him to die.

"So, you're gonna be okay, yeah? The doctors say you're gonna make a full recovery."

"That's what they tell me. You can't count me out just yet."

"So, what the hell happened?"

"It's all a bit fuzzy, to be honest. All I remember was…" He looked up at the ceiling, searching his memory. "I came back from the book thing… I got off the train and… I remember it was a nice day, so I thought I'd walk some of the way back to the flat… I walked round the corner from the station… and then nothing. Then I woke up here with a bloody sore chest. The rest's all a blank."

"You don't remember anything else? You didn't see anyone? You didn't see who shot you?"

"Sorry, Freddie."

"When they brought you into the hospital, you were apparently muttering something about Garfield. Was it the car you've been seeing around? The blue Ford with the Garfield in the window? Did you see it on the street?"

"I don't know. I don't remember coming into the hospital. Or what I was saying. Sorry, I'm not being much help am I? It's the painkillers, I think. They're quite strong, and everything's a bit… funky… fuzzy… well, both really…" He smiled, suddenly amused, like he was slightly drunk.

"No worries," I said. "If anything comes back to you, just let me know. I'd better get off and let you get some rest, otherwise that nurse will have my balls."

"Okay, Freddie," he said, his eyelids hanging even lower, and his voice sounding more drowsy.

"Listen before I go, I need to ask you about your cancer. It's just… I was talking to the doctor here the other night and he said there's nothing about it in your records."

"Really? That's strange."

"Look, I know this sounds weird… but you did really have cancer, didn't you?"

"Of course," he said, his words starting to slur as he fought to stay awake. "The doctor told me. I took… medicine… for months… Made me feel… like shit… but I… got… better."

"I saw the pills in your flat, Dylan. But why would there be no record of it? Why would it be kept out of your file?"

There was no response. Dylan was unconscious again.

******

I left the hospital and headed to the Duke of Argyll pub on Great Windmill Street. I hadn't been there for some years, and I felt like a trip down memory lane. Dylan and I spent a lot of time drinking there in our younger days, and I thought maybe spending some time there might trigger some inspiration in me. Plus, their beer is really cheap.

I took out my notebook and scanned through my list of suspects.

"Thought I'd find you in here. Well… I cheated, really – I've had one of the young DCs keeping tabs on you."

I looked up to see Dick Stone (the real one) standing over me. His grey suit was wrinkled, and his tie hung loose around his neck. He had a dark sheen of stubble on his face and looked like he hadn't slept in two days.

"I thought you weren't speaking to me," I said.

"No, what I said was: I didn't want you wasting my time. Doesn't mean I can't come and waste some of yours."

He sat down opposite me, took a long swig from a pint of lager and placed it down on the table. "Sorry, I didn't get you one," he said, with a slight sneer.

"No problem. So, how's the investigation going?"

He didn't answer. He just stared at me before pulling a notepad from his breast pocket. "Whether I like it or not, it seems you might have information pertinent to a case I'm investigating. So, I need to ask you a few questions."

"No problem," I said, perhaps a little too excitedly. "Happy to help."

"Now, I believe you said you're currently residing with Mr St James."

"That's right," I said, "I told you that the other night. Are you any closer to finding out who did this to him?"

"I'll ask the questions, thank you very much. You just need to worry about the answers."

"Fine. Yes. I'm currently staying with Mr St James."

"You mentioned the other evening that Mr St James thought someone might be trying to kill him. What can you tell me about that?"

"Exactly what I said the other night. Dylan tracked me down a few days ago. He was convinced someone was trying to kill him, and he wanted me to investigate."

"And you believe this threat is real?"

"I didn't at first. I thought he was just being paranoid. But I've uncovered some pretty strange things over the past couple of days."

"Strange things?"

I told Detective Inspector Stone all about my investigation. I told him about the ex-wives, my near-death experience with the blue Ford, and the unfortunate incident of the exploding postman. I told him about my list of suspects, possible motives and how I'd been carefully crossing them off the list.

As I talked, he listened and made notes in his own notebook, in between swigs of his lager. I finished my account and he sat there for a few seconds, looking over what he'd written, stroking his chin.

"How long have you been friends with Mr St James?" he said, after a minute.

"Oh come on, Richard, you know this. I've told you all about Dylan in the past."

He just sat looking at me, his eyebrows raised and his pen pressed against the page of his pad.

"Fine," I said, with a sigh. "I've known Dylan for twenty years or so, since we were at university. We lost touch about seven years ago, and haven't really spoken much since. Then he contacted me again this week."

"And how would you describe your relationship with the victim?"

"Fine. Good. What are you getting at?"

"You don't hold any feelings of animosity towards him at all? Any jealousy over the fact that he's a highly successful, very wealthy author, and you're just... well... not?"

"Of course not," I lied, "Dylan and I are old friends. I want nothing but the best for him."

"Come on Freddie," he said, dropping his policeman's guard for the first time. And, just for the merest second, I thought I saw him smile like he used to when we'd sit chatting over a pint.

"Okay, perhaps I was just a little bit jealous. I mean, the guy's a millionaire bestselling author. And as you so astutely pointed out, I'm not. So yes, I was jealous."

"Hmmm," he said, writing something down in his notepad.

"Hang on a second. You... you don't think I had something to do with this?"

He just looked at me, completely deadpan.

"Wait... no... you can't think I'm involved? I'm investigating it. What possible motive would I have?"

"You said it yourself, Freddie. You're jealous of Mr St James. He's very successful, whilst you spend your time scraping by and leaching off people. I bet you're still pulling that fake book signing scam, aren't you?"

"What? Don't be ridiculous."

"Quite a coincidence, don't you think? You haven't seen Mr St James in several years. You show up, then all of a sudden he ends up in hospital."

"No, Dylan came to me," I said, panicking. "People were already after him. He wanted me to find out who it was."

"Well, I only have your word for that. And there's no record of any previous attacks or murder attempts. How do I know there were any?"

"Dylan told your lot all about the attacks. And you told him to get lost. Said he was just being paranoid. If you'd done your jobs properly in the first place, we wouldn't be in this mess."

"Really?" he said, raising his voice slightly. "And how do I know you didn't just make all this up to cover your back? You could have faked these supposed previous attempts, just to scam some money out of your friend. How much is he paying you, by the way?"

"No," I protested, my heart beating hard. "It's not like that."

"What happened, Freddie? You fired an arrow at him, trying to scare him? But you accidentally hit him. Or was this the big murder attempt? You make Dylan think someone's after him, then you install yourself as chief investigator to deflect suspicion from you. But you missed. You're not as good a shot as you thought you were, and he survived the attack."

"No. I was nowhere near Paddington when it happened. I was with Dylan's ex-wife. You can check."

"Where did you get the explosives for the letter bomb?"

"What... I..."

"How did you make it?"

"I... what? I didn't make any bomb. I wouldn't know where to start..."

"You could have hired someone to do your dirty work for you."

"No," I said, really starting to panic. "No. Besides, if what you said was true, why would I want Dylan dead? Surely it would be better to keep him alive, or I stop earning money?"

"Oh, don't play dumb with me, Freddie. With Dylan out the way, you stand to become a very rich man indeed."

"What?" I said, suddenly more baffled than panicked.

"The will?" he said, raising his eyebrows so high I thought they might detach from his head and float away.

"What? What will? What are you talking about?"

"Mr St James' will. You inherit, what, five million if he dies?"

"What the hell are you talking about?"

"Come off it, Freddie, don't play dumb. We've seen the will. Pretty standard practice when we're investigating an attempted murder – you know, looking for motives. Who has the most to gain from the victim being killed? As it turns out, you're actually pretty high on the list."

I couldn't believe what I was hearing. Dylan had left me five million quid in his will. He'd never mentioned it. I had no idea. I felt sick, ashamed and utterly wretched, at the same time as feeling strangely hopeful and overjoyed. I had to remind myself of the gravity of both Dylan's and my own situation to keep me from wondering what I might spend the money on first.

"I swear to God, I had no idea about this, Richard. You have to believe me. Dylan never told me anything about his will. I'm trying to help Dylan, not kill him."

Richard Stone just sat there looking at me for a good long minute. I was sure my face was bright red with fear. I could feel sweat beading on my forehead and running down my cheeks in thin rivulets. I probably looked about as guilty as any man ever has.

I was waiting for him to pull a pair of handcuffs from his pocket and march me down to the cop-shop for interrogation. But he didn't. He just folded his notebook closed, placed it back into his pocket and drained the last of his drink.

"No, Freddie," he said, "I don't think you are trying to kill Dylan. You're many things – a liar, a cheat, a charlatan, a leach, a crappy friend – but you're not a killer."

"Oh, thank God," I said, exhaling heavily and letting my shoulders drop.

"But five million quid is a pretty good motive. And you're not totally off the suspect list yet. If we don't find the real attacker, you can bet your arse someone higher up than me will be looking back in your direction. And if you don't have a watertight alibi… well, I've seen plenty of people go to prison on less."

"But I didn't do anything."

"Oh, I know that. In fact, you're pretty lucky I'm investigating this one. Some other DI might just have seen that will and pinned it on you for a quick win and an easy life. I bet if someone were to do a bit of digging, they'd find enough compelling evidence to build a pretty decent case. I wonder, what would your Detective Dick Stone do? He's a pretty fucking unscrupulous character, isn't he? Would he follow the evidence and try to find the real killer? Or would he just lock you up and throw away the key?"

I looked at him, blowing air out of my cheeks. "So, that's what this is about. You're still upset about the books? I told you I'm sorry. I don't know how many more times I can say it. I'm sorry. I'm sorry."

"You know, policemen are a funny bunch. Right little gang of stand-up comedians at times. I came in to work this morning, and do you know what I found on my desk?"

He reached into the pocket of his beige raincoat, pulled out a paperback copy of *Stone Cold Murder* – my first ever Dick Stone novel – and threw it down onto the table.

"Blimey," I said, picking it up and inspecting it, "they've done well to find a copy of this one. It's been out of print for years now."

He just stared at me, face like thunder.

"Sorry," I said. "I know I've caused you problems in the past. It was never intentional. And if I can ever find a way to make it up to you, I promise I will. But for now I'm just concerned about my friend. Someone is clearly trying to kill him and I think they're going to try again. We need to work together to find out who it is, so we can stop them before... well, you know."

"Work together?" he scoffed. "Freddie, I don't want you anywhere near this investigation."

"But I can help. I've told you what I know. If you tell me what you've found out, we can help each other. What leads have you got? What suspects are you looking into? Did forensics find anything from the bomb? There must be something I'm overlooking."

"Like I told you the other day, you're not wanted. Not welcome. And we certainly don't need your help. I needed to ask you some questions, and for the time being I'm convinced you're not involved. And that's the end of it."

"But I can help. I know Dylan. I know the business. I'm making headway."

"Headway? You're a second-rate crime writer with delusions of grandeur. You have no idea what you're doing. And if I find out you've been anywhere near my investigation again, I'll arrest you for wasting police time."

"But..."

"No, Freddie," he said, standing. "Time for you to fuck off now. Don't get in my way, or I promise you'll wish you hadn't."

He reached forwards, picked up my pint and drained the rest of glass. Then he winked at me, turned around and walked out of the pub.

I sat back in my chair and closed my eyes, hoping that when I opened them again I might find myself in a far nicer place, with all my problems and worries floated away into the ether. But they hadn't. I was still in the same pub, and not only were my problems still there, somehow they seemed even worse.

Not only was my friend in hospital, I was now a suspect for putting him there. And when it came to motives, I apparently had a pretty bloody good one.

I turned to my notepad. At the bottom of my list of suspects, I wrote my own name. I was pretty sure I didn't have anything to do with the attempts on Dylan's life. But then, as any good crime writer will tell you, you can never completely rule out any potential suspects.

I pulled out my phone and dialled the number I'd saved in it that morning.

"Hello," said the voice on the other end. She sounded nice and pretty. "Dr Miles Shepton's surgery. How can I help you?"

"Ah, yes, hello," I said, affecting a slightly pained, apologetic tone, "I know it's a long shot, but I was hoping you might be able to get me an appointment with the doctor today?"

"Mmmm…" she said, "that is a bit short notice."

"Yes, sorry, it's just that I'm in rather a lot of pain at the moment. I had a bit of a tumble earlier, and I think I need someone to have a look at my ankle."

"We do usually ask our patients to book at least a week in advance," she said, coming over all Nurse Ratchett. Maybe she wasn't as nice and pretty as I thought.

"Well, that's the thing, you see. I'm not actually a patient at your surgery. I'm just visiting London at the moment, staying with my good friend, Dylan St James. He's a patient of yours, perhaps you know him."

"Oh, Mr St James? The author?"

"The author, that's right. Very good friend of mine. It was actually him who suggested I try calling. He thought you might be able to fit me in. I'm sure it's nothing serious, I'd just be happier if I could get someone to take a look."

"Oh well," she said, her voice brightening, "if it's for Mr St James… let me see what I can do."

Honestly, how does one man have this effect on women?

I heard the click-clack of her computer keyboard, then she came back on the line. "It looks like we do have one spare slot that I can give you. Could you be here in an hour?"

"No problem. See you then."

CHAPTER 15

"SO, WHERE EXACTLY does it hurt?"

I was sitting on the cold, grey medical bed in Dr Shepton's office, trying to remember which leg I'd pretended to hobble into the room on.

"It's this one," I said, indicating my right leg. "The ankle is absolutely killing me. I'm sure it's not broken or anything. Probably just twisted it or something."

Dr Shepton pulled up a chair to sit in front of me. He carefully rolled up my trouser leg. He umm-ed and aah-ed, looking at my ankle, squeezing gently it between finger and thumb. "Any pain there?" he asked.

"Ooh... ow... yes..." I said, suddenly remembering the symptoms I was supposed to be faking.

"Hmmm... well, there doesn't appear to be any swelling. Can you try moving it for me?"

"Like this?" I said, slowly rotating my ankle and pursing my lips into a pained expression. "You know, you have a very familiar face. Have we met before somewhere?"

"No, I don't believe so. Can you try rocking your foot back and forwards?"

"Are you sure? I'm sure I recognise your face... have you ever been on..." And then it hit me. "My God, of course. Dr Shepton. You're Dr Miles Shepton. You used to be on that morning telly show."

He looked up at me with an expression more pained than my own pretend one, as if he'd heard this same sentence a million times before. Then he just looked back down at my foot.

"It is you, isn't it?" I said excitedly. "Isn't it?"

Without looking up he just said, "Yes. Yes, I used to be on television."

"Wow," I said, actually feeling a little bit star struck. "I thought it was you. Wow, a bona fide celebrity doctor, looking at my ankle."

His prodding suddenly intensified, and he squeezed my foot just a little harder.

"So, what happened?" I said, pretending not to know all the gory details. "Why aren't you on the box anymore?"

"I'm just not, okay," he said, through gritted teeth.

About three or four years previously, Dr Miles Shepton had been one of the darlings of breakfast television. He was a real doctor, of course, with a side line in guest appearances on ITV's *Get Up and at 'Em!* – a poorly devised early morning news and entertainment show. It was one of a myriad of failed formats in which the channel tried to imitate the American early morning shows, with fast-talking, chirpy presenters, brightly coloured sets and the kind of in-depth news coverage that would leave a toddler demanding more insight.

Despite a raft of format changes, set redesigns and a revolving-door turnover of presenters, the show never managed to attract enough viewers, and it only lasted on air for three years. However, the one and only jewel in its crown was Dr Miles Shepton.

He started out small, with the odd appearance here and there. His job was to talk about the latest disease people were currently worried about; the newest medical breakthroughs; or whichever food the government had that week claimed could either cause cancer, cure cancer, or used to cure cancer, then started causing it, but it was now a cure again. And people loved him. With his tanned complexion, big, shiny smile and calm, reassuring doctor's voice, he was an absolute natural for television. He was good looking, with a very easy way about him. Before long, the papers had labelled him everything from TV's Dishiest Doctor to Housewives' Favourite and the Thinking Woman's Crumpet. The Sun's Bizarre section even started calling him a DILF (doctor I'd like to... well, you get the idea).

The producers of the show were quick to realise to the doctor's comfort in front the camera. And with his growing fan base, they gave him his own weekly slot – *The Doctor Will See You Now*. It was a fifteen-minute segment every Friday, in which Dr Shepton would look at the week's medical issues and take calls from viewers. The segment proved popular and was quickly bumped up to twice weekly. Then, really finding his presenting feet, Doctor Shepton even started filling in to sit on the main sofa and co-present the whole show when the lead anchor, Martin Murray, went on holiday.

Dr Shepton's fame grew, along with his TV appearances, and soon he was doing just one day a week at his fancy Harley Street practice, so he could concentrate on his TV work – much to the chagrin of his rich, private patients, who were forced to see the practice's junior partners, rather than the main man himself.

And it wasn't just TV appearances for the good doctor. He published a number of highly successful books, including his guide to being healthy, a guide to weight loss, and a guide to dealing with stress. In just two years, since his first appearance on *Get Up and at 'Em!* Dr Shepton grew to become one of the country's best-loved TV stars. But it wouldn't last for long. Because the good doctor wasn't quite as good as people thought.

The tabloid newspapers were absolutely delighted to discover that Dr Shepton was not very good at following his own advice for leading a healthy life. Instead, he preferred to spend his time taking copious amounts of Class-A drugs in the company of various high-class prostitutes. The poor GP was subjected to nearly a full week of front-page headlines, including: *Dirty Doc's Call Girl Shock*; *Class-A Physician*; *Creepy GP's Cocaine Sex Shame*; *Sex, Drugs and Waiting Lists*; and in a dreadful pun based on his morning TV segment, *The Doctor Will Screw You Now.*

Although all of the papers ran similarly shocked and appalled pieces, it was The Sun that first broke the story. On day one, they published exclusive pictures of the doctor arriving at, and subsequently leaving, a London brothel. Turn to page five, and you could see a selection of grainy, mobile-phone pictures of the good doctor half-naked, taking drugs and getting up to no good.

On day two, the paper delighted in providing a diary of just what the doctor got up to in one week – six visits with three different prostitutes; an account of the different services he had apparently requested; and a veritable shopping list of illegal substances he was purported to have consumed – including ketamine, cocaine, MDMA and cannabis. And then, to really hammer home the depravity, they provided a running total of all the costs – actually designed in the paper to look like a supermarket shopping list.

By day three, they had an exclusive account from one of the many 'ladies' Shepton had engaged for her services. She was apparently his favourite, and the one with whom he'd spent the most time and money. So, of course she repaid his customer loyalty by snapping pictures of him on her mobile, then flogging them to the paper for the best price she could get. It was a fairly sordid account, in which the young lady did herself no favours by rubbishing the doctor and going into graphic detail about their time together. Most of it was probably fiction, but the tabloid readers absolutely lapped it up. The Great British public love nothing more than an underdog – except when there's a juicy disgraced public figure to lambast.

It took the paper until day four before they started in on Shepton's poor wife – the betrayed mother to his kids – having presumably been camped out on the doorstep of the family home for days, waiting to get any kind of quote or sound bite.

Dr Shepton finally broke his silence on day five, via a statement issued through his lawyer. It told how sorry he was and how he'd let himself, his family, his fans and his patients down. There was then a formulaic promise that he would be seeking professional help for his problems.

By day six the papers had tired of Dr Shepton and moved onto another subject. But the doctor's problems had only just begun. He was suspended, then released from his contract on *Get Up and at 'Em!* A new solo show, which was in pre-production with the BBC, was instantly shelved, never to see the light of day.

A few days later his publisher issued a statement saying that they had parted ways with the writer, and would no longer be releasing his forthcoming (and also fully written and edited) new book.

Of course, it wasn't just his second career that suffered. Shepton was lucky not to be struck off. The General Medical Council ruled that, although his conduct was questionable, to say the least, there was no proof that he had endangered or posed any risk to his patients. As such, he was allowed to continue practicing medicine – but just barely.

That didn't mean his patients wanted to be seen by him, however. And his colleagues wanted even less to do with him. Within just a few months, all the other partners and physicians at the Miles Shepton Medical Practice on Harley Street had gone their separate ways – taking the majority of the patients with them. Only a handful of people were either loyal, stupid or lazy enough to stay with him.

So, Dr Miles Shepton, whose star had been so close to reaching its peak, came crashing back down to earth with a bump. I hadn't heard a great deal about him since. Much like the rest of the world, I suppose. I do remember feeling annoyed and jealous when, at the height of his fame, all three of his books had held spots in the Amazon bestsellers list at the same time. And then feeling equally repulsed, but amused at the irony, when the kiss-and-tell book by the doctor's former paid-for-lover (laughably published by the same firm that had so unceremoniously dropped him) went straight into the chart at number three.

Since then, I assumed the good doctor had been keeping his head down and trying to settle back into the less-than-shiny world of general medical practice.

"Are you a drug seeker, Mr Philpott?" he asked me, dropping my ankle and sitting back in his chair. Obviously, I hadn't given the receptionist my real name.

"Drug seeker? What's that? Sounds like a folk band from the sixties."

"Are you addicted to narcotics?"

"No, just the love of Jesus Christ," I smiled.

He raised an eyebrow and glowered at me. "You've come here claiming to be suffering from an injured ankle, yet there's clearly nothing wrong you. No swelling, no restricted movement, and you've barely shown any sign of pain. I can only assume you've come here to try and trick me into prescribing you strong painkillers."

"Why, have you got some?" I laughed.

"This is a very serious matter, Mr Philpott," he snapped. "I can tell you now that I will not be prescribing you any medication whatsoever. I suggest you leave now, before I call the police."

"Okay," I said, "you caught me. I haven't really hurt my ankle. But I haven't come here trying to con painkillers out of you. I just wanted to talk to you."

"Talk to me? Oh, Jesus, you're not another bloody journalist, are you? Have you got nothing better to write about? It was four bloody years ago."

"No, no," I assured him. "I'm not a journalist. I actually wanted to talk to you about one of your patients. Dylan St James."

"Patient? Nice try. I take it you're from the GMC, then? Come to try and trick me into disclosing private patient information, have you?" His eyes narrowed then, an angry tone to his voice. "You lot have been desperate to get me struck off for years. Did you really think I'd fall for this?"

"I'm not..."

"What is it with you people, eh?" he said, cutting me off. "Haven't I paid enough already? Okay, I made a mistake. A fucking mistake. People do make mistakes, you know."

"Sorry, you don't under..."

"Is it not enough that I lost my book deals? My TV work? My livelihood?"

"Wait, no…"

"Is it not enough that my bitch wife left me and took my bloody kids – who I only get to see every other weekend… and all they ever want to do is sit there playing video games and wasting their life on Facebook? Is it not enough that I don't get to live in my own house, since that fucking harridan took it off me in the divorce? And all I can afford is a shitty little two-bed flat in Tufnell Park?"

"Not enough that half my patients deserted me, and practically every penny I do earn goes on bloody maintenance payments to a miserable old shrew who everybody knows is shagging the gardener…"

I sat silent as he yelled, his face turning red, and a large purple vein throbbing in the side of his neck.

"And now you want to strike me off and take the only thing I've got left…"

"I'm not from the GMC," I said, stopping him before his head exploded.

"What?"

"I'm not from the GMC. I promise. I just want to talk to you about my friend, Dylan. He's a patient of yours. And I'm worried about him."

"What… er… well, whoever you are, I'm certainly not going to discuss any confidential information about my patients with you."

"I'm not looking for confidential information. I'm just concerned. Dylan thinks someone's trying to kill him."

Dr Shepton's face instantly changed. The red drained away, leaving him looking quite pale.

"He's asked me to try and find out who wants him dead. And now he's lying in hospital and I…"

"Hospital? Why is he in hospital?" A look of grave concern flashed in his eyes.

"You mean you haven't heard? Dylan was shot yesterday."

"Shot?"

"Yes, someone shot him with a harpoon."

"A harpoon? Who the hell shoots…?"

"Yes, I know," I cut him off. "Believe me, I know."

"Well, what does any of this have to do with me? I didn't even know he was hurt. I haven't seen him in…" He turned to face the computer on his desk, tapped away on the keyboard and brought up a new screen. "There... three months. His last appointment was three months ago."

"Yes, well, that's what I wanted to talk to you about. What exactly were you treating Dylan for?"

"I told you," he said, clicking a few more keys and turning the monitor to a screen saver, "I'm not going to discuss that with you."

"Because Dylan told me he had cancer," I persevered. "I've seen the medications in his flat. I assume you prescribed them..."

"Please, Mr... whoever you are, you're wasting your time," he said, smiling a smug, satisfied grin.

"Only, the doctor I spoke to at the hospital told me he doesn't think Dylan ever had cancer. He says there's nothing in his medical records."

The grin fell instantly from Dr Shepton's face. Replaced with a strange look, somewhere between shock and confusion.

"And that's pretty confusing, wouldn't you say? I mean, as I understand it, Dylan has had cancer twice. He's been treated for it twice. Yet, there's nothing in his medical records about it at all. Don't you find that strange?"

"Well, er... the doctor at the hospital must be wrong. He must have been looking at the wrong file, or..."

"No, he was absolutely adamant."

"Well, there must be a clerical error... or a nurse has lost something..."

A long, cold silence hung between us as Dr Shepton squirmed slightly in his chair. Then, as if suddenly remembering something, he smiled his sickly TV doctor grin at me and said, "Anyway, as I've already told you, I'm really not at liberty to discuss my patients. Now, I'm very busy, with lots of other people to see. So, if you wouldn't mind..." He gestured towards the door.

"Really," I said, determined not to give up, "that's all you've got to say on the subject? Clerical error? Come on, what's really going on here? Did Dylan ever actually have cancer?"

He just sat there, silent, and smiling that smug grin at me. Then he very calmly reached over to the phone beside his computer and pressed a red intercom button. I heard the young lady from reception answer it.

"Laura," said Dr Shepton, "could you be a dear and get the police on the line for me?"

"Police?" she said, sounding alarmed.

"Don't bother," I shouted so she could hear, "I'm leaving."

I stood for a second, glaring at Dr Shepton, before storming out of his office and slamming the door shut behind me. I wish I could have stood outside for a second, waiting to hear if the good doctor made any quick, panicked calls. But Laura, the receptionist, was staring at me from behind her desk, phone in hand and preparing to dial those three digits. So, I stormed out of the waiting room, and slammed another door behind me.

Out on the street, I took my phone from my pocket and opened up an internet search window. I typed in 'Dr Miles Shepton', marching quickly away from the surgery in case the police really were on their way. I scrolled through the list of results as I walked.

I found several links to news stories from a few years back, covering the doctor's indiscretions and his rapid descent from fame. There was a link to his author's page on Amazon, and below that a link to his surgery's business website. Then, right down at the bottom of the list, was a link to Dr Shepton's personal website.

I clicked through. The site was a few years out of date, featuring a large picture of the doctor grinning like an idiot, sitting on the *Get Up and at 'Em!* Sofa, with the words: *The Doctor will see you... every Monday and Friday, 8.45am on ITV*. It was a professional looking website, with tabs across the top for sections including *About, History, Books, Blog* and *Contact*. I clicked on the *About* section to see a dull potted history of the man's education, qualifications and history to date. Nothing very interesting, and it wasn't giving me the link I was looking for.

I clicked on *Blog* to find a series of short blog posts – mostly self-congratulatory guff, talking about his books, his good work in the community and various cases (mentioning no actual names of course) where he'd made a huge impact on people's lives through his medical prowess. What a bloody saint!

I clicked on *Contact* and found exactly what I was looking for. A short paragraph that read:

For fan mail or general enquiries, please write to me care of Get Up and at 'Em!

For enquiries regarding books, author events or television appearances, please contact my agent, Mortimer Bunkle, at the Mortimer Bunkle Literary and Talent Agency.

Doctor Shepton's agent was Mortimer Bunkle. Well, of course he bloody well was. Or, at least, he had been.

I closed down the browser page on my phone and looked up to see a large brute of a man stood in front of me. I stopped just in time to avoid walking directly into him.

The man was a monster – at least six feet five, with short cropped hair, a nose that looked as if it had been broken several times, and an angry scowl on his face. His large body was crammed into a suit that only just held his frame – like the Incredible Hulk, mid-transformation, just before the seams on his clothes start to rip apart.

"Excuse me," I said, agitated, "you're kind of blocking the way."

The man said nothing. He just scowled for a moment longer, before raising his right arm and punching me square in the face.

CHAPTER 16

PAIN SURGED THROUGH my face like an electric shock. It seared through my cheek and ran along my jawline. My nose felt like a bursting balloon, a thick splatter of bright, red blood exploding out of me. My eye stung with the impact, and my brain rattled around inside my head. The giant man's hand was so big that he managed to punch the whole side of my face with just one blow.

Then I felt myself falling. My legs buckled underneath me and I collapsed. Not the slow-motion timber of a tree, gracefully collapsing sideways. I went straight down, like an imploding building, crumbled down into the spot where I had previously stood. The effect was that I didn't fall and hit the back of my head on the pavement. Rather, I sort of twisted on the way down, and the pavement delivered its blow to the other half of my already throbbing face.

I rolled onto my back, looking up at my attacker through the tears welling in my eyes. Still he said nothing. He just reached down, grabbed a thick handful of my collar and pulled me up onto my feet. Then I felt the sensation of being dragged, my useless legs completely limp and my feet scraping along the floor.

I tried to call out, to plead for help from anyone in the street, but my mouth had stopped working. I couldn't open it, I couldn't scream. I was like a rag-doll, completely immobile.

I heard the sound of keys in a lock. The hydraulic whisper of a car boot opening. Then I was lifted up and tossed in, squeezed unceremoniously into the tight, uncomfortable space. The boot was slammed shut again, trapping me inside the darkness.

I wriggled as best I could, trying to straighten my legs as the driver's door opened. The whole car rocked as the brute climbed in and then slammed the door shut. My hands went to the swollen, bloody pulp that used to be my face, trying to check which of my features were most damaged, but I winced in pain every time my fingers made contact with the hot, battered skin. So, I gave up and just lay there, trying to catch my breath. Trying to figure out what the hell had just happened.

I've been abducted, I thought, as I heard the car's engine roar into life. The whole thing shuddered slightly, before lurching into action and tearing off down the road.

I wriggled around like a contortionist, manoeuvring my hand down to my trouser pocket. If I could just get to my mobile phone, I could make a call for help. Or I could open up the Google maps app and use GPS to track where I was being taken. I struggled and wiggled, finally getting my fingers to my phone. I jostled and shimmied, carefully retrieving it from my pocket and working it up my body to where I could see it. I pressed the button to unlock the screen and... fucking typical! The damned thing's battery had died.

The car continued to drive. The engine roaring loudly as I was jostled, battered and thrown about with every acceleration, brake and corner. I have no idea how long I was in there, or how far we travelled. I remember lots of stopping and starting, like the car was being held up by traffic lights, so I guessed we were still travelling along the busy roads of the city. Then the stops became less frequent, and we were soon driving more freely.

The entire time I was trapped in the boot, my face throbbed and ached. My head pounded and I felt dizzy. I could feel myself drifting nearer to unconsciousness, as if my brain wanted to power down – to reboot my system and wake me up a little more refreshed and renewed.

I fought the urge to sleep. I wanted to stay awake and aware. I tried to pay attention to as much of the journey as I could – trying to remember each turn, creating my own rough timeline – in case I needed to recall any important details later on. And I wanted to be as ready and prepared as I could be for when we finally came to a stop. But I quickly lost count, my concentration inadvertently shifting to focus on keeping me from throwing up.

After a while, I actually did pass out. Because I awoke feeling suddenly much colder. And I had the sense that at least an hour had passed by.

Eventually, the car began to slow. The ride became bumpier and I could hear a crunching sound, like the tyres were moving over gravel or rough ground. Finally, the car stopped. The driver's door opened and the whole vehicle shifted and bounced as the big lug heaved himself out. I heard muffled talking somewhere off in the distance. Then footsteps approaching the rear of the car.

Panicking, I searched all around me, patting the rough carpeted floor of the car boot. Feeling for something, anything that I might be able to use as a weapon. But there was nothing there. The footsteps ceased. The sound of the key in the lock again. And then the boot opened.

Bright light stung my eyes. I tried to clamp them shut, but my swollen face made that too painful. So I opened them, groaning as the world slowly came into focus. Stood above me was the same giant that had thrown me in there. The same mean, angry expression on his face. He reached in, grabbed me and dragged me out of the boot, throwing me down to a heap on the muddy ground.

I looked up, trying to take in as much of my surroundings as possible. I was right; we were no longer in central London. There was mud and trees. I could hear rustling leaves and birdsong. I could smell the thick, earthy scent of nature. We were in the countryside somewhere, parked up in a small muddy car park.

And that's when I really started panicking. My heart beat fast and heavy. Because why else would you attack someone in the street, bundle them into the boot of your car and drive them out into the middle of nowhere, unless you were planning to kill them?

I still had no idea why I was here. Or who had taken me. My mind raced with the possibilities. There were a good few people I'd rubbed up the wrong way in the past. Other authors I'd slagged off – both in person and online. Disgruntled readers who'd said mean things about me on websites. Jealous husbands whose wives I'd entertained behind their backs. Esteemed police detectives whose lives I'd accidentally ruined... in short, plenty of people who had good reason to walk up to me in the street and punch me in the face. But kill me? That seemed a bit harsh.

Oh my God, I suddenly thought. James Patterson. It's James fucking Patterson. He's heard what I've been saying about him. And now he wants me dead.

I heard a noise behind me. The squelching sound of tyres on wet mud as a car pulled into the car park. A large, black Rolls Royce circled round and parked in front me.

Two men in dark suits climbed out of the front. Both were equally as big and mean looking as the thug that attacked me in the street. One of them moved to the rear of the car. He opened the door and out stepped a smaller man, immaculately dressed in an expensive grey suit with a white shirt and pink tie. He was about fifty-five or sixty, with salt and pepper hair combed into a neat side parting. Diamond-studded cufflinks twinkled at the ends of his sleeves.

He walked over and stood in front of me. The other men flanked him either side.

"Mr Winters," he said. It was a deep, rasping cockney tone, like the owner had spent a good forty years as a heavy smoker.

I clambered up onto my feet, standing with all the grace of a newly born horse. I felt weak and woozy, the blood rushing suddenly to my head, my legs swaying in the breeze. I could barely breathe. My nose was blocked with thick dried blood, and my battered jaw was stiff and swollen. I thought I might be sick at any moment.

"Sorry to drag you out 'ere in such an unceremonious fashion," the man continued, "but I needed a quick word. And I really 'ate travellin' into London at rush hour, if I don't 'ave to."

I went to speak, but my jaw clicked loudly as I opened my mouth, sending another electric shock of pain surging through my whole face. The best I could manage was a pained whimper.

"Sorry about that," the man continued, "Tony does pack one 'elluva wallop, don't he? Anyway, where's my manners? I know who you are, but you're probably wonderin' who I am."

I shrugged my shoulders, nodding my head slightly.

"Well, then, allow me to introduce myself. My name is Frank McLeod."

"Oh fuck…" I mumbled.

Frank McLeod burst out with a loud, raspy chuckle. "Oh fuck is right, my friend!"

CHAPTER 17

IT'S AN INTERESTING feeling, knowing you're about to die. It's not at all like you see in the films. I'd always assumed you'd get one of two reactions – either the sudden panic that makes you go running off wildly into the woods, shrieking and crying, desperate to get away. Or, you'd get that calm, nonchalant acceptance that says, 'Hey, my time has come, there's no point trying to put it off any longer, let's just get it over with.'

But it's not like that at all. If anything, it's more of a dull stupefaction. Like you're standing there, trying to understand the punchline to a really clever joke someone's just told, while everyone else around you is laughing. At least, that's how it felt to me. Because at that point, I had no doubt in my mind that I was moments away from being murdered.

Frank 'The Animal' McLeod was by far the scariest person I knew. I mean, I didn't know him – I'd never actually met him. But I knew *of* him. Everyone did. He was one of London's most notorious gangland villains.

McLeod apparently started his criminal career back in the 1970s, as something of an enforcer for a number of London's big organised crime gangs. Whenever someone needed to be silenced, persuaded, taught a lesson or made to conveniently disappear, Frank McLeod was the man they called.

Legend has it that he gained his nickname, 'The Animal', because of his animalistic rages and affection for violence. He apparently never used weapons in any of his interrogations or torture sessions – preferring instead to inflict pain by biting off body parts and tearing away chunks of his victims' flesh with his own teeth. So, all in all, an absolutely lovely guy.

Somewhat unusually, Frank was a freelance gangster, not affiliated to any one particular family. Instead, he was happy to work for whoever paid the highest price. And the various families were happy with this too.

Well, not happy. It wasn't the usual way of doing things. Generally, an enforcer like Frank would need to swear an allegiance to one – and only one – gang. Then he'd be their man, who worked to silence, persuade, teach a lesson to, or conveniently disappear witnesses to crimes, business owners who wouldn't pay up, or anyone else who the family wanted dealt with. And, of course, members of opposing gangs. It was very much an exclusive contract sort of deal.

But Frank preferred to keep his options open, providing services for whichever family paid the most at the time.

To start with, all the various gangs railed against this approach. They all, individually, tried to have Frank killed. But the man just wouldn't die. He'd been shot, stabbed, strangled, run over by cars and even thrown off a building.

Each time he survived, he enacted revenge on the attempted murderer. And to really make a point, he also sent an invoice to the gang responsible for the attempted hit. If they didn't pay, he'd kill more and more of their members until they finally did. And each new death was, of course, followed by a new invoice for services rendered.

In the end, realising they couldn't get rid of him – and couldn't afford to keep paying out for the murders of their own men – they all paid him off. Then they left him to work as, and how, he preferred.

By the 1980s, McLeod was one of the most feared men in London. He set up his own small gang, with interests in everything from drugs to extortion, kidnap, blackmail, prostitution, and just about anything else illegal. Of course, the police knew all about him, and rumours were rife about the various crimes he continued to commit. But he always managed to stay one step ahead of being caught.

In the mid-90s McLeod also became something of a dubious celebrity. There was a strange craze at that time for real-life crime books. Biographies from all sorts flooded the market. Everyone from notorious drug dealers to football hooligans, gangland assassins, crime bosses, murderers and even reformed pimps seemed to have a book out. It's a wonder the crime rates up and down the country didn't suddenly drop to zero – how did the criminals have time to do their day jobs when they were so busy writing?

Unbelievably, people couldn't get enough of them. Whole sections of bookshops were suddenly devoted to them. Some even made it onto the bestsellers lists. And Frank McLeod, keen to claim his own share of the limelight, put pen to paper and wrote his own sordid, seedy memoir.

Many of the crimes featured in the book were from McLeod's

formative years. He gave long detailed accounts of the few for which he'd actually been prosecuted and imprisoned. There were also stories about his time behind bars, or as he called it, his 'education'.

McLeod went into detail about various other unsolved crimes – talking very circumspectly, of course. The book gave enough detail, and added more than a hint at The Animal's involvement, to make readers suspect that he was responsible. But they cleverly just held back, never giving away enough for the police to actually build a case against him.

This was all much to the annoyance of Richard Stone, of course. I could remember various angry, drunken discussions on the subject. I would be annoyed about the number of sales McLeod's book was racking up, whilst all of mine sat dwindling in the bargain buckets. And Richard was absolutely furious that McLeod was bragging over committing murders, assaults and robberies, whilst he could do nothing to prove it. McLeod was number one on the list of people Richard hated. Until we had our little falling out, of course – at which point, I suspect he was relegated to second place after me.

I'd never actually read McLeod's book. But I remember seeing parts of it serialised in one of the tabloids. And I'd heard enough from Richard to know that standing in front of him, in a deserted countryside carpark, with no witnesses anywhere nearby, meant I was probably about to be murdered myself.

"I'm guessin' you do know who I am, after all, then?" said Frank McLeod.

I just stood there, my face screwed up with a ridiculous, dumbfounded expression.

"And you're probably wonderin' why I've dragged you all the way out 'ere?"

"Erm… well… er…" I managed to cough.

"It seems you're a little bit of a nosey parker, Mr Winters. Going around, poking your nose into places it doesn't really belong."

Still I couldn't speak.

"Now, I assume you know enough about me to know that I don't really like people interferin' in fings that don't really concern 'em. Especially when it interferes wiv my business interests. It makes me… angry."

He looked totally calm and serene as he said it. But there was also a glint in his eyes that suggested it wouldn't take much to change that. And I really didn't want to see what he looked like if he actually did get angry.

"And when I get angry," he continued, "people tend to get 'urt. Have you ever 'ad a broken leg, Mr Winters?"

"What... erm... no," I stammered.

"You're lucky. I broke a leg once – some fucker frew me off a buildin'. He's fuckin' dead now, of course, but let me tell you, it's one of the most painful fings that can 'appen to ya. Worse than gettin' shot, I reckon. And did you know, if a baseball bat hits at just the right angle, it can snap the shin right in two. Yer bones come stickin' right out, don't they Terry?"

He turned his head back to the goon stood behind him on the left. The goon, whose name I presumed to be Terry, pulled a large brown baseball bat out from where he'd been holding it behind his back. "That's right boss," he said. "D'ya want me to show ya?"

"What do you fink, Mr Winters," said McLeod, "would you be interested in a demonstration?"

"No, Christ, no," I shrieked. "Please... please don't kill me."

I dropped back to my knees, the fabric of Dylan's suit trousers squelching noisily in the mud. I looked up at the three men in front of me, clasped my hands together in prayer and pleaded desperately with my eyes.

I'm not ashamed to admit it – well maybe a little, I guess – but I can actually be something of a coward at times. I'm really not one for physical confrontations. In fact, one of my main aims in life is try and avoid death, injury and physical harm at any possible cost. In the past this has seen me:

- Hide in the toilets of a pub when my friends got into a bar brawl (instigated by derogatory comments I'd made about one of the other party's fat wives).

- Hide behind an ex-girlfriend as a particularly vicious cat ran at us and clawed at her bare legs.

- Pretend to be my own agent at a book signing and point out a poor, unknowing stranger to a very disgruntled looking old battleaxe who asked where she could find "that bastard Frederick Winters". Apparently, in a moment of less-restrained annoyance at having to do a signing at an old people's home the previous week (something organised by my useless agent), I'd signed a book for her husband, saying: *I hope you have a chance to read it before you die.* A week later, she tracked me down and beat me (or, at least, the innocent party that I'd claimed was me) relentlessly with her handbag.

Now, I know I should probably be more ashamed of these things. And had I had any choice at the time, I probably would be. But they were spontaneous reactions – practically out of my own control. At the moment of every one of these events, I was presented with a split-second choice. And my sub-conscious took control, moving my body to spirit me out of the danger zone – regardless of the consequences for others.

When it comes to the fight or flight response, I guess it's the flight part that has always been strongest in me. And it's worked pretty well, keeping me mostly out of harm my entire life. But it does mean that I'm not brave. And not averse to the odd spot of grovelling. The shame always kicks in later, when I have enough booze to dull the pain of it all.

McLeod smiled, then looked back to his two associates. They joined in the joke, each breaking into a soft, raspy chuckle.

"No, I thought not. Do you know what you are, Mr Winters? You're a sad, scrawny, paffetic little man. You're not even worth the effort it takes to dig the fuckin' 'ole. So, I'm not gonna kill ya. I'm not even really gonna 'urt ya. Sumfin' tells me you already get the message. Am I right?"

"Yes," I said, sniffling with relief. "Yes. Definitely."

"Good, 'cos I'd 'ate to 'afta go through all this again. I mean, it's such a pain, innit lads?" The assembled thugs all grunted and humphed in agreement. "Not the killin', so much. I quite enjoy that, truth be told. It's all the other bollocks that goes with it. Disappearing bodies, digging 'oles..."

"Yes, I can imagine," I said.

"So, take this as a warning, Mr Winters. Stay out of other people's business. Stop all your runnin' round, asking people questions. And keep out of matters what don't concern ya. Otherwise, we'll just 'ave to 'ave another little meeting like this. And I'll show you exactly how many bones you can break with a baseball bat. But I won't kill ya. I'll just 'urt ya. Really bad. It'll be the getting buried alive that kills ya, I should fink."

With that, McLeod turned and walked back to his car. He opened the door and prepared to climb in, then stopped and looked back at me.

"Do me a favour, eh lads?" he said. "Make sure Mr Winters fully understands the severity of his situation."

"But you said you weren't going to hurt me…" I implored.

"I'm not," said McLeod. "They are." Then he climbed into the back seat of the car and closed the door.

I was at once aware of the original face-puncher approaching from behind. So, I immediately collapsed to the floor, curling up hedgehog-like into as tight a ball as I could, and gripped my head in my hands to protect my face.

I felt a large foot collide hard into my left buttock. Pain screamed through it, surging down my leg and up my spine, as I was shunted along the cold hard ground. Another blow rained in onto my shoulder – a punch this time, I think. It came from the other direction. One of the other men. I just lay there, yelping and keeping my body as tense as possible.

Another foot stamped down on my hip with a large crack. The pain was unbearable, and I let out a shriek so loud and high-pitched that I actually managed to scare myself a little. It forced me out of my little ball long enough for a kick to land hard into my stomach. I was instantly winded, all the breath rushing out of me, and I had to fight the urge to move my hands down to nurse my aching ribs. But I knew I had to protect my head at all costs.

Another kick sent a shockwave of pain through my right thigh. Then another blow to my back. I screamed out loud – louder than strictly necessary – hoping they might feel as though the kicks and punches were doing more damage than they really were.

Finally, they stopped, all three men grunting and breathing heavily. They shuffled about on the ground next to me, presumably assessing their work. I dared not look up. I just kept myself concealed, curled up and hoping it was all over.

Eventually, I heard them move away from me and head back to their cars. Doors opened and slammed shut. Then the two cars' engines started up. I remained on the ground, not even daring to peek out, until both had driven away and I was absolutely sure they were gone. Then I unfolded myself and looked around.

I was all alone, in a muddy woodland car park in the middle of God knows where. I clambered up onto my feet. My face still ached, joined now by intense throbbing in my legs, arms, stomach and back. I felt woozy and nearly collapsed back down to the ground, but I managed to hold myself up.

The sun was sinking slowly. It was beginning to get dark in the woods. And those bastards hadn't even offered me a bloody lift home. I pulled my mobile phone from my pocket. Then I remembered the battery was dead. Bollocks.

******

I finally made it back to Dylan's flat about three hours later. It turns out they'd driven me out to a small country car park, hidden out in the woods on the outskirts of a town called Crawley. I'd staggered my way out to the main road and started walking, not actually knowing where I was, or where I was going.

Dylan's suit was completely ruined. Great, dark streaks of mud covered it all over, where I'd lain crouched on the wet, filthy ground. A large butterfly of dried blood covered the lapels of the jacket and the chest of the white shirt, where my nose had exploded all over it. The material covering both of my knees was torn, where I'd dropped to the floor several times.

With practically every muscle in my body aching and pinching, it was difficult to walk straight. I hobbled and clambered along the darkening country road, shuffling like a zombie.

I must have walked for about thirty minutes before a pretty, kind young woman in a tiny silver Ford KA stopped and picked me up. She'd looked pretty horrified, and I guess she immediately had second thoughts, when she saw the state of my face. I explained what had happened – assuring her that I wasn't a random, wandering serial killer – and then she'd wanted to drive me to the local hospital. But I insisted I just wanted to get home. Eventually, I talked her into taking me to the train station instead.

Once again, I'd sat looking out at the glittering lights as the train ambled past Gatwick Airport. And once again I imagined myself sitting on a beach somewhere, a scantily clad babe lathering me with sun cream as I slurped on a large Pina Colada. But the train carried on, and soon the lights were just a distant glow behind me.

I walked in to Dylan's flat and plugged my phone into the charger in the kitchen. It buzzed and glowed as it burst into life. There was yet another voicemail from my landlord, Mr Singh, shouting and screaming and calling me all the names under the sun. He went on to say that I had until the end of the week to pay my rent, or he was going to change all the locks and leave my possessions out in the street. Once again, I simply deleted the message.

Unsurprisingly, there were no messages from Richard Stone. No updates on the case, or anything else that might have helped. Thankfully, there was also nothing from my newest acquaintance, Frank McLeod. I blew out a small sigh of relief.

There was a voicemail from Caroline, and a series of text messages, asking how I was, what I was up to, and whether I wanted any company. With each new message, the language grew increasingly sharp. Almost desperate. The final one simply read: *Call me.*

I clicked reply and typed out: *Sorry. Phone died. Been a long day. Pretty tired. Talk tomorrow?* I turned my phone back off and grabbed a handful of paracetamol and a bottle of wine from Dylan's wine rack. Then I went for a long, hot soak in the bath.

Finally, before I went to bed, just to make myself feel better, I logged onto Amazon and left a particularly scathing review of the latest James Patterson novel.

CHAPTER 18

I SHOVELLED THE last bite of sausage into my mouth and washed it down with the lukewarm remnants at the bottom of my mug of tea. Every part of my body ached – my face worst of all. I glanced at my reflection in the window opposite me. I looked dreadful. My battered nose was swollen and red, both nostrils still caked with dried blood, which made it hard to breathe – especially when eating. My right eye had bloomed into one hell of a black eye – dark purple and black in the centre, blossoming out into a blue-green tinge around the edges.

When I'd first hobbled into the café, the woman behind the counter actually let out a tiny shriek at the sight of me. Not exactly the best customer service I've ever received, and not too great for my self-esteem. But, seeing my own reflection, I could hardly blame her.

My head was throbbing. I wasn't sure whether it was the result of the beating I'd taken, or the three bottles of wine I'd sunk as self-medication the previous night. Or maybe a mixture of both. Thankfully, the fried breakfast was working wonders, and I was starting to feel half human again.

The suit I'd worn the previous day was completely destroyed. I'd snaffled another one from Dylan's wardrobe, and another expensive shirt, so at least I looked respectable from the neck down.

The past twenty-four hours had certainly been eventful. With more than a few new revelations surfacing about the case. I cursed myself, and my own lack of bravery, for not having questioned Frank McLeod. He'd warned me off of doing something, and I could only assume it was something to do with Dylan's case. But how the hell was a notorious gangster mixed up in all this?

He hadn't exactly been very forthcoming with details. All he'd said was that I should stop going around asking questions. Well, that's all I had been doing for the last few days. And I'd spoken to lots of people. So, who exactly had I'd rattled enough for them to get Frank 'The Animal' McLeod involved? And who out of them would actually have known McLeod in the first place?

Had I inadvertently stumbled upon something else – something completely unrelated? Was it all just a misunderstanding? Or had James

Patterson actually hired a London gangster to put the willies up me?

After McLeod's warning, my first instinct was to run away as far and as fast as possible, and never look back. But then I thought of Dylan in that hospital bed and I knew I had to at least try to be brave for the first time in my life.

I was keen to keep digging into the new discoveries I'd made. There were still far too many unanswered questions. But I was going to have to put things on hold for a few hours at least. Because I had another prior engagement.

It was the first day of the Hyde Park Literary Festival – a new event for books, book lovers and writers. A series of events, held in a variety of tents and marquees in Hyde Park, where book enthusiasts could come and meet the cream of literary talent from around the UK. In reality, it was basically another excuse for authors to gather in a big field to chat, schmooze, fawn all over each other and generally act like a load of literary luvvies.

As this was the festival's first year, I wasn't sure quite what to expect. But I've been to a few of these things, and they generally follow the same script. Despite being sick-making, sycophantic literary love-ins, these events are actually a great place to meet up with other authors and see what's happening in the publishing world. They're a unique opportunity to network with publishers and agents, and try to get a new deal. And, of course, they present a good opportunity to engage with the general reading public – and flog them a few books.

I hadn't actually been invited to take part in the festival in any official capacity. Despite my best efforts (and numerous emails and letters to the organisers), I hadn't been asked to take part in any of the panel discussions. I had no private author reading sessions or book signings. I hadn't even been invited to teach a writing masterclass, for God's sake. And because I wasn't technically on the guest list, the only way to gain access to any of the events was to pay. The bloody cheek of it!

However, I tend not to let trifling little matters like that stop me. The security at literary festivals is generally not the most stringent, and the doors tend not to be armed with ex-military, secret-service types. Rather, the people manning (or, more commonly, womaning) the gates are usually dowdy old librarians, or easily-confused, elderly ladies from the local Women's Institute.

I find it's fairly easy to bamboozle them and trick my way in by simply wearing a badge that says 'Author', talking very quickly and throwing a hissy fit that my agent hasn't told them I'm coming. Then I act all sweet and charming, tell them I'm sure it's not their fault, and promise to give them a free signed book from my holdall when my errant assistant deigns to turn up with my special book-signing pen.

They're usually so bewildered that they just smile and coo, and I breeze right past them. Works every time.

I even have my own special author badge, which I made myself, and that I drag out for occasions just like this. I've even had it laminated to make it look more official.

I arrived at the festival at 1.30pm, did the whole 'stroppy author' bit and conned my way in. Then I ambled around, popping my head into the various tents and immersing myself in the literary atmosphere.

A trio of posh-looking middle-aged women wandered past, each nose-deep in their festival programmes. I stopped them, flashed my special author badge and asked to borrow a programme under the pretence that I was supposed to be giving a talk and couldn't remember where to go. At first, they were a bit startled at my appearance. But after I explained that my injuries were the result of a charity boxing match against Julian Barnes – in which we'd raised over £30,000 for disabled children – they were more than impressed. They cooed and clucked, practically falling over themselves to be the one who got to lend their programme to a real, genuine author.

I took the programme from the oldest, fattest one, then pointed off into the distance, telling them I could have sworn I'd just seen my old friend J K Rowling in the crowd. When they were suitably distracted, I wandered off with the programme. Well, these things are ridiculously overpriced. And why would I want to spend £5.99 just to be reminded that my name had been omitted from the list?

Reading through the pamphlet, the line-up was pretty much as I expected. There was a whole tent devoted to dreary women's fiction writers, giving them a platform to prattle on about their poorly-written, uninspiring, insipid chick-lit.

There was a talk by the author of this year's big celebrity autobiography – some no-mark reality TV star from a horrendous sounding show called *Celebrity Enemas*. He was, apparently, the "Anal Cleansing Technician" who had made his name sucking God knows what from the rear ends of Z-list celebs. And he had seemingly written a book all about it. Quite why, I have no idea. And quite why anyone would want to buy it... well, perhaps they need a few more appointments with their psychiatrists.

There was a panel discussion about paranormal fiction; a talk on sports biographies; and a lecture from some travel writer who had just returned from a ghastly sounding jungle in South America. And, of course, there was the usual array of literary figures signing books for the general public.

Sadly, there were none of the big crime authors present, so I wouldn't be able to heckle them through their talks – one of my favourite pastimes. I was once ejected from the Cheltenham Literary Festival for interrupting a reading by Val McDermid, to ask her what she thought would be the best way to kill James Patterson and get away with it. She pretended to be annoyed, but I could see in her eyes that she'd often wondered the same thing.

Otherwise, the list looked fairly promising. There were representatives from all the major publishing houses, giving talks on this and that. And there were several literary agents offering one-on-one tutorials with budding authors – giving advice on how to get published, and presumably looking for new literary talent. You had to pay for their time, of course, but I figured I could hang around at the end and just foist myself upon them.

I turned the page and smiled as another golden opportunity shone out at me. Carlisle Philpott – Dylan's nemesis – was giving a talk in the main tent. That meant he was here, today, at the festival. And that meant I could find him and question him. But all in good time.

I wandered around the field, lugging my heavy holdall of books and looking for a reasonable space to set up. Much like the bookshops, it's generally better if you can commandeer a table to set up on – it makes the whole thing look much more professional than simply selling books out of a bag. At first glance I wasn't sure how easy that was going to be.

As well as the larger tents, where all the author talks, readings and lectures were taking place, there were several others run by various large and small booksellers. They were the obvious place to try and sneak my way in. But they were also pretty small, so it wouldn't be easy to clear a table and set up my own stuff.

Just as I was scanning the arena, looking for the weakest possible point of entry, I felt a tap on my shoulder.

"Freddie, you old swine," said a loud, booming voice behind me, "how the bloody hell did you manage to trick your way in here?"

I spun round to see another face I hadn't seen in many years. It was Matthew Dickson – Dylan's publisher.

"Great to see you, Freddie," said Matthew, grabbing my hand and nearly crushing the bones with his over-enthusiastic handshake. Matthew was one of those annoyingly happy people – always smiling, positive and overjoyed to see everyone. Exactly the sort of person I'm always very distrustful of. I mean, what the hell have they got to be so bloody happy about?

"Yes, good to see you, too," I lied.

"Christ, what happened to your face?"

"Oh, you know, the usual."

He just laughed loudly, patting me heartily on the back. I'm not entirely certain what he thought 'the usual' was.

I'd known Matthew for many years, back since Dylan and I were first published. He was another member of our gang in the early days – always out drinking with us. Another one of our team, fresh from university, embarking on our careers and determined to shake up the literary world with our genius. Very young and completely full of ourselves, of course.

Much like Mortimer, Matthew was also one of the first people to take a chance on Dylan. He was a junior editor at Dylan's publishing house and took a risk signing his first book. The gamble paid off with pretty reasonable sales. And when Dylan's second novel turned out to be a massive success, Matthew's career progression received a huge boost. He quickly rose up the ranks of the company, from Editor to Senior Editor and then Publisher.

His friendship with Dylan went a long way towards securing the rights to all of his further bestsellers, and he soon became part of the biggest literary success story of the past twenty years. Unsurprisingly, Matthew was now a senior partner at the firm, and one of the most powerful men in the business. The smug git.

"So, what are you doing here, Freddie? Are you giving a talk? Or have you sneaked in to try and flog a few books on the sly?" He laughed a loud, hearty bellow and slapped me hard on the shoulder.

"Something like that, Matthew," I said.

"Terrible news about Dylan," he said, his face turning serious. "I couldn't believe it when I heard. My secretary called me in the middle of the night to tell me. And then it's all over the bloody news ever since. Bloody hospital hasn't let me in to see him. Apparently, it's family only at the moment – not that the poor sod really has any."

"No," I said. "They let me in, but only because he was calling for me when he was admitted. And I think they might have let Mortimer see him. Other than that, they're being quite strict, I believe. I heard from the hospital this morning. He's still unconscious, but they're confident he'll make a full recovery."

"Oh, that is good news. I had to come here today, to represent the firm and do a talk. But I'm off to the hospital this afternoon to see him, and I don't care what the nurses say, I'll bloody well barge my way in." He let loose another thunderous roar of laughter. "So, do you still see much of Dylan? I heard you had a bit of a falling out."

"Something, like that," I said. "But we've actually just reconnected. I'm staying at his place at the moment... just for a while."

"Oh, great," he said. "At least he'll have someone to look after him when he gets home."

"Yes, I suppose so..." I said, not overly thrilled at the idea of becoming a live-in nurse. "So, how's business?"

"Oh, you know. Same old, same old. The book business is dying, but we're still hanging on in there."

"Really," I said, slightly surprised. "Things are a little rough?"

"No more so than anyone else. People just aren't buying as many books. In fact – and it sounds absolutely terrible to say it – but Dylan being in hospital has actually been pretty good for business."

"What?" I said, actually quite horrified.

"Oh no, don't get me wrong. It's awful. Absolutely awful. And I'd give anything to go back in time and stop him being harmed in the first place. But have you seen the charts? Every one of Dylan's books has gone shooting up. We're seeing up to two thousand per cent increase in sales on some of them. They're all in the top ten."

"Really?"

"Seriously, you can't buy publicity like that. As soon as the story hit the papers, we started seeing sales go through the roof. I wish all our backlist titles did that well."

"Christ almighty," I said, wondering whether my own sales might benefit from a spell in hospital, or even an elaborately faked death.

I noticed a sudden flash of excitement in Matthew's eyes, as he thought of Dylan's recent sales spike. And he noticed me noticing it.

"But like I say," he said quickly, "it's not about the money. And I'd give anything just to have Dylan back up and healthy."

"Yes, of course," I said, not really believing him.

"Truth be told, though," he said, lowering his voice and leaning in towards me, "we could do with a big hit at the moment."

"Really?"

"Like I say, things are bit rough across the whole business. People buying fewer books, self-published eBooks selling for 10p... You're only as good as your last big success."

"But you have Dylan's new book coming out soon, don't you? That's bound to be a hit."

"That's what we thought. We were so sure of it, we've actually built much of this year's business plan around it. But it's looking less and less likely now."

"What do you mean?"

"We thought we had the winning bid. But since the news broke about Dylan being in hospital, and with his backlist titles doing so well, we're hearing that other publishers have started upping their bids at a ridiculous rate. Everyone wants to cash in on this latest publicity."

"Bids?" I said, confused.

"I mean, interest was high enough already," he continued. "You know it's a sequel to *The Merchant of Sorrow*? The public have wanted this book for more than ten years. Christ, I've been begging him to write it for ten years. And now he has, it's going to be the biggest seller of the year.

"But what if it turned out that, not only is it a sequel to his biggest book ever – a book that the literary world has been salivating over for ten years – it's also the last ever book he wrote? And not only that, it was finished just prior to his untimely death. I mean, God forbid, but think of the press coverage. Think of the legend. People would buy a copy just to say they own one. Never mind Fifty Shades of Fucking Sodomy – this book could be the biggest seller ever. Every single publishing house in the world would cut their arms off to get it."

I was absolutely stunned.

"But what do you mean bids?" I said. "You always publish Dylan's books. He told me you were publishing the next one."

"It seems not," said Matthew, sighing with disappointment. "We've published every one of his previous novels. He's out of contract with us at the moment, but it's usually just a formality. He always signs with us, and we fully expected to get this next book as well."

"So what happened?"

"The book's gone out for auction," he said, shrugging. "Mortimer's trying to get the best price he can."

"But that doesn't make any sense," I said. "I spoke to Dylan only a few nights ago, and he told me you were publishing the book. Mortimer had suggested going to auction, but Dylan told him he wasn't interested. He wanted to stick with you."

"Well, I don't know about that," said Matthew, sighing even deeper. "All I know is that Mortimer is accepting bids from everyone. We've already upped ours a couple of times. And at this rate, we're probably going to miss out. It's all extremely disappointing. I tried calling Dylan, but I can never get through. All calls have to go through Mortimer's office, and he keeps telling me Dylan is holed up at home working. I assumed this was all coming from Dylan."

"No, definitely not. I mean, unless he was lying to me. But if he's not, can Mortimer do that? I mean, can he take bids from other publishers without Dylan knowing?"

"I don't see why not," said Matthew. "Pretty standard practice, to be honest. We very rarely negotiate with authors personally. It's almost always done through agents."

"So, do you think there could me more to Dylan's injury than an accident?" I said, testing his reaction.

"More to it?" he said, surprised. His reaction seemed genuine enough. "What do you mean?"

"Well, you said it. If Dylan doesn't pull through, his book suddenly becomes the biggest seller in years."

"Well, yes, but... what are you getting at Freddie?"

"Oh, I don't know. Just the old crime writer's brain working overtime, I guess."

"Probably, Fred. You always were one to see conspiracies where there weren't any. Although, if Dylan didn't pull through, someone somewhere would stand to make a lot of money. Not a bad motive for murder. Maybe you could use that for your next book?"

He burst out with another huge belly laugh.

"Look, I'd better go," said Matthew, "I'm on stage soon. Take it easy Freddie. And look after Dylan. I think he needs a good friend at the moment."

He gave me another hefty pat on the shoulder and walked off in the direction of one of the large tents.

"Hey, I don't suppose you're looking to sign any new crime books?"

I shouted after him. But he didn't hear me over the noise of the crowd. Or, at least, he pretended not to.

I looked down at the bag of books at my feet. Strangely, I'd gone off the idea of trying to sell any. I didn't even feel like going to heckle the anal cleansing technician in the biographies tent.

******

I sneaked into the main tent just as Carlisle Philpott was rounding up his self-indulgent, self-congratulatory talk, and found myself a seat at the back. I yawned and sneered as he welcomed the usual array of pandering, fawning, sycophantic questions from the audience – 'Where do you get your ideas from?' 'How do you manage to capture the complexities of the female spirit so well?' 'Who do you most admire?' 'Who do you base your characters on?' – all that tired, glib bullshit. And, of course, Philpott responded with the usual inane, pompous, uninspired answers.

A large woman with curly grey hair and a floral dress that looked like she'd woken up that morning and decided to dress in her living room curtains had asked the last question. She sat down with a big grin on her face, seemingly overjoyed with Philpott's response. Arms shot up all round the tent from eager questioners. Another was selected and she stood up on the far side of the crowd. She was too far away to make out what she looked like. But she had a younger voice.

"Mr Philpott," she began, "I was just wondering why you make such a concerted effort to rubbish the work of Dylan St James, when any reader with half a brain can see that he's a far superior writer, and you're just a very poor imitation of him, with barely a quarter of his talent?"

Well, that was a question and a half. Exactly the sort of question I like to hear at these kinds of things. I felt like standing up and applauding her.

The crowd, however, definitely did not share my enthusiasm. The whole room fell instantly silent, before a flutter of audible sighs and intakes of breath flew around the room. A sea of stunned, angry faces turned to see who the culprit was. I still couldn't make her out, thanks to the big head of the overeater next to me obscuring my view. Everyone swivelled again, turning back to the stage and a stunned, open-mouthed Philpott.

"Er... well... I, er..." he stammered.

"I would argue," continued the woman, her voice singing with vindictiveness, "that you are not even half the writer he is. Your plots are lazy, your writing style is long-winded and pompous, and your characters have no emotional depth whatsoever."

Brave words, especially in front of a room packed with Philpott fans. But I guess that was the point.

"I think you only criticise Dylan St. James," she said, "because you're jealous. And you know you'll never be as good as him."

That was it. The crowd reacted with a cacophony of boos, hisses and angry jeers.

"Shut your mouth!" screamed one old lady with blue-rinsed hair.

"How dare you?" shouted a middle-aged woman in a red anorak.

"Fuck you! Fuck you, you fucking slag!" yelled a plump old granny with a face reddened either through rage or over-eating of sausages. I guessed probably a mixture of both.

A wrinkled old crone in front of me threw down her bag of knitting, jumped to her feet and screamed, "Shut your trap, you fucking whore!"

They can be a pretty passionate bunch, the literary groupies.

Carlisle Philpott stood there on the stage, stuttering and stammering, and turning paler with every second. He looked like a light breeze might knock him off his feet. Finally, a woman in a power suit marched onto the stage and told the crowd there would be no more questions. Then she took Philpott by the arm and ushered him away.

As the crowd continued to jeer the troublemaker, the flaps at the side of the tent flipped open and two sturdy old broads – no doubt the brawny enforcers of the local WI – came rushing in. They marched over to the woman, gripped her elbows either side and started to drag her away.

I still couldn't see her face, so I clambered up onto my chair and looked over the heads of the crowd. As the beefy old girls dragged her to the exit, she suddenly broke free of their grip, spun back to face the crowd and raised a defiant middle finger high into the air. And that's when I saw her.

She was an attractive woman with pretty eyes and mousey brown hair. She had a mischievous smile etched across her face, and a devious, slightly psychotic twinkle in her eye. And she had a large picture of a cat on her jumper.

It was Caroline. My 'sort of' girlfriend.

CHAPTER 19

BY THE TIME I'd made my way through the angry crowd and out of the tent, Caroline had already been marched away. I was just about to chase after her, when I saw Philpott exiting the other side of the tent. He was flapping and wobbling, clearly giving the power-suit-woman something of a telling off, as she guided him in the direction of a smaller, much nicer looking tent.

There was a large sign above the entrance that read 'TALENT'. They both walked inside, and I felt like shouting out that he was massively underqualified to enter anywhere with the word talent above the door. But then, I knew this was my best chance to corner him, so I bit my tongue, flashed my author badge at the old biddy at the entrance and bamboozled my way inside.

The interior of the tent was far nicer than anything the paying punters would get to experience. There were comfortable, padded chairs. A stable, laminate wood floor. A long table littered with fruit, pastries, tiny sandwiches, various baked goods, tea, coffee, canned drinks and pre-poured glasses of champagne. Now, this was more like it!

I walked over to the table, filled my pockets with bags of pretzels and M&Ms, and quickly scoffed down three sandwiches and two doughnuts. I can eat remarkably quickly when I'm rushed, or when the food is free. I picked up a glass of champagne, downed it in one and then picked up another.

An old bag at the end of the table glowered at me with disapproving eyes. I shrugged, gripped my author badge between finger and thumb and mouthed the word 'nervous' at her, with a look of mock terror on my face. She quickly softened, coming over all mumsy and concerned for me. So, I downed the drink in my hand and picked up another.

I scanned the room. There were four other authors in there, sitting on the padded chairs and looking rather pleased with themselves. I didn't recognise any of them. Each one had a corresponding power-suit-clad minion next to them – no doubt their agent or representative from the publishing house.

Carlisle Philpott sat in the corner, red-faced, angry and clearly on edge. Was it just annoyance and embarrassment that had made him so upset? Or was there a tinge of guilt there as well?

His hands shook as he held his glass of champagne. His power-suited companion flipped between consoling him and tearing a strip off a very apologetic looking WI lady. Shouting at an old woman was clearly not good enough, however. I could just make out the words 'organiser' and 'now' before the old lady walked sheepishly out of the tent, with power suit stomping along behind her.

I walked over and sat down next to Philpott, forcefully chinking my glass against his. "Philpott, old mate," I said, "fancy seeing you here."

"Bloody hell," said Philpott, flinching like he might topple off his chair. "As if this day wasn't bad enough already. How the hell did you get in here, Freddie?"

"Nice to see you too," I said. "What's it been... ten years?"

"Not fucking long enough," he sneered.

"Well, at least you haven't lost any of your charm," I laughed.

"What the hell happened to your face?"

"I accidentally bought one of your books and had to give myself a severe thrashing as a punishment."

The last time I saw Carlisle Philpott, we were still sort of friends. He was one of our gang – back in the day, before all the rivalry, back-stabbing and mean spiritedness.

We were a little group of newly published authors – Me, Dylan, Carlisle, a scrawny guy called Anderson Taylor and a young womens' fiction writer called Tabitha Martin. It was a fun little clique and we used to hang out in the Duke of Argyll pub on Great Windmill Street pretty much every day. We had our own little corner where we'd drink, laugh, talk about literature and generally feel very impressed with ourselves.

It was a great place to feel inspired, right at the heart of Soho. We could sit for hours, watching the world go by outside the large glass windows. And because we were all young, struggling artistes, the fact that the beer was cheap was also a huge bonus.

It lasted a few years, and we were like a little support network for each other. Reading early drafts of each other's work. Offering hints, advice and proofreading services. We celebrated each other's success, and we consoled each other when we received bad reviews, poor sales or rejected manuscripts. We were convinced we were the new face of literary London – and we didn't mind telling anyone who happened to sit at the table next to us.

Dylan, Philpott and I were the heaviest drinkers. After the others had called it a night, the three of us were usually still at it, drinking late into the night. Many was the time we'd wake up in an unexpected location, with no reasonable explanation as to how we got there. They were some of the happiest days of my life.

Then Dylan's career really took off. At first, Philpott was every bit as happy for Dylan as the rest of us. I guess he assumed that Dylan was just the first of us to make it big, and the rest would follow in his stead. But when Philpott's own star failed to ascend to the same dizzying heights, jealousy began to rear its ugly head.

It first came in the form of drunken, barbed comments disguised as good-natured ribbing. But then the comments became more personal. The drunker Philpott got, and the more he felt like he was in Dylan's shadow, the less he bothered trying to pretend they were jokes. He stopped coming to pub as regularly, and when he did, he'd all but blank Dylan completely.

Jealousy can do terrible things to people, and soon the friendship had disintegrated completely. As the pair published new books, and became more famous and widely regarded, Philpott showed his true colours and started rubbishing Dylan in the press.

Philpott just couldn't handle seeing his friend get everything he'd always wanted for himself, whilst he languished in second place. So, I guess it was easier for him to invent a conspiracy in which Dylan was the architect of his failure. That way no blame would rest with him. And it was easier to cut ties with Dylan, rather than constantly being reminded of his own shortcomings.

Naturally, I stuck by Dylan throughout all the quarrels and upset. Until, of course, my own jealousy got the better of me, and I ended up cutting ties in a far less dramatic manner – but for very much the same reason.

"That was quite something," I said to Philpott. "I see your fans still love you."

"Very funny," he snorted. "Seriously, though, how the hell did you get in here? I didn't see your name on the programme." He looked at me with the kind of condescension I usually reserve for politicians, traffic wardens and James Patterson fans.

"Last minute addition," I lied. "They asked me to come down and do a signing. And to fill in if any of the other authors wet themselves on stage."

He sneered at me, his top lip curling up and his eyes burning with anger. "What the fuck do you want, Freddie?"

"Oh, you know me, Carlisle," I said, leaning back in my chair and crossing my legs. "Just here for the free booze." I let a short silence hang between us before saying, "Oh, and I did want to ask you one question: Why are you trying to kill Dylan?"

His face crinkled with utter bewilderment. "What the hell are you talking about?"

Not quite the guilty reaction I'd been hoping for. I'd assumed he would recoil in horror or jump up out of his chair and make a run for it. Instead, he just sat there looking confused.

"I take it you know Dylan is in hospital with a bloody great harpoon hole in his chest?" I said.

"Of course I do, it's been all over the news. I had my assistant send flowers. But what's that got to do with me?"

"You hired a hitman to take him out."

Philpott stared at me with a blank look. Then he burst out laughing. "Take him out? Hitman? What the hell are you on, Freddie? Why on earth would I want to kill Dylan?"

"Revenge," I said, letting the word hang in the air. "You've always been jealous of him. He stole the life you want, and you want to make him pay for it. And you want him out of the way so you can sell more books."

Philpott really started laughing then. "Christ, Freddie, I think you've been reading too many of your own books. I don't want Dylan dead. It doesn't make any sense. In fact, it's the exact opposite of what I'd want."

"Opposite?" I said, now my turn to be confused. "I... er... what?"

"I don't know if you've noticed," he said, looking around the tent, then picking up his glass of champagne from the small table in front of him, "but I'm not exactly doing too badly. Not quite up to Dylan's standards, maybe, but my last book has already sold half a million. If Dylan doesn't pull through, I'll be lucky to sell another half dozen."

"What do you mean?"

"Have you seen the Amazon chart today? Dylan's got two books in the Top Ten. His sales have spiked since the news of the attack and his books are flying off the shelves."

"Actually, yes, I did hear something about that," I said.

"We live in a truly morbid world, you know. If Dylan were to actually die, the sales would go through the roof and no other sod would get a look in for months. I've got a new book coming out in two weeks, and it'll sell bugger all.

"Besides, if I was going to hire a hitman to kill Dylan, I'd find someone slightly more competent than some numbskull that uses a harpoon. I mean, who tries to kill someone with a harpoon? In central London?"

The flaps of the tent opened and Philpott's power-suited companion appeared with an apologetic, weasly-looking man in glasses and an ostentatious blue blazer.

"I'll put my hands up and admit that Dylan and I aren't exactly on best terms," said Philpott, standing up from his chair. "I've said things I probably shouldn't have, and yes, I have been jealous of him. But I'd never want to see him hurt. And I'd certainly never try and kill him."

"I... er... I'm..." I stumbled, not knowing what to say.

"Maybe you should get your facts straight, and actually think things through before you go accusing people of murder. Now, I suggest you fuck off before I call the police."

He turned and walked towards his companion, then stopped halfway and looked back to me.

"When you see Dylan," he said, "give him my best. I really hope he's okay. And tell him I'm sorry. For everything." There was a genuine look of remorse in his eyes.

I nodded as he turned. Then he walked through the tent flap and disappeared.

CHAPTER 20

I LEFT THE festival, jumped on the Tube and headed back to Dylan's flat. It had been quite a day. And I was more than a little confused at having seen Caroline there, standing in front of a crowd and berating Carlisle Philpott.

I took my phone out of my pocket. No messages. And I couldn't send her any, because I obviously had no signal down there. Instead, I took out my notebook and crossed Philpott's name from the list. I was certain now that he had nothing to do with the attack on Dylan. I couldn't really see him wanting Dylan dead just out of spite. And I know how much he values his book sales – he'd never do anything to jeopardise those.

I turned to a blank page in my pad and wrote down:

MOTIVE
Money?

As Matthew had said, Dylan's death could stand to make someone very rich. But who? According to Richard Stone, I was currently the only one with a plausible reason for killing Dylan – I was bitter about his success over the years and I actually did stand to inherit a large sum of cash. But I was still pretty sure I wasn't behind it all.

I tapped my pen absent-mindedly against my pad, much to the annoyance of the passenger sitting next to me. She was a chubby woman with a red face and several bags of shopping at her feet, blocking the way for other passengers to either stand or move past.

She was already annoyed at me for having demanded she move the shopping bags from the seat next to her, so that I could plonk myself down onto it. There were, of course, about five other empty seats on the train that I could have chosen to sit in. But I was in a bad mood and felt like taking it out on someone else. Now the pen-tapping was really making her angry.

She huffed and puffed, blowing air out of her cheeks, making a point of looking down at my pen rat-tatting against the pad. Then she shook her head violently from side to side, glancing around at the other passengers as if to say, "Who does this clown think he is, making all this noise?" As if I had a full mariachi band strumming along next to me, or something.

The more she huffed, the louder and faster I banged my pen, until she finally picked up her bags and trundled off to find another seat at the far end of the carriage. I immediately halted the tapping, and she glanced back to glower at me. I blew her a kiss and smiled as she hissed at me and wobbled away, muttering under her breath.

One-nil to Winters. Mean? Yes. Childish? Definitely. But it's the little things in life that keep you going, isn't it?

I exited the train and made my way through the station, deliberately kicking the pathetic little wheeled bags people were dragging along behind them. It's one of my favourite games – kicking the bags, watching the owner wince in pain as their wrist is twisted with the impact. Then, when they turn to confront me, I clutch my ankle as if they've just run me over. I tell them to mind where they're going, and they hobble off holding their wrists and offering a confused apology. It really is fun – you should try it yourself!

I made it back to Dylan's flat, headed straight for the office and turned on his laptop. I opened his email browser and checked for any recent correspondence. Right there at the top of the list, almost blinking out at me with its bold font and unopened envelope symbol, sat a new email from DylansBiggestFan. The subject line read: *Your biggest fan defends you!!!!!*

The ridiculous overuse of exclamation marks told me the message was of high importance – at least the sender seemed to think so. It also told me that the sender was something of a simpleton who didn't understand how to use exclamation marks correctly.

I clicked it open:

Dearest Dylan,

I hope you're bearing up well, my love. I was so devastated when I heard the news about your attack. I was beside myself with sadness and fear. Who could do such a thing to such a lovely, warm, talented man? I'm sure they'll catch whoever shot you soon. And when they do, I hope they lock him up with the most evil, violent, horrible men that will beat him and bugger him every day. Although that won't come close to what he really deserves.

Beat him and bugger him? She sounded absolutely charming. I

carried on reading.

I did try to come and see you at the hospital, my darling. But they wouldn't let me in because I wasn't family. I tried to explain how close we are, but they wouldn't change their minds.

Instead, I went to the Hyde Park Literary Festival. That gasbag Carlisle Philpott was there, sounding so bloody impressed with himself. Well, don't worry my sweet baby, I put him back in his place. I got up in front of a big crowd and told him he could never be the writer you are, and that he'd better stop bad-mouthing you in the press. He practically ran off the stage crying. So don't worry, I'm sure he'll realise the error of his ways and stop being so mean to you.

Holy crap! I'd seen the protest against Philpott. I practically had a front row seat for it. And it had been Caroline standing there shouting the abuse. The realisation hit me like a bucket of cold water. Caroline was DylansBiggestFan. My 'sort of' girlfriend was Dylan's bloody stalker. Fuck!

I'm sorry I haven't written in a few days, but I've been busy seeing another man. Please don't be jealous though – he means nothing to me. I have no feelings for him, and being with him will only help to bring us closer together. I can't explain how, but all will become clear soon enough, my love.

Well, that's fucking charming, I must say. Talk about feeling used.

Please believe me when I say that every time I've been with him I was really imagining that I was with you.

Nice! What a classy lady.

I hope you feel better soon, my darling. I can't wait for us to be together. I've started knitting you a new jumper to make you feel better when you get out of hospital.
All my love
Your biggest fan

I closed the laptop, sat back in the chair and blew air out of my cheeks. Caroline, the woman I'd been sleeping with, was Dylan's stalker. And not just that, she'd only been sleeping with me as part of some crazy, deluded scheme to get closer to him. She'd literally just said so in her own words.

I don't mind admitting my feelings were a little hurt. I mean, I had no intentions of taking things any further with Caroline, other than the odd bunk-up here and there. And I was effectively doing the same thing to her that she was doing to me. But still. Seeing it in print, it all seemed a bit mean.

In fairness, I should have known from the start. The way she approached me at the reading, then followed me to the coffee shop afterwards. All the questions about Dylan, and how upset she'd been when she heard about the attack.

I mean, I should have known she was cracked in the head the moment I saw that fucking cat jumper.

No wonder she'd been so keen to come back to my place the first night we met. I'd told her straight away that I was staying with Dylan. The whole thing must have been some warped scheme just to get a peek inside her favourite writer's home.

If she'd been willing to shag me just to get a peek at Dylan's wallpaper, and find out what kind of loo roll he used, what the hell else was she capable of? Maybe it wasn't such a bad thing I'd found out about her, before she got the chance to chop me up into bits and wear my balls as earrings – or whatever it is these deranged stalker types do.

******

I was sitting on the sofa, drinking a glass of wine. I was still reeling from the revelations I'd read in the latest email from DylansBiggestFan, when I heard the mechanical buzzing of the door-entry system. I walked out into the hallway, pressed a button on the door-entry phone and the screen lit up with a picture of Caroline.

I held the phone up to my ear and said hello.

"Hi Babe," said Caroline, suddenly looking up into the camera, her face beaming with a large, excited smile. "I thought I'd pop over and say hi. I've brought food."

She held a hand up, showing the camera a carrier bag with the letters KFC emblazoned under a grinning picture of The Colonel.

"It's KFC," she said.

No shit, I thought. I was still feeling raw after seeing what she'd written about me. Without saying anything, I pressed the buzzer to let her in. I watched the screen go blank as she went out of shot and then hung up the phone.

In the past, people have called me unscrupulous. They've called me far worse things too, but I prefer to think of myself as enterprising. I like to turn a situation to my advantage wherever possible. And when I have the upper hand over someone, I figure it's only sensible to exploit that to get what I want or need.

Clearly, Caroline had no idea what I'd found out about her. How could she? And there was no need to reveal my hand just yet. So, when I heard her footsteps on the landing outside, I opened the door and welcomed her in with a big smile.

"Hey, you," she said. Then she suddenly recoiled in horror. "Christ, what happened to your face?"

"Oh, it's nothing. Just had a bit of an altercation... You should see the other guy."

"Oh," she said, leaning in and kissing me gently on the lips. "Are you sure? It looks really sore. Maybe you should call the police, or see a doctor?"

"No need for that," I said. "I feel fine. And I might have a few more leads in Dylan's case."

"Well, as long as you're sure. Sorry to just pop round unexpected, but I thought you might like some company. I can go, if you'd rather be alone."

"No, of course not. It's great to see you," I lied. I closed the front door and led her through to the kitchen.

"I picked up a bucket of chicken. Naughty, I know, but I just fancied it. And a little of what you like..." she said, smiling and winking seductively.

"That's really thoughtful," I said. "But I'm not really very hungry, I'm afraid." I took the bag from her and placed it on the kitchen counter.

"Oh, okay," she said, trying to hide her disappointment.

"But... perhaps you could help me build up an appetite," I said, winking.

She smiled coyly, as I took her hand and led her through to the bedroom.

Forty-five minutes later, we were lying next to each other in bed. "That was amazing, babe," she said.

"Thanks very much," I replied. "At least two other women have said the same thing to me in the past!"

Okay, so I probably shouldn't have shagged her again. It certainly wasn't chivalrous. Or ethical. And I wouldn't be winning any awards for feminism any time soon. But I was genuinely upset at her, and this was as good a way of punishing her as any. It was also pretty obvious that I wouldn't be getting another shag once I'd confronted her about the contents of that email. So, I figured why not get a last one in while I still could.

"I hope you've worked up that appetite now," she said. "I'm absolutely famished. How about I heat up some of that chicken and we can curl up on the sofa together?"

"Sounds good," I said.

She pulled back the covers and slipped out of bed. She then scurried about, scooping her clothes up off the floor before putting on her knickers and shirt.

"You know," I said, sitting up in bed, "I could have sworn I saw you today."

"Really? I don't think so." She didn't flinch. Not even the flutter of a guilty eyelash.

"Hmm… No, I'm sure it was you."

"I don't see how," she laughed, "I've been in meetings all day. Never even left the office. I even had to get one of the girls to go out and pick me up a sandwich."

She turned her back to me, walked towards the bedroom door and gripped the handle.

"Strange," I said. "So, you didn't happen to pop to the Hyde Park Literary Festival, at all?"

She stopped dead. I couldn't see the expression on her face, but her head dropped slightly.

"You didn't stand up in front of a crowd of people and verbally abuse Carlisle Philpott?"

Her hand fell from the door handle.

"I guess that must have been another woman in a cat jumper being dragged off by security…"

She turned to look at me, her face pale, her eyes totally lost.

"Don't bother with any more lies," I said. "I know it was you."

"It's not what you think," she said.

"Really? Because what I think is that you cosied up to me, got me drunk and then got me into bed in the deluded hope that it might somehow get you closer to my friend, Dylan."

"Erm… I…"

"Tell me something, how did you even know that I knew Dylan?"

She stood for a second, looking blank. Her eyes twitched, scanning from left to right, as if she were searching her brain for the perfect excuse. Then a look of resignation fell over her.

"I saw you," she said. "Drinking coffee together, the day before we met at the library."

"Of course, you did," I said, smiling as it suddenly dawned on me. "You're his stalker. You were following him."

"I'm not a stalker," she snapped, suddenly angry. Her eyes shone like they had when she was being dragged from the tent. "I hate that word. I'm a fan. And I was not following him. I just happened to see him going into a coffee shop. And I happened to pop in myself. For a coffee. There's no law against that."

"Hmmm… so how did I get mixed up in all this?"

"I was in the library the next day and I saw you in there. I recognised you. And when I saw you setting up to do a talk, I thought I'd come and listen. When you got kicked out I followed you. I just wanted to say hello and ask you a few questions about Dylan. But when I found out you were actually staying with him… well, I knew it was too good an opportunity to miss out on."

"So you got me drunk and seduced me, just so… what? So you could get a sneaky look inside Dylan's home?"

"You didn't seem to be complaining at the time."

"Well… no… but…"

"What did you think was going to happen, Freddie?" she said, her tone harsh and cold. The keen girlfriend act was completely gone. "That we were going to fall in love and live happily ever after?"

"No. Well… maybe…" I lied.

"Be honest, you were using me just as much as I was using you. I bet you were planning on shagging me a few more times and then conveniently losing my number."

"Absolutely not. That's a horrible thing to say. I can't believe you'd think that of me." Well, I was hardly going to admit it, was I? And I so very rarely get to occupy the moral high ground.

"If you must know, I thought you were a very special woman. And I'm not saying I was planning a future with you, exactly, but I thought maybe there was something special between us."

Her gaze dropped and she looked at her feet, slightly ashamed.

"And then I find out you're just a fucking nutbag stalker, using me to get a peek inside my famous friend's flat."

"I am NOT a stalker," she shouted.

"I've seen the emails, you crazy cow. I've seen the jumpers you knitted. And after your recent behaviour – following Dylan, shagging me on the off-chance of bumping into him over breakfast coffee… not to mention standing up in front of a crowd of people and publicly berating his competitors. I'm sorry love, but if that's not a stalker, I don't know what is."

"I am NOT a fucking STALKER!" she shouted, her face turning bright red and her eyes shining with absolute menace. The noise was so loud it rattled the little trinkets on top of the chest of drawers. I suddenly became very aware that I was stark bollock naked, with nothing but a 10-tog duvet between my most valuable assets and a crazy stalker bitch.

"D'you know what? Fuck you!" she said, kicking the end of the bed. "I don't care about you. It's Dylan I love. You were just a means to an end. Just a shag to get me closer to my Dylan. And a pretty crap one at that!"

Why do women always say that in the heat of anger? Who is it supposed to offend? Not me. I couldn't care less how much they enjoy sleeping with me, as long as I've had a good time.

She searched around on the floor, picking up the rest of her clothes, and marched out of the bedroom. She hopped along down the hallway, putting on her skirt and shoes. Then she picked up her bag and coat from the kitchen and headed for the front door. I jumped out of bed and ran down the hall after her.

"So, are you behind it?" I called out, as she started to open the door.

"Behind what?" she said, turning back to me.

"Are you the one trying to kill Dylan?"

"What? No, of course not." Her face was one of total shock and confusion. "How could you possibly think that?"

"Well, the stalker thing for a start," I smirked. "Your temper tantrum at the festival. Sneaking your way into Dylan's home. It's not that much of a leap."

"I would never hurt Dylan. Never."

"Well, pardon me for saying so, but you're not exactly averse to the odd lie or two. Why should I believe you?"

Her eyes glistened. One small tear rolled down her cheek. "I could never hurt him. I love him with all my heart."

"But if you can't have him, maybe no one should, eh? Maybe you want him dead so you don't have to feel jealous seeing him with someone else."

"No," she shouted, physically shaking with the emotion. Her tears started falling heavily, running great streaks down her face. "I would never do that. I only want Dylan to be happy – no matter what tramps and floozies he takes up with. Besides, as soon as Dylan gets better we're going to be together."

"What?"

"I love him. And he loves me. He just doesn't know it yet. He's had too many distractions. Too many cheap whores throwing themselves at him. But once he's better, he'll realise how he feels about me. He'll see that I'm the right woman for him and we'll be together. I certainly don't want him dead."

"No, I don't believe you do," I sighed, mentally crossing another name from my list of suspects. She might have been as mad as a box of frogs, but I could see she only had affection for Dylan. A bit too much, that was for sure. But it was obvious she didn't really want to hurt him.

So, another lead was dead. I sighed heavily as, once again, it felt like I was taking one step forward and three steps back. Dylan was still in hospital with a bloody great hole in his chest, and I was no closer to finding the person who put him there. Then I had a sudden flash of inspiration.

"Listen, I need to ask you one last thing."

She raised an eyebrow and smirked at me. "I've had quite enough of your questions for one night."

"It's important. It could help me figure out what's been going on. It could help to protect Dylan."

She breathed out a long sigh, softening slightly. "Fine. If it will help Dylan."

"Okay, when you were stalking Dylan…"

"That's it," she said, reaching for the doorknob.

"Wait. Please. It's important."

She sighed again, staring right at me.

"I know you said you weren't following Dylan… but if you *had* been, did you see anything strange? Any odd people? Somebody else following him? Anything bizarre or unusual at all?"

She thought for a second.

"If I did *happen* to see Dylan out and about – and I'm not saying I did – well... Actually, now you come to mention it, there was this one guy I kept seeing all over the place."

"Guy? What did he look like? Where did you see him?"

"Well, it was actually the car I noticed first. Blue one... not sure what kind... a Ford maybe. I just kept seeing it everywhere I went. I knew it was the same one because it had one of those stupid things in the back window."

"A Garfield?"

"That's right, bloody Garfield. Do you remember, it was like everyone had those things in their car at one point? But you never see them anymore, do you? That's why it stuck in my mind."

"That's the same car I've seen," I said. "Dylan mentioned it too. Fucker nearly ran me over."

"Oh my God," said Caroline. "I just figured he was a paparazzi or something. Following Dylan to get a picture. They do that, don't they? Do you think he might be the one trying to hurt him?"

"Could be," I said, getting slightly excited at the possible breakthrough. "Did you happen to see the licence plate number?"

"No, sorry. Didn't really think about it. I wish I had now."

"And the man – what did he look like? Would you recognise him if you saw him again."

"Sorry, I didn't see him that well. He was always in the car and I only saw him from a distance."

"Dammit," I said. "That car definitely has something to do with all this. I've got to figure out who the driver is."

A cool silence hung between us as we both thought about the car. Then Caroline suddenly remembered how angry she was with me. She curled her lip into a sneer and raised an eyebrow at me.

"Well, don't let me keep you any longer," I said.

"Fuck you, Freddie," she said, as she unlocked the front door and yanked it open. I watched her step through the door and out into the hallway.

"Hey, listen," I called after her, softening my voice to a reconciliatory tone. "I'm not one to hold a grudge. So, if you fancy one last quick shag before we part ways, I'd be up for that."

She gave me a look that told me just how disgusting she thought I was. Then she marched out of the flat and slammed the door behind her. I retired to the living room, flicked on the telly and tucked in to the bucket of chicken she'd brought round.

CHAPTER 21

A LOUD NOISE woke me. I lifted my head from the pillow, confused. It was dark and I was still slightly drunk.

I scanned the room, my eyes barely open. A dense fog of half-sleep clouded my mind. My booze-soaked brain was working on half power, struggling to get up to speed. The bed felt strange under me, the sheets softer and fresher than the ones I was used to. A thin stream of moonlight cut across the room from a gap in the curtains, illuminating a streak of blue, fluffy carpet and striped wallpaper.

For some reason I was in Dylan's bed. I had a vague memory of sitting in the living room, eating cold chicken and drinking red wine. Then I'd decided look through Dylan's room to see if there was anything obviously missing – or even anything that shouldn't be there.

Caroline had been snooping in there just a few nights previously and I'd swallowed her lies about sleepwalking. Now that I knew her real identity, it occurred to me that she might have had more sinister intentions. She could have been in there pinching all manner of keepsakes. She might have been leaving Dylan some freaky little love tokens. Or she might have installed closed circuit surveillance equipment. So, I'd gone into Dylan's bedroom to investigate and I must have fallen asleep.

I rubbed my eyes, shaking my head at the confusion, and collapsed back down onto the pillow. Then I heard another noise.

This one was louder, more menacing somehow. A hard, crashing sound, like furniture being thrown around a room. And it was coming from inside the flat.

I snapped up in bed, my eyes wide open. Instantly awake. Another noise followed, like metal scraping along the ground. And then the unmistakable sound of hushed voices.

My heart started thumping. A shiver of fear coursed down my spine as my stare remained fixed on the bedroom door. There were people in the flat. And not only that, they were noisy people. Angry people. Furniture-throwing people.

I heard the voices again. The sound of footsteps as they moved around in the living room, lifting objects and throwing them back down. I couldn't tell how many of them there were. The voices were muffled, no more than soft vibrations in the walls. I couldn't make out what they were actually saying.

Who were they? And what did they want?

Were they here to rob the place? Opportunistic burglars who'd broken in, believing the flat was empty, and were now busy ransacking the place?

Had Caroline somehow managed to get back into the flat, and now she was tearing the place apart in some kind of revenge against me?

Or perhaps it was someone here for another reason entirely. McLeod's men – breaking in to give me a follow-up warning. Or the people responsible for Dylan's harpoon attack. If so, they could be plotting their next murder attempt: planting a bomb in the microwave; filling the shower pump with hydrochloric acid; hiding a school of merciless, bum-biting piranha down the toilet... My mind raced with the horrible possibilities.

Worse still, they might be here to tie up loose ends. Like a sleuthing pal, currently residing in the flat they'd just broken into. And who was close to unmasking them and their murderous ways.

I needed to call the police. I clambered out of bed, throwing the covers to the floor. I looked all around for my mobile phone. I scrabbled around on the carpet. I checked the bedside cabinet. I couldn't see it anywhere. I must have left it plugged in to the charger in the kitchen.

My heart beat faster. The only way I could get to it would be to leave the bedroom and try and sneak past them. If they caught me, I wasn't sure they'd take very kindly to me interrupting their ransacking and asking if they'd just keep it down for a second whilst I called the cops.

But I couldn't just stay in there. It wouldn't be long before they made their way to the bedroom and found me. Dylan's bed was one of those low to the floor things, so I couldn't hide under it. There wasn't even a decent-sized wardrobe to cower in – Dylan's ones were all shallow and space-saving, and couldn't conceal a cat. I took a deep breath and a hearty gulp, and resigned myself to foolhardy bravery. Or, at the very least, silent, terrified sneaking. But I wasn't going out there empty-handed.

I sprung to my feet, darting across the floor, scanning for the room for anything I could use as a weapon. Sadly, however, one thing that seems to hold true for the majority of novelists I know, is that we don't tend to own a particularly large quantity of weaponry.

I looked around me, hoping to find a baseball bat, a pair of nun-chucks, a machete or a flame-thrower with which to defend myself. Even a chainsaw would have done at a push. I rummaged through the wardrobe, checked under the bed, and ransacked the contents of the small cupboard in the corner of the room. But there was nothing. Dylan didn't even have so much as a Samurai sword, for God's sake.

I checked the chest of drawers, rummaging through clothes until I found it. It wasn't perfect. In fact, it was probably no use at all. But it was all I could find, so I lifted it out and gripped it tight in my fist.

And so I found myself dressed in just a pair of tatty Y-fronts, gently squeezing down the handle of the bedroom door, with nothing but a bright pink 'rampant rabbit' to protect myself with. Quite why Dylan had a vibrator hidden away in his sock drawer, I couldn't really say. And I wasn't entirely certain I wanted to know. Besides, I had slightly more pressing matters at hand.

I inched the door open slowly. The narrowest crack appeared between it and the doorframe. I opened it a little more. Then a little more, careful not to make a sound. I peered tentatively out, holding the sex toy at head height, ready to defend myself.

The long hallway was dark and empty. No one in sight. My heart beat hard and my breath came in short, ragged gasps. A thin beam of light suddenly shot down the hall, streaking the floor and climbing the wall as the burglars turned on the kitchen light.

Cheeky bastards! I thought. Where were their torches? Where was the skulking and the secrecy? They didn't even have the common decency to burgle the place properly – they'd just burst in, thrown on the lights and strolled about the place, casual as you like. What kind of burglars were they? And then I remembered – they might just be the type of burglars who were actually here to kill me.

I held my breath. My legs felt weak. I'm not too proud to admit that I felt a little bit like crying. I looked back at the bed, briefly entertaining the idea of jumping back under the covers and cowering there until they'd gone. But it was no good. I had to get to that phone.

I took a long, calming breath, slowly pulled the door open and eased my way out into the hallway. I pressed my back tight up against the wall, holding my weapon high, swivelling my head to look this way and that. I inched along the hall – creeping silent and stealthy. In my head, I was a ninja. Outside of my head, I was an overweight, middle-aged man in his pants, gripping tight to a bright pink sex toy.

From down the hall I heard cupboards opening and slamming shut. Footsteps. Muttering. Loud, disgruntled sighs.

"Where the hell is it?" a voice suddenly said. A man's voice. Frustrated. Probably in his late 20s or early 30s. He spoke in a soft London accent – not terribly threatening or scary.

"Where's the stuff?" he said. "Where's the money? The jewels? Anything?"

"I dunno," a second voice replied. Female this time. Also a London accent, all high-pitched and squeaky. "Just keep looking, it must be here somewhere. He always keeps a few grand in cash around the place for emergencies. And the jewellery has to be here too."

So, they were definitely burglars and not just here to kill me. Not that they wouldn't still kill me if they caught me skulking around the flat. But at least that wasn't their primary mission. My heart slowed from a rampant thudding to a mild, panicked throb.

Not only were they not lethal, maniacal assassins, one of them was a woman. Not that women can't bludgeon you to death, or stab you in the kidney, or shoot you in the face, or reach down, grab your balls and yank them off... but I was slightly relieved to know that one of the burly men I'd been afraid of wasn't actually a man. A touch sexist? Probably. But this was hardly the time to worry about that.

Besides, I reckoned I could probably punch a woman in the face and run away screaming. I mean, if I absolutely had to. If she was trying to yank off my balls, for example. I know you're not supposed to punch women, but needs must, and all that. I made a mental note to be slightly ashamed of myself at a later date. Then I breathed out hard and gripped the pink dildo tighter in my hand.

The biggest revelation, of course, was that they clearly knew Dylan. They knew he wouldn't be here. They knew what sort of stuff they'd be likely to find. And from the way they went easily from one room to the next, I guessed they also had more than a cursory knowledge of the flat.

I inched my way another step down the hall.

"Where the bloody hell is it all?" the male burglar complained, slamming another cupboard door. Then there was another crash, like one of the sofas was being tipped over. "There's gotta be a safe here or something..."

"I dunno," said the female accomplice. "He had a safe in the big house, but that's burned down now, hasn't it?"

The big house, I thought to myself. Another damning piece of evidence. Not only did this woman know Dylan, she'd obviously been here at the flat before. She also knew about his former residence. She knew where he kept things.

"There might be something in the bedroom," she said. "He sometimes kept money in the bedroom."

"Fine, let's go and look," he said.

Oh shit! I thought. I was standing just a few feet from Dylan's bedroom. There was no way to get down the hall and past them without them seeing me. And if I ran back to the bedroom, it wouldn't take them long to find me. I heard footsteps on the laminate flooring. I looked behind me, then forwards to the living room. The footsteps moved closer. I couldn't even dash across to the other bedroom in time.

They were nearly on me. I took a deep breath, gripped the dildo tighter and raised it high above my head.

They moved into the hallway, flicked on the light switch and froze as they saw me. The man did a quick double-take and nearly fell over his own feet as he blurted out, "What the fuck?"

The female burglar stopped dead in her tracks. She wobbled slightly on a pair of ridiculously high-heeled shoes and let out a shrill, piercing squeal. Not a scream exactly, more of a squeak – the kind of noise a small dog makes when you stand on its foot.

I gripped the dildo tighter, accidentally pressing one of the buttons. It jolted into life, emitting a loud buzzing sound and juddering violently in my hand.

"Don't fucking well come any closer, you fuckers," I shouted. "Or I'll fucking fuck you!"

Not exactly the most eloquent of utterances, but I was tired, scared and confused. And I thought it got the message across quite effectively. Then it suddenly dawned on me that I was thrusting a large, buzzing sex toy towards them. And I realised my words could have been misconstrued.

"You fucking what?" said the man.

"What are you doing with my rampant rabbit?" said the woman.

I instantly recognised her. She was petite and blonde, with a stunning face, a slim body, long legs and big boobs. It was Dylan's fourth wife, Chantelle Star.

"Who the fuck are you?" said the male burglar. "What are you doing here?"

"And what are you doing with my rabbit?" asked Chantelle. "I've been looking everywhere for that."

"Who am *I*?" I said, thrusting the pink device in as threatening a manner as I could. "Who the fuck are *you*? And what are *you* doing here?"

They both stared back, silent.

"Actually, forget that," I said, "it's pretty obvious what you're doing here. You're taking advantage of a poor, sick man and robbing him blind while he's laid up in hospital."

"It's not robbing, actually," said the woman. "We're allowed to be here. I have keys."

Chantelle held up a set of shiny, silver keys, as if to illustrate the point. They twinkled and glinted in the light, a furry pink keyring hanging off them, like they'd just been stolen from a seven year old.

"Oh really," I said, "I wonder if the police would agree with you. What have you been doing in there? Turning over sofas? Ransacking drawers and cupboards, looking for cash? It's not as if you've just popped round to water the plants, is it? What do you think; shall we call them and find out?"

A look of guilty terror flashed across both their faces. The man opened his mouth to speak, but no words came out.

"No, I thought not," I said.

"Look, we don't want any trouble," said the man. "This is Dylan's wife; we've only come for what she's owed."

"Ex-wife," I corrected him. "Now, I'm no lawyer, but I'm pretty sure she got everything she was owed in the divorce. And the fact that you don't seem able to find whatever it is you've come here looking for, leads me to suspect that you're actually just here to get your hands on whatever cash and valuables you can find."

"No, we wasn't," said Chantelle, the sudden panic making her voice sound even more squeaky and cockney, "we was looking for something I left here."

"And what's that exactly?"

"Er… for… for…" she looked around the hallway, her eyes searching this way and that. "Er… for that," she said finally, her eyes resting on the sex toy in my hand.

"This," I said, once again thrusting it menacingly in her direction, "you came here for this? In the middle of the night?"

"Well... I needed it," she said.

The man at her side rolled his eyes.

"Nothing to do with the spare couple of grand you were saying Dylan keeps around the place?" I made a mental note to go in search of the money myself, once I'd got rid of these two. "Or the jewellery?"

Her face went blank, her eyes flickering slightly as she searched for a clever reply. "Fuck off," she said, finally.

"Look, we don't want no trouble," said the male burglar. "No need to call the police. We're sorry to wake you up and startle you. We really didn't mean any harm. We're just a bit skint, and we thought we could sneak in and get some cash without anyone knowing."

"Hmmm..." I said.

"And you may as well put that thing down. What were you gonna do with it, anyway? Vibrate us to death?"

"Fair point," I said, pressing the button to turn the dildo off and handing it to Chantelle. She took it and placed in her big, pink handbag.

We stood for a few seconds, looking gormlessly at each other, no one quite sure what to do next.

"So," I said, breaking the silence, "now that we've established that you're not here to kill me, and I'm not letting you leave with anything more valuable than a plastic penis... can I offer you a tea or coffee?"

CHAPTER 22

OBVIOUSLY, IT'S NOT standard protocol to make hot beverages for people that break in and ransack your house at 2am. But I was already up and buzzing with adrenaline. So, it was highly unlikely I'd get back to sleep any time soon.

Besides, I figured while I had Dylan's fourth wife as a captive audience, it was the perfect opportunity to carry on with my investigations and quiz her. Chantelle and her friend were somewhat confused at the sudden change of tack, but reluctantly accepted when I reminded them that I could still call the police. And when I told them their faces were being captured by hidden CCTV cameras as we spoke, they practically raced me to the kitchen. Whether or not Dylan actually has CCTV in his flat, I have no idea. But they weren't taking the chance.

I flicked on the fancy coffee machine, instructed the male burglar to get back in the living room and bloody well turn the sofas the right way up, then we all stood in the kitchen drinking coffee.

The man's name was Simon Clarkson and he was Chantelle's new boyfriend. At least, that was the story they gave at first. However, it didn't take a genius to realise they were trying to hide something. And then Chantelle slipped up and told me they had first met during a modelling assignment – at least a year before she'd started being photographed in all the papers with Dylan. So, clearly Simon wasn't just a new acquaintance.

It didn't take a great deal more probing to find out that, not only had their relationship begun before her marriage to Dylan had ended, it had actually been going in secret throughout their whole relationship.

"So, you were just using Dylan and carrying on behind his back?" I said.

"No, it wasn't like that. It was more about the money," she admitted, sounding strangely pleased with herself. "You know, like a business arrangement."

"The money? So, you're a whore?" I snapped.

"I am not a whore," she shouted. "And there's nothing illegal about it. I had a proper contract and everything."

She nodded her head in defiance, a smug look glinting in her eyes. Her boyfriend sighed and shook his head.

"Wait, hang on a second," I said. "You had a contract to sleep with Dylan?"

"Sleep with him? No, to marry him. The man told me to treat it just like any other acting job. Only real life. Like that film... The Truman Show."

"You're saying Dylan paid you to marry him? He paid you to be his wife?"

"I think you've said enough, darling," Simon cut in. He raised his eyebrows, glaring hard at Chantelle, as if trying to convey some psychic message to shut the fuck up.

"Wait, what's going on here?" I said. "What's she talking about?"

"It's nothing. She's just a bit confused."

"Nothing?" I said, raising my voice. "My best friend – your ex-husband – is lying in a hospital bed with a bloody great hole in his chest because someone shot him with a harpoon gun. This is after he tells me he thinks someone's trying to kill him. Then I catch you two breaking in here, trying to rob the place. And now you're telling me that you were paid to marry Dylan. Call me a conspiracy theorist, but I can't help feeling like all these things are connected somehow."

"We had nothing to do with what happened to Dylan," said Simon.

"Really? Well, why don't we get the police round here after all?" I said, picking up the phone. "I'm sure they'll be very interested in talking to you?"

"It's not what you think," he said, a chord of panic ringing in his voice.

"What isn't?" I said, raising my thumb and theatrically pressing down on the '9' key.

"We're not involved in anything," he pleaded. "We can't say."

"Can't say what?" I said, pressing the second '9'.

The two of them looked at each other, worry darting back and forth between their eyes.

"Last chance," I said, my thumb hovering over the key, ready to press again.

"All right, all right," he said, raising his palms to me. "I'll tell you. But it's not what you think."

*****

KILLING DYLAN

Chantelle and Dylan first met on the set for the film adaptation of Dylan's novel, *Once Upon a Never*, in which she'd landed an acting role. It was a bit part, with just one line, but she'd been over the moon to get an actual part, in an actual movie – starring alongside Keira Knightley, no less. At least, that's what she'd told people. The fact that Keira didn't actually appear in her brief scene, hadn't been on set that day, and had never actually even met Chantelle was entirely beside the point.

It was her big break – the thing that was going to take her away from flashing her boobs in the lads' mags, and get her on the road to Hollywood stardom. Of course, the role basically just involved her looking pretty and flashing her boobs, but everyone has to start somewhere.

During a break in filming, Chantelle had approached Dylan, under the mistaken assumption that he was one of the film's producers. She'd flirted with him, hoping he might be able to get her a few more lines in the movie, or maybe even a bigger, better part in one of his other films. She'd thought he seemed nice, but when she found out he was only a novelist, with no direct connections to casting, she'd moved on to someone else who looked even more important.

A few days later, however, she started receiving invitations to lots of different events. There were book launches, art gallery shows, movie premieres and showbiz parties. And she was thrilled to go to every single one of them. They were great places to network – you never knew which celebs, agents or producers you might bump into. And if the paparazzi happened to snap her picture, so much the better.

At first she had no idea who the invitations were from. But when she kept bumping into Dylan at each event, she assumed he had taken a shine to her and had her name added to the guest lists so that he could see her again. Every time she bumped into him at a party, however, he always acted surprised to see her. It was as if he wasn't the one getting her invited at all.

A few weeks went by and Chantelle attended a few more awards ceremonies and star-studded events. The whole time, Dylan kept up his act of surprise. Then she received a phone call out of the blue, asking her to come in for a meeting with a lawyer.

"It wasn't Charles Walker, of Walker, Hawkes and Byrne, by any chance?" I asked, remembering the name I got from Corinne Handley.

"Yeah," said Chantelle, "how d'you know that?"

"Call it an educated guess."

191

"So, anyway, we go to meet this guy," said Simon. "Posh lawyer at this big firm in the city. We sit down in his office, and he starts talking about Dylan and how he's taken a shine to Chantelle. Then he says he has quite an unorthodox proposal to make. He wants her to marry Dylan."

"Really?" I said. "And what did you say?"

"Well, I wasn't having any of that, was I? I said to the guy, who does this Dylan St James think he is, going around proposing to other men's girlfriends? I mean, in fairness, Chantelle hadn't ever actually told him she had a boyfriend – but that's still not the point."

"Why did she never mention you to Dylan?"

"It's business. She has to keep our relationship a secret. For one thing, the lads' mags readers prefer it if they think the model they're ogling is single. It makes them seem more attainable. So, Chantelle has always kept her relationships secret. Haven't you babe?

"Also, it helps when you're trying to get movie parts. A lot of these producers prefer it if the actresses are single. So Chantelle kept me a secret. But it's still a bloody liberty."

"Quite," I said.

"Besides, I told the lawyer, if this Dylan bloke's so keen to marry Chantelle, why isn't he here asking her himself?"

"And?" I asked.

"Apparently it was a bit more complicated than that. The lawyer tells me that, technically, Dylan didn't actually know that he was proposing."

"Technically?" I said, getting more confused. "What the hell does that mean?"

"Well, the lawyer says that Dylan is really shy when it comes to meeting women. So, he's been hired to 'make arrangements' for a suitable match." He curled his fingers into quote marks. "He says that Dylan really likes Chantelle and he thinks she's a perfect candidate."

"Right..." I said. "So, he wants to pay Chantelle to marry him? For the rest of her life? And you're fine with that?'"

"Well, that's it. It's not for the rest of her life. The lawyer tells me it's only for a 'contractually obligated period of time'." Again, he waved his finger quotes at me.

"What period of time?"

"Well, that's what got me," Simon laughed. "It was only six months. I said to him, what's the point in that? But the lawyer tells me it's more common that you'd think. All the celebs are doing it. They marry someone else famous, or sort of famous, so they can get their face in the paper. All good publicity for the latest film, or album, or book. Then at the end of it they split up, get back in the papers and, hey presto, more publicity for the next film."

"No. I'm not buying it," I said. "I've known Dylan for more than twenty years, and he certainly never had any problems picking up women. He wouldn't play that sort of press manipulation game, either. What's in it for him? His books sell already millions of copies."

Chantelle and Simon both shrugged.

"And I don't believe he did marry you just for publicity," I continued. "He had feelings for you. He was really upset that you'd split up – I could see it when I spoke to him."

Chantelle looked to the floor, a hint of remorse flashing in her eyes.

"Yeah, well," said Simon. "That's where it gets a bit tricky. The lawyer tells us Chantelle's never allowed to mention anything about the arrangement to Dylan. In fact, it's all part of the deal. She's not allowed to talk to him about any of it – the contract, the money, the lawyer, nothing. She's not allowed to tell anyone. Although, now that people are nearly being murdered, I suppose it hardly seems important to keep secrets."

"Besides," cut in Chantelle, looking even more sorrowful, "we've spent all the money, anyway."

"This in unbelievable," I said, anger burning in my chest. "So, how did it work? How did you end up getting married if Dylan didn't know anything about the deal?"

"They told me I should continue bumping into him at events," said Chantelle. "Flirt with him. Ask him out to dinner. That sort of thing. I was supposed to come on to him, and everything would fall into place."

"So, Dylan had no idea. As far as he was concerned, you were genuinely interested in him. Genuinely flirting with him. He really thought you liked him. You deceived him."

"No, it wasn't like that," she protested. Then a flash of shame and sorrow eclipsed her face. "At least... at least... oh, I don't know. At first, when they asked me to do it, I figured he knew all about it. I thought it was one of those rich bloke's fantasies, where he needed a wife but didn't want to admit to paying for one. He wanted to feel like the woman was chasing him. They told me to treat it like an acting role, so I assumed he was doing the same. Just pretending."

"Pretending?" I laughed.

"Yeah, I thought he knew exactly what was going on. But then…"

"Then?"

"Well, after we'd been dating for a few weeks, and things seemed to be going well, I did start to wonder. Then he proposed, just like he was supposed to – like I was expecting, because of everything that was in the contract. But suddenly it didn't seem right anymore."

"Why not?"

"It was… well, he put so much effort into it. I'd assumed it would be very straightforward. You know, like the contract had been. But he did it all romantic. He took me out for this lovely day out and we had a picnic down by this beautiful river. And then he pulls out this ring and proposes. But he seemed so shy, like he was worried that I might say no. But why would I? He must have known I'd signed the contract, so of course I'm gonna say yes. So then I started wondering, what if he didn't know?"

"But you still said yes?" I asked her.

"Well, of course I did. I had to. I'd signed the contract, hadn't I? And he seemed so happy when I said yes, that's when I figured something was up."

"And what did you do?"

"Me and Simon went to see the lawyer. He told me the deal was still on, and still the same. Now that Dylan had proposed, I was to tell him I wanted a quick wedding. After we tied the knot, we'd stay married for six months and then I'd be free to divorce him."

"And you asked him whether or not Dylan knew anything about the deal?"

"Of course. He just told me Dylan was eccentric, and I should play along with it. But I definitely wasn't allowed to ask him about it, or mention anything to do with the contract, or I wouldn't get any of the money."

"So, what did you do?"

"What could I do? I told you, I'd already signed the contract. And I really wanted the money."

"Of course you did," I sneered. "How much money are we talking about, by the way?"

"A million pounds," said Chantelle, more pleased with herself than she really should have been. "Half after the wedding, and then the other half after the divorce. And they made me sign another thing… a pre-natal."

"Pre-nuptial?" I corrected.

"Yeah, preenupshall," she repeated. "Said I couldn't sue Dylan for any more money after we split up."

"A million quid," I said, my voice dripping with disdain. "You sold yourself, you conned a good man, and you ruined his life for a measly million quid?"

I made a mental list of all the downright horrible things I would probably do for even a quarter of that sum.

"Well, I'm not exactly proud of it," she said. "But I really thought Dylan was in on it. And I needed the money."

"Hang on," I said, "if you got a million quid for marrying and divorcing Dylan a year ago, what the hell are you doing breaking in here looking for cash?"

"It's like Chantelle already told you," said Simon. "We've spent it."

"You spent it? A million quid in a year? That's disgusting."

I made another mental list of just how quickly I would have burned through a million pounds – what with all the sports cars, fancy meals, five-star hotels, booze, parties, gadgets, trinkets, holidays and nights out with women who charge by the hour (if you know what I mean). I figured it was about six weeks.

"You should be ashamed of yourselves," I said, indignantly.

"Paying for an acting career don't come cheap, you know," countered Chantelle. "I have to buy expensive clothes so I look the part for auditions. I have to travel up and down the country doing readings. And I wasn't getting any parts. So, with no earnings coming in, the money soon disappeared. I didn't get any of the work the lawyer said I'd get. He told me marrying Dylan would raise my profile and the roles would come flooding in. But it was exactly the opposite. All the producers said I was too famous, and they didn't want the wrong kind of press for the movie. Some of them even had the nerve to say I couldn't act good.

"So, I paid to go out and spend six weeks in Hollywood, trying to get work there. But I couldn't even get an agent."

"Oh, what a shame," I said.

"Now we're back home," continued Chantelle. "We're completely skint and staying in my mum's spare room."

"What about this million pound apartment of yours that I've read about in the papers?"

"That? That was never mine. Not owned, anyway. It was just rented.

As soon as we couldn't pay the rent, they kicked us out."

"Can't you go back to your modelling work?" I asked her.

"I don't do that anymore," she said defiantly, "I'm a serious actress now, not a lads' mag model. Besides, they won't offer me any shoots. They reckon I've been away too long. There's a load of new girls that the readers like now – all 19, fresh-faced and stealing my jobs. Imagine that, twenty-five years old and I'm already past it. The only thing I've been offered is getting my bits out in Mayfair for three hundred quid – and I'm definitely not doing that!"

"And what about you?" I said to Simon, who had gone suspiciously quiet. "Where's your money? Or are you just happy leaching off your washed-up, twenty-five year old girlfriend and stealing from invalids?"

"If you must know," he said, "I'm an artist. I'm close to being discovered. We just need some extra money until Chantelle gets an acting job, or I sell one of my paintings."

"Paintings?" I sneered disapprovingly. "What do you draw?"

"Draw?" he said, screwing up his face like the word tasted bad in his mouth. "Draw? I don't draw. I create experiential mind landscapes. I explore the depths of my soul and regurgitate my emotions onto canvas. And I use my own bodily fluids – sperm, saliva, blood, hair, skin and nails – in every piece, to make it even more real, personal and vivid."

"Regurgitate?" I said. "Mind landscape? Sperm? I can't imagine why you haven't sold any."

He gave me a look that suggested he'd quite like to punch me in the face. I know that look well. I've seen it on the faces of quite a few people in the past – usually just before they punch me in the face.

"So, you earned a million quid for marrying Dylan, but you don't think he knew anything about it?"

"At first I did. I swear, I thought he was in on it. But after we got married, and I moved into the big house, a few things made me suspect he might not be."

"What things?"

"Little things, really. He was always so affectionate and caring, buying me little presents and taking an interest in me. It was like he really did love me, not a marriage of convenience at all. And he was always up for the... you know... sex. Quite insatiable, actually."

"You were sleeping with him?"

Simon looked away, grimacing hard as if repeating some well-worn mantra in his head.

"Well, yeah, of course," said Chantelle. "We *were* married. When that lawyer first asked me if I was interested in marrying Dylan, I asked him if I was expected to have sex with him too. He told me it was completely my choice. I was a bit wary at first, but then I thought, well I am getting a million quid. So it only seemed fair, really. And it's not as if he's exactly horrible to look at…" A mischievous grin flashed across her lips.

"But she was only doing it as part of a role. Like a sex scene in a movie," snapped Simon.

I don't think any of us really believed that. Especially not him.

"And that doesn't make me a whore," said Chantelle, defiantly. "Like I said, I had a contract."

"If that's what you wanna tell yourself, love," I said. "And where were you, Simon, while all this was going on? Sitting at home, watching your spunk paintings dry?"

He breathed hard out of his nose, his mouth curling into a grimace.

"And I presume you two were still seeing each other behind Dylan's back?" I continued.

"Look, we know none of this is right," said Simon. "And we're not exactly proud of ourselves. But it was a million quid. A million quid."

"Let's get this straight," I said. "If Dylan didn't know about this, it's fairly obvious the money didn't actually come from him. So where did it come from? Who would want to pay you to marry Dylan? And why?"

They both stared at me blankly. "I dunno," said Chantelle, "we only ever met the lawyer bloke? Do you think it was him?"

"Well, no. Most likely someone he was working for. I think I might have to go and pay this Mr Walker a visit."

A silence hung between us in the kitchen, as we stood there sipping Dylan's expensive coffee.

"Right then," I said quite abruptly, "you two had better fuck off before I really do call the police."

I showed them to the door. "And if I see either of you around here again, or anywhere near Dylan, I'll be straight on to the papers to tell them all about your little sham marriage. I can't see the serious acting roles flooding in when they find out what you're really like."

I was expecting an indignant outburst, but they both just stood there looking forlorn and a little sorry for themselves.

"And no more emails begging for money, either," I said. "Dylan's been through enough thanks to you two parasites, without having to deal with that as well."

I watched them walk out of the flat and slammed the door behind them.

CHAPTER 23

MY HEART WAS still pounding a bossa nova in my chest. There was so much adrenaline in my blood I could have syphoned some off and marketed it as a new energy drink. I was far too wired to get any sleep. Aside from the fear, the caffeine and the utter bewilderment at what had just happened, my mind was absolutely racing with details of the case. I was in desperate need of calming.

I made myself a hot chocolate from one of the pods in Dylan's fancy coffee machine (this thing really was marvellous. I was going to have to look into buying myself one when I left – or maybe see if I could take Dylan's with me) and went through to the living room. I sat on one of the recently turned-back-over sofas and flicked on the television. There really is nothing like a spot of mindless TV to numb the senses.

It was just after 4am, so of course there was nothing on. At least, nothing worth watching. There must have been about a thousand channels on the fancy subscription TV box, and absolutely bugger all shows of any interest whatsoever. I preferred the good old days, when there were just four channels to pick from – there was still sod all on, but at least you didn't risk getting a repetitive strain injury from all the channel flipping.

I flicked through the list until my thumb started aching. I gave up when I reached one of those channels that only shows crap from the 80s and 90s, re-packaged as 'classic TV'. The programme on was a British detective show that I vaguely remembered from the early to mid-90s. It was called *Parish and the Priest*, and followed the unlikely adventures of DCI Steven Parish. It was your typical lazy cop show, with one key twist – the detective solved cases with the help of a super-sleuthing priest. You'd think it was a comedy, but no. It took itself far too seriously.

The Priest in question, Father Seamus O'Malley (as if they couldn't find a more generic, ridiculous name), was an amateur crime-solver. He always had his ear to the ground, and an uncanny ability to find himself in dangerous situations. He also heard plenty in confession and, although he was forbidden from revealing any of the details, he was able to point DCI Parish in the right direction. Seriously, who makes this shit up? If James Patterson did TV shows, this is what you'd get.

I remember the programme being universally panned, receiving some of the worst ratings ever, and being cancelled after just one series. Classic television, my arse!

I sipped my hot chocolate and let my eyes glaze over as I watched the show.

In the episode I was watching, DCI Parish was on the trail of a gang of armed robbers who'd been knocking over banks and jewellery shops all over town. One of the gang's henchmen just happened to be – you guessed it! – a religious type who couldn't help but reveal every single detail of a forthcoming job to his local priest. Who just so happened to be Father Seamus. I mean, for fuck's sake.

The trite dialogue and terrible acting did its job, however. Before long, my heart rate returned to normal and I felt a great deal calmer. Detective Parish was waiting to ambush his prey. I was drinking my last sip of chocolate and getting ready to turn this drivel off and head back to bed. And then I saw him.

It was almost imperceptible at first. Like a switch being flicked on in my head, but I wasn't sure what the switch was for. Then I saw him again. Another one of the show's characters. Father Seamus's sidekick, Father Christopher.

He was a younger man, under the tutelage of the older priest and his questions often sparked within Father Seamus the eureka moment that helped him crack whatever case he was working on.

When Father Christopher appeared on screen, it was like déjà vu, or some strange awakening. It was as if my brain was telling me to sit up and pay attention. I put down my cup, focused hard on the TV. There was something strangely familiar about the man. I was certain I knew his face, but I couldn't tell where from. And there was something in his voice – a whiny, nasal intonation that I knew I'd heard before. I just couldn't put my finger on it.

The conversation ended and Father Christopher exited the shot. And now my mind was racing. Why did I recognise this man? And why did it matter? I had no idea, but I knew I had to find out.

I fumbled for the remote control, quickly rewound it, and watched intently as Father Christopher repeated his five lines of dialogue. I watched it again – two, three times, but still I couldn't get it. Like an itch deep in the centre of my brain and I couldn't reach to scratch it.

I clamped my eyes tight shut. I searched my brain, playing the words over and over again. I scanned the image of the man's face in my mind's eye. And then it came to me. Of course!

Excitedly, I opened my eyes, rewound the programme again and paused it with a full-sized image of Father Christopher on the screen.

My God, it was. It really was him.

Add about ten years, a few flecks of grey hair and a stupid goatee beard. Replace the priest's dog collar with a roll-neck jumper and... yes. It was him. It was definitely him. Dr Michael Jeffries. Dylan's shrink.

I ran through to Dylan's study, powered up his laptop and clicked onto the Internet Movie Database (IMDB.com). It's an incredibly useful site that chronicles movies and TV shows from throughout the years. It has a wealth of useful information from the shows' plots to when they were made, who directed them and, most importantly, who played the various characters.

I typed Parish and the Priest into the search bar and clicked go. As the show was pretty old – not to mention a bit of a flop – I wasn't sure there'd be much information. But I scrolled down the list of search results and, sure enough, there it was. I clicked on the link, found the show's detail page and scrolled down the list of actors.

There he was. Father Christopher played by Douglas Moone.

Next to the entry was a picture of the actor. It was one of those professionally-taken portfolio shots – all teeth and eyes trying to convey every single possible emotion in one snap. The man in the picture was a few years older than Father Christopher had been in the show. He had greying hair, a few extra wrinkles and a slightly chubbier face. There was no beard, or roll neck, but there was absolutely no doubt in my mind that the man in the picture – Douglas Moone – was Dr Jeffries.

What the hell was going on? Who was this guy? I knew there had been something a bit fishy about him when I met him, but why the hell was Dylan's therapist listed as an actor on a website? And why the different name?

I clicked the hyperlink on the actor's name and went through to another page dedicated to him. The biography section had been left blank, but it did list the actor's other appearances throughout the years. There were a handful of listings – *The Bill*, *EastEnders*, *Men Behaving Badly*, *Minder* and several others. Seemingly all bit parts.

The most recent entry was for a show called *Dark Days, Dangerous Nights* in 2004. He'd appeared in three episodes. And nothing since.

Who was this guy? An actor who had retrained as a therapist? Somehow it seemed unlikely. And why would he have changed his name?

I typed 'Douglas Moone Actor' into Google and got a selection of hits. The first was his Wikipedia page, listing his roles to date and a short biography. Apparently, he had grown up in Woking, moved to London and spent the last twenty years as a 'highly successful' star of stage and screen. Well, not if his IMDB page was anything to go by.

It was also proof that you can write literally anything you want on Wikipedia and get away with it. It's something I've been known to do myself in the past, and the reason why the James Patterson Wikipedia page used to chronicle his involvement in war crimes, and at one point claimed that his publishing empire was funded by blood diamonds. The things you do when you're drunk!

I scanned a few more search results and found mentions of Douglas Moone on several other sites. There was a Facebook page about him, saying much the same as the Wikipedia page. There were tiny mentions on a few other actor type sites. And some sad loser had even set up a fan site dedicated to *Parish and the Priest*. Seriously, do people have nothing better to do?

Not one of the sites, however, featured any mention of Douglas Moone retraining as a shrink and changing his name.

I tried 'Douglas Moone Therapist'. Nothing. I tried 'Douglas Moone Dr Jeffries'. Nothing. I tried multiple combinations of the two names. Absolutely nothing.

It was looking very much like Dylan was currently being counselled – and given some very bad psychiatric advice – by a failed actor, using a fake name, with apparently no professional qualifications at all.

Bizarrely, it was now all starting to make sense. The poor, typo-ridden emails. The psychiatrist who sets up his own appointments. The unorthodox home visits. This guy wasn't a shrink at all; he was just 'acting' like a shrink. But why?

I clicked open Dylan's emails and re-read the first one he'd received from Dr Jeffries:

Dear Dylan,

I have been provided your details by your agent, Mr Mortimer Bunkle, who feels I may be of some assistance to you. Mortimer tells me you've been feeling a bit down recently, and asked if I would consult with you...

Mortimer. Did he have something to do with this?

I went back to the Wikipedia page and scanned through the entry. Nothing stood out.

I clicked back to Douglas Moone's Facebook page. Nothing. Nothing. Nothing. Then finally, there it was. A tiny entry at the bottom of the ABOUT section:

If you are interested in hiring Douglas Moone for any acting roles, please contact the Mortimer Bunkle Literary and Talent Agency.

******

There were a number of reasons I could think of for someone hiring a fake shrink:

1. Competition was heating up over who would get to publish Dylan's new masterpiece book. Was it really beyond the realms of possibility that one of the big publishers would use underhand tactics to get their hands on the rights to one of the biggest books of the year? Maybe even the decade. They could have hired Douglas to unsettle Dylan, make him paranoid and depressed, and steer him towards signing a deal with their company.

2. Dylan has lots of ex-wives. Maybe one of them had hired Douglas to fuck with Dylan's head as part of some twisted revenge plot.

3. Maybe Douglas's role was part of an elaborate financial scam. He could have been hired to unsettle Dylan, convince him he'd be happier without his vast fortune – that the money was the thing bringing him down, and the only way to ever be happy was to give it all away. In that case, the culprit could have been anyone from the ex-wives to Douglas himself. Or even the local Cats Protection League – some of these charities can be really underhanded in their fundraising tactics.

4. Dylan could have personally harmed Douglas in the past – said something mean about him in the press, or written a bad review of *Parish and the Priest* – and this was all part of some personal vendetta.

5. It could have been one of Dylan's literary rivals, messing with his head to try and stop him from writing another book. Thereby taking out their biggest competition for the end of the year hardback sales.

The more I thought about it, the more theories I came up with. Admittedly, some were more ridiculous and fantastical than others.

There was also that link to Mortimer. Now, just because Mortimer's name had been linked to this charlatan, it didn't mean he was necessarily involved. In his heyday, Mortimer had represented hundreds of clients. He could have been duped into providing Douglas's services. Or he might not even know anything about it.

The same went for Dr Shepton. There was a clear, tangible link between him and Mortimer. It wasn't proof of any wrongdoing on Mortimer's part, but in a little over forty-eight hours, I'd discovered two supposed medical professionals providing Dylan with advice that was, at best, misguided and incorrect. At worst, it was dangerous, suspect and potentially life-threatening. And both of them had been indisputably linked to Mortimer Bunkle. It was far too big a coincidence to ignore. I'd have to go back and ask Mortimer a few more questions.

I continued Googling for another half an hour, searching for any further information on Douglas Moone. But I couldn't get any closer to a definitive motive.

Finally, I logged into my own email account. There was disappointingly little of any interest – a handful of PPI emails and a spurious offer to earn thousands of pounds from the comfort of my own sofa.

There was also an email from my publisher, asking how I was getting on with my new book, and why the hell they still hadn't seen a first draft. The answer was quite simple – because I hadn't written one.

I heard the distant sound of my phone beeping in the kitchen. I retrieved it and carried it through to the bedroom, checking the messages as I went.

There was another voicemail from Mr Singh, asking why I hadn't returned any of his calls, and threatening me with the bailiffs. From experience, I knew I had at least two more of these phone calls to come before I actually needed to start worrying.

There was a message from my agent – the first one this year – asking why the bloody hell I hadn't sent a first draft to the publisher yet. I deleted it straight away.

Finally, there was a text message from Caroline, calling me a prick, telling me I was the worst shag she'd ever had, and then still having the audacity to ask if I'd introduce her to Dylan when he finally got out of hospital. Crazy fucking stalker.

I leaned back and rested my head against the pillow. It was 6.04am and a golden haze of sunrise was beginning to creep in through the gap at the edge of the curtains. I closed my eyes and fell fast asleep.

CHAPTER 24

"I'M SORRY, BUT Mr Walker's schedule is completely full today. It doesn't look like you'll be able to get an appointment to speak with him until at least next week, I'm afraid. Can I ask what it's concerning?"

I was stood in the reception area of Walker, Hawkes and Byrne Solicitors. After the previous evening's excitement, I'd slept in until after lunch. So, I'd lost a good half a day of detecting, and my plan to drop in on the lawyer Chantelle had told me about wasn't running as smoothly as I'd hoped.

I'd chanced my arm at getting a last minute appointment, like I had with Dr Shepton. But the snooty, busybody receptionist wasn't being at all helpful. She looked to be about fifty years old – short and haggard, and wearing a frilly blouse. She had one of those faces that suggested she was not to be messed with. I guessed this was about the extent of the power she had in the world – refusing people access to see lawyers – and she was relishing the delight of turning me away.

"Are you sure you can't squeeze me in?" I said. "It's really rather urgent and I need to see a lawyer today. My friend recommended Mr Walker. I'm sure he's the only one who can help me."

She just looked up at me, her face puckered with smug condescension, like she wouldn't lend me a thimbleful of water if my head was on fire.

"As I say, he's really not free. If you like I can call through to Mr Walker's assistant, and she might be able to book you in for a meeting next..." She looked down at the onscreen calendar, then clicked a few times on her mouse. "Next Thursday? Is it to do with your...?" She pointed at my black eye and swollen nose.

"Actually, no. It's a rather delicate matter, which I'd prefer to discuss with Mr Walker in person."

This really put her nose out of joint. She raised one eyebrow, folding her arms defiantly across her chest. I could see I wasn't going to get her to budge, so I did the next best thing – I started coughing. Loudly. As loud as I could. I gripped my throat, coughing and rasping, my face turning a bright, violent shade of red.

The woman looked up at me, concern suddenly flashing in her eyes.

I laid it on even thicker, hacking and spluttering, and practically shrieking. Cough. Hack. Cough.

I gripped onto the edge of the reception desk, like my legs were going to collapse under me. Cough. Hack. Cough.

I pointed at my throat, mouthing the word 'water'. Cough. Cough. Hack.

"Please," I managed to rasp, "water…" Then I dropped to my knees.

She jumped up from her seat, panicking and flapping. She gazed over the desk, looking down at my dying swan act on the floor. "Oh Goodness," she said. "Oh my goodness. Wait right there." Then she pressed a door release button on the underside of the reception desk and ran off, disappearing out through a set of now unlocked security doors to the right of the desk.

I jumped up from the floor, dashed for the door and managed to catch it just before it clicked shut again. I took a good look at the schedule the receptionist had left open on her computer screen, then sneaked through, moving as quickly and quietly as I could.

Beyond the doors was a large office space, lined on either side with trendy, glass-walled meeting rooms – luckily all vacant. A long corridor, with plush, expensive carpet, led off into the distance. I stepped carefully along the hall. As I neared an open door, I heard the sound of cupboards opening, glasses clinking and then a tap being turned on – presumably the life-saving glass of water the receptionist was fetching for me. I darted into one of the absent meeting rooms, hiding behind the door, as she came out of the little kitchen area and breezed past me.

I heard the mechanical click of the door unlocking. It was quickly followed by an exasperated, "Well, where the hell did he go?" Then the security door clicked shut and I was all alone.

I waited a few moments until the coast was clear, then emerged from the room. I sneaked up to the security door and peered through the little window. The receptionist was looking down at the floor in front of the desk. She looked over at the main entrance, shook her head in confusion, then returned and sat back down in her seat.

I blew out a sigh of relief, turned back to the office behind me and crept along the corridor. It came to a T-junction at the end, with signs on the far wall indicating Mr Hawkes and Mr Byrne in one direction, and Mr Walker in the other. I followed the sign for Mr Walker, which led me along a further corridor. At the end was a rather grand, mahogany door. In front of the door sat a brown leather sofa. And opposite that was another desk, with an attractive, young blonde woman sitting behind it.

"Good morning," I said, approaching the woman. "I'm afraid I'm a little early for my appointment. It's at three o'clock."

"Oh yes, good morning Mr…?"

"Mr Adamson," I said, recalling the name I'd seen on the receptionist's digital calendar.

The woman looked at the computer in front of her and smiled, satisfied with my answer. "Yes, of course. Hello Mr Adamson. Mr Walker is still in with a client. But he should be done in about fifteen minutes or so. You can wait here, if you'd like. Would you like me to get you a cup of tea or coffee, whilst you wait?"

"No, thanks, I've just had one," I said, sitting down on the sofa. Quite what I was going to do when the real Mr Adamson showed up, I wasn't sure. But at least I'd got this far.

Eleven minutes and fourteen seconds later, I heard a distant electrical clicking sound as the main security door by reception unlocked.

"Actually," I said, to Walker's assistant, "I am a bit parched. I don't suppose I could trouble you to get me that coffee after all, could I?"

"No problem," she said, smiling and standing up from her desk. "How do you take it?"

"White with one, please."

She smiled again, walked round from behind her desk and disappeared off along the corridor. I took my chance, dashing round behind her desk and sitting down in her chair, as the real Mr Adamson appeared around the corner.

"Mr Adamson?" I said, standing as he approached. "I'm terribly sorry, but there's a problem with your appointment. I've been trying to call all morning, but I couldn't get through."

"Problem? What problem?"

"I'm afraid Mr Walker has been taken ill. Terrible flu. And we're not quite sure when he'll be back in the office." I walked around from the behind the desk, taking Adamson by the shoulder. I turned him around and started leading him away, terrified Walker's office door might open at any moment.

"Flu? The woman on reception didn't say anything about it."

"Yeah, she's… well, I'm not sure I should really say, but… well, she's not quite all there, I'm afraid. We've been telling her all morning to explain to Mr Walker's clients what's happened, but she just doesn't seem to be getting it. She's been like this for months now. Same thing happened to my auntie, and she ended up with Alzheimer's, so... well, what can you do?"

"Goodness. That's terrible. So, what about..."

"Don't worry, Mr Adamson. As soon as Mr Walker is back in the office we'll give you a call to reschedule your appointment. Sorry again for the inconvenience."

Adamson looked slightly bemused, then wandered off down the hallway. I darted back to towards Walker's office and threw myself down onto the sofa, just as Walker's secretary reappeared from around another corner with my coffee.

"Here you go," she said, handing me the expensive looking cup and saucer.

Walker's door opened and a small man in an expensive suit walked out, carrying a leather brief case. He thanked the assistant and disappeared along the corridor. I sipped my coffee, waiting to be summoned in for poor old Mr Adamson's appointment. The sucker.

Walker's secretary answered her phone, then looked over at me and told me I could go in. I left the coffee on her desk, pushed open the large wooden door and strolled into the office.

"Good afternoon, Mr..." said Walker, leaving me to fill in the blank.

"It's Winters," I said. "Good afternoon."

"Oh?" said Walker, his face crinkling with confusion. He looked down at the computer screen in front of him. "I was expecting a Mr Adamson."

"Yes, I'm afraid Mr Adamson couldn't make it today. I'm his associate. You can discuss any of his matters with me."

"Of course, please take a seat."

I sat down in the leather chair opposite his desk. Everything in the room looked expensive, from his antique mahogany desk to the leather seats, another leather sofa in the corner and, again, thick, plush carpet. The walls were adorned with certificates in frames. A bookcase in the corner held large, leather bound books of some kind – presumably legal texts.

A glass-fronted display cabinet behind Walker's desk occupied a number of shiny awards and trophies. Some were obviously prizes for golf – little golden men holding golf clubs high above their heads. I couldn't tell what the others were for. In pride of place was a large framed photograph of Walker posing casually on the deck of a yacht.

The man himself was trim and in good shape. He must have been in his fifties, but had the physique of a man at least fifteen years younger (unlike me, who has the physique of a man at least fifteen years my senior). He looked like he probably spent his weekends running and cycling, and doing all those boring, healthy things that people with little imagination do.

Walker had short-cropped dark hair with flecks of silver along the sides. He wore a blue shirt with white pin stripes and thick red braces. His tie was bright red too, and looked expensive. I couldn't see his legs behind the desk, but I assumed he was wearing equally expensive trousers.

"Okay, let's cut the crap, Mr Winters, if that's your real name," he said quite abruptly. "Who are you, and what do you really want?"

His accent was posh, but still slightly common. Like he'd worked his way up from a humble background, made it to upper-class status, and had changed his voice to fit in with his posh, rich friends. But try as he might, there was still the slightest twang of a working class, guttural tone that he just couldn't get rid of.

"I don't know what you mean," I lied.

"Well, you've admitted you're not Mr Adamson. And you're clearly not an associate of his. Even if you were, I certainly would not be discussing his private affairs with you. So, who the bloody hell are you, and what do you want?"

"Fair enough," I said. "I want to talk to you about Dylan St James."

"The novelist? Why would you want to talk to me about him?"

"Because someone's trying to kill him. And I don't know quite how yet, but you're mixed up in it. Right up to your eyeballs."

He didn't look shocked. He didn't look panicked. He just sat there smiling at me.

"Okay," he said calmly. "I'll play along for a moment. I can assure you, Mr Winters, I have nothing to do with any plot to murder Mr St James. I've never even met the man."

"Well, of course you'd say that, wouldn't you? But I know different. For example, I've met with all of Dylan's ex-wives. I know about the contracts. They all signed pre-nuptial agreements, drawn up by you."

"Well, there's certainly nothing illegal about drawing up a prenuptial marriage agreement. And I don't see how that would constitute part of a murder conspiracy."

"What about the contract you drew up for Chantelle Star? The one that said she'd get a million quid for marrying Dylan and then divorcing him. What about all the meetings you had with her and her dick of a boyfriend? Where you explained about the plan to for her to marry Dylan. And you told her she had to keep all the details from him."

His voice and his face remained completely calm, as if he'd been preparing for this conversation. Or maybe he was so crooked that conversations like this happened on a daily basis, and he was just a master at them.

"Mr Winters," he said, "I'm afraid I have absolutely no idea what you're talking about. And even if I did, whatever I discuss with my clients is privileged information. I'm certainly not going to share any of it with you."

"Who hired you to do it? How much did they pay you?"

"Mr Winters, I…"

I cut him off, trying to keep up the momentum. "I was paid a visit by Frank McLeod the other day. But you might know him better as 'The Animal'. Is he one of your clients? Is that why you sent him after me, to try and stop me from getting to the truth?"

"Frank McLeod? The gangster? I can assure you I have no dealings with people of his kind. And I'm afraid your argument falls completely flat. How could I possibly have sent anyone to silence you, if I didn't even know who you were until today? It's not even logical."

He had a fair point there. But I wasn't giving up now.

"Who hired you? Why are they paying you to get rid of Dylan's wives? And why do they want him dead?"

"I've already told you, I have no idea what you're talking about. And even if I did, I am not going to discuss it with you."

"Okay, how much?"

"How much what?" he said, sighing and rubbing his eyes, like he was getting very tired of the conversation.

"How much do you want? I'll pay you to tell me what's really going on here. Tell me who hired you, and why, and I'll pay you. I won't even tell the police you're involved."

"Mr Winters," he said, "you are aware what I do for a living, aren't you? I mean, it can't have completely escaped your attention. And yet, you still think it's a good idea to come barging in here, accusing me of… well, I'm not quite sure what you're *actually* accusing me of… but you must realise this is not a good plan. Whatever you know or whatever you think you know, you are wrong. And if you go around making unfounded accusations, especially to people in the legal profession, you'll find yourself being sued for slander before you can even finish your next sentence. I'll have you for everything you're worth, which I'm guessing, by the state of your face, is not a lot."

"You don't scare me, you know."

"Please leave now, Mr Winters. Or I'm going to call the police and have you removed."

"Yeah, well, the police don't scare me, either," I lied.

"Very well," he said, "opening up a notebook and clicking a pen. Perhaps you could give me your full name, address and billing details. If you're going to stay there, I'm going to charge you. My usual fee is £600 an hour, and I'm quite happy to cancel all my other appointments for the day. So, how would you like to pay?"

Now, that did scare me.

"Fine," I said, standing up from the chair, "I'm leaving anyway. I've got as much out of you as I wanted – you just don't realise it yet."

"Is that so?"

"Yes it is," I sneered. "I hope you enjoy playing the harmonica. I hear there's little else to do in prison."

Walker stared at me, his face scrunched up in confusion. Admittedly, it was a pretty weak line – which definitely sounded better in my head before I said it – but it got the point across.

I stepped forward, sneering at Walker, and tipped over the little pot of pens on his desk. Then I ran out of his office, slamming the door shut behind me.

******

I set up in the Starbucks across the road from the lawyer's office. I picked out a seat by the window so I could keep track on all the comings and goings. Then I sat there nursing a caramel macchiato, looking over the notes and lists in my notepad.

I wrote down *Charles Walker, Lawyer*. Then, next to the name, I wrote: *Guilty as fuck*. He'd clearly written those pre-nuptial agreements and the contract for Chantelle to marry Dylan. If only I could get my hands on a copy of that paperwork, I might be able to prove the lawyers involvement.

But involvement in what? As he'd said himself, it's not exactly a crime to draft legal documents. That's just his job. So what exactly was he up to? And who was he working with?

My notepad was a mess of questions, with very few answers. There was clearly some kind of conspiracy here. I could see all the various threads. I just couldn't see how or where they connected. I needed to see that paperwork, but how was I going to get in there? I'd already tricked my way past the receptionist and Walker's assistant once. And that tactic wasn't going to work again.

As I was sitting there, trying to figure out the best way of breaking in, I suddenly saw a very familiar figure waddling down the street. He was old, fat and dressed in a billowing suit with a high-collared shirt and bright pink bow-tie.

Mortimer Bunkle passed in front of the coffee shop window. I hid my face in my hands in case he glanced in and spotted me. He turned and waited for the traffic to cease. Then he crossed the road and walked in through the main entrance to Walker, Hawkes and Byrne Solicitors.

What the hell was that old sod doing here?

Thirty minutes later, I was still nursing the same coffee, holding my head in my hands at my own ineptitude. One of the waitresses was skirting around the tables, pretending to wipe them with a manky cloth, sneering at me as she inspected the contents of my mug – I mean, seriously, is this a customer turnover tactic that they teach at the coffee shop academy?

I looked up and out of the window, trying my hardest to avoid eye contact with the waitress, just as the main door to the solicitor's office opened up. Mortimer Bunkle's wide frame moved into view as he stepped out onto the street. He was red-faced and sweating, and clearly a little flustered. Like he'd received some very bad news. What exactly had the lawyer told him?

Mortimer turned left and started walking along the pavement. I jumped up from my seat, downed the last dregs of my cold coffee, and stepped out onto the street. I waited for a lull in the traffic, then darted across the road, making sure to stay out of Mortimer's sight.

I kept an eye on him up ahead, following along stealthily behind – which proved to be more difficult than I had imagined. In the films, the detective or spy always keeps a watch on the bad guy, following on quickly, stopping to look in shops to avoid suspicion, and then dashing along afterwards. But following Mortimer was nothing like that.

Trailing a man who walks slower than a snail is incredibly difficult. To say that Mortimer Bunkle was unfit would be an insult to unfit people. He hobbled along the road, carrying his massive girth, huffing and wheezing the whole way. He stopped on practically every fourth step to take a breather and mop his brow. At one point he was even overtaken by an old lady with a Zimmer frame.

Following on ten yards behind was practically impossible. Because I had to stop every three or four paces as well, then stand stock still in the middle of the pavement until he started moving again. Which meant I had to try and look interested in the window displays of New Look, Ann Summers, Lush, The Early Learning Centre, a lingerie shop, Mr Simms Olde Sweet Shoppe and a pet store. At least I didn't look like a spy or private detective carefully following his prey. Instead, I just looked like a very confused pervert.

Finally, I got into a rhythm, walking as slow as possible to stay a reasonable distance back. Then Mortimer turned a corner, so I ran up, pressed my shoulder against the edge of the wall and carefully peered around.

I looked round just in time to see Mortimer climbing into the passenger seat of a dark blue Ford. In the driver's seat was another face I recognised. A man I'd briefly met a few days before in Mortimer's office. He was dressed all in black combat clothes and had an anxious, agitated look on his face.

The car rocked as Mortimer bundled himself in and shut the door. Then I heard the engine rev loudly and the car pulled out sharply into the street. I ducked back behind the corner, hiding my face in case they saw me as they passed.

I looked back to see the car racing along the street and disappearing off into the distance. As it did, I saw something stuck to the rear passenger window. It was orange and black, with plastic suckers on each paw. It had lazy, half-closed eyes and a big white grin. It was Garfield.

CHAPTER 25

I HAILED DOWN a passing taxi and jumped in. For a moment, I considered asking the cabbie to 'follow that car'. But I didn't really need to follow them; I had a pretty good idea of where they were going. Besides, the cab driver was a fairly gruff, miserable-looking type, and I suspected he might just tell me to fuck off.

I had a few other things to check on, anyway, so I gave the driver the address for Dylan's flat and asked him to take me there. Fifteen minutes later, I raced up the stairs, two at a time, and burst in to Dylan's apartment. I went straight to his office and started pulling open the drawers of the unit at the end of the desk. I pulled out wads of papers, letters, bank statements and documents of all kinds. I thumbed through them, but I couldn't find what I was after.

I was way out of my depth now, I knew that. As soon as I saw Mortimer in the car with that man, I knew I needed help. Real help. Police help.

Mortimer had clearly been lying to me. He'd introduced me to that man in his office, but lied about knowing the car. And the Garfield.

No wonder Sanders had rushed past me in the office, desperate to get away. He obviously recognised me from when he'd tried to run me over. And he must have been worried I'd recognise him as well.

I'd already heard about Sanders' own dubious past. He clearly wasn't averse to lying. But was he also capable of murder?

My meddling and amateur investigations had got me so far. They'd helped me uncover some kind of plot – although I was still unsure of all the details, or what the outcome was supposed to be. But they'd also led to me being kidnapped and threatened by a gangster.

People's lives were at stake. If I wasn't careful, I could end up getting myself or someone else killed.

I looked around the office, hoping to find a filing cabinet or some kind of lockbox, but there was nothing. "Where the hell would Dylan keep contracts?" I said to myself.

If Mortimer was a client of Walker's, then maybe he'd used him to draft up other legal documents, as well as the marriage contracts. Book contracts, or agent agreements for Dylan. If I could find anything tying

Mortimer and Walker to Dylan, plus my eye witness accounts from the last few days, it might just be enough to convince Richard Stone to believe me.

I emptied out all the drawers. I checked the book shelf. I even looked down the back of the sofa, and behind that ridiculous penguin poster, just in case Dylan had a concealed safe. But there was nothing.

I flopped down onto the sofa, breathing heavily and looking up at the ceiling. I had a real sense of dread that time was running out. Mortimer had looked panicked when he left Walker's office. And he'd got straight into a car with my number one suspect. Maybe they knew the net was closing in. If I'd managed to piece together the clues, it was only a matter of time before the police started banging down their door. Would that lead them to take drastic action? Had I just put Dylan's life in even more danger?

And then it dawned on me. Of course there were no contracts in the flat. Dylan was only staying there temporarily. Practically everything he owned, and all his paperwork, would have gone up in flames when his house burned down. But there would definitely be copies at Mortimer's office. There had to be.

I didn't have to break into the lawyer's place after all. I was going to have to break into Mortimer's.

I headed through to Dylan's bedroom, searching through his drawers and wardrobes for any clothes that might be suitable for a spot of light burglary. Sadly, there wasn't much – no black leather gloves, no black bomber jacket, no balaclava or baseball cap. With his distinct lack of weaponry and criminal attire, Dylan really wasn't making this easy for me.

After rooting around for five minutes, I managed to find a pair of black suit trousers, a thin, black roll-neck sweater and a pair of black loafers. I put them all on and inspected myself in the mirror. The shoes were a bit tight. And I looked more like the bloody Milk Tray man than a competent working burglar. But it would have to do. And at least I should be able to move about undetected.

I checked my watch. It was 18.23, which meant Mortimer's office would most likely be deserted and I'd be able to get in there easily without being detected. It was now or never.

******

Another fifteen quid lighter, a new, slightly less grumpy taxi driver dropped me at the bottom of Wardour Street, at the junction with Old Compton Street. It wasn't until I exited the taxi, and garnered more than the odd wink from the friendly chaps gathered on the street outside Compton's Pub, that I suddenly remembered what I was wearing.

Dressing like the Milk Tray Man in the middle of London's gay capital was possibly not the best idea when trying to remain inconspicuous. I'm not saying they all fancied me (although, I'd like to think I might have caught the eye of at least one or two), I suddenly realised that I stood out like a clown at a funeral. I thought the cabbie had given me a bit of a knowing look when he pulled up at the kerbside.

"Where's yer chocolates?" shouted one over-eager fellow out on the street. I just smiled, cursed Dylan's wardrobe again, and headed off towards Mortimer's office.

When I reached the building, I stood over on the other side of the street, blending into the background so I could monitor the premises.

"Ha ha, where's your box of Milk Tray?" laughed one drunken reveller as he passed me in the street.

"I left them with your mum," I replied, "she always gets hungry after a good seeing to."

I cursed myself as soon as the words left my mouth. It was bad enough that I looked like a tit – picking fights with random strangers in the street was hardly likely to keep me hidden. Luckily for me, he was just the right level of drunk to find my comment amusing rather than wholly offensive, and he simply carried on past, giggling drunkenly.

I returned my attention to the building. There were no lights on in the windows of the top floor. That meant Mortimer's office was most likely empty. Good start.

The offices on the fourth floor looked equally deserted. And there were no lights showing on the third floor. Unfortunately, several of the windows at Red Monkey Marketing were illuminated and there looked to be a handful of people milling about inside. So typical of marketing people to be working late and getting in the way. I bloody hate marketing people. If they're not busy thinking up new, despicable ways to invade your lives and sell you crap you don't need, they're working late, getting in the way and making it more difficult to burgle a literary agent's offices.

Still, it did make the first part of the mission that little bit easier. I crossed the street, approached the entrance and pressed the buzzer for Red Monkey Marketing. It took a few minutes for someone to finally answer.

"Courier," I said, in my best confused, Polish accent.

"Courier?" replied the voice on the other end. "Who are you here to see?"

"Courier," I repeated, trying to sound even more confused.

"Yeah... who are you here to see?" said the voice. I then heard them shouting out to the rest of the office, "Anyone waiting for a courier?"

"Courier," I said into the intercom.

"Yeah, I get that, mate," said the voice. "Who are you here to see? Dropping off or picking up?"

"Courier."

"Oh for fu..." Then the voice disappeared and the door buzzed loudly as the lock clicked to let me in.

I dashed inside, raced up the stairs past the main entrance for Red Monkey, and hid, skulking in the corner of the stairwell. The marketing agency's door swung open and a young man's head popped out. Seeing nobody there, he trotted down the stairs, flung the main door open and looked out onto the street. Again, seeing nobody there, he cursed and muttered under his breath, then walked back up the stairs and into the office.

Step one complete. I waited until all was quiet again before coming out from where I was hiding. I walked quickly and quietly up the next few flights, making sure to step only on the outside edges of the old wooden stairs, to keep them from creaking. I made it up to the main entrance of Mortimer's office and gently turned the round door knob. As expected, it was locked. Still, it was worth a try.

I looked round to check the coast was still clear, reached into my pocket and pulled out my set of lock picks. I unzipped the leather case, opening it up and laying it out on the floor in front of me. It really is staggering what you can buy from Amazon for under twenty quid nowadays.

It was dark in the hall, the moonlight streaming in through the window barely illuminating anything. I took a penlight from my pocket, clicked it on and held it in my mouth as I set to work.

I first learned to pick locks when I was doing research for *Break and*

Enter, one of my earliest Dick Stone novels, in which the detective was hot on the trail of a home invasion killer. Naturally, I'd wanted to get all the details right, so I'd learned how to pick locks myself, in order to better describe the process. I spent several hours in the company of a nefarious character that I met in a pub in Elephant and Castle. He charged me two hundred quid for his tutelage, and after several hundred hours of practice, I actually became a bit of a dab hand at picking locks.

Nowadays, of course, there's no need to pay criminals to teach you how to do these sorts of things. It's all there for you on the internet. Hundreds of pages of instructions on how to pick locks, break into places, and commit all sorts of crimes – all with handy diagrams, videos and even links to where you can buy the best tools for the job.

I inserted the tension wrench into the lock, twisting the barrel slightly and applying pressure. I then slid my pick into the lock, slowly moving it back towards me as I felt the pins click into place. It took a few goes, but eventually I had all the pins locked in the correct position and I twisted the wrench.

I again turned the round door handle below the lock and this time the door swung open in front of me. I flashed my torch light around the room, double-checking it was empty. Then I darted inside, carefully closing the door behind me.

The office was even darker than the landing outside. My tiny torch lit up only the smallest section of the room at a time. I swiftly moved through the outer office, just managing to avoid bumping into the gaudy, antique bar. I walked round behind the small desk outside Mortimer's office, where the old lady had been sitting. Just as Mortimer had told me, there was no keyboard to the computer. Even worse, it didn't actually appear to be plugged into anything. So, there was no use trying to turn it on and search for computer records.

I opened the top drawer of the cabinet next to the desk and found the keyboard and mouse tucked inside. I slid open the next drawer down. It was absolutely crammed full of wool – all different colours, thicknesses and textures, shoved in higgledy-piggledy until the drawer would barely close. Finally, I opened the bottom drawer and wasn't even surprised to find that it contained nothing but packets of tissues, loose Werther's Originals and a collection of previously-used stamps, all cut from envelopes. Quite what anyone was going to do with them, I have no idea.

I scanned the rest of the room, looking for filing cabinets, folder organisers or anywhere that important documents might be kept. There was nothing, so I moved to Mortimer's inner office.

I flashed my tiny torchlight around the room. The horrendous wallpaper and brightly coloured carpet streaked into view in narrow patches. I crept round behind Mortimer's desk. The floorboards creaked and squeaked as I moved through the room, so I had to slow right down, literally tip-toeing.

I sat down in Mortimer's chair, the leather squeaking and farting loudly as it had the other day. I cursed myself for not remembering. How much noise was I making? Enough to alert anybody still left in the building below?

I looked around, holding my breath and listening out for any signs that people had heard me. Thankfully, it was all silent, so I carried on with my amateur burglary.

I scanned the contents of Mortimer's desk. It was unusually tidy. A dated computer screen sat to the left of the desk – this one actually plugged in, with a mouse and keyboard in front of it. It looked to be at least ten years out of date. And by its position on the desk, I guessed it wasn't used for anything more than checking emails and the odd bit of web surfing. Next to the computer monitor sat a phone.

A number of framed pictures lined the desk. There was one of Mortimer and Dylan – both of them wearing black suits and bow ties and holding a copy of *Once Upon a Never*. It must have been the night of Dylan's first Booker prize win.

Next to that was a group shot of staggeringly famous people – Marlon Brando, John Lennon, David Bowie, Robert Redford, Twiggy, Burt Reynolds, Stephen King and famed 1980s wrestling star Big Daddy. A smiling Mortimer Bunkle held pride of place in the middle of the group. I was sure he couldn't have represented all of these people – but it made for one hell of a picture.

A third framed picture showed Mortimer sitting on a sofa drinking tea with Margaret Thatcher. It actually sent a little shiver down my spine.

Aside from a desk tidy that held several pens, and a blank, leatherbound A4 notepad, there was nothing there to show that this was a desk used for daily business. It was more like a tragic shrine to a man's former glory days.

I slid open the top drawer at the side of the desk. It was absolutely crammed full of letters – some opened and some unopened. I pulled a handful out, gripped my penlight between my teeth and inspected the contents. Letter after letter featured the words *Final Notice* in bright, red type across the top of the envelope. Having received many similar pieces of mail myself over the years, I know that these are never good. And I can fully understand why Mortimer had chosen to leave the majority of them sealed.

I tore one envelope open. It was a demand for over nine hundred pounds arrears on the electricity bill for Mortimer's office. Another one was demanding payment for Gas used at Mortimer's home. A letter from Mortimer's bank asked him to contact them urgently to arrange a meeting to discuss the unpaid mortgage on his house. A letter from a bailiff company urged Mortimer to phone them within the next seven days to discuss the urgent payment of rent for his office. If they didn't hear from him, they would be sending an agent round to assess the value of his possessions. The letter was dated two days previously.

As I dug through the contents of the drawer, I found more and more damning evidence of Mortimer's woeful financial situation. Once a rich, powerful man, he now apparently owed money here, there and everywhere. He looked like he was close to losing his house, his office and pretty much everything he owned.

There were letters from three separate debt collectors. All his utilities companies were demanding money. There was even an angry letter from the Cats Protection League, enquiring when they were going to receive the proceeds from a charity fundraiser Mortimer had run six months previously – auctioning off lunch with the famous novelist Dylan St James as a prize. They were even threatening legal action if they didn't see the funds within thirty days (I told you those bastards can be pretty underhanded).

Finally, I fished out a letter from HM Revenue & Customs, dated nine months previously. The letter thanked Mr Bunkle for his payment of outstanding taxes owed, in the amount of £4,534,672.24. It went on to assure him that, with full payment received, they were no longer interested in pursuing criminal charges against him.

I laid the letter on top of the pile. It was in very stark contrast to all the others. He was paying off over four million quid in unpaid taxes, and yet he was failing to pay his mortgage, utilities bills, and even stiffing the poor old sick and unwanted cats on charity donations. Clearly, the man had big money problems. So where the hell did he get a spare four and a half million pounds?

I shone my torchlight around the room, catching sight of an old, grey filing cabinet in the opposite corner. I stood up carefully, minimising the chair farting as best as I could, and crossed the room. I opened the top drawer. It was crammed with files, all alphabetically ordered into clients' names. There were authors, TV presenters, models, movie stars, celebrity chefs and even a few random reality TV 'celebrities'. It was a veritable 'who's who' of the rich and famous.

I scanned through the names. Each one had its own file containing various papers – files, contracts, printed spreadsheets, sales figures. There were printed agreements with publishers, producers, directors and TV and film companies. As I delved further I found a number of other odd documents – everything from invoices for dog-sitting services, private jet hire, receipts for lunches, villa hire and other miscellaneous payments, services and expenses. Someone could have made an absolute fortune selling this information to the press. I made a mental note to break back in once everything had died down with Dylan and see what juicy titbits were worth stealing.

Dylan's section was all the way down in the bottom drawer of the filing cabinet. Unsurprisingly, being one of Mortimer's biggest, most successful clients, his was also the largest set of papers – taking up nearly the whole drawer. Thankfully things were filed in sections, and also pretty much in chronological order. I went to contracts first and found his original contract with Mortimer along with the one for his first published book. There were agreements for two- and three-book deals, with separate papers outlining each individual book. All of Dylan's obligations in these deals were fulfilled, and it confirmed that Dylan was currently out of contract. No wonder there had been something of a race to sign up his latest novel.

I fingered my way through all the various sections in the drawer – from sales figures to contracts for movie rights, and all the other bits of random paper. Then, tucked in right at the back of the drawer, I found another divider labelled simply: *Wives*.

I pulled it out and laid it on the floor in front of me. Clutching the small torch between my teeth, I lifted the first document from the pile and flicked through it. It was a prenuptial agreement drawn up between Dylan and his second wife, Georgina. The details seemed fairly standard, as she had described. I flicked to the back page and saw that the footer copy held the name of the law firm that had drafted it –

Walker, Hawkes and Byrne Solicitors.

Next, I found the pre-nups for both Corinne and Chantelle. Again, both seemed fairly standard and the details were those that had been described to me. I placed them to the side and then I found what I was looking for. Again, drawn up by Walker, it was a contract between his firm and Miss Chantelle Heath (presumably Chantelle Star's real name). It was more like a contract of employment, laying out a length of service during which she would technically be employed jointly by the law firm and by Mr Mortimer Bunkle. Under duties, it simply listed: *Marriage to Mr Dylan St James. And any other reasonable duties as required by advance agreement with Mr Bunkle.*

This was it. This contract proved Mortimer's involvement in the marriage and separation of Dylan and Chantelle. I looked down at the remaining papers on the floor. There was a printed collection of emails between Mortimer and Walker. The first few were fairly innocent, discussing the pre-nup between Dylan and Georgina. Then I found one which really caught my interest. It read:

Dear Charles,

I fear I may need your assistance with a new matter. As we recently discussed, Dylan's output is as feared – far below average. The new book he just delivered to me is… well, to call it chick-lit clap-trap would, I fear, be doing a disservice to the genre. It is bad. Very bad.

This new wife of his is having a very ill effect on his career. We must think up a way to be rid of her. Something must be done – and quick. We must get Dylan back on track. We must get him writing again.

Please contact me at your earliest convenience to discuss the matter fully.

Yours

Mortimer

I wasn't sure what I was looking at. I checked the date and made a quick calculation in my head. It had been sent around the time Dylan was married to Corinne. "Get rid of her," I whispered to myself. What did it mean? I placed it on the pile, and reached for the next printout.

Just then I heard a noise behind me – the unmistakeable sound of a floorboard squeaking. I felt a sudden dull pain as something large and heavy collided with the back of my head. Then everything went black.

CHAPTER 26

I AWOKE, SLUMPED in a chair. My head was pounding – short, sharp electrical shocks of pain surging through my brain. The back of my head was throbbing. It felt wet and I could feel a strange, sticky trickle of something running down my neck. My mouth stung, too – the cuts on my lips having re-opened when my face collided with the floor. I reached up to clasp the back of my head, but my hands wouldn't move. They were stuck down at my sides, tied to the legs of the chair I was sitting in.

My eyes slowly came into focus. It took me a few seconds to figure out where I was. Then I realised what I was looking at. I was in the chair opposite Mortimer Bunkle's desk. I heard a noise behind me and twisted my head just far enough to see Mortimer standing by the door to the office, talking with a man dressed all in black.

"Go and get it taken care of," I heard Mortimer saying. "It has to happen tonight. And no more mistakes."

"And what about that one in there?" replied the man in black.

"Don't worry about him. Get to the hospital and take care of our more immediate problem. Then come straight back here, and we'll figure out what to do with the other one later."

The man in black grunted with disapproval, then stepped outside the door and disappeared. I heard Mortimer sigh loudly, then he slowly walked round behind his desk and sat down opposite me. We looked at each other for a few moments. Said nothing. The pain throbbed in the back of my head. Mortimer sighed again.

"You seem to be proving a bit of a problem, Freddie," he said.

I straightened up in the chair, sniffed and spat out a mouthful of metallic-tasting blood onto the floor.

"Imagine my surprise when I received a phone call this evening, to say that there were strange lights and noises coming from my office. Then my associate comes here to find you snooping around the place, going through my files."

I just sat there, not speaking.

"Of course, he had no idea who you were, being that it was so dark. So he had to subdue you. How's the head, by the way?"

"Bit fucking sore, as it goes," I snapped. "Probably gonna leave a scar. Or a big fucking hole."

"Well, that's what you get for breaking into people's private offices. What were you looking for, anyway?"

"Evidence."

"Evidence? Of what?"

"That you're trying to kill Dylan. Or, more accurately, your friend has been trying to kill him. I know he's the one in the blue Ford. He tried to run me over. He's the one who shot Dylan, isn't he? As soon as I get out of here, I'm going straight to the police to tell them what you've been up to."

"Kill Dylan? Freddie, you've been reading too many of your own books. Why would I want to kill Dylan? You're talking nonsense."

"I know it's you. And I'm gonna prove it. You've spent your life hanging off the coattails of Dylan's career. And now everything's gone wrong for you, you wanna cash in by killing him."

"Career?" he shouted, suddenly angry. "If it wasn't for me, that man would have no career. I discovered him. I got him published. And what thanks do I get? He wouldn't listen to me when I tried to get him the best deals. He just insisted we stick with the same publisher – Matthew bloody Dickson – even though others were offering double."

"Really?"

"And that was just before. With this new book, the offers coming in are ridiculous. You know it's the long-awaited sequel to his biggest hit. Everyone wants to get their hands on it. But Dylan's a loyal person, and he wants to stay with the same publisher. He says it feels more comfortable for him. And he doesn't really need the money, anyway." Mortimer screwed his face up in disgust.

"Well, it's *his* book. He can do what he wants with it."

"No," Mortimer shouted, anger coursing through his voice and his face turning bright red, "it's not just *his* book. He can't just do what *he* wants. I've put too much into this not to get my rewards. If you only knew what I had to do to keep that man writing over the years..."

He stopped short, as if suddenly realising that he'd let something slip.

"Keep him writing?" I said. "What do you mean, keep him writing?"

"What? Oh... er... nothing," he said, sounding defensive.

"It *was* you, wasn't it? The lawyer... the wives... you paid those women to divorce him. I know you did, I've seen the contracts and the email."

"What? Pay what? You're talking nonsense, Freddie."

"You sabotaged his life. You paid women to marry and then leave him. You made him miserable, then sent that bogus shrink round to give him bad advice and make sure he never got the help he really needed."

Mortimer squirmed in his chair, fingering his tight shirt collar. The cracked leather chair wheezed and farted with each slight movement.

"The cancer," I said. "That was you as well. He actually had it, did he? You paid that doctor to misdiagnose him on purpose. And all that medication he was taking... Christ, you could have killed him."

"It... it wasn't like that," he finally spat out. "I was... helping him."

"Helping him?" I laughed. "You convinced him he had a fatal illness – twice. You made that man utterly miserable. But why?"

Mortimer looked at me, then down at the desk in front of him. His eyes closed as he blew out a long deep sigh, then he looked up at me again.

"You know what Dylan's like," he said, "such a sensitive soul. And he needs that sensitivity. It's what makes him such a great writer. I could see that the first time I met him. He thrives on it and it gives his writing so much depth and beauty."

"So what? Lots of writers are sensitive. Most of the ones I know are a bunch of cry-babies."

"Yes, but with Dylan it goes so much deeper. He reflects his whole life, all of his emotions onto the page. And well... the fact is, he can only write when he's depressed."

"What?" I laughed.

"Seriously, all of his big successes have come about following various stages of depression."

"Fuck off! That can't be true. I'm depressed 99% of the time, how come I'm not a bloody millionaire?"

Mortimer rolled his eyes in a fashion I found rather offensive. "Trust me, it's true. When Dylan wrote his first book, he was struggling, broke and desperate for his first big success. He took all that angst and wrote a good book – good enough for me to take a chance on him.

"But it really came after Sonia died. A part of him died too, I think. He went inside himself for a while, shutting himself off from the outside world. And when he finally came back to us, he'd created an absolute masterpiece. His first book was good, but this was something else. He took all that pain and suffering, and he channelled it into his writing to create something absolutely beautiful. That was when I realised just what he was capable of.

"When he wrote his third book, he was suffering with writer's block. Nothing he was writing was good enough and he couldn't replicate his previous success. The stress got to him, and his marriage to Georgina fell apart. Again, he fell into a deep depression, and when he came back out of it, he'd written *Once Upon a Never*. He won the bloody Booker Prize for that one!

"It's just what he needs. For some reason he has to be depressed or he can't write."

"Bollocks!" I said.

"Trust me, you can chart every one of his books and correlate it with a low point in his life. Whenever he's depressed, he writes phenomenal books. Whenever he's happy, he writes absolute crap."

"But all of his books have been bestsellers."

"The ones he's had published. Believe me, there have been several novels that were rejected. Some were so bad that I daren't even show them to editors – I knew they'd laugh me out of their offices."

"I can't believe it," I said. Then I thought back to Dylan's laptop. The folder of books I'd never heard of. "But Dylan's a fantastic writer. I can't believe being happy would suddenly stop him from being able to put a sentence together."

"Oh, the writing was okay, I suppose. It was the stories. Dylan's books appeal to a certain audience. They're dour and depressing. They're melancholy. But they're absolutely beautiful because of it."

"And the other stuff?"

"Dreadful. It's all happy families, people falling in love, young men finding themselves. All that happy-ever-after nonsense."

"Yeah, that doesn't sound like Dylan. But they can't have been that bad."

"They were fit for purpose. But they would have got lost in the sea of all that other dreadful chick-lit. They certainly weren't Dylan St James novels. And the publishers didn't want them. One of them even featured the story of a woman who was visited by a magical unicorn in her dreams."

"Jesus," I said.

"I've no idea what happened at the end. I couldn't make it more than halfway through."

"Couldn't you have published them under a pseudonym?"

"What would have been the point? The publisher wasn't interested in pretending they came from a new writer. They didn't want the expense of building up a new author profile. They'd never get any return on investment.

"The only way these books would have sold was if we released them under a fake name, and then," he formed his fingers into air quotes, "'leaked' the real identity of the writer. Like Rowling did with those crime books she wrote. And trust me, that was the last thing we wanted. The books were so bad we didn't want anyone finding out that Dylan had written them. He'd have been a laughing stock. He'd have been rubbished in the press. His whole reputation would be in tatters.

"The publishers were only interested in a *real* Dylan St James novel. Which meant I needed Dylan doing what he did best. So... I took measures."

"Took measures? You ruined his fucking life."

"Yes, but it worked, didn't it? I stopped him producing that awful writing. I steered him back onto the right path and he produced literary classic after literary classic."

"Put him on the right path?" I laughed. "You call convincing a man he has cancer putting him on the right path? Somehow you tricked Corinne into thinking he wanted a divorce. And that's helping him?"

"Corinne was always trouble," he snapped. "So, I had to get rid of her. It was easier than you'd think, actually," he said, a wry smile forming on his lips. "I sent each of them divorce papers, and made sure they couldn't contact each other. They both thought the other one had left them. And they both just accepted it."

"Why the hell would you do that?"

"When I stepped in and got rid of her, I put Dylan back on track. He went on to win his second bloody Booker. Look, I know it's unconventional, but it worked."

"You're out of your mind."

"Maybe," said Mortimer, deflating slightly and looking down at his hands. "But I was just trying to help him. You have to believe me. I just wanted him to be the best writer he could be."

"And make plenty of money for yourself along the way. Speaking of which, where did you get the money to pay Chantelle to marry Dylan?"

"What... er...what?"

"The money you paid Chantelle Star to marry Dylan. You paid her a million quid. Where did it come from?"

"I took it out of Dylan's royalties," he said, ashamed.

"Jesus Christ," I coughed, indignantly. "So, not only did you pay a woman to seduce, con and marry Dylan, you also used his own money. You're evil. That man's just a source of revenue to you, and you don't care what you do to him."

"I... er..."

"What about the money Corinne got to divorce him? That was Dylan's too, I take it?"

"Yes... but it really wasn't like that, Freddie."

"No, of course not. You just wanted to help him. That must be why you're trying to kill him as well."

Mortimer just sat there, staring into his hands, breathing in shallow, ragged breaths. "It has to be done," he said, in a near whisper.

"But why? Okay, I can understand all this other stuff. Pretty fucking awful thing to do, but I get it. But how could it possibly benefit you if Dylan dies?"

"Because I need the fucking money," he shouted. He looked up at me, his face bright red and tears glistening in his bloodshot eyes.

"I don't get it. Dylan's books are still making money, aren't they? With your... what, fifteen percent... you must still be making a fairly tidy amount?"

"Fifteen percent? Fifteen percent? Look around you, Freddie. I have nothing. Do you see? Nothing. The bank want to take my house away. I can't afford to pay any bills. Any money that comes into this place goes to... him. And it's never enough. Every month he wants more. And I don't have it.

"Every single penny I get in from my clients gets completely swallowed up. He takes all of it. And yet he demands more. So I need the money. Now. I need enough to pay him off and get him out of my life once and for all. If I don't then... then..."

"Him? Who the fuck are you talking about?"

"Him, Freddie. Him. Frank bloody McLeod."

I sat, staring blankly at him for a second. Of course it was Frank McLeod. It certainly explained my recent abduction. And my black eyes, squashed nose and the stinging pain in my ribs.

"Frank McLeod?" I said. "The gangster? What has he got to do with any of this?"

"He's my… business partner."

"What? But how?"

"He used to be a client."

Of course he did. Why was I not surprised?

"Do you remember back in the day," said Mortimer, "when all those real-life crime books became so popular? The Krays, Dave Courtney, Mickey 'The Blade' Jones, Steve 'Stab-em-up' Spencer, Jimmy 'The Hat' Folan… Dreadful people writing dreadful books that revelled in their sordid, shameful, illegal activities. But they were damned popular."

"Yes, I remember."

"When Frank 'The Animal' McLeod came to me looking for representation for his own memoir, I knew it would be an easy sell. So, I took him on and got him a deal. His first book was actually pretty good and racked up a few decent sales. Since then, he's brought out a new book every other year."

"Okay, but why is he demanding money from you?"

Again, Mortimer sighed heavily. "You may remember a few years ago, I had a bit of trouble with the Inland Revenue."

"A *bit* of trouble?" I laughed.

"They cleaned me out, Freddie. Took everything. It looked like I was going to have to declare bankruptcy and lose the business. And I couldn't do it. I spent too many years building this firm up; I wasn't going to lose it just like that. So, when Frank came to me and offered to help me out… well, I didn't have a choice. He gave me money, so I could pay off my tax bill. In exchange for fifty percent of the business."

"You gladly went into business with a man nicknamed 'The Animal'?"

"Not gladly. But I had no choice. And it would have been fine. There's a clause in the contract allowing me to buy the business back from him. So, I took the money. And when I got the business back on track, I was going to pay him off and get rid of him."

"But all your clients left you."

"The fucking rats."

"Didn't you have them all tied in to contracts?"

"Yes, but nothing their slimy lawyers couldn't argue their way out of. After all the business with not paying my taxes, I was apparently deemed to be untrustworthy. And there were a few minor issues with… payments. Which meant several of the clauses in the contracts were broken by me. I didn't have a leg to stand on. I tried reasoning with them, of course. I mean, we're talking about people I'd been representing for years. Decades, even. People I put on the bloody map. Slightest sign of trouble, and they run for the hills. The fucking ingrates."

"But you still have some clients. You have Dylan. The royalties from his books must be enough to keep you afloat."

"They would, except for McLeod. Every week he comes round with one of his goons – giant of a man, like a shaved gorilla."

"Yeah, I think I know the one," I said, a sudden jolt of pain surging through my swollen face at the memory.

"It's all intimidation, of course. But he comes round once a week for a so called 'board meeting' just to scare me. He says he's owed his dividends, and the business isn't performing well enough. At first, they had me transferring every single penny I earned to them. Now they've taken total control of the company and all its finances. They think I don't know what they're up to, but I'm not fucking stupid."

"What?"

"Huge sums of money coming in, then a few days later it all goes out again to other bank accounts. Payments received for clients I've never even heard of. Offshore accounts in lots of different countries. And there's all these huge payments, all going out to various businesses owned by McLeod. Services I've never heard of. Payments I've never made – but it's all there in the books."

"Money laundering?" I said.

"Of course it is. Why else would there be so much money moving through the company? He doesn't even really try to hide it. I guess he thinks nobody would ever suspect a literary agent of laundering money for criminals."

"No, because you're all so bloody honest, aren't you?" I sneered. "So, why don't you just call the police?"

"Are you mad, Freddie? The man is nicknamed 'The Animal' for a reason. Have you read his books? The things he's done to people... they're... terrifying. Just look at yourself. That was just a warning to stop poking your nose in."

"So, I have you to thank for all this, then?"

"You were seen at my office. They didn't want you asking any more questions and finding out what they were up to. They were going to kill you, but I talked them out of it. If they find out that I've been anywhere near a policeman, I'll end up in a shallow grave with large bits of me hacked off."

I looked down at the ground, my heart beating fast. I really had been close to death.

"So, that's why you want Dylan dead," I said. "If he dies, his next book also becomes his last book. The last novel the great Dylan St James will ever produce. The sales will be through the roof and whichever company publishes it will make an absolute fortune. They'll pay through the nose to get their hands on the rights. Then, with money from the sales... combined with royalties from all his other books, which are guaranteed to sell plenty more copies... your fifteen percent will be worth..."

"Millions," said Mortimer, shame tingeing his voice. He hung his head, looking like he might actually burst into tears. "More than enough to buy off McLeod and get him out of my life for good. Then I can concentrate on getting this place back up and running. I'll get my clients back. I'll be as big as I used to be."

"You're out of your mind. The only thing that's ever going to be as big as it used to be is your fucking waistline, you lunatic."

"Well, that's a little uncalled for, I must say. I'm actually quite sensitive about my weight," he huffed.

"Do you really think McLeod is ever actually going to let you buy him out of this place? He's got you over a barrel. Any money you get from whatever deal you make, McLeod's just going to take it. He's got a good thing going here. Like you said, who'd ever suspect a literary agency of money laundering? And if they ever do, he can just close down that part of his business and take all the legitimate profits that come in."

"That's not true... I'm going to... to..."

"You seriously planned to kill Dylan for this? Your best client? The only one who stood by you? Your friend?"

"It wasn't like that. I just wanted him to sign a better deal. At first we were just trying to scare him. That's why Sanders burned his house down and started following him. We thought it would be enough to... unsettle him. Then he'd see reason and let me arrange the best possible deal with the biggest publisher. But he wouldn't budge. I even got that dreadful actor Douglas Moone to pile on the pressure and try to convince him. But the more we pushed, the more stubborn Dylan became. He just wasn't willing to change his mind."

"You could have told him the truth."

231

"Then it would all have come out. The wives, the cancer, the fake doctors. He'd have found out about everything I'd done over the years. He wouldn't have understood. He'd have left me and signed with another agent. And then where would I be? I'd have nothing, and no way out of this."

"So it was easier just to kill him?"

"I didn't do this lightly," he shouted. "I didn't want any of this. But the only way to make any of it work was to get Dylan out of the way. Then I'd be free to sell his book for whichever deal I thought was best."

"Of course, you oversaw all the pre-nups he signed, didn't you? You made sure the wives would get nothing. And as his agent, you'd have control over all the rights to his books."

"I'm not proud of any of it. But it's done now. My associate is on his way to the hospital to finish things. It's too late."

"You have to call him," I pleaded. "You have to stop him."

"No, Freddie. I can't. In a short while it will all be over. It's better this way."

"And what happens to me? Are you going to kill me as well?"

"That's entirely up to you. We could be in this together. I've seen Dylan's will and you already stand to make a lot of money. You'll be a millionaire. All you have to do is let things happen. Dylan dies and you're rich. Tell me you don't want that?"

I have to admit, a few million quid would have come in rather handy at that particular point in my life.

"And you can be my first new client," continued Mortimer. "I still have contacts, Freddie. I'll take you on. I can get you deals you couldn't even dream of. I can do for you what I did for Dylan. Sign with me and I'll make you a literary star."

I also have to admit, I did rather like the idea of being a literary star. And if Mortimer could make it happen...

But then...

"Fuck you Mortimer, you bloated old has-been. I wouldn't sign with you if you were the most successful agent on earth. I'd rather never sell another book again."

"Then I'm sorry, Freddie. But as soon as my associate gets back, he's going to kill you as well." He paused for a second, then said, "How did you know it was me, by the way? Just out of interest."

"A few things, I suppose," I said, sitting back in the chair and sighing. My throat felt dry and rough. My voice sounded coarse. "But the thing that first tipped me off was the harpoon."

"The harpoon?" he said, smiling with intrigue.

"I came here and told you that Dylan had been shot with a harpoon. And you barely blinked. Everyone else I told about it could barely believe me. I mean, who the hell shoots someone with a harpoon? But you didn't flinch. You weren't surprised at all. It didn't really dawn on me at the time, but later on I figured the only reason something like that wouldn't have surprised you was because you already knew about it. And if you already knew about it, you must be involved in some way."

"Very clever," said Mortimer. "Very clever."

"But you can't actually think you're going to get away with this," I said.

Mortimer sighed again. "You see, Freddie, that's why nobody likes your books. You're a walking bloody cliché, and you fill your second rate, hackneyed detective novels full of the same obvious, clichéd drivel. 'You can't think you're going to get away with this?' Of course I am. Who's going to stop me?"

"Me for a start," I said. "I might be a bit of a hack. And my books may not be the best in the world. But when it comes to crime, at least I do my fucking homework." Then I yanked my hands up, pulling them clear of the restraints.

In the same way that I learned to pick locks in order to create a realistic description of it in *Break and Enter*, I also carried out similar research for another of my books, *Killer Maze*. In this novel, Dick Stone had to hunt down and catch a psychotic killer, who kidnapped his victims and held them captive for two weeks before murdering them and dumping the bodies in the city centre late at night. As part of the plot, one of the victims manages to free herself from being tied up. She escapes from the room and makes her way out, screaming and crying, and calling for help.

The twist, of course, is that, although she thought she was being held in a normal residential house, the killer had actually decorated one room of an abandoned industrial building to look like an ordinary living room. When the victim gets outside, she realises she's still trapped in the confines of a large industrial building, which the killer has transformed into a giant, deadly maze. And that's when the fun starts – will she be able to make her way through the maze and actually escape, before the killer tracks her down and kills her?

In order to make sure that the escape part was realistic, I spent two weeks with Exodus: The Master of Escapology. His real name was Barry Watkins and he was a mediocre magician and escapologist working the club circuit. He taught me everything there was to know about escaping from handcuffs, zip ties, rope, duct tape and pretty much anything else somebody might choose to tie you up with. As part of his magic act, Barry's 'escapes' usually included a key or small knife secreted somewhere on his person, which he'd use to escape his bindings out of sight of the audience. But my victim wouldn't have any of that, so he also taught me how to escape with no tricks or secret help.

The key to escaping from rope is essentially to create some kind of extra space in the bindings in which to manoeuvre. You then move your hands and wrists like crazy, yanking this way and that to destabilise the knots, loosen the bindings, and eventually work your hands free. If you're awake and aware when the restraints are being tied, you would tense your muscles as much as possible, and hold your wrists out at angles. That way, when the person tying you up thinks they've got a good tight seal, you relax your arms and you have that little bit of space to work with.

Unfortunately, I'd been unconscious when I was tied up. So I hadn't been able to do any of the preparatory work. Luckily for me, however, the genius who did the tying had made one very crucial mistake. He'd used the wool from the old lady's drawers.

Unlike rope, wool has a tendency to stretch. Not a lot, but just enough. So, as Mortimer sat talking, I very quietly and discreetly moved my hands from side to side, all the while loosening the restraints. After just a few minutes, what had started as a reasonably tight binding had stretched just enough that I could pull my wrists away from the chair legs. After that, it was just a case of pulling, yanking, tugging and squeezing until I managed to work my hands up and out.

"What the...?" said Mortimer, bouncing back in his chair in surprise.

"Little trick I picked up writing one of my hackneyed detective novels," I said, standing and rubbing my aching wrists.

"But... you... but..." he said, pointing to the wool, now fallen to the ground around the chair legs.

"Are you really surprised," I said, "that your fake SAS expert, who's proved himself so inept at running people over, blowing them up or shooting them in the street, can't even manage to tie someone up properly?"

I marched round the desk, stood over Mortimer, raised a hand into the air and threw my fist into his fat, round face. "That's for ruining Dylan's life," I shouted.

I lifted my hand and threw it back at him, punching him hard in the chin. "And that's for trying to kill him."

I raised my hand for a third time, punching straight down onto his fat, bulbous nose. "And that's for calling me a fucking cliché."

CHAPTER 27

"CALL YOUR FRIEND," I said, one hand gripping tight round Mortimer's throat, the other one high in the air, threatening another punch. "Call him off. Tell him you've changed your mind. You don't want him to go through with killing Dylan."

"I can't," snivelled Mortimer.

"It's over," I yelled. "You've been caught. I'll tell the police everything. You'll never get away with any of it. If you kill Dylan now, you'll only go to jail for longer. There's no reason to go through with it."

"No, I mean: I can't! Sanders doesn't have a mobile phone. He won't carry one. He thinks the government are using them to track his movements. He's not quite right in the head, you know."

"Fuck me, what lovely people you associate with."

It had taken me a good thirty minutes to work my way free from Sanders woollen restraints. So he had at least half an hour lead on me. At that time of night, it would probably have taken Sanders around twenty minutes to get from Mortimer's office to the hospital – depending on where he parked his car. So it could already have been too late. Sanders could have made it to the hospital, killed Dylan and already be on his way back to where I was.

However, if he'd hit any traffic, roadworks or other hold-ups, I might still have time to make it to the hospital and stop him. I dug my mobile phone from my pocket and dialled Richard Stone. Unsurprisingly, it went straight to voicemail.

"For fuck's sake, Richard," I screamed at the phone in annoyance. Mortimer flinched back in his chair, making the leather squeak and fart loudly. "And you can fucking pack it in and all," I said to him.

I waited for Richard's voice to stop and the tone to let me know it was my turn to talk. "Richard," I yelled into the mouthpiece, "I need your help. It's Dylan. Dylan St James. He's in trouble." I was breathing heavily, panic twisting my voice and making it hard to get my words out. "I found the killer. I tracked him down. But he got away. And now he's on his way to the hospital to finish him off. You've got to get there, Richard. You've got to stop him. Please."

I pressed the little red button to hang up and clutched the phone hard in my hand. Then, just to relieve a bit of tension, I punched my hand hard into Mortimer's fat stomach. He wheezed and gurgled at the impact.

"If that man harms Dylan in any way, I'm gonna come back here and fucking kill you," I screamed.

I looked around the office, panicking. I had to get to the hospital and stop the killer. I could run to Piccadilly Circus and jump on the Bakerloo line to Paddington. But it would take too long. And I didn't want my phone signal to cut out on the underground, in case Richard Stone tried calling back. I didn't have a car I could use, or, in fact, the driving licence or necessary skills I'd need to make the damn thing move. So, I was going to have to risk it in a taxi.

I ran out to the old lady's desk and pulled open the drawer she kept her wool in. I knew I was wasting time, but I couldn't leave Mortimer to escape. Not after what I'd discovered. I ran back through to the inner office with a great handful of wool, and round behind Mortimer's chair.

I couldn't get his stubby little arms to bend round behind him, so instead I tied each wrist to the arms of the chair. I tied both his ankles together as well. And then, for extra security, I ran a great length of wool all the way round his chest, tying him firmly to the chair's back rest. I was sure he didn't have my skills at escaping bindings, but I made sure to tie all the knots extra tight – partly to guarantee he'd never get out, and partly just to inflict extra pain on him.

"I never meant for things to go this way," he said weakly, as I started towards to the door. "Please believe me; I only had Dylan's best interests at heart. And things got out of hand. It was Sanders. He convinced me. He made me do it."

"Save your plea bargaining for the police," I said. "They'll be here soon."

I ran out of the office, down the stairs and out into the street. Luckily, a taxi was pulling up right outside Mortimer's office, having been hailed down by a pregnant woman struggling with three or four heavy shopping bags. I ran over, tapped her on the shoulder, and told her that she'd dropped something behind her. When she turned to see what it was, I jumped in the taxi, told the driver to get me to St Mary's Hospital, and said there would be a twenty quid tip if he wasn't too bothered about sticking to the speed limit or stopping for red lights.

The taxi pulled out into the road and sped away in a screech of tyres. The pregnant woman turned back to see my apologetic face peering out the rear window of her taxi as it disappeared down the road. She dropped her shopping to the floor, threw her middle finger up in anger, and shouted out something that sounded like 'shunt'.

I did feel bad. But my friend's life was in danger. And the killer had about a forty minute lead on me now.

As the car raced along Wardour Street, I pulled my phone from my pocket again. I checked the display. There were no messages or missed calls from Richard. I dialled 999 and, when the operator came on, I told her what had happened. I asked her to send a car immediately to St Mary's Hospital, and also one to Mortimer's office, where they could find him tied up and very much in need of arrest. Finally, I asked her to try and get a message to Richard, asking him to call me immediately.

I've no idea how well my message got across. I was highly stressed, sweating and still a little woozy from the knock I'd taken to the head. I remember her asking me repeatedly to calm down and speak more slowly, but I didn't have time to calm down or speak slowly. My friend was in danger and I was the only one who could save him. I rattled off my message as quickly as I could, reiterating the emergency of the situation. Then I hung up before she could really make much of a response. I sat back in the taxi, happy at least that the driver had taken my offer seriously, and was speeding along as fast as the roads would allow.

Twenty minutes later, the taxi pulled up in traffic at the bottom of Norfolk Place. The road was completely gridlocked.

"What's happening?" I asked the driver. "Why have we stopped?"

"Sorry mate, stuck in traffic," he shouted back over his shoulder.

"Well, can't you go around it? I need to get to the hospital now."

"Sorry, chief. Looks like there's some kind of temporary traffic lights up ahead. We'll get moving in a minute."

"I don't have a minute. Is there no way to get around it? I have to be at the hospital now. It's a matter of life and death."

"That may be, mate. But this is a one-way road. I can't go forwards, I can't go back. Just have to wait until the traffic moves."

"Dammit!" I yelled, digging two twenty pound notes out of my pocket and shoving it through the little gap in the window to the driver. "I'll go the rest on foot."

I threw open the door, clambered out onto the pavement and ran down the street. My lungs started burning as I sprinted, a hot pain in my chest. I made it about one hundred yards before I had to stop, bend over and hold my knees, as I wheezed and coughed.

As I crouched there, thinking I might throw up, I looked up at the road ahead of me. It must only have been a few hundred yards, but it seemed to stretch on for miles. I placed my hand on the back of my head, feeling for the first time the hot, sodden lump where I'd been hit. Then something on the other side of the road caught my gaze. A bright orange something, smiling menacingly from the rear passenger window of a blue car in a parking bay.

"Fuck!" I said to myself. "He's already here."

With my head still swimming, and my hair wet from the blood and sweat, I straightened myself up and set off again. I ran down to the corner of Norfolk Place and Praed Street, crossed the road and ran in through the main gate of the hospital. I found the entrance, deciphered the myriad of confusing signs and bolted off towards the lift.

I made it up onto the right ward, trudging along the corridors like a marathon runner five hours into a race, and finally burst into Dylan's room. It was empty.

"Fuck!" I shouted. "Fuck!"

Where the hell was he? The bed was empty – rumpled and untucked. The machines at the side of him were all still there, still turned on but completely inactive. The IV bag still hung from the large metal pole, but the tube that had previously been plugged into Dylan's forearm now trailed limply down to the floor.

I clambered into the room, sitting down roughly on the bed, as I wheezed and gasped. A nurse came bundling in after me. She was a fat woman with a face like a bulldog.

"What's going on in here?" she yelled at me in an officious tone. "What's all this shouting? We've got people trying to sleep, you know."

"Where the fuck is my friend?" I said.

"What are you talking about?"

"My friend. The previous occupant of this bed. The man with the big fucking stab wound in his chest? Where is he?"

"Well… I don't know…" she said, suddenly looking worried.

"You don't know? What do you mean you don't know? You mean you've lost him?"

"No, of course not. I think I saw one of the doctors coming in to see him. Though, come to think of it, I didn't recognise him. And then he wheeled him away in a wheelchair, which I remember thinking was a bit strange, but…"

"But? But fucking what?"

"But I got called away to another patient," she said, indignantly. "It's only me and Kelly on tonight. We can't see to everyone at once, you know."

"Oh, well that's all right then. Remember and tell that to the police when they ask you why nobody stopped a murderer coming in and abducting my friend. 'I would have, officer, but it's only me and Kelly on tonight.' Fucking idiot!"

"Murderer?"

"The same man that put Dylan in here. He's come back to finish the job. Now, which way did he go?"

"Erm… well… he went off in that direction," she murmured, pointing down a long hallway outside the room.

"What's down there? Where does it go?"

"Nowhere, really. It just leads to the lifts at the end."

"When did you see him?" I yelled.

All the woman's previous authority had drained out of her. She looked like she might burst into tears. "It was… about… five minutes ago. I'm sorry, I really am. I had no idea. And we really are busy tonight…"

"Only five minutes," I said, crossing the room to the door.

Only five minutes. He couldn't have got too far. But where would he have taken Dylan? Of course he wouldn't want to kill him in his hospital room. There was too great a risk of someone coming in and catching him. He'd wanted to take Dylan somewhere private and secluded.

In fact, I thought, he wouldn't want anyone to think it was murder at all. It would be much better to disguise the death as an accident. Then he could slip away without suspicion. And if nobody thought Dylan had been murdered, there would be nobody looking for the killer.

"You said he was a doctor." I turned back to look at the nurse, who was now actually weeping slightly. "Why did you think he was a doctor?"

"Well… he was wearing scrubs."

Of course. Sanders had disguised himself. He must have sneaked in to the hospital, stolen the medical clothing from somewhere, and then changed into it. That explained why I'd managed to reduce his lead down to just five minutes. Then he'd come in here, put Dylan in the chair and wheeled him off somewhere.

"Where would he go," I asked the nurse, "if he wanted to take Dylan somewhere and make it look like he'd had an accident rather than been murdered? How would he do it? How would he make it look like an accident?"

"Well... erm..." she said, breathing deeply and trying to gather herself. "There's lots of ways, I suppose. Depending on how much medical knowledge he has... he could inject him with something..."

"So, he'd go the pharmacy, or somewhere he could get drugs?"

"Yes, I suppose so. But he wouldn't go that way; the pharmacy is in completely the other direction. And he wouldn't be able to just get his hands on some drugs. He'd need a prescription."

"Don't you keep drugs on the wards?"

"Yes, but they're all locked away. He'd need to know where they are. And he'd need a key. And he'd need to know what meds to give him in the first place."

"Dammit!" I said, my theory crumbling in front of me. "Then where the fuck has he gone?"

I poked my head out of the room, looking down the corridor into the ward. Then I looked the other way – the long, sterile hallway leading down to nothing but the lift.

"Fuck!" I shouted. "He's not going to make it look like an accident. He'll try and make it look like a suicide. He's going for the roof."

CHAPTER 28

I JABBED HARD at the silver call button, pressing again and again until my finger ached, willing the lift to hurry up. Finally it came, and I dashed in through the half-open doors. I found the button for the top floor and started my continuous jabbing again. "Fucking come on," I muttered under my breath.

The lift took me to the top floor and I dashed out, looking this way and that for any sign of Dylan. It was colder up on this floor. There were no wards up here, no patients, just a long eerie corridor. A broken tube light flickered on the ceiling, intermittently lighting the space before plunging it back into darkness. There was something at the far end of the corridor. I couldn't quite make out what it was.

Carefully, I started towards it. The flickering light gave me short, sharp glimpses. It was a solid shape. Dull metal and some kind of fabric. I got closer. I could see something circular. It was an abandoned wheelchair, tumbled over onto its side. It had been deserted outside a door which sat slightly ajar.

I ran over and looked down at the wheelchair. It must have been the one Sanders had used to wheel Dylan around. I looked closer at the door. It was smashed at the lock. Small shards of loose, cracked wood hung off it. A big red sign on the door read: *MAINTENANCE STAFF ONLY. STRICTLY NO ACCESS TO PATIENTS.*

It had to be the stairs to the roof. The lift wouldn't take him all the way to the top, so he'd kicked the door open and had to continue on foot. That's why he'd abandoned the chair – he couldn't get it up the stairs. He would have had to carry Dylan the rest of the way, which would have slowed him down even further. There might still be time.

I kicked open the door and stepped through into a tight, dark stairwell.

"Sanders?" I called out. No reply.

Tentatively, I placed my foot on the first step, gripping tightly to the handrail. It was pitch black in there, the broken tube light from the hall doing nothing to light it up. I made my way carefully up the stairs, clutching the handrail the whole way. I knew time was of the essence, but my head was still pounding from the knock I'd taken, and I felt woozy in the dark. I made it up one flight of steps on wobbly legs. Then I climbed a second, and a third. Finally, I reached another door at the top.

I threw it open and bounded out onto the roof of the hospital. It was windy up there and the bright twinkling lights of the city stung my eyes, momentarily disorienting me. A large generator buzzed and hummed noisily to the right of me.

"Sanders?" I yelled out. "Dylan?"

To my left, I saw a flicker of movement. I dashed after it, following a narrow pathway, rounding the small concrete block I'd emerged from. I turned the corner and came out onto the main roof area. Over in the corner, stood Sanders, dressed in pale blue medical scrubs, dragging Dylan towards the edge of the roof.

"Sanders," I screamed. "Don't do it!"

He stopped, then turned to look at me. Dylan looked up at me as well, a foggy, pained, confused look on his face. "Freddie," he yelled, his voice slurred from the morphine. "Freddie, help me."

"It's over, Sanders," I shouted. "There's nowhere to go now. You can't get away with it."

"Who is this fucker, Freddie?" yelled Dylan. "What the hell's going on?"

Sanders lifted a hand and brought it down hard, thumping Dylan's chest, right where the spear had wounded him. Dylan screamed out in pain, then went limp, his legs flopping about beneath him like two damp lengths of the rope.

"Shut up, you!" shouted Sanders. Then he looked up at me. "You can't stop me, Winters. It's too late."

I edged across the roof, slowly moving closer to the two men. "Look, just give up, will you? You've already been caught. The police are downstairs and they're on the way up here now. Another team are on their way to pick up Mortimer. You'll never make it out of the building."

"I don't believe you," he shouted.

"It's true," I said, moving to within just ten feet of him. "You're only making things worse for yourself. So far, you're only going down for a bit of assault and kidnapping. If you kill Dylan now, you'll go to prison for murder. You don't want that."

"It's not going to be murder. Everyone knows about his depression. He's suffered with it for years. When they find his body on the ground, they'll just think he killed himself."

"Don't be a fool, man. I'll tell them what you've done."

"You don't have to. Nobody has to know I was even here. You tell them you came to the hospital to see him. You find the room empty, so you figure he's come up here to top himself. You run up after him, but you're too late. Mortimer will take care of you. We'll all be rich. You know it makes sense."

"Mortimer? What's he talking about Freddie?" whimpered Dylan, still struggling to hang on to consciousness.

"Oh yeah," I said, "this guy works for Mortimer. He's the one trying to have you killed. And you wouldn't believe what else he's been up to."

"What about it, Winters?" said Sanders.

"Oh, fuck off, Sanders. Of course I'm not gonna let you kill my friend. Now give it up, before someone really gets hurt."

"Shame. Looks like I'm just gonna have to throw your friend off the roof, then throw you off after him. Double suicide. Much neater, actually."

He edged further back, dragging Dylan to the very lip of the roof.

"Freddie," yelled Dylan, too weak to move or fight back. Terror sparkled in his eyes.

"Wait," I shouted, "wait. At least tell me why."

"You know why," snapped Sanders. "The money. It's all about the money."

"No, why the harpoon? Why did you use a bloody harpoon?"

"What?"

"Why did you shoot Dylan with a harpoon? It's been bugging me this whole time."

"It's not a harpoon, it's a spear fishing gun."

"All right, spear gun, then. Why did you use that? Why not get a proper gun?"

"Do you know how hard it is to get your hands on a gun? You can't just go and buy one in Tesco, you know."

"Well, couldn't you just get one... on the street?"

"Street? What street? I live in Surrey. The only thing you get on the street is fast food, overpriced shops and charity muggers."

"Oh, tell me about it," I said. "I fucking hate those guys!"

Dylan flashed me a confused look, as if to indicate that I'd strayed slightly off topic.

"Anyway," I said, forcing myself back on track, "I thought you used to be in the SAS. You must have a secret stash of guns somewhere. Or a gang of ex-forces mates, who could sort you out. I mean… unless you weren't really in the SAS, of course."

"I was in the SAS," he screamed.

"Really? That's not what they say."

"I *was* in the fucking SAS!"

"Don't they teach you to build bombs in the SAS? I mean, ones that actually kill the people they're supposed to?"

"I'm an expert bomb maker," he said, indignantly.

"Really? Tell that to the postman you blew up by mistake. Where did you learn how to build that thing? Build-a-Shit-Bomb.com?"

"Well, it fucking worked, didn't it? He did blow up."

I couldn't fault him on his logic. "Yeah… but the wrong bloody person. Surely they don't teach you that in the SAS – *it doesn't matter who you blow up, as long as someone explodes.*"

Sanders eyes shone with anger. His mouth pursed up into a tight little pucker and his face flushed bright red.

"Admit it," I said, "you were never in the SAS. That's why you were dropped by the papers, and your publisher, and all your TV appearances. That's why you're a fucking laughing stock. Because everyone found out it was all just a pack of lies."

"It's not lies," he screamed again, his eyes wild and his face glowing pink. "I was in the SAS. They just wanted to silence me. They didn't like me being a public figure, and they didn't want people to know what I know. So they said I was lying, to discredit me."

"A likely story. If any of that's true, how come there's no evidence?"

"They destroyed it all. It's all part of the cover up."

"Cover up? They? Who are they, exactly?"

"The Government," he said, his voice cracking with anger. He was so adamant, so emotional, as if he truly believed it. Like he'd spent so long lying about it, he'd somehow convinced himself it was all true. "They told lies about me. They destroyed all the records. They broke into my house and stole pictures. All so they could…"

He went quiet, his crazed eyes twitching as he thought. Then his face straightened and he smiled at me.

"Very clever, Mr Winters," he said, in a slow, calm voice. "Trying to distract me. Buying time until the back-up arrives. But not clever enough, I'm afraid."

He grabbed Dylan hard under the arms, lifting him slightly off the floor. Then he spun around, twisting his body and throwing Dylan towards the edge of the roof.

Dylan skittered along the floor, his limp, battered body unable to move. He twisted and turned, the rough asphalt screeching and crackling beneath him, as he bumped along. He had a terrified look in his eyes, as one arm scrabbled on the floor, desperate to find something, anything to grab hold of.

His fingers clawed at the hard ground. I tried to move, to run to him, but I wasn't quick enough. His legs disappeared over the edge of the building. His mouth opened wide as he tried to scream. And then he was gone.

"No!" I screamed, as I watched my friend disappear over the side of the building.

I looked up at Sanders. A wave of pure anger washed over me. Without thinking, I ran at him.

I crossed the space between us in three giant strides. Shock flashed across Sanders' face as I raised my hand, drew it back in one fluid movement, and then threw my balled up fist at him.

It hit him square in the side of the face, sending him off balance. The sickly sound of my knuckles cracking against his cheek echoed around the roof. I balled up my other fist, drew my hand behind me and launched another punch at him. But he was too quick this time. He ducked his head to the side and my fist went flying straight past. I tried to pull it back, but it was too late. I was off balance now, and I stumbled forwards with the momentum of my loose punch.

Sanders side-stepped, moving out of my way, and threw his left hand into my side. The punch landed hard in my ribs, making me squeal with pain. He followed it up quickly with a second fast punch. Then he raised his leg and kneed me hard in the buttocks.

I skipped away from Sanders, one step, then two. I turned to face him, just in time to see him running towards me, fists high in the air.

I had just enough time to react, throwing my arms up in front of my face to protect myself. Sanders' fist bounced off my forearm, and I took a step back to steady myself. I saw him winding up for another attack, and I shifted left, hoping to avoid his hands.

I didn't. His knuckles collided hard with my chin. Pain exploded in jaw and cheek. My teeth and brain rattled in my head. He punched me again, but I managed to twist just in time so that it missed my head and bounced off my shoulder.

Sanders took a step backwards, planning his next move. And that's when I pounced. I'm not much of a fighter. I have no skills to speak of. But even if you can't punch very well, everyone is susceptible to an out-and-out flying attack.

So, that's what I did. I launched myself at Sanders, literally diving towards him, and grabbed him hard around the waist. My weight knocked him back a step. Then he stumbled and tripped, and we both fell to the ground. He landed on his back, and I flopped down a second later, landing on top of him.

He wheezed and screamed as the landing knocked the air out of him. Then I fought dirty, punching and thumping him in the face, ribs, and chest. He squealed and coughed, as I caught him again and again. He raised his hands to defend himself, but I batted them back down. Thump. Splat. Thump. Whack. I rained blow after blow down upon him.

My hands were singing with pain. My breath ragged. Sweat soaked my head and my muscles were quickly tiring. But I couldn't stop punching.

Sanders raised his hands to protect his face. And then my fists were hitting nothing but the hard bones in his forearms. I felt him breathe hard and squirm beneath me. Then he shifted his weight, flicking a leg up somehow and driving it hard into my balls.

I stopped instantly, screaming out in agony. All the breath whooshed out of my lungs, pain surging through my groin and stomach. My hands went straight to my privates as I collapsed sideways, falling off Sanders and rolling onto the ground. I was vaguely aware of Sanders picking himself up off the floor. Then he kicked me hard in the ribs.

"You fucking arsehole," he shouted. Then he kicked me in the leg. A surge of pain streaked through it.

"All you had to do was go along with the plan." Kick. This time in the back. It was so hard it made me spasm wildly on the ground.

He stopped for second, bending over to catch his breath and spit out a mouthful of blood. "You think you can beat me?" he shouted. "Well, now you're going to die!"

He stood over me. He raised his foot high into the air. Levelled it with my head. Readied himself to smash it down into my face.

I looked up at him, once again expecting that moment of curious bliss as my life flashed before my eyes. Instead, I saw a very different sort of flash. A thin streak of silver light that rose up behind Sanders head, then crashed down onto it.

Sanders looked down at me with a confusion. Then his leg dropped, his body went limp, and he collapsed onto the floor next to me.

I peered up through squinting, bloodied eyes to see Detective Richard Stone. He had an extendable police baton in his hand.

"You all right, Freddie?" he said.

"What? Fuck… shit… Dylan," I said, suddenly remembering.

I clambered up off the ground and hobbled to the edge of the building. I didn't want to look. I didn't want to see my friend's mangled body lying dead on the ground far below. But I knew I had to.

I took a deep breath, trying to calm the rapid beating of my heart, and peered over the edge.

"Oh, for fuck's sake," I said, turning back to look at Sanders, bloody and beaten on the floor behind me. "You really are the worst fucking hitman in the world."

I looked back over the edge. About eight feet down, and protruding roughly four feet out from the edge of the building, was a narrow, grey ledge. Dylan lay there looking up at me, dazed and winded, and very much alive.

"Don't worry mate," I called down to him. "It's all over now. We'll get you up from there in just a jiffy."

CHAPTER 29

"SO, IT WAS Mortimer all along. I can't believe it."

I was perched on the edge of Dylan's hospital bed, a cool breeze tickling my back as it whistled in through the gap of the poorly-tied hospital gown. After all the excitement of the previous evening, and seeing the deep, bloody gash on the back of my head, the hospital staff had decided to keep me in overnight for observation. All I'd wanted to do was head to the closest pub and dull the pain with a several large scotches. But apparently, that's not the best thing to do when you have a possible concussion.

Dylan's offer to sweeten the deal by paying for me to spend the night in the private hospital room next to his finally persuaded me. He didn't actually know he'd offered to pay — he was unconscious at the time. But I'd figured it was what he would have wanted.

Sadly, my dreams of what private healthcare provides were cruelly dashed. Contrary to my hopes, the doctors don't actually give you first dibs on the coolest, strongest painkillers. And there are no gorgeous, busty, blonde nurses in short dresses and stockings, administering blowjobs at the press of a call button. But the bed was fairly comfortable, the food was edible and the staff did prevent me from slipping into a coma. So, I wasn't complaining too much.

"Yeah, sorry mate," I said, "but that's what I found out. Mortimer's been behind everything. He's been screwing with you for years."

I'd just got through reporting the results of my investigations to Dylan. I told him all about Mortimer's scheming over the years. About the man who had thrown him off a building the previous evening. And how Mortimer was behind the plan to have him killed. Understandably, Dylan was more than a little shocked.

"So, I really never had cancer?"

"No, Dr Shepton lied to you. He faked the test results and prescribed drugs you never needed. He'll be struck off, for sure. And probably end up inside for a stretch, too."

"I've been through two courses of chemotherapy. Taking those pills every day. Puking, feeling dizzy, sweating and shaking for weeks on end. And there was never anything wrong with me?"

"That's right."

"And Dr Jeffries wasn't even a real psychiatrist?"

"Nope. Just an actor. And not a very good one, either."

"I always knew there was something dodgy about that fucker," said Dylan, shaking his head with disappointment. "No wonder he was always asking me to read through plays and scripts with him. I thought it was some kind of confidence building exercise. The fucker was just using me to read lines with him."

I clamped a hand to my mouth, holding in the smile that I could feel spreading across my face.

"Still," I said, "I suppose you do kind of have to hand it to Mortimer."

"You what?" said Dylan, outraged. He sat up in bed, so he could look me directly in the eye. Then he winced, coughed, clutched his chest and fell back into his pillow.

"No, I mean, utterly reprehensible, of course," I said. "And he's gonna get what's coming to him. But he did kind of have a point. You wrote all your bestsellers when you were depressed."

"So, you agree with him? You think I can only write when I'm depressed?"

"No... yeah... no... oh, I don't know. All I'm saying is, he had a plan – a fucking horrible, evil, despicable one – but it seemed to work. You won two Bookers. You've made millions."

"Well, he didn't have to make me think I was dying. He didn't have to ruin my marriages. He didn't have to try and kill me. He could have just told me to focus on the darker storylines."

"Well, there is that," I said. He had a point. As far as constructive criticism goes, Mortimer's approach was more than a touch extreme.

"So, what happens next?" asked Dylan.

"I don't know," I said. "They caught Sanders up on the roof last night. And I left Mortimer tied up in his office for the police to arrest. I'm sure they're both going to prison for a very long time. You'll probably need to get yourself a new agent, though."

"Yeah, a slightly less murderous one, I think," said Dylan, forcing a smile.

"I'd give that Chantelle a miss, too," I said. "Really not a very nice girl. You know, I caught her and her boyfriend breaking into your place the other night, looking for money."

"Jesus," said Dylan solemnly. "You know, I can't believe I ever married her. I guess I always knew she didn't really love me. And I knew it would never last. I was just lonely, and still missing Corinne, I think. Just an old fool, flattered by the attentions of a young, pretty woman. And I let it all go too far."

"Hey, we've all been there, mate. Given half a chance, I'd have been right in there myself. But maybe stop giving her money, eh?"

"I guess I just felt sorry for her," he said. "Of course, that's before I knew the scheming bitch was being paid to pretend to like me."

"Oh, I don't think it was all pretend. Seriously, I think she really did like you, in her own weird way. Just not as much as she likes herself. Or money. At least you can take solace in knowing what kind of a clown she picks with her own free will. The guy's a complete dick. He makes paintings out of spunk, for God's sake."

"Makes paintings out of what?" said Dylan, baffled.

"Never mind," I said. "Best not to know. Anyway, I have to go now. They've said they're ready to release me, but I just wanted to come in and talk to you before I left. The doctors reckon you could be out of here in about a week. But I'll stay on at the flat for a little while, if you want? And I'll be there to look after you, as long as you need."

"Thank you, Freddie," he said. "You really are a good friend."

"Well, maybe not," I sighed. "I certainly haven't been. But I'm trying to make up for it."

Dylan looked up at me, smiling, battling to keep his eyes open.

"Although, having said that, it might be a good idea to move house, if you can. I accidentally shagged your stalker. The one that knits those jumpers. And now she knows where you live."

"You accidentally did what?"

"Shagged her. So, she's been to the flat a few times. I caught her wearing your pants the other night, and going through your drawers, the crazy bitch. And, do you know what; I swear there's still little bits of postman in the bushes. Those cleaning guys haven't done a very thorough job, if you ask me. So, you know… maybe see about getting another flat, I guess."

Dylan just stared at me blankly.

"Anyway, I'm gonna push off. But try not to go to sleep just yet. I've asked someone else to pop in. I thought you might want to see her."

Dylan glanced over to see who I meant. Stood in the doorway was Corinne Handley.

I'd called Corinne the previous evening. I told her what had happened to Dylan, and explained how I'd saved his life. As I'd hoped, she'd been completely beside herself with worry. She really did still love him.

I explained about all the recent goings-on and what Mortimer had been up to. I told her how he and the lawyer had colluded to get rid of her. How the payment and the divorce papers had not come from Dylan. And how, as far as Dylan had known, it was her that wanted rid of him, not the other way round. When she'd tried to contact Dylan, to ask for an explanation, or to seek reconciliation, Mortimer had acted as some kind of evil middle man, intercepting all of Dylan's calls and refusing to put her through. And he'd done the same to Dylan, telling him Corinne had not been in touch, and was refusing to answer Dylan's calls or emails. Dylan had been so depressed at the news and in such a vulnerable state. It had taken only the slightest push from Mortimer's fake psychiatrist to send Dylan further back into himself, so that he trusted no one but Mortimer and did pretty much what he told him.

Mortimer had effectively ended their marriage, leaving each of them thinking it was the other one that had wanted out.

I told Corinne that I thought Dylan still had deep feelings for her. His marriage to Chantelle Star, although not ideal, had been another one of Mortimer's deceptions. I told Corinne I thought Dylan had only gone along with it because he was still so crushed over the break up with her.

"Hi Dylan," said Corinne, crossing the room, her eyes filled with a mix of happiness and distress. "I'm so glad you're okay. Are you in much pain?"

"No, I'm okay," said Dylan. "Thanks to Freddie. He saved my life. Sort of…"

"Thank you Mr Winters," said Corinne. "Thank you so much… for so many things."

I went to answer, but Dylan cut me off.

"Freddie has been filling me in on everything that Mortimer did. I can't believe he'd do that to me. But worst of all…" His eyes filled with tears, and his words caught in his throat. "I can't believe what he did to us."

I looked at Corinne. She too had tears glinting in her eyes.

"When I came home to find those divorce papers," she said, "I couldn't believe it. I tried calling you for weeks, but you wouldn't answer. I was going to fly out to America to talk to you, but Mortimer said you wouldn't see me. He told me you wanted out of the marriage, and there was nothing I could do to change your mind. I should have known it wasn't true. But I... I... you broke my heart. And I didn't know what to think."

"No," said Dylan, "I should have known. Mortimer told me it was you that wanted out. He told me you only married me to keep your profile high. And once you had, you didn't need me any more. I shouldn't have doubted you. I should have known."

Things were getting a bit emotional in the room, and there were way more tears than I generally like to deal with. So, I decided this would be a good time to leave.

"I think you two need a little time alone," I said. "To get reacquainted. So I'm gonna shove off and leave you to it."

"Thank you Freddie," said Dylan. He reached out and took my hand, squeezing it gently. "For everything." The tears were now rolling slowly down his cheeks.

"Yes, thank you, Mr Winters," said Corinne. "You've done a great deal for both of us. It won't be forgotten."

"Hey, that's what friends are for," I said smiling.

I stood up from the bed and walked to the door, a sense of pride glowing in my chest – just next to the bruised ribs.

"Oh, before I go," I said, turning back to them. "Any chance you could log into your bank account and pay me the money you owe me. It's just; I really should go and pay my rent. Or they're gonna kick me out."

"No problem," said Dylan, with a weak, tired smile. "I'll log in and send the money in a minute."

"Cool. So, that's... eight days at £500 a day... plus, I should probably get some kind of bonus for solving everything... catching the bad guys... getting beaten up... twice... oh, and saving your life, too... so... call it six grand?"

"Cheap at twice the price," said Dylan, with a tired laugh.

"Or you could just give me your password and I'll do it myself. If that's easier? You know, save you getting up and going to find a computer."

"Nice try, Freddie," said Corinne. "Dylan can log in using my phone. You'll have the money in a few minutes."

"Fair dos," I said, turning and walking out the door. "Just trying to help."

******

The doctor came to see me for a final check, then told me I was free to go home. He said I should rest for a few days and lay off the booze. He also gave me a small bottle of codeine pills. I tried to haggle him up to something a bit groovier, like Tramadol or Vicodin, but the miserable sod was having none of it.

I dressed in Dylan's torn, blood-stained suit, and headed off. As I walked out of the main entrance I bumped into Detective Richard Stone. He looked slightly less angry than usual.

"I wanted to thank you," said Richard, grimacing slightly, as if the words tasted bad in his mouth. "And to apologise. As much as it pains me to say so, I should have listened to you when you asked to help with the investigation. You followed leads we'd never have thought to look into. You figured out what was going on. And you caught the killer. Well, sort of…"

"Yeah, thanks for last night," I said, my hand inadvertently reaching up to touch the wound on the back of my head. "You saved my life."

"I'm only glad I was there in time to catch Sanders. Before he could do anything else."

"Is he going to prison?" I asked.

"Oh, definitely. We've got him on assault against you and attempted murder against Mr St James. And that's just the start. We found his car where you told us to look. There was a spear-fishing gun in the boot, along with a number of spears. We're still waiting on forensics, but I think it's a good bet it's the one he used to shoot your friend. So, we've got him on two counts at least.

"We also found trace residues of a number of chemicals that can be used in bomb-making and a six-pack of padded envelopes, with two missing. Oh, and when we searched his home, the first thing we found on his internet history was a page that describes how to make letter bombs. I mean, talk about bloody amateur."

"SAS, my arse," I said. "So, you've got him for the murder of that poor postman as well?"

"At least manslaughter, we reckon. He'll be going away for a very long time, don't worry about that."

"And what about Mortimer?"

"Yes, thanks for that little parcel you left us? Very nicely wrapped. We picked him up last night. And thanks for your tip about checking through his accounts. It definitely made for some very interesting reading."

"So, you've finally got something on Frank McLeod?"

"More than something. We woke him up at 4am with a nice cold pair of handcuffs. We can tie him personally to dozens of cases of money laundering. And we're also looking at multiple charges of fraud, tax avoidance, living off the proceeds of immoral earnings… he didn't even make much of an effort to hide what he was up to."

"Too cocky," I said.

"Your friend Mortimer has been spilling his guts all night. He's gonna testify against McLeod. So, I think we've really got him this time. Shame we couldn't get him for anything bigger, though."

"Hey, they got Al Capone on tax avoidance, didn't they?" I said. "But if Mortimer's testifying does that mean he's gonna get some kind of deal? You're not letting him off, are you?"

"Don't be daft. He'll share the fraud and money laundering charges, as it was all run through his business. And we have him on conspiracy to commit murder, perverting the course of justice, as well as a host of other things. We've promised him the judge will look favourably on his case after his testimony against McLeod. So, he'll probably end up in a fairly cushy, low-security prison. But he'll still be going away for a long time."

"What about the doctor and the lawyer? And that fucking actor pretending to be a shrink?"

"Not sure yet. We're rounding them all up today, after I've been upstairs to talk with Mr St James. We'll probably have the doctor on malpractice and negligence. But the lawyer's a different matter. It all depends on what he knew and, more importantly, what we can prove he knew. We're gonna drag the actor in, sweat him for a few hours and see what he cops to."

"That's brilliant, Richard," I said. "Quite a big day for you, then. Solving an attempted murder and taking down a crime boss. Good result."

"Yep, I've definitely had worse. And I couldn't have done it without your help. I'd never have thought the likes of McLeod would be involved with a literary agent. Just goes to show."

"So, does this mean I'm forgiven?" I asked, hopefully.

"Not a fucking chance," said Richard, smiling. "I still think you're a prick. But maybe there's hope for you. Anyway, I need to speak with Mr St James, so I'd better get on."

To my surprise, Detective Richard Stone reached out a hand to me. I nearly flinched, such was the shock. But I reached out my own hand and shook his.

"Take care of yourself, Freddie," he said smiling. "And thanks again." Then he patted me hard on the back, and walked off into the hospital.

I stepped out into the cool, lunchtime air and felt the heat of the sun warming my face. I smiled and reached into my pocket, pulling out the bottle of codeine pills. I threw two into my mouth and swallowed them. Then I headed off to find the nearest pub.

EPILOGUE

TEN MONTHS LATER

I WAS SITTING in my favourite Starbucks, sipping a hot caramel latte. Marta, the Polish barista – and my coffee shop nemesis – was wearing a badge that informed me she was now Manager. As if the red-haired harridan wasn't cocky enough before, she had now graduated from wiping tables and sneering at customers, to standing behind the till and sneering at the poor young girls struggling to work the coffee machine.

However, she wasn't sneering at me, for a change. And she had no reason to. Because I was drinking my coffee at the regular pace of other customers. And I was onto my second cup.

Things had been going rather better for me of late. My latest novel, *Death of a Mailman*, was actually doing quite well in the charts. And for the first time in a long time, I had a bit of money in my pocket.

When the story broke about Dylan's attempted murder, and the arrest of his agent, I became something of a minor celebrity in my own right. The story was carried in all the big tabloids. And when they found out that I had been an integral part in cracking the case and getting to the bottom of Mortimer's nefarious schemes, I was interviewed several times by newspapers, on the radio and on TV. I'd learned my lessons, of course, and every time I sang my own investigative praises, I made sure to follow up with an even bigger endorsement for Detective Richard Stone, assuring the interviewer that he was the real hero of the piece – I was just a novelist with several very reasonably priced books, currently available from many reputable shops and online retailers.

Richard, of course, was deservedly celebrated for being the man who finally managed to put the notorious gangster, Frank 'The Animal' McLeod, behind bars. He received a promotion at work, along with a special commendation. Best of all, people again started to think of him as a highly-skilled police officer, and not just the man from the crap detective novels.

My own fifteen minutes of fame was followed up very quickly by offers from several agents, all keen to represent me. And *they* came to *me* – not the other way around. So, I parted ways with my useless, former agent and signed with one of the biggest agencies in the country. Within a week my new agent had secured me offers from three big publishers, provided I could get a new book out quickly – in order to capitalise on my new-found, and quickly dwindling, fame.

I locked myself away and got to work. Although the publishers gave me free rein to write whatever I wanted, I decided the time had come for a change. So, I said goodbye to Dick Stone.

They say you should write what you know, and I knew it had the makings of a fantastic book, so I decided to write a fictional version of Dylan's story. Again, learning my lessons from the whole Dick Stone debacle, I checked and double-checked with Dylan that he was okay with it. His view was that the papers had already covered the whole thing anyway, so there was no harm in using the story as material for my book.

When I told my new agent what I was planning to write, he even managed to get the publishers to up their initial offers. No doubt they saw the potential for extra sales and publicity, based very much on the great British public's shameful desire to find out all the sordid details of the story. I'd made no promises to include that in the book, but my agent saw no reason to correct the publishers' false assumptions.

With the fictional Dick Stone out of the picture, I had to create a new protagonist to tell my story. Again, following the mantra of 'write what you know', my lead investigator became a grizzled, grumpy crime writer, who called on his own sharp intellect and problem-solving skills to investigate and uncover the truth. I then told the story pretty much as I remembered it – adding quite a bit of artistic licence, of course, to beef up the dull parts and keep the reader guessing until the end.

I wrote the first draft in just over six weeks. It then went through a number of revisions with my new editor, and I even let Dylan read a copy before I handed a final version over to my publisher. The book was proofread, typeset and had a really cool cover designed. And just six months after I had cracked the real case and saved Dylan's life, my fictional version of events hit the shelves.

The release date cleverly coincided with Mortimer Bunkle's trial, so my book received plenty of coverage alongside the court reports in the tabloids. Say what you like about marketing people (and I invariably do), they do know what they're doing sometimes. They ambushed a new wave of public interest in the case and then plugged the hell out of the book.

They had me lined up for two whole weeks of book signings,

readings and appearances up and down the country. I was more than happy to do it, of course. It was something of a novelty to actually be invited to appear somewhere, rather than sneaking in with my duffel bag and setting up unseen. And I got to use my special 'Author' badge honestly for a change. I was interviewed by some of the papers again – this time about the book, and not just my involvement with Dylan. And the Guardian even asked me to write a guest blog post for their website.

The book garnered a number of good reviews in the papers, and readers and critics alike really seemed to enjoy it. For once I had an actual, genuine hit on my hands. There were a few dicks who gave me one-star reviews on Amazon, and attacked the minutest, most insignificant, petty little things. But I consoled myself that they were either jealous, illiterate or just plain idiots. And I figured at least one them must have been James Patterson getting his own back on me.

I stayed on at Dylan's flat for a couple of months after the attack at the hospital, but Dylan never returned there himself. Instead, when he was released, he went and stayed with Corinne Handley, who even cancelled her own book tour to look after him. And that was definitely for the best. As willing as I was to chip in and take care of my old mate, I'm not a particularly gifted or patient nurse. And I would probably just have made him worse.

Truth be told, I was actually quite glad to have the peace and quiet. It was nice living in luxury for at least a bit longer. Dylan, being Dylan, made sure groceries were delivered for me on a weekly basis. I protested that he didn't need to, but he just kept claiming they were a thank you for everything I'd done.

I never saw Caroline again. Despite suspecting she might have tried to pop round, or even break in, in an attempt to see Dylan, she never did. Which was a shame. I'd actually grown quite fond of her, in a strange Stockholm syndrome sort of a way. But maybe she'd found someone else to follow around and knit jumpers for.

I eventually moved back to my own flat – Mr Singh having been appeased with the eventual payment of my back rent, the next two months in advance, and a promise not to be (in his words) "such a bloody bastard" in future.

For the first time in a long time, I actually felt quite happy.

******

It was nearly noon and the coffee shop was starting to get busy. A long line of people queued, either waiting to place their order, or waiting at the other end of the counter for their coffee. Marta was standing behind the till, sneering and muttering in Polish, while two young, blonde women scrabbled about, steaming milk, loading and unloading the coffee machine, and pouring out drink after drink.

The number of people in the queue greatly outnumbered the available tables remaining in the place. It was clear that before long I'd have to protect myself from all the stumblers and mumblers, hobbling around like zombies, looking for somewhere to perch.

I spread my coffee cup, laptop and notepad out to fill up as much of the table as possible, then moved my bag down from the empty seat onto the floor. It was my own, subtle way of saying: 'Please by all means take the empty chair, but don't even think about joining me.' I've mellowed a little, of late. I at least attempt to be nice before launching into out-and-out rudeness.

I focused my attention hard on my laptop screen, in an attempt to avoid eye contact with anyone in the place. I clicked open my emails. There were five new ones. The first was from my agent, full of praise over how good the latest book was and how well sales were doing. It was still riding high in the Amazon bestsellers list, and he had been speaking with publishers who were keen to know what I was working on next.

As usual, I hadn't even thought about what I might write next. Usually, at this point after the release of a new novel, I'd be sitting there licking my wounds, lamenting people's inability to know a good book when they saw it, and cursing James Patterson for stealing all my readers. It was a new experience for me to be doing this well. I hadn't had time to stop and think about any new stories. But I was confident I would.

I went to open the next new email when I heard the shuffling of feet and felt the presence of someone stood in front of me. I looked up, readying my hand to shoo them away, when I saw Dylan stood there, clutching a fancy white envelope to his chest.

"Hello Freddie," he said.

"Dylan," I replied, smiling. "How the hell are you?"

"I'm well thanks. In fact, I'm very well."

"What brings you over this way?"

"I went to your flat and you weren't in, so I figured this was the next most likely place. I wanted to come and personally hand-deliver this." He passed me the envelope. "It's an invitation to my wedding... our wedding... Corinne and I are getting married. Again."

"Oh, that's great news," I said. "I'm really pleased for you."

"Thanks mate. And listen, I want you to be the best man. No excuses. We wouldn't be doing this if it wasn't for you. You're the reason we're even back together in the first place."

"Oh, I don't know," I said. "I'm not very good with all that organising…"

"Corinne wants it. I want it. You're bloody well doing it, all right," he snapped. I hadn't seen him talk like this in years. He seemed more confident, more assertive. More like the old Dylan I used to know. "Besides, Corinne's three bridesmaids are all stunning, all single, and all used to be models. And as best man, you'll have to spend a lot of time with them on the day."

"Well, when you put it that way…" I said, laughing. "So, how are you now? Sorry I haven't been round in a few weeks, they've had me traipsing up and down the country doing book signings and things."

"No problem, Freddie," he said smiling. "You deserve every second of this. I couldn't be happier for you. It really is a good book, and I'm glad people have taken to it."

"So, you're okay?"

"I'm really good, Freddie," he said, beaming. "Thanks to you. I'm really happy."

"And things between you and Corinne are obviously good," I said, holding up the envelope.

"Never better. As soon as we found out what Mortimer had done to us, we both realised how much we still love each other. It wasn't easy at first, and there was a certain amount of water under the bridge…"

"Chantelle?" I said.

"Yes, Chantelle…" he said, slightly annoyed.

"And Corinne's a good-looking woman, so she wouldn't have struggled to…"

"No," he said, stopping me. "But we worked everything out. And we're doing better than ever."

"I'm really pleased for you," I said. "Any news on Mortimer?"

"I believe they've set a date for his sentencing now. I don't think he'll get as long as he should. But he's in prison, and hopefully they'll keep him in for a good while longer."

As Richard had predicted, Mortimer did see the inside of a prison, albeit a low-security version thanks to his testimony against Frank McLeod. Sanders, however, had no such trump card to play. The evidence against him was damning, and his own former adversary,

Mortimer, made things worse by turning on him and trying to blame him for the whole scheme. Sanders, too, was awaiting sentencing. But Richard Stone was confident he'd go away for at least twenty years.

McLeod was also held on remand, along with a number of his henchman, as Richard Stone and the CPS built a solid case against him. And things looked good. Due to his own sloppiness and over-confidence, he'd left enough physical evidence to put him away for a good long while.

"Have you heard from Mortimer?" I said.

"He's written to me. But I tore the letters up. And he's asked me to visit him in prison. Says he wants to explain himself. But I don't care. I just want to put that all behind me."

"Quite right, mate. Quite right."

"Corinne asked if she could have the visiting invites, so she can go there and give him a piece of her mind. But I don't think it will do either of us any good if she goes down for murder as well."

We both laughed loudly. The other people in the coffee shop turned to see what had set us off.

"I see your latest book is up for another raft of awards," I said.

"Yes, it's done pretty well. The publisher certainly seems happy. And they've optioned it for another film, which is nice."

Pretty well? My book had done 'pretty well'. Dylan's was an out-and-out bestseller all around the world. God knows how many hundreds of thousands of copies it had already sold.

Dylan smiled, then his face dropped slightly. It was almost imperceptible, the slightest flicker in his eyes and the corners of his mouth dipping the tiniest bit.

"And what are you working on at the moment?" I asked

"Oh, you know, nothing really. I've been tinkering with something... but I've been spending time with Corinne, and getting over everything that happened. And now we've got the wedding to organise... there isn't really the time..."

"Come off it," I said, "I've never known you not to be writing something. Even when your wives left you and you thought you had cancer, you were always tapping away at something."

Dylan sighed, letting out a long breath. His shoulders hunched and his head dropped a little.

"Well," he said, "I have been working on something, recently. And I thought it was going pretty well. But I showed the first half to my new agent, and he wasn't really impressed. He said it doesn't read like a Dylan St James novel, whatever that means. I mean, it is a Dylan St James novel. I wrote it, so of course it is. But apparently it's 'too happy'," he said, raising his fingers into air quotes, "if you can believe that."

I quickly clamped my hand to my mouth for fear that I might actually burst out laughing.

"He says he'd struggle to find a publisher who would take it," continued Dylan. "So he's advised me to start fresh with a new idea."

"What are you gonna do?" I asked.

"I don't know. To be honest, I think I might pack up writing for a bit. I think maybe I need a break from it. And it's not as if I really need the money at the moment."

"Sounds good, mate. So what next?"

"Well, I'm going to get married. And then we're going on holiday for a couple of months. To tell you the truth, I'm quite happy just being happy for a change. So I think I might just give that a go."

"Well, that sounds like a very good plan to me," I said, smiling. "I really couldn't be happier for you. And I'd love to be your best man. Now, can I buy you a coffee?"

"That would be lovely. But I'm afraid I can't stay. Plenty to do and no time to do it. But it was lovely seeing you again, Freddie. Come round for dinner next week, and we'll talk about the plans for the wedding."

"Will do," I said.

Dylan stood up from the table, smiling like an idiot and strolled off, practically skipping out of the coffee shop. I sat there smiling, a happy glow warming my chest. Then I suddenly realised I might be giving off a far-too-friendly demeanour that might encourage one of the plump, older ladies looking for somewhere to sit to come and join me. So, I slipped my face back into its more comfortable grimace mode, and fixed my eyes back on my laptop.

I checked the rest of my emails. Nothing interesting. Then I opened up a crisp, new page in Word. At the top I typed out *NEW BOOK IDEAS*. Then I sat there, looking at those three words, wondering what scrapes and adventures my newest character could get into next.

Just as I was starting to plot out the very genesis of an idea, I again felt a presence looming beside my table. I lifted my hand, poised in its affirmative dismissal position. The presence didn't move away. Instead, it cleared its throat in annoyance.

I looked up to see a face I hadn't seen for some years. A face I wasn't sure I'd ever see again.

"Hello Freddie," said my wife. "I think we need to have a little chat about money."

THANK YOU

Thank you very much for deciding to buy my book. In a world where there are so many books being published on a daily basis, it means a very great deal that you decided to buy my quirky, comedic crime book.

Since I started reading at a young age, it has been my dream to write a book and to have it published. I achieved that with my first book, The Unexpected Vacation of George Thring. And enough people liked that to make me think I'd have another go. So here it is. I hope you enjoyed reading it.

If you did like it, then please feel encouraged to leave a review or a few good words on Amazon, Goodreads.com, Facebook, Twitter, any social networking sites you regularly use… or even good old word of mouth!

And make sure to come and say hello at: www.facebook.com/alastairpuddickauthor. It would be great to hear from you.

Alastair Puddick

ACKNOWLEDGEMENTS

This book would not have been possible without the help of some very nice, lovely people, who I would like to thank.

Firstly, my good friend Gavin Walker and my mum, Elizabeth Puddick, for reading early drafts of this book and offering the invaluable help, advice and tips that enabled me to get it up to scratch. Thanks for the long chats, phone calls and, of course, all the time it took to read the book and make lots of useful notes.

Thank you to Karen Street, who listened to my daft questions and gave me some very useful information about different kinds of medication and what they do to you. I hope I remembered it all correctly and didn't get anything wrong.

Thanks, too, to Helen Edgington, whose help and advice guided me through a pretty tough time. She also endured a number of daft questions, and offered invaluable advice about the effects of depression and how psychotherapy can help (all of which enabled me to write about how it definitely should not be done).

Thanks, as ever, to my good chum Helen Brennan, who always loves being mentioned at the back of books. In truth, she is one of my biggest supporters, and without her help, advice and encouragement, I would never have managed to get a second novel published.

The biggest thanks has to go to my lovely wife, Laura, who puts up with me disappearing off to the study for hours on end (which I suspect she secretly quite likes). She reads more drafts than anyone else, helps me with ideas and inspiration, and always has plenty of insightful tips. She never loses enthusiasm for my writing (even when I sometimes do), and offers the faith, encouragement, praise and the good kick-up-the-arse I sometimes need to keep going.

Many thanks to my Dad, Iain, for being a one-man marketing machine, encouraging everyone he meets to buy my books. Every time I see him, he tells me how people are dying to read the new book – so thanks for keeping their enthusiasm up.

Thanks to all the lovely people at Raven Crest Books, who believed in this novel enough to publish it, and who put up with all my demands on covers, formats and many other things. And thanks to you lovely readers for picking up a copy and taking a chance on it – I really hope you enjoy it!

Finally, and I know I've already said it, but huge apologies to James Patterson. It's Freddie's opinion, not mine. I'm sure you're a very lovely man, really.

ABOUT THE AUTHOR

Alastair Puddick is a writer and editor who lives in Sussex with his wife, Laura. *Killing Dylan* is his second novel. His first novel is called *The Unexpected Vacation of George Thring*.

CONTACT DETAILS

Visit Alastair's website: www.alastairpuddick.wordpress.com

Visit Alastair's Amazon author page: Author.to/APuddick

Follow Alastair on Twitter: www.twitter.com/HankShandy

Like or join Alastair on Facebook:
www.facebook.com/alastairpuddickauthor

Cover designed by: László Zakariás.

Published by: Raven Crest Books
www.ravencrestbooks.com

Follow us on Twitter:
www.twitter.com/lyons_dave

Like us on Facebook:
www.facebook.com/RavenCrestBooksClub

Made in the USA
Lexington, KY
20 October 2018